Susan Madison was born in Oxford and lives there now, following spells in Paris and Tennessee. A novelist of considerable experience, *The Colour of Hope* marks an exciting new direction in her writing career.

THE COLOUR OF HOPE

Susan Madison

CORGI BOOKS

THE COLOUR OF HOPE
A CORGI BOOK : 0 552 14772 9

Originally published in Great Britain by Bantam Press
a division of Transworld Publishers

PRINTING HISTORY
Bantam Press edition published 2000
Corgi edition published 2001

1 3 5 7 9 10 8 6 4 2

The author and publisher are grateful to the following copyright owners
for permission to reproduce extracts of lyrics:

Words by Bob Dylan taken from the song 'Tambourine Man'.
By kind permission Special Rider Music/Sony/ATV Music Publishing.

'Shall We Dance', words and music by Richard Rogers and Oscar
Hammerstein II. © 1951, Williamson Music International, USA.
Reproduced by permission of EMI Music Publishing Ltd,
London WC2H 0EA

'Witchy Woman', words and music by Don Henley and Bernie Leadon.
© Kicking Bear/Benchmark Music, USA. Warner/Chappell Music Ltd,
London W6 8BS.
Reproduced by permission of IMP Ltd.

Set in 10/12pt Sabon by
Falcon Oast Graphic Art.

Corgi Books are published by Transworld Publishers,
61–63 Uxbridge Road, London W5 5SA,
a division of The Random House Group Ltd,
in Australia by Random House Australia (Pty) Ltd,
20 Alfred Street, Milsons Point, Sydney, NSW 2061, Australia,
in New Zealand by Random House New Zealand Ltd,
18 Poland Road, Glenfield, Auckland 10, New Zealand
and in South Africa by Random House (Pty) Ltd,
Endulini, 5a Jubilee Road, Parktown 2193, South Africa.

Printed and bound in Great Britain by
Cox & Wyman Ltd, Reading, Berkshire.

For who else but
MARK LUCAS

THE COLOUR OF HOPE

1

All her life, Ruth Connelly had feared death by water.

Once, standing as a child at the sea's edge, foam covering her feet, she had been filled with the sudden knowledge of terror, clear and sharp as the knife her parents sliced bread with. She held their hands, as water heaved away from her and lunged back again, heavy with intent. Wrinkles of water, glinting where the sun caught them. Diamond fingers, beckoning.

Terrified, she tried to move away, out of its reach, but they urged her forward. Go on, don't be frightened, it won't hurt you. Unconvinced, she pulled at their hands but they held her tight, stepped nearer themselves. It's the sea, the sea, they said in high bright voices, come on, honey, the sea.

Pebbles shifted under her toes. Slippery. Cold. The ground gave way. She stumbled and fell. Mommy! Daddy! She heard them, miles above her, laughing. She tried to stand but an unexpected wave slammed into her, green and glassy, determined. Daddy! She screamed again and the sea poured through her, swamped, deluged her. The gasp, the choke, clutching at green, at water which slid through her fingers: she remembered it still, salt stinging in her eyes, burning the back of her

9

throat. She would never forget the purity of her panic, the premature step into adulthood as she sensed something of which she should not yet have been aware.

Death. Oblivion. Nothingness.

You were only under the water for a second, her father soothed, big, jovial, as he swung her up against his chest, it's all right, baby, it was only for a second.

It was a second that would last a lifetime.

All her life, she had feared death by water. All her life, she had imagined that the death would be her own.

Standing on Caleb's Point, the low bluff which marked the ocean-most edge of their property, she looked down at the scene of that unforgotten moment. Beyond the fallen boulders was a tiny strip of sand, not even sand, small pebbles really, ground over the centuries to the size of peas. A beach, that was all. Nothing to be frightened of. But all these years later, she still feared the sea. At some instinctual level, she knew that it would destroy her if it could. And yet she loved this place. Up here, with the murmur of the waves, the honey-colored air, the waving grass brilliant with devil's paintbrush and field daisies, she found solace. She had come here so often during the years of her growing up. She did the same now, as an adult, a mother, a wife.

The Point pushed out into water dotted with lobster-pot buoys. Arms of green woodland curved round the horizon on either side, trees falling down to narrow shorelines of rocks crushed and scarred by the fierce winter tides. The woods were broken here and there by the shingled roofs of summer cottages. Further out, in the open channel, lay the gray hump of Bertlemy's Isle, a barren piece of granite which rose from the water like a turtle shell, crowned with a small stand of spruces. Tomorrow, as they always did, the four of them would be sailing out there to celebrate Will's birthday. She grimaced, thinking that they needed something to celebrate.

Wind flattened the dry grass of the bluff. Hawkweed leaves scratched the back of her thighs as she lowered herself to the ground. Behind her, a granite boulder reared out of the earth; the rain-formed dip at its center provided a toehold for reindeer moss and sphagnum, a creep of bearberry, asters, blue flags. Ruth leaned against it and closed her eyes, turning her face up to the sun, smiling as she remembered how, as a little girl, Josie had believed that the boulder was a pixie's garden. She sighed. It was so peaceful up here. No arguments. No bickering. No tension. Ants scurried over her feet. Maybe she should get one of the local carpenters to make a bench so she could sit in comfort.

Every time they came up to Maine from the city, she toyed with the idea of suggesting that they move here permanently. Paul already held a part-time visiting professorship down at Bowdoin; he would surely find it easier up here to finish the book he was writing than in the Boston apartment, spacious though that was. The children, it went without saying, would be ecstatic. What held her back were her own needs. She would probably find work with one of the legal firms in Portland or Bar Harbor, but she had worked too hard, for too long, to want to start again at the bottom.

She stared at the distant whaleshapes of Mount Desert Island on the horizon. Triangles of white sail were scattered across the water, heading out to sea from the little yacht club down at Hartsfield. One of them belonged to the children, though at this distance it was impossible to say which. Could they see her up here,

11

watching from the bluff like a new-made widow still scanning the heaving sea for the drowned sailor who would never again come home to sweep her into his arms, smelling of salt and wide horizons? Though she did not feel like smiling, she waved, just in case. Smiled. Just in case.

At her back, higher up the slope, were the pinewoods. Spruce, red and white pine, balsam, hemlock. The hot resin-scented air always recalled the simplicity of summer days when she was still just a mother and not a lawyer as well. Picnics under the trees. Hide-and-seek. Swimming in the pond. All the innocent things which, as a child, she had done in this dear and familiar place with her own parents.

Where had it all gone, that security, that sweetness? Time had rushed by, leaving her to wonder what had happened to the chirping voices of her children, to their unconditional love, their trust. There had been so many picnics here, so much fun. The slipperiness of pine needles under her feet, the taste of crab cakes and fresh-made wholemeal bread, chocolate brownies and carrot-sticks. She had been happy then. Consciously happy. Glad to subsume ambition in the treasure of her children. Will, with his freckled face and cowlick; Josie, hair tied back in pigtails on either side of her head, smiling, adorable in tiny raggedy shorts and a stripy top. They had filled her world. Had *been* her world. Often, overcome by a rush of love, she would squeeze the little creatures close and murmur, 'I love you, I *love* you,' pressing the words into the nutty fragrance of their hair, breathing them in while they squealed and wriggled and said they loved her too, they would always love her, she was their mommy, she was squeezing too tight, she was *hurting*.

12

Will had not changed much since then, but Josie had grown so secretive, so distanced from them. She knew this was only to be expected, part of her daughter's reach toward adulthood, a necessary element of parenting, something to be endured. But even so, Josie's hostility was hard to live with.

She got to her feet, brushing at the back of her shorts. Her spirit sagged. Time to go back into the real world. She took the trail which led down through the woods, past the boulder from which Josie, playing King of the Castle, had fallen and torn open a gash above her eyebrow which had required six stitches. Across the tree trunk which spanned a shallow ditch; the tree had toppled one winter during her childhood and, years later, watching her own children cross it with shrieks of thrilled terror, she recalled how huge it had seemed then, how deep the chasm it crossed. Through moss and fern, blueberry and wild ginger, into the sunshine and out of it, stepping over the thin lines of fallen sapling birches. Halfway down the hill the trail forked, one path leading on further into the woods, the other descending sharply toward the house, passing the wild cranberry bog, and the bend toward the freshwater pond, before ending at the rear porch and the door which led into the mud room at the back of the house.

The boundaries of their property were wide – though, strictly speaking, it was not *their* property but hers alone, deeded to her on her marriage by her parents, who had thankfully retired to Florida after a lifetime of New England winters. There was hardly a square yard which did not hold special memories of her own childhood and that of her children, as well as those of the people who had lived here over the years, legends handed down through the generations.

'That's where Grandma's wedding hat was blown into the pond, isn't it, Mommy.'

'That's where Great-Great-Grandmother was stuck in the bog.'

'Over there's where Great-Uncle Reuben fell off his horse 'cause he was drunk.'

Again, the prattling voices filled her mind, and behind them were echoes of her own voice when she herself was a child, and all the children who had been here before her. One day Josie's children, and William's, would listen just as eagerly to the same stories and, in their turn, pass them on.

As she came out of the trees, the house stood before her. Carter's House – *her* house. Foursquare, white clapboard, wraparound porches, shingled roofs and turrets. It had been built more than a hundred and fifty years earlier by Ruth's seafaring great-great-grandfather, Josiah Carter, who spent thirty years on the China run before making his final landfall. He had worked his way up from ship's boy to owning his own clipper, probably indulging in more than a little piracy on his way to amassing a considerable fortune. A prodigious womanizer and a legendary drunkard, it was said that he would drink until reason left him and then, rolling about the upper decks of his boat, he would spy all manner of wonders: frozen demons in the rigging and angels setting the sails, mermaids riding the crested waves, Neptune rising from the deep. Then came the day that God himself, albatross-shaped, admonished him from among the shrouds – 'Josiah, Josiah, why hast thou forsaken me?' – calling upon him to forswear the demon drink and the loose living. Accepting the inevitable, for even he could not fight with God and hope to win, Josiah had made his last voyage and retired.

A canny businessman, he had over the years purchased a number of fields and a large acreage of wooded hillside above the little cluster of stores and houses which comprised the village of Sweetharbor; there he built his cedar-lined house and filled it with the spoils of his many voyages. Having found himself a virtuous wife, he spent his life thereafter preaching hell-fire and damnation to terrified but appreciative audiences, who came by the cart- and carriage-load to quake deliciously at his descriptions of the afterlife they would endure for all eternity if they did not repent – and perhaps even if they did. Paul called him the nineteenth-century equivalent of a horror movie.

On the landward side of the property, there was no sign of other human habitation, for, in his misanthropic Yankee way, Josiah had bought to the horizon on all sides, in order not to be disturbed by sight or sound of his neighbors. Succeeding generations had cared lovingly for the place. There had been some modernization, of course. Ruth's grandfather, Jeremiah Carter, had brought electricity in. Wringers and iron tubs had given way to washing machines and dryers. The plumbing had been updated several times, the septic system overhauled. Her father, Jonathan Carter, had installed central heating, glassed in the two side porches, planted a small garden of exotic shrubs, but in its essentials the house had remained unchanged. Were old Josiah to rise again from beneath the white marble cross which marked his final resting place down in Hartsfield, he would find his home very much as he had left it, still smelling of cedar, still full of the curiosities he had brought back from distant shores.

2

'I'm not coming tomorrow,' Josie said.

'Of course you are,' said Ruth.

'I have better things to do, thanks, than go off on some stupid kid's picnic.'

'I'm not a kid,' said Will.

'Says who?'

'What kind of better things?' Ruth asked.

Josie looked belligerent. 'I said I'd drop by the Coombs.'

'Who're they?'

'You wouldn't know them, Mom: they're only year-rounders, not worth your while cozying up to.'

Josie's contemptuous tone was infuriating. 'You're coming with us,' Ruth said shortly.

'Why should I?' Josie had been working on one of her canvasses; there was a smudge of blue oil paint on her face, and more on her fingers. When she moved, her clothes gave off a faint whiff of turpentine. 'Anyway, I've had it with sailing.'

'What do you mean by that?'

'I'm not interested anymore. It's all kind of meaningless.'

'But you've been sailing since you were a little girl.'

'Yeah, and now I'm all grown up, Mom, in case you hadn't noticed.'

'I want you to come with us,' Ruth said. She felt helpless in the face of Josie's determined strength. 'It won't be the same without you.' When Josie made no response, she added: 'Besides, it's your brother's birthday.'

'So what?'

'So he'd like to take the boat out one last time before we go back to the city.' Ruth began spreading chocolate butter frosting on the cake which Will, with a little help, had made earlier in the afternoon. 'We all would.'

'Not me. I don't care if I never set foot on a boat again in my whole life.'

'That's nonsense, Josie. You were out sailing yesterday. I saw you.'

'Only because Will forced me.'

'If you don't come, you'll ruin Will's day.'

'Yeah, and I'm the birthday boy and you have to do what I want.'

'You're nuts, Will. I mean, who'd want to listen to Mom and Dad screaming at each other all afternoon? I sure as hell don't, I can tell you.'

'Thank you, Josephine.'

Will, the peacemaker, flashed his dental braces at the two women. 'I'd really like it if you'd come, Jo-Jo, but if you don't want to, you don't have to.'

'Don't call me Jo-Jo.'

'Josie, then.'

Will was always so equable, so reasonable. Like his father used to be, Ruth thought. She slapped at his wrist when he snuck a finger into the bowl of frosting.

'Count me out,' Josie said.

'Aw, c'mon,' said Will. 'It'll be cool. Besides, it'll be our last chance to go out in the boat.'

17

'Jeez, you are such a wimp.'

'Am not.'

'Are so.' Josie wrinkled her nose. 'You and your dumb braces.'

Ruth felt her temper rise. Will was sensitive about the ironwork on his teeth. So was she, for that matter: it had cost a sizeable fortune. 'That's enough out of you, young lady,' she snapped. More than enough, to tell the truth. She tried to tell herself that her daughter had been zapped by adolescence, that inside she was a mass of bewildered hormones, but it did not help much. She decided there was no point in even trying to be an understanding mom. 'You're going to come to Will's picnic – and you're going to behave yourself.'

'I'm nearly seventeen: why do you still treat me like a kid?'

'Why do you still behave like one?'

'How come we have to go to this friggin' geekfest at the Trotmans' first?'

'I already told you why.'

'But *why*?'

'Because it's important. Because Ted Trotman wants me to come.'

'Since when did we all have to kiss Ted Trotman's ass?'

'Don't use language like that in this house. Ted has put a lot of business my way.' Ruth wanted to slap Josie hard across the face. 'Besides, he's asked someone specially to meet me.'

'What, another rich gross-out like himself?'

'I'd prefer it if you didn't talk about my friends like that,' Ruth said. 'This is someone who could be a very useful contact. He and his wife are driving up from Brunswick especially to meet me. I can't just not show up.'

'Jesus Christ, don't you ever stop brown-nosing?'

Furious, Ruth slammed the knife back into the bowl and put her hands on her hips. 'I'm warning you, Josephine. I won't tolerate you speaking to me like that.'

'Networking, then,' Josie conceded, unwillingly moderating her language. 'Sucking up to people like this guy, in the hope of getting business from them. I'll just bet he's fat. Bet he's wearing nerdy shorts, white ones.'

'And a baseball cap,' added Will. 'On backwards.'

'I don't know about his taste in hats,' Ruth said lightly. 'Just that I have to be there to meet him.'

'We're supposed to be on vacation.'

'Time doesn't stop just because we're up here,' Ruth said.

'Why do we always have to do *your* stuff, but you never do ours? Like, *we're* supposed to show up at some nerdy party, but *you* couldn't be bothered to come to the school art exhibition last semester, which had no less than *three* of my paintings, as if you cared, and you missed Will's last game, and at Christmas you didn't even—'

'I explained why I couldn't come, Josephine. I have a responsible job, I can't just take time off whenever I feel like it.'

'Dad seems to be able to manage it.'

'Dad doesn't have the demands on him that I do.'

'You mean he's not as interested in making money.'

Once again Ruth put down the frosting knife. 'You know as well as I do why I work so hard. It's because I want you two to have—'

'Don't say it, Mom,' Josephine said loudly. '*Please* don't tell us you're only working your buns off for *our* sake.'

'Why not? It's the truth.' Ruth's face was flushed with rage. She pushed back a lock of hair. It *was* the truth.

'The truth is, we'd rather have you around so we could fuckin' *talk* to you just *some*times, just every now and *then*, instead of having all this money piling up in some bank.'

'Mom,' Will said, changing the subject. 'Why can't we live up here all the time?'

'Because we live in the city.'

'But we're year-rounders, really. I mean, Grandad was the local doctor for years. You and Dad are the first Carters—'

'Dad's not a Carter, thank *God*,' said Josie nastily.

'—the first ones not to live up here all the time.'

'First off, although your grandad was the doctor here, we moved down to Boston when I was little. After that, we only summered here, so I don't think we count as year-rounders, especially since your dad's from California. And secondly, your father and I had to go where the work was. Which was not up here.'

'You could have found something if you really wanted,' said Josie.

'Just be grateful the work we found wasn't in Little Rock or Kansas City.'

'Or Oshkosh,' put in Will.

'That is *so* not funny,' Josie said witheringly. 'Anyway, I thought the whole point of coming up here in the summer was to get *away* from work. So you can spend *quality* time with your kids.'

Nobody did contempt like Josie. 'I thought that's what we were doing,' Ruth said, as mildly as she could.

'Except you *so* can't bear to be cut off from your office for even a single day that you have to bring *zillions* of computers and modems with you. Anyone would think you'd rather be at work than with us.'

'That's ridiculous,' Ruth said.

'And now we've got to hang around while you schmooze with some fat guy because he'll be *good for business*. Even though you and Dad are always going on about opting out of the rat race.'

'Your father is. I don't recall that I've ever said much on the subject.'

'We all know that's because you'd rather be in some stuffy office in downtown Boston,' Josie said. 'You'd have thought you could forget the job just for *one* day. Will's birthday.'

'To which you've just announced you won't come,' said Ruth.

'I guess I will in the end.' Josie made a face at her brother.

'Which is why, as soon as we decently can, we're going to leave the Trotmans', come back home, pick up the picnic hamper and take the boat out to Bertlemy's.'

'You don't *have* to go to the party first.'

'I *do*.' Ruth tried to touch her daughter's face, but Josie shied away. 'Darling, you shouldn't frown so much. You'll get lines between your eyebrows if you're not careful.'

'Who cares?'

'You'll care, ten years down the line. So will your husband.'

'*Hus*band?' Josie spat out the word as though it were synonymous with smallpox.

'He'll say: "Didn't your mom ever tell you not to frown?" and when he does, I just hope you'll tell him the truth.' Inwardly, Ruth sighed. Friends with daughters had frequently warned her that the transformation from Growing Girl to Monster Maiden was

21

an overnight thing, and when it happened, better hang on to your butt. That had not made it any easier when it finally occurred. Especially given that, until recently, Ruth had really hoped that Josie was going to pass more or less unscathed through the frenzy of puberty.

'I'm *never* going to get married,' Josie said.

'Good decision,' said Will.

'What's that supposed to mean?'

'Who'd want you? He'd have to be blind. Or crazy. Or both.' Will grinned. He looks like one of those deliberately cute screen kids, Ruth thought, the way his hair springs up on the crown of his head and his ears stick out sideways. 'Unless Dad bribed someone.'

In the days before Josie had grown so antagonistic, Ruth might have made some lighthearted comment about not even Bill Gates having *that* much money. Now, she did not dare. Josie would take it personally and then there would be more sulks, more black moodiness.

'I love you too, *dork*,' said Josie. She stuck out her chin. 'If we go to the Trotmans', you know Dad'll just drink too much.'

'Yeah,' said Will.

'That's "yes", William, not "yeah". And where did you two pick up the idea you could talk about your parents like that?'

'It's true, though, isn't it?' demanded Josie. 'And if he does, we shouldn't be going out sailing, it wouldn't be safe.'

'If we're going out on the boat, obviously your father's not going to drink too much,' Ruth said. 'Anyway, I don't know why you're making such a fuss about going to the Trotmans'. All your friends'll be there.' She scraped the knife against the edge

22

of the bowl. 'You used to enjoy those parties, Josie.'

'That was before I discovered what a *murderer* Ted Trotman is.'

'How do you figure that?'

'All those companies he's on the board of? I bet you don't even *care* that they're all releasing dangerous toxins directly into the environment.'

Looking at her daughter, Ruth felt a kind of anguish. Under the tan, Josie's face was pinched and there were shadows beneath her eyes. Was her truculence due to something more than her age? Was she, God forbid, experimenting with drugs? With boys? It was hard being adolescent these days. Let me help you, Ruth wanted to say. Tell me about it. I'm your mother.

'Is anything upsetting you?' she said.

'Apart from the mess this country's in, do you mean? Not to mention the rest of the globe.'

'You always seem so uptight.' Yesterday, Josie had been so exasperating that Ruth had eventually threatened to send her off to one of those attitude-adjustment schools for wayward kids which seemed to be springing up all over the place. She had meant it as a joke but sometimes, such as right now, it seemed like a darn good idea.

'Well, I'm not.'

'She's right, Jo-Jo,' said Will. He ran his finger round the bowl which held the remains of the frosting and stuck it in his mouth.

'Who asked your opinion, schmucko?'

'You act like you're coming apart at the seams.'

'Shut up, you little wuss.'

'Are you sure you're okay?' asked Ruth.

'I said so, didn't I?' Josie moved restlessly round the kitchen. Her arms were sunburned, crackle-glazed with

23

salt from her earlier sail with her brother. The faded T-shirt she wore clung to rounded breasts. Does she know how heartbreakingly pretty she is, Ruth wondered? And, with a pang, thought: Where was I, what meeting was I chairing, when she turned from a girl into this almost-woman?

'Mom.' Josie pulled open a drawer and examined the contents before slamming it shut.

'Yes?'

'Do you think the end ever justifies the means?'

'What?' Ruth was thrown by the question. One minute sulks and hostility, the next, philosophical discussion.

'I mean, like, suppose someone's got good intentions and can only achieve them through violent means, would that be justified?'

'It would depend on the end. And the means, of course. But in my opinion, violent means are almost never justified.'

'What about Hitler? I mean, if they'd managed to kill him.'

'Would it really have made any difference to the course of the war if the Stauffenburg plot had succeeded? I doubt it: some other monster would have stepped into his shoes.'

'Or like,' Josie said, scratching at a blob of paint on her arm, 'you deal drugs big time, in order to fund a soup-kitchen for street-people.'

'Kind of a contradiction in terms, isn't it?'

'So you don't believe in the greatest good for the greatest number?'

'In theory, that's a defensible position, but in practice it never works out like that.'

'Yeah, right. Like, the haves always find a way to keep down the have-nots.'

'What *is* this, Josie? Some garbage you've picked up from your Save the Entire Universe group?'

'Typical of you to mock something you know squat about,' Josie said scornfully. 'At least we've got ideals, unlike *some* people round here.' She tugged open the drawer once more, slammed it shut again.

As she pulled at it for the third time, Ruth said: 'Are you looking for something specific?'

'No.'

'If you want something to do, you could go down in the basement, take the clothes out of the machine and put them into the dryer for me.'

It seemed to be the cue Josie had been waiting for. She turned, leaning against the cooking surface, her sunbrowned hands resting on the counter behind her. 'God, I *hate* the way we are,' she said. She pressed her long hair back behind her ears, exposing neat lobes pierced by a pair of turquoise studs which set off the gray of her eyes.

'What way's that?'

'The way we live.'

Ruth's heart sank. Please, not another argument about the rainforests and tuna fish and the Silent Spring, all of which Josie seemed to think was personally down to her mother. 'Which particular aspect of it do you have in mind?'

'*All* of it. Do you know how much damage people like you are doing to the environment?'

'People like me, huh?'

'Yeah. Like all that yucky foam you see in the rivers and on the edge of the ponds? That's because people like you use so much laundry detergent. I bet you don't even think about all those phosphates damaging the aquifer, do you?'

Aquifer? Where was Josie getting all this stuff? From

listening to the crackpot environmentalists in that group she had joined last fall? What did they call themselves: For a Cleaner Earth? Ruth sighed. There was nice Rob Farrow from Harvard who had been trying to date Josie for several months now, without any success: why couldn't she go out with him? 'Not very often, to be honest.'

'See what I mean?' Josie said.

'If using a machine is no longer acceptable, how do we keep our clothes clean?'

'Wash them less often. Wash them by hand.'

'Josie, if you want to take your clothes down to the creek and beat the hell out of them between two flat stones, feel free. I'm going to go on using modern conveniences because I haven't time not to.'

'You've never got time for *any*thing. Why can't we at least hang our clothes out to dry outside, like the year-round people do? The Hechsts, for instance. Or the Cottons.'

Ruth made a face.

'God, you are so *mean*!' screamed Josie.

'How do you figure that?'

'Just because Mrs Cotton's a bit slow doesn't mean she isn't just as good a human being as anyone else. And *way* better than some.' She glared at Ruth.

'Did I say that? Did I say anything like that?'

'You didn't need to,' Josie said sulkily, realizing she might have jumped to a mistaken conclusion. 'Anyway, sunlight is a natural bleach, did you know that? If everybody did it, the chlorine industry, people like your *buddy* Ted Trotman, would soon feel the pinch.'

'That's a great idea, Josephine. What are we supposed to do in winter?'

'Chlorine causes cancer,' insisted Josie. 'Especially in

women. I should think you'd worry about that. The risk of contracting cancer is now one in three, did you know that? And it's all because of the toxins and dioxins Ted Trotman's producing. It's all preventable, if we'd start using viable alternatives. Drying the laundry outside is just one. Besides, it's so much more natural.'

'Like I said, feel free to use the clothesline. You'll find some clothespins in the basement. Or perhaps,' Ruth added, 'you'd rather protect the environment and hand-carve your own.'

'Yeah, great,' said Will, trying again to ease the tension. 'You could sell them, door to door. Like those guys who come round with onions and stuff. Gypsy Josie.'

'Shut up!' Josie yelled, as though she were back in kindergarten, instead of pushing seventeen. Her face went red.

'Shut up yourself.'

'Be *quiet*, both of you.'

Josie curved her hair behind her ear again and folded her arms across her chest. 'The way we live's so artificial. I mean, the people here live *real* lives, sort of close to the land, and the water. They're part of it all. Not like *us*, only interested in *money*.'

Ruth had a sudden flash of foreknowledge. Josie at college, a student politician, running for office, rallying her peers round the flag of some unlikely cause, some doomed issue, infectiously enthusiastic. The way Paul used to be. The way she herself used to be. Engaged with life, idealistic. Ready to fight battles for those who could not fight for themselves. She wished she had not treated Josie's questions so lightly just now. Had not mocked her ecogroup. 'Did you say real lives?' she said.

27

'Yes.'

'I hope you realize that there's more than one reality.'

'As you'll appreciate when you grow up,' put in Will, quoting his grandmother.

'Shut up,' Josie said. She frowned yet again at her mother. 'And there's another thing,' she began.

'I don't want to hear it,' said Ruth. Gaahd . . . what was she going to be accused of *this* time?

'See what I mean?' Josie said. 'You never talk to me. Never. Not about anything *real*.'

'Oh Josie . . .' Ruth shook her head. 'That's not true. So why don't you just tell me whatever it is you want to say.'

'You know what it is.' Josie touched her ear studs with long paint-stained fingers. 'I want to leave school.'

'Don't we all?' said Will.

Ruth sighed heavily. 'Not this again, Josie. I've already told you what a ridiculous idea that is. I really can't be bothered to discuss it any further.' Ruth looked at her watch. 'Come along, kids, we've got—'

'I mean it, Mom. *Really*.' Josie's voice rose. 'I want to leave school right now and go to art school instead. I want to paint.' Some of her belligerence had faded, giving way to a kind of pleading. 'It's all I ever wanted to do, right from when I was a little kid.'

'She's really good,' Will put in.

Ruth drew a deep, exasperated breath. 'And for the hundredth time, I'm telling you that you don't have the slightest idea how difficult it is to make a living as a painter.'

'Money isn't everything. What about job fulfillment?' Josie straightened. 'Besides, if you took the slightest interest in what I do, if you ever bothered to *look* at my work, you'd know I could make it.'

'There's no way I'm allowing you to leave high school without graduating.' Ruth could feel her own voice rising. 'That's an absolute given.'

'What friggin' use is a high school diploma to an artist?'

'If my parents had allowed *me* to leave school every time I wanted, do you think I'd have been—'

'It's *my* life we're talking about here, not *yours*,' Josie said angrily. 'I don't need college, I don't need certificates. All I want is to be a painter.'

'What you do with your life once you've left home is your business,' Ruth said coldly. 'But while you're in my care, Josephine, the answer's no.'

'Fuck you!' Josie shouted. Kicking one of the chairs as she passed, she slammed out of the kitchen, leaving a space charged with negative electricity.

Ruth was exhausted by being kept constantly on the defensive. In the office, nobody questioned her, nobody disputed what she said. Who gave this furious feisty adolescent the right to argue about everything all the damn time?

'Dad'll be back soon,' Will said. He had a smear of frosting on his chin which he was trying to reach with his chocolatey tongue. 'We're going out in the *Lucky Duck* – want to come along?'

'I've got some papers to look at,' said Ruth. 'And some reading to do before we meet this man tomorrow.'

'Sure.'

Ruth said defensively: 'I need to be prepared. Otherwise I would.'

'That's okay. Just thought I'd ask.'

That evening, after another bad-tempered discussion about the sterling qualities shown by the year-rounders, as opposed to the decadent lifestyles of summer people like her parents, Josie bounced off the couch in the living room. 'You two are so *smug*,' she declared. 'You think you know it all, don't you? You and your rich materialistic friends.'

'Rich? Who's rich?' Paul said, not looking up from the *New York Times* book pages.

'Ted Trotman, for a start. Mom's big best buddy. Half the companies his corporation owns are known industrial polluters. And on top of that, he's got interests in a logging company down in the Amazon basin which is destroying thousands of square feet of rainforest every single *day*.'

'He probably doesn't even know.'

'Sure he does. Everybody knows. And he's just had that *gross* deck built onto the back of his summer cottage, out of Honduran mahogany, for God's sake. He should be thrown in jail. People that rich have a duty to others.'

'Is that all you've got against our friends?' asked Paul. 'That they're rich, materialistic, have no sense of duty and like to improve their property? Or is there more?'

'It's not funny, Dad.'

'What else do you object to?'

'Like, none of you ever talk about anything interesting. It's always yak, yak, yak about stupid things like movies and vacations and recipes and stuff. Not about *important* things.'

'Give it a rest, Josie.'

'I bet you couldn't even name more than three local families. To you, they're just specimens, like something in a museum.'

'Tell me, Josephine, what gives you the right to sit in judgement on your parents like this? How would you

30

like it if your mom and I nagged you the way you feel free to nag us? Who says *we're* not real?'

'At least the people up here aren't destroying the planet every time they get out of bed. And they don't just sit about marking student essays or whatever. They're making a living from their *hands*. Using their *skills*.'

'And when you finally run away from home to live with the *real* people, as you've threatened to do ever since you could walk, what skill would *you* use, Josephine, if you had to?' Paul asked in a softly reasonable voice intended, Ruth knew, to infuriate.

'I could sell my paintings.'

'Oh yes?' Paul raised his eyebrows.

'And if that didn't work, I could – I could help on the lobster boats.'

'Like they're *really* looking for extra crew,' said Will sarcastically.

Josie flushed. 'At least I wouldn't be working in a fucking bank or selling stocks and shares, for God's sake. Or poisoning the environment. Or tearing up the rainforests with a fucking bulldozer.'

'Moderate your language, Josephine.'

'Dad used to make those neat wooden bowls and boxes and stuff, didn't you, Dad? That's pretty real,' put in Will.

'He gave that up years ago. Anyway, he wasn't trying to live off it. It was just a stupid *hobby*.'

'Not that stupid,' said Ruth. 'He was really good at it.'

'And *I'm* really good at painting.'

'Not that again,' Ruth said sharply.

'Not what?' Paul asked.

'Your daughter has decided she wants to leave school right this minute and set up as an artist.'

31

'I could do it, too,' said Josie, 'if you'd let me.'

'Uh-uh.' Paul shook his head.

'Let's talk about this again when you've got your high school diploma,' said Ruth.

'How often do I have to tell you I don't need one?' said Josie. 'If you'd take me a bit more seriously, you'd realize I could make it. All I need is a little help to get started.'

'And suppose you didn't?' asked Ruth.

'I *will*.'

'You'd find yourself out on the streets without even a high school certificate, let alone college or university degrees.'

'I don't *need* degrees,' said Josie.

'You do,' Ruth said.

'She's right,' said Paul.

'You two make me *sick*.' Josie got up and flounced out of the room, managing to catch with her bare foot the base of one of the two Chinese porcelain vases which stood on either side of the door. It toppled against the wall and then rolled down on to the broad pine planking; although it did not smash, a large triangular chip broke from the rim.

'Josie!' Ruth was furious. She picked up the chip and ran her finger across the ragged edge. '*Damn* it. Can't you be more careful?'

The depth of her rage surprised her. After all, the vase could be mended, when she found time to take it to someone who knew about such things. Nor was it simply frustration over her deteriorating relationship with her daughter. The broken vase was more than that: it seemed symbolic of a rupture she only partially understood, yet another rip in the fabric of their lives.

Josie walked away without responding. Ruth ran out

into the hall to find her halfway up the stairs. 'Josephine!' she shouted.

The girl stopped, one hand on the banister. Her shoulder blades were defiant. She did not look round. 'What?'

'Get back here this minute,' Ruth said.

'Why?'

'You know why. The very least you could do is apologize.'

'Sorr-ee, Moth-er,' Josie said, with singsong insolence.

Ruth bounded up the stairs faster than she would have thought possible, and grabbed hold of her. 'How dare you,' she said, shaking the girl. Josie turned her face away. 'How dare you speak to me like that. Especially after damaging my property through your own sheer bloody-minded carelessness.' A bubble of her spit landed on the girl's cheek. Just below her hairline, Ruth could see the faint scar left by her fall from the boulder up in the woods. What had happened to that skinny little girl, with her ready smile and her loving personality?

Josie rubbed at it, smiling contemptuously. 'That's the trouble with this family,' she said.

'What is?'

'Objects matter more than people.'

'You're talking crap.'

'Am I?'

Ruth stared at her. Josie's eyes were blank with hostility. And something else. Behind the truculence of her daughter's expression Ruth glimpsed uncertainty. Maybe even fear. Which was fine by Ruth. Uncertainty was good. Fear was better. She opened her mouth to argue, then closed it. The wall between them seemed all of a sudden too high for her to climb.

She let go of her daughter and turned on the stair. 'It's not because it's an *object* that I'm upset,' she said wearily. 'What bothers me is that it's that particular object. Not only is it beautiful in its own right, but Great-Great-Grandfather Carter brought it back in his boat all the way from China. It's been here as long as the house. Don't you see you've broken something more than a vase? In a way, you're breaking the continuity between him and us.'

'I said I was fucking sorry, didn't I?'

Paul came into the hall with the newspaper in his hand. He stared up at the two of them over his reading glasses. 'Don't use language like that to your mother, Josephine,' he said. 'And don't be so discourteous. Can't you see it's not the vase she regrets? It's the way you've violated the spirit of the house.'

'The *spirit* of the *house*?' sneered Josie.

'That's what I said. Now, apologize to your mother.'

Both her parents could see Josie contemplating further belligerence before she eventually decided to mutter an ungracious apology. Then she marched on up to her room.

'Jeez,' Paul said, staring after her. 'What did we ever do to deserve this?'

His support was more than Ruth could have hoped for and she was grateful. These days she felt she seldom had it. A rush of affection swelled inside her. She put her hand on his arm. 'Thank you, darling,' she said.

He looked down at her and patted her hand absently, almost as though she were a student in one of his classes.

'Do you think I should give up my job?' she said suddenly.

'Why do you ask?'

34

'Maybe the price is higher than I realized.' The knowledge that she could never recapture the days of her children's growing was like a bruise which hurt when pressed. 'Maybe I should stay home, grab the years while I still can.'

'Get real, Ruth. You'd hate that.'

Ruth was reluctant to admit it. 'I don't know . . .'

'The time when they really needed you is long gone.'

'I suppose so, but—'

'And let's face it,' Paul said dispassionately, 'the money you make keeps us in the style we've grown accustomed to. God knows, my salary doesn't come anywhere near yours.'

'So you think I should go on working?'

'As with so much in this family, it's your decision, Ruth, not mine.'

'Sometimes I wish you'd just give me an ultimatum. Put your foot down.'

'If I did that, you'd stamp on my instep so hard I'd be on crutches for the rest of the year.' Paul made a face. 'Besides, don't you think it's a bit late now for you to go back to being a mommy?'

Like all the Trotman parties, the Labor Day Weekend cookout was an elaborate affair. Although in his invitation Ted had described it as a barbecue, Mindy's from Augusta had been called in to handle the catering. As well as two pits outside, one with piles of charcoal-broiled ribs slathered in Mindy's Famous BarBQ Sauce, and another where whole racks of lamb were cooking, there were also long flower-decked tables inside the house containing all kinds of other dishes, from local crab and lobster to sushi and tortillas. The furniture was all good – and expensive – Americana: oak, maple, cherrywood. The Trotmans were wealthy and had no objection to spending money.

Even though fog was billowing along the horizon, the air-conditioning was turned on in the house. Blinds were pulled down over the porch to alleviate the glare and a temporary canopy had been erected over the new deck. It was one of those rare Maine days when the temperature hits the nineties, and everyone outside was bathed in a light sheen of sweat. This would be the last party of the season: tomorrow the vacationers and summer visitors would begin heading back to New York City, Boston and Philadelphia. School would be starting, university semesters getting under way. Most of the people with cottages up here had already begun packing them up for the winter.

Although the weather would not deteriorate for a while longer, and there were families who would continue to spend weekends up here before winter gripped the state, the party had a nostalgic air. People, all of them from away – Ruth was not sure the Trotmans knew any of the year-rounders – drifted languidly across the well-watered lawns and elaborately planted gardens. Even the rocks thrusting up through the grass between the sculpted shrubs looked as though they had been set in place by the world-famous landscaper the Trotmans had hired up from Atlanta. Perhaps they had. Standing on the huge new deck – Honduran mahogany, right? Or was it Peruvian? – Ruth knew she preferred the more rugged look of the land around her own cottage.

'Ruth! I've been looking for you.'

She fixed a smile to her face and turned. Ted Trotman, dapper in Madras shorts and a polo shirt, was coming toward her, accompanied by an older man. 'Ted,' she said warmly. 'Wonderful party.'

'I want you to meet Phil Lavelle, who's driven up from Brunswick specially to meet you.'

'Hi.' Ruth put out her hand and shook the beefy paw which Lavelle extended. As her children had predicted, he was short and fat, in white shorts and a baseball cap. At least he was not wearing it backwards.

'Ted's been talking you up a storm,' he said.

'With good reason.' Ruth eased back her shoulders, knowing she looked good in her beige linen shorts and navy halter top.

'I'll leave you two together.' Trotman patted Lavelle on the shoulder. 'Watch out for her, Phil: she's as sharp as an ice pick.'

'So.' Lavelle hoisted a plump buttock onto the deck rail. 'Ted's obviously hooked.'

'He gives us a lot of business.'

'Persuade me that I should, too. For a start, what do you think your firm can do for me that the others can't?'

'You probably have a pretty good idea already, or we wouldn't be talking,' Ruth said. 'There's a lot of companies out there, but our particular strength lies in helping corporate clients at a turning point in their development, assisting them to identify market position and to form strategic alliances.'

The heat was getting to Lavelle. Sweat rolled down his face and gathered in the folds of his neck. His knees glistened. 'Any firm touting for new accounts would say the same. But what can LKM do specifically for *me*?'

'For a start, we aren't generalists,' Ruth said. She loved moments like this, playing the mark, reeling him in. 'We specialize in mergers and acquisitions, debt refinancing, contract negotiations, real estate development.' She looked at him shrewdly, persuasive and in control. 'But you already know that. Perhaps a better question would be to ask what *you* think we can do for you that another firm can't.'

'I like the fact that you specialize. I like the fact that so many of your partners serve on the boards of public and private companies.'

'Company policy,' Ruth said smoothly. 'Doing so gives us a unique insight into management perspectives and that can help us to deal with issues on the shop floor, as well as operate effectively in banking and government circles. Now, when I was looking into the background of your firm, I noticed that a couple of years ago you were involved in some fairly complex union negotiation which didn't work out as successfully for you as it should have.' Ruth knew there had been serious boardroom disagreement because yesterday she had read an account of the acrimonious discussions in *Business Week*.

Lavelle frowned. 'I told my board that's how it would pan out.'

'And you were proved right.'

'You've done your homework.'

'I'd have been a fool not to.' She smiled slowly at him, and shifted a little so he could see the curve of her breast inside the halter.

Lavelle removed his cap, wiped an arm across his forehead, and put it on again. 'Hot enough for you?'

'We don't often get temperatures this high up here.' Ruth moved in for the kill. 'If I'd been involved in those negotiations, I'd have approached the problem from a different direction.'

'Tell me about it.'

For another ten minutes, she outlined an alternative strategy. He nodded, occasionally throwing her a calculating glance; she could see him wondering why his legal advisers had not come up with the same idea, and wincing as he contemplated the money his company could have saved. By the time their glasses were empty, he was sold. When they shook hands he told her that he would phone to make a lunch date. When he did, she would be prepared, would have identified a particular problem that needed solving, would be able to forestall some of his questions. He would see just how secure his interests would be once he had placed them in the capable hands of Landers Keech Millsom. Thereby not only justifying her salary but also ensuring her a substantial end-of-year bonus.

When he had moved off to join his wife, she stood looking at the crowd of guests. Conversational snatches from the grass below reached her in bursts, like the sound of a warning buoy, now close by, now far away. The talk was of insignificances. The slow trek down Route 1 back to the city. The problems of dry-docking boats for the winter. The price of vegetables up here, compared to city supermarkets. Movies. Little things. And why not? Old friends, these people were already well acquainted with each other's views on wider issues such as the President, the economy, world peace, right-wing militias, abortion.

Listening to them, Ruth remembered Josie's outburst. What was wrong in talking of nothing very much, in the face of so much unalterable consequence: war, famine, hatred, intolerance? There was something terrifying about the puritanism of adolescence: she had been just the same, constantly questioning the attitudes of her own loving parents, castigating them for the easy lives they led.

She pressed her ice-filled glass against her cheek. Her mission accomplished, they were now free to go.

Automatically, she checked on her family. Will was playing Frisbee with Ed Stein and one of the Trotmans' golden retrievers. Josie was standing with her friends Tracy and Shauna; normally she would have been animated and noisy, leading the conversation, but today she stood with head bent, just listening to the other two girls. When she moved her head, responding to something Tracy had said, the sun caught the shining highlights of her hair, somewhere between clear honey and maple syrup.

In spite of herself, Ruth smiled, remembering a rare moment of empathy with her daughter. Last fall, Josie had dyed her hair a raw bright orange which made it look like a wig discarded at a clown convention. Running out of the bathroom, she had collapsed dramatically against the kitchen table. 'I can't go to school like this,' she said, her voice throbbing with self-pity. 'I'd rather *die*.'

Ruth, knowing that she must treat this as the tragedy it was, had soothed and comforted, all the while trying not to laugh, and, eventually, had gone down to the nearest drugstore with instructions from Josie to buy another shade of hair dye nearer her natural color.

The next day Josie had come back from school carrying a sheaf of white freesias. 'Thanks, Mom,' she had said.

'They're beautiful, Josie.' Ruth had admired the delicate white blooms on their thin green stems.

'They're my absolute favorite flower.' Josie had stroked one, sniffed the overwhelming fragrance. 'Don't they smell fantastic?'

'Just wonderful.' Ruth had hugged her tightly. 'Thank you, sweetheart.'

'Thanks for coming to the rescue last night.' Josie

started to laugh. 'I guess I looked pretty stupid with that orange hair.'

'I wouldn't say that. But I did wonder whether you were going to have to run away and join a circus.'

As Ruth recalled the moment, Josie looked up and caught her mother's eye. She scowled and turned away. Don't do that, Ruth wanted to call. You cannot imagine how much that hurts. She longed to bridge the gap which lay between the two of them but the task seemed beyond her at the moment.

Standing in the shade of a juniper tree, Paul watched his wife. A classy lady. He'd always thought so, from the very first time he saw her walking across College Green, her books clutched to her chest, laughing with a friend, glancing sideways at him, catching his eye. Catching his heart. Innocent: that was the word which had sprung into his mind. She had a quality of innocence about her. So unlike the other coeds. He'd walked after her and seen her smile shyly over her shoulder as she slipped into her dorm.

He batted away the no-see-ums which hovered round his face. Wiped his forehead. Jeez, it was hot. He wondered if Ruth had impressed the fat little man from Boston in the white shorts. Lavelle, was that his name? She was good, no question about it. No wonder Bob Landers kept increasing her bonus, promoting her, telling her how much the firm valued her.

Chris Kauffman strolled into sight, at his side the young woman who had taken the Prescotts' cottage for the summer. As he chatted, he looked up at Ruth and the side of his mouth lifted briefly as she caught his eye. They'd become lovers for a brief few weeks last summer, both of them left temporarily spouseless in the

41

city. Several people had made sure Paul knew about it. No. Not lovers. Fuckers, because fucking was all there had been between them. In the incestuous world of Boston law firms, he guessed it'd been dangerous and, consequently, intensely thrilling for Ruth. At that point, she'd only recently been made a partner and Chris was already a highly respected figure in the world she was hoping to conquer.

The ice in Paul's glass had melted. He swallowed the last drops, throwing back his head, looking up through the branches to the sun overhead. He had never let on that he knew about Ruth's affair. He guessed it would mortify her, perhaps even precipitate some action on her part which he was not prepared to accept. Besides, there'd been a couple of episodes on his side, too. He was not going to stand in judgement on her. At least, not yet. There were ups and downs in every marriage. How could there not be? They got along at least as well as most of their friends, and considerably better than many.

A pleasant alcohol-induced blur sat inside his head. Lovely day. Reasonable job. Pretty wife. Beautiful children, even if Josie was sometimes a pain in the butt. On the whole, a good life. He pushed himself away from the tree. Time to get another drink.

Where was Paul? Ruth hoped he was not drinking too much. She watched Josie detach herself from her friends and walk across the grass. She passed Chris Kauffman without noticing him and stomped up the steps of the deck. Setting herself wide-legged in front of her mother, her pose belligerent, she said: 'I asked Mr Trotman if he knew that Honduran mahogany was protected. Wanna know what he said?'

'No, Josephine, on this particular day, at this particular time, I do *not* want to know what—'

'He said: "What do I care, sweetheart? I just sign the checks." Nice guy, huh?'

'Almost as nice as you, confronting him in his own home. That was extremely rude of—'

'I asked him about his magnesium plant, too.'

'You what?'

'Which emitted thirty-five million pounds of chlorine gas last year.'

'How do you know?'

'I read it in a Greenpeace article,' said Josie. 'I asked him what he thought about that, and he said he wasn't breaking any laws because chlorine pollution isn't part of the Clean Air Act. Said in any case the Department of Health issued a report saying chlorine emissions aren't a health hazard. He's obviously been asked about it before.' Josie tilted her chin aggressively. 'Still gonna send him a Christmas card, Mom?'

'This is neither the time nor the place for this discussion,' Ruth said. 'Standing here, eating Ted's food and—'

'Oh no. Not me.' Josie put out her hand in a warding-off gesture. 'I haven't touched one thing of his – I'm only here because you made me come.'

'You're a real pain these days, Josie.'

'I'm amazed you even noticed, Mom.'

Mother and daughter faced each other. For a startling moment, dislike pitched around in Ruth's gut. She was shocked at herself. How could she not like her own child, even for the tiniest fraction of time? Yet, for that second or two, she undoubtedly did not.

3

Ruth stowed thick sweaters in a duffel bag. In the refrigerated cooler she packed the birthday food she had prepared for Will, who had fairly sophisticated tastes: cocktail sausages, chicken legs baked in saté sauce, cold cooked lobsters, a ginger-and-lime dressing for the avocado. She added local raspberries, plates, toothpicks, forks, plastic glasses, a bottle of chilled wine, cans of Diet Pepsi and Sprite. Finally she slipped the chocolate cake into a Tupperware container, hoping it would not look too battered when they finally ran up onto the stony beach of Bertlemy's Isle.

Josie came in and flung herself around the kitchen. 'You don't like me much, do you?' she said suddenly.

The words pierced Ruth. 'What a terrible thing to say.'

'But it's true, isn't it? You'd never send Will away to one of those boarding school type places, would you.'

'That was just a—'

'I saw the way you looked at me, when we were at the Trotmans'.'

'And I saw the way you looked at *me*,' said Ruth. 'As if you hated me.'

'Maybe I do.'

Ruth gripped the cooler tightly, suddenly close to

tears. 'Why, Josie? Why would you hate me? What have I done?'

'It's more what you haven't done,' muttered Josie.

Ruth shook her head. 'Well, I don't hate you.' She held out her arms. If only Josie would run into them, the way she used to. 'I *love* you.'

'Yeah. Sure.'

Ignored, Ruth let her arms drop. I love you, she had said, and meant it. Yet Josie was right: she did not *like* Josie much. Not at the moment. Not the alienated Josie she had been this summer. It makes no difference, she wanted to say, love is the important thing, and the love was still there. The liking was only resting, only in abeyance until the former Josie came back from wherever she had been. But she did not say it.

'Would you love me whatever I did?' Josie asked. She vibrated with a restless energy, wanting something, anything, but not knowing what it was or where to look for it.

'Love is unconditional.'

'Would you love me no matter *what*?'

'Of course I would. You don't turn love on and off.' What on earth was Josie about to come out with? Could she be – oh Lord, no – pregnant?

'You're saying you'd love me whatever I'd done?'

'I guess I'd have to rethink my position if you told me you'd been alone in the Oval Office with Bill Clinton,' Ruth said.

'Droll.'

'How would you feel if I accused you of not loving me?' Ruth demanded.

'Who says I do?'

'Josie!' Ruth felt lost. Was her obviously unhappy daughter simply looking for reassurance? Was she

45

trying to explain why she was so much at odds with her family this summer? In her ears glinted the earrings Ruth had bought for her last Christmas, small silver rectangles with a copper heart set in the middle. Was it a signal of some kind, that she should have chosen to wear those particular earrings? And if so, what was the message? She had badgered Ruth to let her have her ears pierced since she turned ten; on her fourteenth birthday, a worn-down Ruth had agreed, wishing her daughter was not in such a hurry to leave childhood behind. How terrified Josie had been, finally confronted with the gum-chewing woman at the ear-piercing place, and her metal implements.

'If you didn't love me, I wouldn't blame you,' Josie said. 'Parents get stuck with their kids, don't they? The same way children don't get to choose their parents. Just because they live in the same house doesn't mean they have to like or love each other, does it? I mean, why should they?' She looked at her mother with careful indifference.

'I can't speak for how you feel about me.' Ruth tried not to show her hurt. 'I can only assure you that I – and your father – love you and Will more than we can possibly say. Surely you know that.'

'You'd give your life for Will, wouldn't you?'

'Of course.'

'Would you give your life for me?'

'Of *course* I would.' Trying to lighten the conversation, Ruth added, 'Let's hope I never have to.'

The angle of light slanting over the trees already spoke of autumn. Although it was still warm on land, it would be chilly out on the water. The motionless heat had given way to sudden gusts of wind which were catching

46

the cedars and hemlocks up on the hill. Rain was on the way.

The sea was her enemy; it would destroy her if it could. Knowing that unless fear was conquered, it would consume, at college Ruth had made herself learn to swim, and found that the containment of a swimming pool somehow eased her terrors. Nonetheless, as they walked in single file along the catwalk, she felt the old anxieties surge. It was safe enough here, close to shore, but once they left the confines of the land-encircled water, the sea would have her at its mercy.

The children's Beetle Cat bobbed restlessly on the water as they climbed aboard the *Lucky Duck*, the thirty-five-foot, wooden-hulled sloop Paul had bought ten years earlier.

Ruth shaded her eyes against the sun and looked apprehensively up at the sky. 'You don't think the wind's going to get any stronger, do you?'

'Don't worry, darling.' Paul put his arm round her shoulders. 'The worst we'll get is a bit of a blow.'

'Which is fun, right?' Will said, reaching for the cooler and the picnic basket. 'It's a perfect day for sailing, isn't it, Dad?'

'You bet.' Paul tripped over a rough plank in the pontoon. 'Absolutely.'

'Okay.' Once she and Paul had become engaged, Ruth had forced herself to crew for him: in Maine, off Cape Cod, down in North Carolina or in California, summer after summer, until she was pretty competent around a boat. But she was always going to be a fair-weather sailor.

As they cast off, Josie produced her Walkman and slipped on the headphones, blotting her family out in a manner which proclaimed she was only here because

47

she had been forced to come. Ruth wanted to tear them off. Tell her to stop behaving like a spoiled child. To grow up. What held her back was the wry knowledge that growing up was exactly what Josie was, in her own awkward way, trying to do.

They got up a fair speed once they reached open water. Sunshine glittered along the ridged surface of the sea, blue-gray under the bow. Ruth sat back in the cockpit with her eyes closed, listening as Paul and Will discussed tactics for tomorrow morning's race. 'If we come in the first three,' Paul said, 'I'll be happy.'

'I want to do better than that,' said Will. 'Last race of the summer, Dad. You and me, we gotta really go for it.'

'The *Duck* doesn't stand much chance against the Steins' new boat,' said Paul. 'Much as I love her, I have to admit she's getting to be an old lady now.'

'We could beat them. We're much better than they are. Mr Stein only bought the boat because Ed nagged him to. He doesn't know port from starboard.'

'Ed's pretty good, though.'

'Yeah, but not as good as we are. Team Connelly,' Will said. 'We're the ones to beat.'

Josie had finally pulled off her headphones and decided to rejoin the family. 'Fat chance,' she said, her expression challenging.

'Get outta here,' said Will.

'Sam Hechst could run rings round all of you,' Josie said. 'And with me crewing for him, that's exactly what he'll do.'

'In his dreams,' said Will.

'Sam Hechst?' Ruth said. She pulled her baseball cap further over her eyes to shield her face from the sun's reflection. 'Is he related to Gertrud and Dieter?'

Josie sighed heavily. 'He's Dieter's nephew, Mom.

Surely even you knew that.' She spoke to her brother again. 'First three? You'll be lucky to be in the first ten.'

'Wanna bet?'

'Yes,' said Paul. 'Are you merely boasting, Josephine, or are you prepared to put your money where your mouth is?'

'Up her butt,' said Will.

'That's enough,' said Paul. 'Come on, Jo: how about it? Team Connelly versus Team Hechst. I'll put twenty bucks down that says we'll beat you.'

'You're on!'

'Winner buys lobsters all round,' said Will. 'Okay?'

'Okay, you greedy little dweeb.'

Ruth smiled sleepily, warmed by the fine salt-flavored air. Below her, the water chuckled and splashed against the hull. The sun was hot on her shoulders. This was how it should always be. Just like this.

'We'd better get going,' Paul said. The weather had taken a sharp downturn and out to sea the water was unpleasantly choppy. Thunderheads were piling up along the horizon; the sky had turned the dark purplish color which announced an approaching storm. Nothing very unusual for this time of the year, but nonetheless it would be best if they reached land before it broke.

'Okay.' Will started packing away the empty wine bottle, the soft drink cans, the remains of the food. 'Great picnic, Mom,' he said. 'Thanks.' He and Josie stowed the stuff in the flat-bottomed dinghy which they had used to row ashore. Small waves slapped ill-temperedly at the sides of the sloop and set the dinghy rocking. Already water was breaking high up the shallow beach.

Will pointed. 'Some storm brewin',' he said, sounding passably down east.

49

'Ayuh,' agreed Josie. Brother and sister grinned at each other.

Getting into the dinghy, Ruth envied them their insouciance, their familiarity with the water. In a small boat, she always felt vulnerable. The sea was so much closer: it had only to reach out and grab hold of her.

Paul waded in waist deep and shoved them off and then scrambled in over the stern. The two children rowed the dinghy to the sloop, anchored a hundred yards offshore. A mile away, the last of the afternoon's regatta competitors were slipping toward harbor, leaving the sea almost empty of sails. On the highest part of the coast, the lighthouse above Sweetharbor stood like a white finger against the swollen clouds which seemed to be hanging only a few feet above the surface of the sea.

Even as they prepared to cast off, the gusting wind changed again. Standing at the wheel, Paul cursed as it blew straight off the land toward them. The squall was closer now, and the seas were running heavier. A dark line of wind whipped toward them along the surface of the water. Behind them, the high seas had covered the lower part of Bertlemy's Isle, and the spruces which crowned it were whipping frantically to and fro.

Paul spoke, his voice calm: 'Okay, crew. First thing we're gonna do is shorten the sail.'

'Right.' Will grinned, peering down at the gray water racing past the hull.

'Put your safety harness on first. You too, Josie. We'll set the small jib and put two reefs in the mainsail. After that, I want you to check the halyards and sheets, make sure they're free to run.'

'Aye, aye, sir.'

Paul spoke to Ruth without taking his eyes off the

50

weather. 'Ruth, go below and make sure everything's secured.'

'Fine.' It was a struggle for Ruth to match his calmness. She stumbled down the companionway, hating this, wishing it were over. Having checked that there was nothing loose in the cabin, she stood on the bottom step and looked forward across the deck to where Josie and Will were struggling to control the flogging canvas, huge folds of sail whipping about them. There was an unseasonably cold edge to the air. Will was suddenly knocked off his feet. Josie shivered as she caught the cringles in the luff of the sail and forced them over the hooks on the mast while Paul kept the boat to the wind. Ruth heard his voice, authoritative and strong, and felt relieved. If anyone knew what he was doing, Paul did. He had been out a thousand times in weather far worse than this. It began to rain, blinding sheets of water flying horizontal to the sea.

With the sails set, the children clambered back into the cockpit, sliding their safety harnesses along the jackstay. 'There are dry clothes in the cabin,' Ruth said.

'In this kind of sea, I'll probably throw up if I go below,' Josie said.

'Me too.' Will touched his mother's arm. 'It'll stop blowing soon, Mom. We'll change then.'

Josie took the wheel while Paul went up on the foredeck and got the anchor up. The chain rattled; at the same time, a clap of thunder seemed to split the heavens in two.

'Watch out!' Paul yelled suddenly and the boat heeled over, the lee rail almost submerged. Ruth ducked down again into the cabin, trying to make herself as small as possible, only to hear, over the buffeting wind, Paul yelling for her to come up. 'Bring the life jackets, too, while you're down there,' he commanded.

'Life jackets?' Her eyes widened with panic. 'Oh, my God, Paul, what does—'

'We need to put them on before we leave Bertlemy's,' he interrupted. 'Always best to wear them. It doesn't mean anything.'

Ruth fastened her own life jacket and brought the other three up into the cockpit. In the short time she had been below, the afternoon had undergone a complete transformation. Overhead, the clouds were now the color of a wet coalface, and visibility was down to no more than a few yards. Whitecaps rolled relentlessly across the sea, each one slamming against the hull, tossing the boat around as if it were made of paper. Somewhere a bell-buoy clanged, the single note sounding like the accompaniment to a tragic opera. Soaked through, Paul and the children fought their way into their life jackets against the rolling pitch of the boat.

'Okay, the anchor's up,' Paul said. 'Let's do it.'

Wind filled the sail as he sheeted it in. As they moved off, Ruth took the wheel, feeling the deck buck beneath her feet. Spray from an oncoming wave slapped across her face and sloshed into the cockpit, covering her Topsiders, but she forced herself to stay calm, told herself that this was nothing to worry about. Below her feet, the sea sucked greedily at the boat.

'The wind's still straight off the shore,' said Paul, after a while. 'Even if we try tacking, we're not going to go anywhere. I'll put the engine on: we'll have to motor-sail home.'

'Aw, Dad,' said Will, his cheeks reddened by the wind and the salt spray. 'This is fun.'

'Yes.' Josie was animated by the scent of risk. 'Let's not use the engine.'

52

'We have to. There's not enough sail up.'

Though they protested, Paul turned the key in the ignition. The engine coughed, sputtered, died. He tried again. Again it died. He muttered something about the line being blocked. Ruth fought rising panic: she knew that there was always a lot of crud in the bottom of the fuel tank and in this sea it had probably been shaken around. He tried once more and this time the engine caught and began chugging away.

Ruth could see he was relieved. Paradoxically, this only made her more frightened. She knew she ought not to express her fears, for the children's sake. Moving closer to him, she caught the smell of wine on his breath. The hysteria she had been trying to batten down took over. 'Jesus, Paul,' she said angrily, keeping her voice low. 'How much have you had to drink?'

'Only some of the wine you packed, to drink to Will's health.' He kept his eyes on the horizon as the rain flattened his hair.

'Some? Most of the bottle, if we're being honest here. How much at the Trotmans'?'

'Not a lot.' He grinned, face roughened by the fierce wind. 'But they do make awful strong martinis.'

The boat heeled violently to port, and all four of them grabbed onto anything solid they could find. 'Clip on, kids!' Paul shouted at the children, and added brusquely to Ruth: 'You too. And watch out for the boom, will you? The last thing we want is you getting knocked overboard.'

'How long before it calms down?'

'What the hell does it matter?'

'How long, Paul?'

He shrugged. 'I don't know . . . fifteen minutes? Half an hour, tops.' He did not hide his irritation at her question.

Half an hour? Ruth breathed deeply, hoping nobody would realize how scared she was.

They motored for a while, parallel with the coast. Through the drumming rain, Ruth could see the green wooded shoreline and the white stub of the lighthouse, so close she could almost have reached out and touched it. Behind them, the distant trees on Bertlemy's had disappeared from sight. The sky was night-time dark. Over to starboard, Ruth saw the lights of a lobster boat. 'Look,' she said excitedly. 'Couldn't we attract their attention?'

'What the hell for?'

'They could give us a tow in or something.'

'For God's sake, woman. We don't need a tow,' Paul said.

'Are you sure?'

'Of course I'm fucking sure. And will you, for Pete's sake, let go my fucking arm.' He shook her off violently.

Ruth was cold and wet and frightened. 'Don't talk to me like that!' she yelled. 'You bring us out here when you're completely smashed and—'

'You're being a pain in the ass,' Paul said angrily. 'Did it ever occur to you that—'

'Shut up! Shut up!' Josie screamed at them. 'Can't you two stop quarrelling for even five minutes?' Her face, screwed up against the rain, was full of animosity.

Exasperated, Ruth turned on her. 'Shut up yourself!' she shouted. 'You self-righteous little prig.'

'You make me sick,' Josie said. The hostility in her gaze was chilling.

Ruth did not reply. They were not making much headway and, although he would never admit it, Ruth could see that Paul was growing concerned. On his own, he would have been fine; with his family on board, the

54

situation was more complicated. There was already a five-foot swell and waves were pounding the boat relentlessly. The cockpit seemed to be inches deep in water.

Ruth knew from experience that the seamanlike thing to do would be to head further out to sea and ride the storm out there. She knew too that without her, that was unquestionably what Paul would have done. But she could not stop her mouth going slack with fear when he suggested it. 'No!' she said. 'For God's sake, let's get home.'

'We'll have a hard time, with the wind dead on the nose like this. The best thing we can do is either ride out the weather or head round the coast a bit to Ellsport.'

Ruth kept her eyes on the wheel. If she looked at the sea, she would be paralyzed by the sight of those angry, hungry waves. 'Why Ellsport?'

'The harbor there faces north-east, which means we could make some use of the wind. Our sails are so short, we're scarcely moving.'

'Can't you put more up?' Josie called.

He shook his head, frowning. 'Can't risk it. We could overpower her and then she might sloop over.' As he spoke, the boat smacked heavily into the space on the far side of a wave and Ruth screamed, clapping her hands to her mouth.

'Knock it off, Ruth, for God's sake,' Paul said. He had always praised her for the way she fought to overcome her pathological fear of the sea; she could see that now he felt nothing but impatience. After all, she was a grown woman, not a child: she ought to be able to control herself.

Will took her hand. 'It's okay, Mom,' he said. 'We're gonna be okay. You know what they say: *The sharper*

55

the blast, the sooner it's past. It's not nearly as bad as you think, is it, Dad?'

'It's just a bit of a blow, that's all,' Paul said. 'Happens all the time in these waters.'

'Why don't we put out to sea?' the boy asked. He had been sailing since he was a baby and was not frightened by anything. 'Wait it out.'

'I already said we should. But your mom apparently knows best and thinks we should head for shore . . .'

'You're the skipper, Dad,' Josie said. 'We should do what *you* think's best – which everyone except Mom knows is putting out to sea.'

Ruth longed to give in to her terror. She wanted to scream at them to get her home, get her off this quivering, heaving, dangerous vessel. 'I'd . . .' Her lips were trembling. 'I'd rather get back, if we can.'

'Then Ellsport it'll have to be,' Paul said.

'Da-ad,' complained Josie.

'We can make it.' Shouldering Ruth aside, Paul took the wheel and bore away to starboard and began heading parallel to the shore up the coast toward the next harbor. At this angle, the wind's scream died down, and the smashing of the waves seemed milder, so that for a while, with the wind on the beam, they motored in comparative quiet.

There was a sudden clunking sound from somewhere under the boat. The engine stopped dead. Without power, the boat veered round and the fierce weather caught it again, throwing it from side to side. Each crashing wave seemed higher than the previous one.

'What the hell was that?' Paul said.

'Did we catch a trap line?' asked Will.

'I'll check.' Paul leaned over the rail on one side, and then on the other. 'Can't see any pot buoys.'

'There's some netting floating about,' Josie called out, hanging out over the stern.

'Shit.' Ruth watched Paul steady himself with a hand on Josie's shoulder. 'Some fucking amateur fisherman, I'd guess, cutting his net loose. Not a local, that's for sure.' The boat wallowed heavily, clumsy as a walrus, and he clenched his fists with frustration. 'Damn it all to hell!'

'What?' Ruth said, her voice loud. 'What's happened, Paul?'

'The fucking prop's fouled.'

'What's that mean?'

'We've got something wrapped round the propeller. Which means the engine's fucked.'

'Can it be fixed?'

He laughed a little grimly, wiping ineffectually at his wet face. The vicious wind lifted his rainsoaked hair and let it drop again. 'Only by going over the side. It's the only way we'd be able to free the prop. Not something I want to do in these conditions.'

'So what now?'

Paul glanced up at the sail. 'I don't know.'

'You don't *know*? Jesus, Paul, you're supposed to be the damned expert. How can you be so irresponsible? I don't know why you ever brought us out in these conditions.'

'Shut the hell up, Ruth.' Paul turned away from his wife and spoke to the children. 'What do you think, kids? More sail?'

'Wind's awful strong,' Josie said.

'Unless we head out to sea,' said Will.

They all stared at Ruth. Tears gathered in her eyes and mingled with the rain, warm against her cold skin. She felt excluded by the other three. Which was bizarre, really. If anyone was the outsider, it was Paul, not her.

She was a Carter; her family had lived around these waters for generations. She knew, absolutely, that they were going to drown. The sky overhead was the color of night. Black with moisture, clouds hung above the trees on shore, only a few hundred yards away. Lights twinkled on the low bluffs and in among the trees. It looked so comforting. So safe. She wanted to be there, staring out to sea, thinking that it was a wild evening. Fighting for self-control, she wiped surreptitiously at her eyes.

The boat had turned in the water so that once again the wind howled round the sails. The sheets were thrashing back and forth, cracking like whips. Ruth knew that, without her aboard, the others would have been enjoying the elemental feel of it, man pitted against nature.

'Dad,' Will said suddenly. 'We're getting kind of close in to shore, aren't we?'

They had been drifting with the current. Paul glanced overboard. 'Christ! You're right. *Much* too close. Jesus!'

Under these relatively shallow waters was a whole slew of hidden rocks and shoals. As though to prove it, there was a second thunk beneath them, much more severe than the last. All four were thrown heavily forward against the cabin bulkhead. Blood started to trickle down Paul's face from a cut above his eyebrow.

Josie screamed, clutching at her left arm. 'My wrist!' Her face screwed up with pain. 'Mom! I think it's broken.'

'Hang on,' Paul said. There was a split second of uneasy quiet and then, somewhere beneath the boat, a noise like a giant chewing glass began down in the bilges. The boat groaned.

'Paul!' Ruth felt numb. As she moved toward Josie,

the cold rain drove against her face, forced itself down her throat. 'What's that noise?'

'Sounds like we've been holed,' Paul said, his voice unnaturally calm. 'Take the wheel, Ruth, while I try to see what the damage is.'

Josie was sobbing. 'My wrist, it really hurts.'

Clinging tightly to the wheel, Ruth knew that a more competent mother would have found something – a knife, a flashlight, anything – and tried to splint the wrist. What were they going to do if the boat capsized? Josie would not be able to swim. 'Don't worry, Josie,' she said shakily to the chalky smudge of her daughter's face. 'It'll be okay.' She did not believe it.

They were not moving forward at all, though the wind continued to tear at the sails. Waves bore down on them in solid ranks, each tremendous crash of water knocking the boat further onto the rocks. With every wave, the boat reared several feet out of the water and smashed down again with a splintering sound. Ruth looked down into the cabin. Water was pouring in with each shuddering crash of wave against keel. The boat was lying at an angle of forty-five degrees, wallowing from side to side. There was a mighty crack as the mast suddenly snapped off and disappeared over the side, dragging the sails with it.

'We're sinking!' Ruth screamed. 'The cabin's full of water.' Her knees faded under her. She tasted salt at the back of her throat. This was the end, then. They were going to drown. My children, she thought. My darlings. Pictures passed rapidly through her mind: Will's funny little face as he lay against her breast after nursing, Josie leaping off the dock into the pond, wearing a cranberry-colored swimsuit, the two of them listening while she read them a story. The smell of their skin, the softness of their hair. Her children. The images lined the interior of her head; the sense of anticipated loss was unbearable.

Paul was back in the cockpit, looking distraught. 'Oh God,' he moaned. 'My beautiful boat.'

'Guess that's us out of the race tomorrow,' said Will.

'Which makes Sam and me twenty dollars richer,' Josie said. Her face was white with pain but she gave a crooked smile.

'Great. Lobsters all round.' Will looked at his father's face and stopped grinning. 'What now, Dad?' he asked soberly.

'Best get into the dinghy, son. We need to get away from these rocks.'

'But if we're already on them . . .' The wind snatched the words away from Ruth. 'Won't they tear the bottom out?'

'Now!' Paul pushed her roughly toward the rear of the cockpit. He ordered Will to climb down the ladder into the little boat and motioned Josie after him.

'I can't, Dad,' Josie said. She was holding her injured wrist at an odd angle against her chest. It took much longer to lower her down than seemed reasonable. All the time, the sea hammered at the hull, demanding entrance, demanding sacrifice.

'I'll give you a hand,' Paul told Ruth. His eyes were cold and condemning. This is your fault, they seemed to be saying. We'd be safely out to sea if it weren't for you and your stupid hysterics.

'But—'

'Just get in the fucking dinghy.'

'Shouldn't we stay with the boat?'

'Do it,' he snapped.

She tried to follow his orders. Standing with one leg over the stern-rail, she saw her children below, their white faces upturned in the near-dark. Josie was curled up against the side, moaning, her teeth pressed into her lower lip. Will was reaching up for her. Below, the tiny craft pitched about on the black water which foamed and crashed around it. Fear locked Ruth's legs to the rail. 'I can't,' she said.

'Come on, Mom, come on, it's okay, you'll be okay, I promise.' Will's voice was gentle, calming. She held tightly to the rail, unable to let go.

Paul was behind her. 'Take my hand,' he said.

'Paul, I . . .'

'You'll be okay, Ruth. I'm right here. I'll steady you. Just get in the goddamned dinghy.'

The sea reached up toward her. 'I can't.' Terror had trapped the breath in her throat. 'I *can't*, Paul.'

'Ruth, get a grip, will you? Will's down there. I'm right behind you. Jump, for chrissakes. We don't have much time.' He reached into his back pocket and brought out his cellphone. '*Do* it, Ruth.'

The boat lurched, the beaten timbers shrieked. Water poured up from the cabin into the cockpit. Paul pushed her and, screaming, Ruth fell toward the sea before landing awkwardly in the bottom of the dinghy, banging her head against the side. Her right knee flamed with pain. There was a ringing in her ears. Will put his arms round her. She felt his cheek against hers and his breath warming her neck. She closed her eyes, willing all this away. Above them, the stern of the boat lifted with the motion of the sea, four, five, six feet above their heads before five tons of wood and metal came crashing down again only inches away from them. Next time, or the time after, they might be crushed beneath it.

Ruth saw Paul's hands on the rail as the stern lifted again high into the air. He dropped toward them and scrambled to untie the painter. The dinghy swirled away into the gloom. A mighty wave suddenly swelled out of the black sea and caught the underside of the dinghy, lifting it endways so that it stood almost perpendicular, tipping them out in a tangle, thrusting them down under the surface. Ruth heard Josie's shriek of agony as the force of the water caught her damaged wrist.

Ruth's head was full of blinding pain. The cold was unbelievable. It forced the air out of her lungs so that breathing was suddenly impossible. This was every nightmare she had ever had come true. As she broke the surface and snatched in some air, the sea rushed into her mouth, choking her.

She closed her throat against it, forced it out again. She could see neither of her children. Where were they? 'Will!' she shrieked. 'Will! Will!' Frantically she reached out, felt something under her fingertips before it was snatched away by the movement of the water, reached again and this time caught something. The webbing of Will's safety harness. She pulled it close. 'Will. Thank God.'

Paul was beside her, his hand strong over hers on the rope. 'The Coast Guard ... I managed to get through . . .' he shouted above the noise of the water. 'They're on their way.'

They heard another scream. 'Dad! Mom! Help me! I can't hold on . . . I can't . . .'

In the near-dark, Ruth could see her daughter's terrified face, white against the thrashing sea. Her mouth was open, a dark circle against her pale skin. In the curious half-light, her silver earrings glinted.

And then she disappeared.

'Josie!' Ruth screamed. 'Oh, God, *no*!' Desperately she lunged toward the space where only a moment ago

62

Josephine had been. 'Josie! Where are you?' Her hands were so cold that she could feel nothing at all. If they did not get out of this water soon, they would all die.

The sea crashed down on her again, forcing her below the churning water. For a second, there was something solid under her feet before she was fighting her way upward again, gasping for breath. She yelled again but the only answer was the whack and groan as the boat crashed down again onto the reef. As she and Paul and Will clung to the safety ropes around the dinghy, they all three shouted Josie's name, but there was no answer.

'She can't have gone,' Paul said. 'She can't.' He took a deep breath. 'Hang on, Jo!' he shouted, his voice cracking with strain. 'Hang on.'

Ruth felt consciousness fading. The bone-chilling cold had taken over her body, had removed all feeling, was creeping toward her brain. How long could they endure it? Will already seemed to be unconscious. Fingers clumsy with cold, she wound the floating strap of his harness around her wrist so that he would not drift away if his grip loosened. 'Josie,' she screamed desperately. 'Come back. Josie!'

'Josie!' Paul yelled. 'Can you hear us? Where are you? Answer me, Jo. I'll come and help you.'

Anguish was building under Ruth's ribs. None of this was happening. How could they be so close to safety and yet be in such danger? Where was her daughter? How long could she survive in water which, even in high summer, was bitter cold? For a fantastical moment, she wondered if Josie could be trying to punish her by not answering their frantic calls. Above her, the boat was half-lifted by the incoming waves, and smashed down again. Once more they heard the crunch of the keel as it connected with solid rock.

Ruth began to shiver, huge tremors running through her body. 'She's gone, she's not here, oh Paul, where is she, where's she gone?' My girl, she thought, my beloved daughter. Images fluttered about in her head like tattered rags: it can't be, the unthinkable, the ultimate horror, she can't be dead, not Josie, not my girl, my Josie, my darling daughter, it isn't true, it isn't . . . She saw again the arch of her daughter's lean tanned body and the summerfruit-red of her bikini as she fell into the unruffled surface of the pond. 'Josie! Come back!'

Afterwards, none of them knew how long had passed before they heard the throb of a helicopter overhead. For all of them, the only reality was that Josie had vanished. Paul kept repeating like a mantra that she had her life jacket on, she couldn't possibly drown, the crew of the helicopter would find her, there was every chance that she would be picked up.

Overhead, a powerful beam arced across the sky before moving over the water to focus on them. With an effort, Ruth forced her frozen body to function and looked up at it. A figure in a survival suit was swinging down toward them. Help had arrived – but was it too late? The crashing all around them had lessened. The sky lightened. Along the edge of the massed thunderheads, the emerging sun gleamed white and gold; the line of the horizon was as sharp as a blade against the bruised sky. The storm was passing.

'We're going to be all right,' Paul said but Ruth knew that what he said was a lie. Because if Josie had . . . her mind could not take in the fact . . . if they had lost Josie, then nothing, ever, was going to be all right again.

4

News of the accident spread quickly through the little community. The Connellys' friends telephoned, or came by, urging them to say if there was anything they could do to help. But although their offers were sincere, time pressed on them, and they had no choice but to take up again the rhythm of their lives back in the city. Though less vocal in their sympathy, the year-round people were more practical. There was scarcely a family in Sweetharbor which could not tell the story of a lost lover, a widow who watched and waited, a father who had never come home. The loss of someone of Josie's age was especially tragic. There had been Carters in Sweetharbor for longer than any memory could stretch, and it was seen as a duty for the local community to rally round.

There were flowers: bunches of summer blooms from their gardens, lilac branches tied with a ribbon, pots of geraniums. But for the most part, they brought food. Paul and Ruth would get up to find the back porch set with covered casseroles, like sacrifices of appeasement. In some corner of her misery-sodden brain, Ruth could see that the proffering of food was an almost ritualistic expression of the human desire to comfort. Every day Gertrud Hechst came up to the house, carrying a dish of dumplings or a sauerbraten, or a blueberry pie, and stayed to brush down the porches, scrub the kitchen floor, wash the outside paintwork free of salt residue. Their nearest neighbors, Ben and Marietta Cotton, the brother and sister whose forebears had lived on the Point for twice as long as the Carters, dealt with other practicalities. Ben chopped wood, pruned trees, began the task of bagging the precious shrubs in burlap, ready for the winter, while his poor crazed sister carried out the simple tasks he gave her to do, dusting, washing, making coffee, all of these kindnesses performed without the use of words.

Ruth was aware of their presence, of their compassion. For the most part, these were people still living the same hardscrabble lives as their parents and grandparents had, lives shaped around the seasons: blueberry picking in the summer, Christmas wreath-making in winter, lobster fishing, clam digging, carpentry, quilting, and she was grateful for a generosity which some of them could ill afford. Nonetheless, they seemed insubstantial to her, inhabitants of another world to which she no longer belonged. Each day, she went through the motions of normality. She got up, showered, dressed, drank the coffee that someone – Marietta? Gertrud? – put in front of her, but could not have said at any one moment where she was or what she was doing.

Her whole being was concentrated on two things. First, on keeping hold, in whatever way she could, of her sanity. Secondly, on the certainty that somewhere, Josie was still alive. She spent hours up on Caleb's Point, a pair of field glasses round her neck, scanning the blank face of the ocean for the sight of a white arm, a piece of wreckage to which her daughter might be clinging. Sometimes she screamed Josie's name to the heavens, Josie, Josie, oh come back to me, come back, as though it might reach her lost daughter, might call her home. Other times, she went down to the shoreline and clambered over the rocks and boulders, searching, searching, wild-eyed, hands bleeding where she cut them on the stones, body bruised from falling onto the sea-slippery rocks, emotions wound tight with desperate expectation. A branch of bleached driftwood, a tangle of seaweed, and her heart jumped into her mouth in the hope that it was her daughter – Josie! My darling – washed ashore, unconscious, maybe, but alive. She took the car along the coast, and doggedly searched the beaches and coves until her tearless eyes were raw with looking.

She refused to accept that her search was futile. The blue-and-white Coast Guard cutters had swept up and down the coastal waters a dozen times, to no avail. All along the coastline, from Portland up to the Canadian border, the locals had been alerted, fishing boats had been asked to keep a lookout, pleasure craft warned. But she would not give up. Every night, she stumbled home, picked at one of the dishes she found in the ice-box, climbed the stairs to her bedroom and lay sleepless until the next hard shafts of daylight hit the window screens. Then she got up again and started over. Her physical self had lost any meaning; she was unaware of its discomforts, the cuts and bruises she sustained, the sleep she missed. Each day, she drove herself onward in her hopeless, desperate quest for her daughter. Even when hope began to fade, she continued the search because to do anything else would be to consign Josie permanently to the past and she was not ready to do that.

As the days passed and there was still no news, Paul rang Will's school principal. Mr Fogarty, expressing his deep sympathy, suggested that since the semester was about to start, it might be a good idea if Will came back to the city; he was sure that Will would be welcome to stay with the family of his best buddy, Ed Stein, and that way he wouldn't miss out on too much school.

'I agree with him,' Paul said. 'I've called Carmel Stein, okayed it with her.'

'It's not okay with me,' said Will. He looked up from the Gameboy he had been restlessly fiddling with ever since they had been rescued and brought back home.

'It would be best,' Paul said.

Will stared at his mother, who sat hunched with misery in the kitchen. 'Don't make me go. Tell him, Mom.'

'I think your dad's right,' Ruth said expressionlessly.

'He's *not*.'

'You shouldn't miss school,' said Paul.

'Who cares about school? She's my sister. I want to be here when they . . . It's not *fair* to send me away.'

'It might be days before . . .' Ruth swallowed. Oh God: such a slim chance, such a meager hope. '. . . before they find her.'

'I want to be *here*.'

'I know how you feel, Will,' said Paul gently. He put a hand on his son's shoulder. 'But it'd be best, son, if you went back.'

'I want to be with *you*.' Will was trying not to cry, his freckled face flushed red with the effort of holding back the tears. All his former ebullience had vanished.

'Oh, Will.' His distress broke through Ruth's own. She got up and put her arms round him. 'My poor little Will.'

He turned his head into her breast. The heat of his

tears burned through her shirt. 'Don't send me away, Mom, *please*.'

'I think it would be best,' Paul repeated tonelessly.

'Please,' said Will. 'If it hadn't been for my birthday—' He began to sob.

With a terrible anguish, Ruth realized that he was blaming himself for Josie's loss. If it had not been for the picnic, none of this would have happened. She looked at Paul, scarcely aware of who he was, so concentrated was she on holding herself together. 'Will, it's not your fault,' she said. 'It's absolutely not.'

'It's nobody's fault,' said Paul, his voice dead.

'I think he should stay here with us,' Ruth said.

'What good can it do?'

'I don't want him to go.'

'Ruth, it would be better for him not to be here.'

Paul had given up on Josie, she could see. Too exhausted by grief to argue, she turned away. Paul pulled Will close against him. 'I promise we'll call you, son, the very minute there's any news.'

'But I want to '

'You can come right back here as soon as . . . as she's home.'

As if recognizing that arguing with his father was futile, Will gave in. 'Okay,' he said quietly. He stood up, looking at them both. In his eyes Ruth saw that he too had already accepted the truth she herself refused to concede: Josie was lost to them.

The Steins were leaving for the city that afternoon. Paul drove a silent Will over to their cottage, set deep in the woods a mile away.

'I hope we've done the right thing,' he said, when he returned.

'How can we know what's right and what's wrong?'

69

'I just don't think it would be good for him to hang about while we wait for news. He'd only brood, and go on blaming himself.'

'It might have been better to keep him with us.'

'I disagree.'

Ruth scarcely heard him. Buried deep in their grief, the two of them exchanged no more than half a dozen sentences a day. Nonetheless, Ruth was aware that while she was gone, Paul stayed within earshot of the phone, taking refuge in numbness, waiting for the call that would eventually come – *had* to come – the one to say that somewhere Josie had been found, damaged but nonetheless alive.

Two weeks after the accident, someone pounded at the front door. It was early. The turning leaves were netted in a sea mist which would not burn off the horizon for another couple of hours. On the pond, the mallards still floated, asleep.

In the kitchen, Ruth felt her body swell with anticipation. 'They've found her!' she said. 'Paul, she's come home!' She pushed back her chair, stumbled down the passage and across the hall. This had simply been a test: they had passed with flying colors, had proved their love, and now Josie had come home. She turned the key, stiff from disuse, and flung open the door.

'Miz Connelly?' The young man on the porch tipped his cap.

'Yes.' Ruth looked beyond him. 'Where's my—'

She heard Paul's footsteps behind her on the pine planking, and his voice, desperate. 'What've you found?'

'Coast Guard, sir, ma'am.' The young man looked awkward. 'Lieutenant Edwards. Mind if I come in?'

'Where's Josie?' Ruth said, as he stepped past her into the hall. 'Where is she?'

The young officer pulled something from a zipped navy holdall. 'Do you recognize this?'

Paul looked down. His hand sought for Ruth's. 'It's her life jacket,' he said. 'Josie's. See? It's got her name printed on it.'

'It was found washed up among the rocks miles further up the coast, almost at the border with Canada.' The lieutenant's weatherbeaten face was solemn.

Ruth took it from him. 'No,' she said. 'Please. No.'

It was waterlogged, the red canvas covering torn by the pounding it had received from the sea. The weight of it in her hands finally put an end to the hope which had sustained her over the endless hours of searching. Looking down at the ripped, sea-stained life jacket, something broke inside her. She forced her mind away from the questions which beat inside her skull. Why Josie? Why us? She held the jacket to her chest, pressing it against her breastbone as though she might squeeze one last precious drop of Josie from it. This was the final connection she had with her daughter, the last she would ever have. She remembered bringing it up from the cabin, Josie struggling into it as the waves crashed about them.

Paul wept, pressing his fingers against his eyes. Lieutenant Edwards patted his shoulder, murmured something. All three of them were acutely aware that there was nothing to be said. Ruth knew she ought to hold her husband, comfort him, but she was too immersed in her own pain. When Paul put his arm round her, she moved away.

'They'll find her, eventually,' the officer said in a low voice. 'Might not be for a while. Tricky waters round

71

here, as you'll be aware, Mr, Miz Connelly.' He did not add what they all knew: that occasionally bodies never did show up. Avoiding their eyes, his expression was nonetheless eloquent: all this couple had left to hope for now was the chance to give their daughter's corpse a Christian burial.

Ruth and Paul could not speak, numbed by the realization that there was no longer any way to avoid the fact that Josie was dead. Ruth watched the dark blue Coast Guard vehicle drive away. She looked at the field grass which spread down toward the sea, the bright flowers dotting it, the lichen-yellowed rocks emerging from ancient earth. 'I will never come here again,' she said. 'Never, ever.'

She stepped off the porch and walked away from her husband, toward the freshwater pond behind the house. Hands tucked under her arms in an attempt to ease the pain which constricted her chest, she paced slowly round its perimeter. Never again. There would be no more memories attached to this house. To these places. The Point. The woods. The pond.

Every summer Paul towed the wooden raft out to the center of the pond and tethered it there; from it, both of the children had learned to swim, as Ruth herself had done years before. As she walked the reedy borders, disturbing dragonflies and katydids, the mental snapshot of her daughter's sunburned body as she dived from the dock into the water was so clear that she almost expected to hear the splash and the sound of Josie's laughter as she pushed upward again into the summer afternoon.

She picked up the trail and followed it through the woods up to Caleb's Point. She wanted views, wide horizons, to prove that there still remained something more than the stifling imprisonment of grief. Needed, too, the confirmation that in these woods, on this bluff, Josie had been happy. She remembered being pregnant, the wonder and the fear she experienced at knowing that something had begun which could not be reversed. She had dreamed of the baby swimming in her womb. She remembered how it had felt as, new-formed and naked, the child had dived from her body into the new world.

How long had Josie struggled a week ago, choking as the sea rushed in, desperate for breath, battered against the rocks? Had she known which was her last gasp? Had death come as a relief? Or had it been the cold which killed her, and not the water? Ruth thought of the girl's body floating deep below the surface of the sea, imagined crab and dogfish nibbling at her face, at her eyes, tender as shelled eggs. *Those are pearls which were his eyes*. I will never come here again. There was only one way she was going to survive the rest of her life and that was not to think about the past, simply to get on with the present.

Memories. Josie. I shall never . . . At the top of the main stairs in the cottage, where the landing widened, two further flights of stairs curving away from the main stem to left and right, there were photographs from former summers. Most of them were group pictures, showing different generations of the Carter family posed in front of the house: sailor-suited boys, girls in white cotton pinafores, young people with disaffected expressions, fat old men wearing three-piece suits and straw hats.

'How did they bear it?' Josie had asked, passing Ruth on the stairs one sunny afternoon and pausing briefly on her way to some more urgent errand. She wore a baseball cap over her hair, skimpy shorts, a torn tank top. Ruth had been filled with a sudden rush of love for her, for the long legs, the coltish knees, the curves which showed she was beginning to move away from them into womanhood. 'It must have been just as hot then as it is now, how did they *bear* all those clothes?'

Ruth had said that they probably only put them on for the occasion, to mark an anniversary or a special visit.

Josie had nodded. 'I'm glad I live now and not then,' she said.

Under the warm blue sky, Ruth shivered. She had never been so cold. Was there any pain worse than this loss? Not able to forget the hostility between them over the recent summer weeks, her mouth loosened and twisted. Death had come so suddenly, there had been no time to explain that it would not always be like this. No time, either, to describe the never-ending ache of parental love or the way in which it saturated the heart.

She bent over the accidental garden in the dip of the big boulder. If she were to kill herself, this tearing grief would be over. There was the pond: she could swim out to the middle and let herself sink. Dispassionately, she imagined the light fading above her, the water growing chillier, the cold mud closing over her. There would be something fitting in such a death. Or it could be done right here. She moved to the very edge of the bluff and looked down at the rocky beach. Soil, small stones, detached themselves from beneath her shoes; for a minute, the earth wheeled in front of her and she thought – hoped – that she was falling. One more step would end it all. Right now.

But there was Will. Her son's imagined grief at her death, and her own irresponsibility in causing it, made her realize she did not have a choice. She had to live, and suffer this endless loss. It would be her punishment.

She lay on her side in bed, staring at the round shadow of the lampshade on the wall. The room was scented by the two sandalwood chests which had come from China a hundred and fifty years ago. Through the open windows she could hear the sea, gentle now, momentarily appeased, no more than a whisper down on the shore. Josephine. My child, my firstborn, lost in that salty underworld, pierced by the spines of the sea urchin, stung by the cruel ribbons of jellyfish. Her heart felt as though it was made of lead, heavy as a coffin. Misery pressed down on her, weighting her to the bed.

Paul came out of the bathroom and she listened to him moving about the room. Heard his breathing, his bare feet on the hooked rugs. They had been married for nearly twenty years, she knew him as well as she knew herself. He would be naked except for the towel round his waist, his hair damp, sticking up. He would pick up a brush from her dressing table and smooth it down, so that he looked like a little boy ready for Sunday school. She heard the soft thud as he dropped the towel on the floor. The bed dipped as he climbed under the covers. She felt the long weight of him as he stretched out beside her. He tried to put his arms round her, as he had done a thousand times before. 'I'm here,' he whispered. 'We'll get through this, Ruth. Somehow we'll—'

She whipped round. 'Don't,' she said, her teeth clamped together. 'Don't touch me.'

He raised himself up on his elbow. His eyes were red, and she guessed he had been crying. She ought to have been moved, but the sight only inflamed her anger.

After what he had done, he had no right to tears.

'What are you talking about?' he said, bewildered.

'It's your fault.' She dropped her voice, forcing herself into a facsimile of calm. 'It's your fault that Josie's dead.'

'Ruth,' he said sadly, 'come on, honey. I understand how you feel but—'

'You don't understand anything,' she said. 'Nothing.'

'We have to support each other, we have to. No one else can.'

'If you hadn't been drunk . . .'

His body stiffened. 'Yes,' he said. 'If I hadn't, what then?'

'You'd have been more careful.'

'You mean I wouldn't have allowed a storm – a freak storm – to catch us like that, is that what you mean?' He was using his pleasant voice, the soft professorial one which screwed her up inside.

'You'd have left Bertlemy's before it started. You'd have taken more notice of the weather.'

'So it's all down to me.'

'Yes.' Her throat tightened. '*Yes.*' It had to be, didn't it? Someone had to be responsible. Otherwise, there was no justice in the world, no reason for anything. Only chaos.

'You're telling me that if I hadn't drunk three martinis, we'd still have Josie?'

'And most of the wine.'

He sighed, the sound almost a sob in his throat. 'If you hadn't forced her to come,' he said, ticking the points off on his fingers. 'If you had let us ride out the storm at sea, instead of insisting that we make a run for home. If you hadn't been knocked down by a wave when you were a kid. If you . . . what the hell good are

76

"ifs", Ruth? Where are they going to lead us? It happened, and now we have to find a way to live with it.'

'Listen to you. You sound as though all that happened was we broke a dinner plate or something.'

'That is such crap.' His face softened and he tried to pull her closer to him.

Again she twisted savagely away. 'This is our daughter we're talking about, our *daughter*, goddammit, and you act like it doesn't matter.' She pulled herself to her knees, her body trembling. 'Don't touch me. Just *don't*.' She began pummeling his chest, her fists slamming against the sunburned skin, feeling the bones beneath, trying to hurt him. Screaming abuse. Yelling at him. 'Murderer, murderer!'

In the mirror over the chest, she could see her reflection. Not her anymore, but a maenad, a fury. Hair streaming over her face, mouth distorted with hatred and rage. With grief. Did she mean what she was saying, or were her accusations simply fueled by her loss, and by a desire to make some sense out of a senseless tragedy?

5

The Medical Examiner came up from Bangor to hold an inquest in the little wood-lined room behind the Cabot Lodge Inn. Fingers peaked in front of his mouth, he listened impassively to the evidence presented by the Coast Guard. A meteorologist described the climatic conditions prevailing at the time of the accident. A marine expert who had examined the wreckage of the *Lucky Duck* declared that as far as could be ascertained, the boat had been sound and seaworthy prior to the squall.

Finally the ME nodded at Ruth. 'Mrs Connelly, I know how difficult this is for you, but could you tell us in your own words what happened in the moments leading up to your daughter's disappearance?'

Seated at a scarred wooden table, Ruth opened her mouth. Her hands clutched at the table's edge as she tried to force out the words. 'I – I . . .' she began. 'She . . .' She shook her head. It was impossible for her even to think about Josie's last moments, let alone speak about them.

The ME turned to Paul. 'Professor Connelly?'

Voice husky with grief, Paul explained about the storm, the netting which had fouled the propeller, the drift toward the rocks.

'And once you were all in the dinghy?' prompted the ME. Ruth gazed expressionlessly at him. His fingernails were very clean.

Paul cleared his throat. 'We were overturned,' he said. 'We were s-swept overboard. My wife and s-son were able to hang on but Josie ... m-my daughter was ...' His voice cracked and he broke down in tears, sobbing wretchedly as he tried to explain how it had been.

Will was absent. Having already given a written deposition, he was spared the ordeal of describing once again how his sister had vanished before his eyes.

While the sound of Paul's tears filled the little room, the ME shuffled the reports in front of him. He stared at his fingernails then looked round the room over his rimless glasses. Finally he spoke. 'The circumstances are unusual,' he said. His voice was grave and fitting. 'We are holding an inquest without a body. We have heard the witnesses describe the condition of the boat and the weather conditions prevailing on the afternoon in question. All proper safeguards appear to have been taken by the skipper and crew. Life jackets and safety harnesses were worn. We know that this is a treacherous coast.' He paused. He coughed, looking over at the Connellys. 'In my opinion, there is little to be gained in waiting, in the hope that the missing girl's body will appear. I therefore propose a verdict of death by cause or causes unknown.'

The locals who had crowded into the makeshift courtroom nodded in agreement. They had all lived too close to the sea for too long not to know that sometimes it refused to yield up what it had snatched.

'I offer my deepest condolences to the bereaved family,' continued the ME. 'It should always be remembered that even with the utmost diligence, accidents can happen. Nobody could have foreseen the violence of the storm which caused this present disaster, and I find that the Connelly family acted with all due precaution.' Smiling gravely in the direction of the Connellys, he stood up.

Someone led them away. Paul leaned against a stranger's shoulder and cried but Ruth could not weep. So swiftly was Josie's death disposed of.

A few days later, they held a short service in the little Episcopalian church in Hartsfield. 'It's not a funeral,' Paul explained to Will, who had traveled up from Boston with Ed Stein and his parents, Franklin and Carmel. 'Because there's no . . . no body.'

'Does that mean she could still be alive?' Will's voice shook as he asked the question.

'No.' Paul held his son close. 'I'm afraid not. The area's been thoroughly searched.'

'But she could have been swept ashore,' Will said stubbornly. 'Maybe she's lying somewhere unconscious.'

'After all this time? She'd have been found by now.'

'You can't be sure, Dad. Suppose someone picked her up and took her somewhere,' persisted Will. 'A Libyan tanker. Or – or a fisherman from New Brunswick.'

'They'd have contacted the Coast Guard.'

'Maybe she can't tell them who she is. Maybe she's lost her memory.'

Paul squeezed Will's shoulders. 'I don't think so,' he said quietly.

A plaque was placed on the Carter tomb in the graveyard alongside the church. Josie's friends stood in a red-eyed group, holding each other's hands. Ruth's parents and Paul's mother and brother came too, along with almost the entire population of Sweetharbor. Faces impinged themselves for a few seconds on the Connellys' awareness and then vanished: eyes, mouths, tears. Chris Kauffman and his wife Aileen stood uneasily at the edge of the huddled mourners. There was someone in a wheelchair. Someone with a beard. Dark coats, checked shirts, working boots. The trees had begun to turn by now; red leaves and orange eddied across the graveyard as they stood beside the Carter family plot. There was the chill of Arctic ice on the wind blowing down from Canada. Small flags, left over from Memorial Day, fluttered on the graves of war veterans.

Ruth stood between her husband and her son, pinched and silent. Beside her, Paul wept. Will, stiff in a borrowed black jacket, carried a sheaf of white freesias. He rested his head against his mother's sleeve, his face wet with tears. Ruth's heart continued to beat, to pump blood round her body, but she felt detached from it all, as though her capacity for emotion had been destroyed. Josie had been so full of life, and now she was dead. Since her body had not yet been recovered, this was not even her last resting place. Somewhere, out in the deep, she still floated. Ruth could see her pale drowned face every time she closed her eyes, the long hair rippling, the paint-smudged, nail-bitten hands riding the movement of the tides.

'In the midst of life, we are in death,' intoned the pastor. His voice was rich and sonorous. 'This young life . . . fulfilment of potential . . . so tragically taken from us . . . we must have faith . . . put on this earth for a purpose . . .'

For what purpose? Ruth wondered. Why should we have faith? And in what? The words meant nothing.

81

'Josie,' she said once, aloud, cutting through the pastor's prayers. It was the only sound she made. What hurt most at that moment was the fact that she had not thought to buy white freesias, Josie's favorite flower. She had not thought to buy flowers for her daughter.

After Paul had gone back to Boston with Will, Ruth made an appointment with Dee's Realty in Sweetharbor. As she walked along Old Port Street, people came up to her, faces she half-recognized, and murmured softly of how sorry they were, what an exceptional person Josie had been, so helpful, so concerned, so thoughtful of others. Ruth heard them, smiled acknowledgement, took nothing in. Their words seemed meaningless. Josie was dead.

Dee's Realty was housed on the second floor of a weathered shingled building opposite the 7-Eleven in Sweetharbor. Belle Dee, the proprietor, was a tiny energetic woman with blond hair cut close to her head. She shook hands with Ruth and poured for both of them from a pot which filled her little office with the pleasing smell of fresh coffee. She pushed over a packet of Sweet'n'Low, and tore one open for herself before stirring the contents into her cup. 'Now, how can I help you, Mrs Connelly?'

'I'm planning to close my house – Carter's House – for a while.'

Mrs Dee's pug-like face showed concern. 'I heard about what happened,' she said. 'I'm just so sorry for you. What a terrible thing to have—'

'We don't expect to be using the house for some time,' Ruth interrupted. 'I'd like your firm to take over the maintenance of it.'

'Maintenance?'

'That *is* what you do, isn't it? One of the services you offer?'

'Yes, but—'

'Then please give me the paperwork and I'll fill it out,' Ruth said.

Mrs Dee put down her cup. 'You said you plan to close the house for some time,' she said carefully.

'That's right.'

'For how long, exactly?'

'I don't know. A while.'

'Will you be back next summer?'

'No.'

'But the one after that, you'll surely want to come back.'

'I doubt it.' Ruth felt very small and cold. The possibility of stepping once again into the high wood-scented rooms of Carter's House was unimaginable.

Mrs Dee was not put off by her prospective client's brusqueness. 'Then have you considered renting? Our books are full of people anxious to rent for the summer.'

'I don't want strangers in my house,' Ruth said.

'I hate to sound fanciful, Mrs Connelly, but to my way of thinking, houses have personalities just as much as people do, and if you neglect them, they suffer.'

'I appreciate what you say.'

'Carter's House has been occupied continuously for over one hundred and fifty years.' Mrs Dee tapped the surface of her desk with her teaspoon to emphasize the time span. 'Now, for the first time in its history, you're planning to let it stand empty, long term.'

'You're used to managing properties for the out-of-towners, aren't you?'

'Yes, but—'

'And you're able to maintain houses which are left empty.'

'Of course. There's a good living to be made in care-taking the empty camps and cottages through the winter.'

'Then please add Carter's House to your list.'

'Perhaps you'll reconsider,' Belle Dee said, foraging for paperwork in the drawers of her desk.

'Perhaps.'

'Mrs Connelly—'

'Here you are.' Ruth pushed papers back across the desk and stood up. 'It was good to talk with you,' she said, then turned on her heel and went out.

Stepping into the street, she ran into a tall bearded man in flannel shirt and jeans, who took her hand and held it against his chest. 'Mrs Connelly. I'm Sam Hechst.'

'How do you do,' Ruth said tonelessly. She recalled Josie's voice telling her that Sam Hechst was Dieter Hechst's nephew and for a moment felt nauseous with grief.

'I'm so desperately sorry,' Hechst said. 'So very very . . .' His voice trailed away.

'Yes.'

'There's so little to say, isn't there?'

'There's nothing, really,' Ruth said. She gave a mean-ingless smile and stepped past him.

Later that day, driving away down the track, she did not look back. Behind her, Carter's House stood mellow in the sloping autumnal sunlight, the black shutters fastened across the windows, incarcerating her memor-ies. An era was ended. That part of her life was over.

In late September, Paul told Ruth that while he was up

84

in Brunswick one afternoon, he had run into Sam Hechst.

'And?'

'We talked. I told him we wanted something to remember Josie by. A kind of memorial.'

'Did you?'

'Something more than a piece of stone in a graveyard. He said, why not make a bench?'

'He's a carpenter, isn't he?'

'Yes, Ruth.' Paul sighed. 'He replaced the dining-room floor at Carter's House five years ago.'

'I remember now. I met him in the street.' Ruth did not want to think about graveyards and memorials to a dead girl.

'I asked him if he'd do it and he asked why I didn't make it myself.'

'Sam Hechst said that?'

'What do you think?'

'A bench.'

'My tools are all up there in the barn. I could do it. Get Will to come along, maybe.'

'She loved the sea,' said Ruth.

'I know. Will and me – we could make a good strong bench, put it somewhere where we can sit and re-member her. Sam said he'd be glad to give us a hand setting it when it's ready.'

'Caleb's Point,' Ruth said.

'Sam suggested teak.'

'She loved it up there.' Ruth remembered the after-noon when she had stood on the little bluff and thought about setting a seat there.

'Something that will last,' said Paul. 'Something that will still be there when you and I are long gone.'

'She loved it up there,' repeated Ruth. She felt like

someone walking across a frozen pond, not really sure if the ice would hold. Even the roomy apartment had taken on an air of unreality: their familiar possessions, the solid old furniture, the Tiffany lamp Paul's grand-mother had given them for a wedding present, the drapes and carpets they had chosen together, seemed scarcely recognizable now, as if they belonged to an entirely different family. Which, of course, they were. Weeks ago, she had asked Bess, her cleaning woman, to pack up everything in Josie's room and take it down to the storage area in the basement.

She thought: we shall have to move away from here, there is too much happiness gradually turned sour, the corners are full of it, it lurks under the tables and behind the drapes. I want to be somewhere else, I want all this not to be.

Most weekends that fall, Paul and Will drove up Route 1 to Sweetharbor and worked on the bench. Ruth insisted that they were not to go into the house so they sometimes stayed overnight at the Cabot Lodge Inn. Although Paul tried to get her to come with them, she always refused, shaking her head, not meeting his eyes.

'It's a great bench, Mom,' Will told her, just returned from Maine. 'Dad's carved the middle part in the back into the shape of a heart. He's really good.'

'You're not bad yourself,' Paul said, ruffling his son's hair.

Will ducked away from the hand. 'Knock it off, Dad.' He smoothed down his hair which he had been trying to shape into a movie-star quiff.

Paul said to Ruth: 'Will's a killer with the sanding machine. Smoothest wood I ever did see.'

'You should see the way Dad shapes the slats,'

countered Will. 'I gotta admit I'm impressed.'

'Never knew the old man had it in him, did you, son?'

'You told me you made that box for Mom's earrings one summer. Remember that?'

'So I did. I'd forgotten all about it.'

Father and son, united, they stared at Ruth and she looked away, hating them for being so contented with each other. Hating them, too, for being able to return to Carter's House when she knew she never would. Going to bed that evening, she took the small heartshaped wooden box from the back of a drawer and put it out on her dressing table, next to her grandmother's silver-topped jars and brushes. Paul had made it for her when Josie was born.

When the bench was finished, Paul had a small brass plate set into the top rail engraved with Josie's name, and underneath, the dates of her birth and her death. He tried to show it to Ruth, but she would not look at it. The finality of that second figure was too much for her, he guessed.

She refused to go to Maine so Paul and Will drove up without her. At Carter's House, Sam Hechst was waiting for them. Between the three of them, they heaved the bench into the back of Sam's pickup and took it up to Caleb's Point.

'I never realized how heavy teak is,' said Will.

'That's because it's durable,' said Paul. 'Hope we didn't use the wrong kind, like Ted Trotman.'

'We'd have got it in the neck from Josie if we did.'

'Tell me about it!'

'As long as you didn't buy it from one of Mr Trotman's outlets,' Will said. He laughed. 'Boy, she was really mad about that deck of his, wasn't she?'

'Sure was.'

The three of them poured concrete and set the bench fair and square, facing out to sea. They bolted it down and, when it was ready, rubbed linseed oil into the wood until it gleamed.

Finally Sam touched a finger to his fur-lined leather cap. 'Guess I'll leave you two,' he said. 'You'll want to be alone to do your grieving.'

'Thanks, Sam.' Paul shook his hand. But when the old Chevy pickup had bumped away into the distance, he could not grieve. He gazed bleakly at the gray winter-water of the Sound. Was it his fault that Josie had died? Could he have done more, done something else which could have saved her life? He would never know. The wind blew in off the sea, cold and salty, and tears ran down Paul's face, but his heart was empty.

'It's okay, Dad,' Will said. He slipped his hand into his father's, his own eyes full of tears. 'We'll be okay.'

'I hope so.'

'I kinda wish Mom would talk about it, though.'

'Not talking is her way of handling it,' Paul said.

The next morning, before returning to the city, Paul and Will went up to Caleb's Point to give the bench a final coat.

'Smells good,' Will said, when they were done.

'It does that.' Paul reached over and touched his son's shoulder. 'You miss her?'

'Of course I do. She was my . . . she was my friend, as well as my sister.' Will bit his lip. 'Yeah. I miss her lots.'

'Me too. All the time.'

'Dad . . .'

'Yup?'

'Do you think she could be . . . might she still be . . . I

88

mean, sometimes I really wonder if she's out there somewhere, still alive.'

'Oh, Will.' Tears came into Paul's eyes. 'I wish I
thought she was. I could almost bear never seeing her
again, if I thought that. But she's not, son. We just have
to accept it. She's not.'

'I guess you're right.'

They drove back to the city without mentioning
Josie's name again.

'I didn't feel a thing,' Paul told Ruth later. The two of
them were in the living room, together but, as always
these days, apart, Paul on the sofa nursing a glass of
wine, Ruth at the table, papers spread in front of her.
'The bench was there, for her, *because* of her, and none
of it made any sense at all.'

'I can see that,' she said, not looking up. The Tiffany
lamp shed a pattern of jeweled light onto her office
papers.

'I put my arm round Will's shoulders,' said Paul. He
was not even sure she was listening but the need to
talk was overwhelming. 'And he kind of squeezed my
waist, you know? Burrowed his head into my jacket,
like a puppy. We just stared at the bench there, overlooking the ocean.'

'He used to burrow like that when he was just a little
boy.'

'I know.' Paul was silent for a long moment. Then he
went on: 'I couldn't cry. I mean, there were tears
running down my face but they were tears of cold, not
of grief.'

'A bench.'

'With her name on. And a heart. The thing is, Ruth,
I haven't cried since the memorial service.'

'A carved heart.'

'I've always been in touch with my own emotions. But up there, with Will, with the bench, I couldn't cry.'

'I don't want to think about it, Paul.'

'All that macho shit about Real Men Don't Cry doesn't bother me. So why don't I cry for her? For my own daughter? Is it my sense of guilt?' His face crumpled, beseeching her. 'Oh Ruth, you don't know how often I wonder what I could have done differently.'

'What happened after that?'

'After what?'

'After you and Will looked at the bench. Up there on the Point.'

'Oh.' He looked defeated. 'Yeah, well, we stood there for a while, then went back to the car and drove back here. Stopped at Dunkin' Donuts for a coffee. Will talked about his history assignment, and the basketball team. And I told him about one of my students who wrote a screenplay during the summer vacation and managed to get a Hollywood development deal.'

'What's his history assignment?' asked Ruth.

'What?'

'Will's assignment.'

'Abraham Lincoln.' Paul frowned. 'Why couldn't I cry, Ruth?'

'She loved it up there.'

'Ruth, I . . .'

Ruth gazed at him expressionlessly then picked up her pen and returned to making notes on her papers.

She would not look back into the past. Never again. Only forward. She had found a way to manage. She worked late nearly every evening and came home too tired to talk, with a legitimate excuse for going early to bed, taking a sleeping pill an hour before she did so, to ensure that there was no chance of her lying awake, brooding over the past. On weekends, she brought papers home with her, crowding out the spaces in her life where Josie might otherwise have lurked.

She was very conscious of the fact that Will needed her more now than before. Every day she made time in her schedule to talk with him, discuss his concerns, be there for him. She tried to factor in weekend treats for him: movies, ball games, trips to New York. He was now an only child: because of this she told herself she must make allowances when he argued with her or refused to go along with some plan she had made.

'I'm going to eat vegetarian from now on,' he told her one morning.

'No, you're not.'

'Why not?' He was truculent.

'You're still growing, Will. Vegetarianism doesn't provide all the nutrients you need.'

'I can take vitamins and stuff.'

'Why not just eat meat occasionally, instead?'

'I don't want to.'

'But Will, you know how much you enjoy cooking.'

'I'll cook vegetarian. There's a lot more to it than lettuce and bean shoots.'

'But you always used to make fun of . . .'

It was a sentence impossible to conclude. Josie had decided she was a vegetarian at the beginning of the summer, becoming adept at producing combination salads and meatless dishes. Ruth had grown increasingly irked by the way she wrinkled her nose at the food the rest of her family were eating and exclaimed, 'Gross!' at least three times during every meal, gazing at her parents and brother with disgust, as though they were feasting on human rather than animal flesh.

'I know.' Will turned awkwardly away, hunching one shoulder. 'Now I wish I hadn't.'

'You do realize, don't you, how much longer it takes to shop and cook for a vegetarian diet? I'm stretched as it is.'

'I'll do it myself,' Will said.

She was wrung by the expression on his face, a mixture of need and dread, but at that moment she did not feel able to deal with either. She was needy enough herself. 'You've got other things you should be doing,' she said irritably. 'Like studying.'

She was being unfair to him. And also to Paul. Once, the book which Paul had been commissioned to write by one of the academic presses had been a shared bond between them. Now she never asked about it, knowing that he went up to Hartsfield and Sweetharbor to gather material for it, and terrified that memories of her daughter might suddenly emerge from his conversation. Withdrawal was the only way she could handle the molten heat of her grief.

Communication between the three of them had all but broken down. She fulfilled her maternal duties, made sure Will had clean clothes, that he got to his extra classes on time, wore his orthodontic brace. Her real life was lived at work. Often, reluctant to return to the aching spaces of her home, she would call to say she could not get away from the office, and remain at her desk, working on her papers.

On the nights when she did come home, she would prepare supper for Paul and Will, sit with them while they ate it, say little or nothing. Her appetite was minimal: swallowing food was too keen a reminder that her body needed fuel to keep it functioning. It seemed wrong that she was alive when Josie was dead.

'Eat something,' Paul said one evening when Will had gone to bed. 'For God's sake, Ruth.' He pushed the cold dishes toward her, offered to warm them up, but she shook her head.

'I don't feel hungry.'

'You've got to get something down. You're looking terribly thin. What good is it doing, acting like this?'

'I'm not acting.'

'You know what I mean. Harming your health won't help Will, will it? He still needs looking after.'

'I do look after him.'

'Barely.'

'That's not fair, Paul. I don't see *you* doing a lot with him.'

'I took him to the ball game last weekend. When you, if I recall, had to go into the office. Ho, ho, ho.'

'What the *hell* is that supposed to mean?'

'I think you know.'

Ruth ignored him. 'I took him to see the new Robin Williams movie the other day. And to the museum. Besides, he's too old to want me fussing round him, for God's sake. Half the time he's over at Ed's place. Or with that band of his. He doesn't need me the way he used to.'

'I wonder.'

'Even so, I can't help worrying about him.'

'Then talk to him, Ruth. That's what he really needs.'

'I can't. I just can't.' Suddenly, after all these weeks of iron self-control, she felt herself crumbling. Breaking apart. She bent over her plate and let the pain rip through her. 'Paul, I keep wondering if it's my fault she died.' She groaned, clutching her stomach. 'That's all I can think of, that I could have saved her if I'd done something different.'

'I thought I was the one who was supposed to be—'

'I know I said things to you. I shouldn't have. It was just as much up to me to see that she was safe. I was down there in the water with her. Maybe if I'd reached across to her – done something . . .' Josie's pale face floated inside her mind, the black waters rushing in to overwhelm her.

'Whatever either of us could have done or not done, she's gone,' Paul said gently. 'I know that sounds harsh, but it's true.'

'That doesn't make it any better.'

'Ruth, Ruth. We can't bring her back. So we have to continue as best we can.'

'I don't want to continue, as best I can or as worst. I don't, Paul.'

'I feel like that too, sometimes. But we have to. For Will's sake. For our own.' He glanced at her and smiled faintly. 'You've changed your hair.'

'Yes.'

'When? Should I have noticed before?'

'I only had it done yesterday. I went clothes shopping, too. Bought a whole heap of new stuff.'

'That's why you're looking so good.'

She wanted to scream at him. Could he not see that she did not care about looking good, only about looking different? Which was why she had had her hair tinted several shades darker, why she took her clients to restaurants where she had not been before, why she had given away most of her wardrobe. She was no longer Josie's mother. She wanted not to be the person she had once been.

94

6

Toward the end of October, Bob Landers came into Ruth's office. 'Do you know what the time is?' he asked.

'No.' She looked up blindly, then glanced at her watch. 'God, is it really eight?'

'Ten after. You're working too hard, Ruth.'

'Probably.' She glanced down at the papers spread over her desk. 'But there's a lot to do.'

'Haven't you got a family to go home to?'

'Actually, no. Paul's taken Will to visit his mother.'

'So you're all on your own.'

'That's right.'

He leaned over and swept her documents into a heap. 'Time to call it a day,' he said. 'Come and have dinner with me.'

'Um . . . I'm not sure I can.'

'If the family's out of town, of course you can. And I warn you, it's not just for fun. I've got a proposal to put to you.'

She flushed. 'A proposal?'

'We'll discuss it over dinner.'

They took a cab down to a harbor-front seafood restaurant. Bob ordered a Californian Chardonnay. The waitress poured it, greenly golden, into tall glasses, and they sipped it quietly, looking out at the reflections from the other side of the harbor rocking on the water. Ruth ordered the crab cakes; Bob had lobster. When they were halfway through their food, Bob said: 'How's it going, Ruth?'

She knew that he did not mean her work. 'Fine.' She put down her fork and sipped her wine. 'Just fine.'

'Is that the truth?'

'As fine as it could be, in the circumstances,' she amended.

'I know you have good cause, but recently you've been looking extra stressed. I'm not the only one who's noticed it. It's none of my business, but is everything okay between you and Paul?'

'Of course. Why do you ask?'

'You've lost a lot of weight and the Lord knows you didn't have much spare in the first place.'

'I don't seem to have time to eat these days,' she said. 'Which is why I'm grateful to you for suggesting we go out. Hey, these crab cakes are—'

'Don't try to change the subject,' he said. He put a hand out toward her, strong and square, with black hair sprouting on the back. She looked down at it, fighting inexplicable tears. She and Bob went back a long way, to college days, to before she began dating Paul. 'It's natural that you should be under strain. Losing a child must be the worst thing that can happen. I can't begin to imagine how I'd cope if it were one of mine.'

'Nobody can.'

'I guess you have to accept that you're never going to get over it, as long as you live.'

'I'm coping,' she said. 'You didn't bring me here to complain about anything I've done, did you?'

'Quite the opposite.' He lifted a forkful of lobster to

his mouth and chewed it thoughtfully for a moment. 'How's the Phillipson takeover coming?'

She shook her head. 'I know Jake likes things to go his own way, and in the past they usually have. But the unions are baying for blood. This time round he's not going to find it so easy to ignore the labor contracts.'

Bob nodded. 'I agree. Incidentally, I should have said before now that you did a fine job bringing Phil Lavelle on board. A very fine job indeed.'

'Thanks.' That summer day at the Trotmans' party came back to her. When Josie, belligerent, feisty, had been so much alive. Her throat closed; she put down her fork and tried to swallow.

'You're doing me a lot of good in the firm,' continued Bob. He looked at her affectionately. 'You're more than justifying my choice. Frankly, at the time, some of the other partners thought you were too young to be promoted.'

Ruth forced herself to speak. 'I wish.'

'And having a family is always difficult for a woman who wants to move up.' Bob loaded another fork with lobster meat and held it halfway to his mouth. 'Now listen, Ruth. I'm going to say what I brought you here to say. Unweighted. Unloaded. Then you go home and think about it. No obligations attached, no strings. It's entirely up to you, and accepting or refusing will make no difference to your career prospects with us.'

'Intriguing.'

'As you already know, some time in the new year the McLennan Corporation is scheduled to be fighting an anti-trust infringement case through the British courts. The hearing's supposed to last about three weeks but might take as long as six, and during that time we're – LKM, I mean – going to need someone on the ground over there.'

'I can't appear in a British court.'

'I know that.'

'Anyway, I don't do litigation work.'

'You'd be there as an adviser. You've worked on McLennan's affairs for nearly five years now. Nobody knows the ins and outs as well as you do. Besides, you have a phenomenal grasp of detail – which is why we promoted you, and why Dave McLennan pays our bills without too much bellyaching. And also why I thought – *we* thought, because I've discussed this with some of the other senior partners – that you'd be the ideal person to have *in situ* over there. In an advisory capacity. You've always got along well with Dave – as a matter of fact, he specifically asked for you to be part of the team. On top of that, although I'm not in the business of providing my partners with therapy, I have the feeling it might do you good to get right away from here.'

'I'm a married woman. And a mother. I can't just take off.'

'I'm aware of that fact. But Paul's around a lot of the time. And it might not be that long. Especially if the Brits can be made to see that they don't have a case.'

'It's tempting,' Ruth said slowly. A breathing space: it was exactly what she needed. There was only Will to worry about. 'I'd have to talk to Paul, obviously.'

'Do that. Take a while, consider the angles.'

'How long a while can I take?'

'Like, till the end of the week?' He grinned at her.

She took a deep breath. 'That soon? I'm very grateful, but—'

'Don't say anything now,' he said, tipping his glass at her. 'And don't be *grateful*. The decision to ask you was based on purely professional grounds. We're paid to protect the client's interests. We all love you, Ruth, you know that, but it's nothing to do with you as an individual and everything to do with wanting the best person for the job.'

When she told Paul about Bob's offer, he seemed almost relieved. 'You should go,' he said.

'What will Will think?'

'Ask him.'

'I don't want to upset him. What I mean is, am I being unfair, leaving him? Will he feel neglected if I go? After all, it's barely six months since . . .'

'You could always take him with you. Put him in school in London for a month. It'd be a real experience.'

'It's an idea. But from what Bob said, I'll be up to my eyes with work. It's going to be difficult to find time to do it all, let alone have to cope with Will. Not that he's any trouble, but he'd be an extra consideration.' Paul was raising sardonic eyebrows and she said: 'Do I sound horribly selfish and self-absorbed?'

'You could say that.' His lip had curled in the contemptuous way she remembered from their college days when, as a student politician, he dealt with right-wing hecklers who opposed his liberal policies.

'You're his parent too,' she said, stung by his disapproval.

'I think I fill my role adequately, given our circumstances.'

'God, you're a self-satisfied bastard.'

'But I'd like to think I wasn't a selfish one.'

'Look, if you disapprove of me leaving you two here for so long, why are you urging me to go?'

'Because it's obviously what you want to do.'

He was right. The thought of getting away from her

familiar places had a bracing kind of comfort about it. Somewhere new. A fresh start. 'I have to say . . .'

'So you'd better go, hadn't you?'

His voice was so inimical that sudden tears came into her eyes. She turned away so that he would not see them. What had happened to them?

When she suggested that he come to England with her, Will was adamant that he did not want to. 'I'll miss too much school,' he said.

'Maybe you could go to school over there for a few weeks. Might be fun to see how those British kids hack it. Pick up an English accent.'

'I don't want to. I'm American.' He looked down at the ground. 'And I want to be with my friends.'

'You might make some new ones.'

'I've got enough already,' he said. 'Besides, I just want to go on the way I am now.' He looked at her with a carefully neutral expression on his face. 'Do you have to go, Mom?'

'I don't *have* to. But it's quite an honor to be asked. It'd certainly be a good career move to go.'

'Right.'

'Would you rather I stayed here, Will? Because if so, I'll tell Bob Landers I can't do it.'

'Hey, good career moves don't happen that often, do they?' The effort he was making wrenched Ruth's heart. How could she leave him? Bob had said there were no strings attached, no obligations, that it would make no difference to her career prospects. She was not sure she believed him, but Will had to come first. She opened her mouth to say this but before she could do so, Paul spoke.

'I think us two guys could manage for a while, don't you, Will?'

'I guess.' Will spoke halfheartedly.

100

'Look,' Ruth said, 'I'll tell Bob I can't go.'

'If you do that, you won't be able to bring us back some of that nice warm British beer,' Paul said.

'Or a deerstalker hat,' said Will. 'With the ear-flaps? So you gotta go, Mom. I really want one of those.'

Hugging him, Ruth asked: 'Will you miss me?' and realized as she said it that the moment to turn down Bob's offer had passed.

'What do *you* think?' Will managed a grin. 'I'll have a ball while you're gone. Dad lets me get away with a lot more stuff than you do.'

'Hey, you little fink,' said Paul. 'You promised not to tell.'

'Guess I'd better not ask what went on while you two were at Grandma's.'

'*Much* better,' Paul said.

'And what will you do while I'm gone, Paul?' Sometimes they almost sounded like an ordinary family, Ruth thought, instead of a three-sided wound.

'What I usually do. Work, write, deal with my students, the ungrateful—'

'—sonsabitches.' Will came in on cue. It was a long-standing family joke.

'Visit friends from time to time,' Paul continued. 'Work out at the gym.'

He sounded as if her absence would be an ideal opportunity for him to have some fun. Once, just being together, doing stuff together, had been fun enough. Since when had being apart become better than being with each other?

She stroked Will's hair.

'Don't *do* that, Mom,' he said. 'Jeez. You don't think this kind of chic comes natural, do you?'

'Sorry.' She laughed. 'Listen, you could always come visit me in London.'

'Sure. That'd be neat,' he said politely.

The next day, Ruth told Bob that she would accept the offer and go to England.

'. . . isn't that right, Ruth?' Jim Pinkus, Ruth's associate, was raising his eyebrows at her, aware that her concentration had lapsed.

With any luck, none of the other people round the conference table had noticed. Briskly, she straightened the papers in front of her. 'I'm sorry. I was just thinking about the Internet,' she said. In fact, she had been worrying yet again about whether she had made the right decision in accepting the assignment to London. 'As we're all very much aware, it's a market segment that's going to play an increasingly important role in banking in the next decade.'

Nathan Yancey, President of Merchants' Commercial, slapped his hand down on the table. 'Precisely. We can't afford not to keep up with the current explosion in information technology.'

'Simply keeping up isn't good enough,' Ruth corrected him. 'The math doesn't work like that. These days, to stay even is to fall behind. If you want to be players, you've got to be ahead of the game. Right now, you're not. That's why the market value of your company shares is shrinking faster than a jellyfish in the sun.'

Don Seigel, Yancey's assistant, agreed. 'Which is why we desperately need this proposed acquisition. It all comes down to the combining of complementary strengths. If we're going to survive into the next century, we've got to expand.'

'You know what they're going to say, though,' said Pinkus.

Seigel groaned. He was a small, balding man with a

102

bad-tempered face and a brain like an electric drill. 'As if we haven't heard it all before, a hundred times. The banks behave how they like because they know they're protected by their market size, and they only got that big in the first place through protection legislation. Blah blah blah.' He rolled his eyes. 'Give me a break.'

'The way I see it,' Yancey said, squaring his big ex-quarterback's shoulders, 'it's like football.'

Seigel closed his eyes. He had heard the football thing before. They all had.

'Football,' repeated Yancey. 'That's what it's all about, right, Don?'

'Absolutely, Nate.'

'Gamesmanship. Figuring out what the opponent's going to do next. Exploiting the other guy's weakness. Talent and teamwork.' Yancey smiled round the table. 'Life, business: it all boils down to football – right?'

'Right, Nate.' Ruth often wondered how this man, with his gridiron metaphors and his playing-field mentality, had reached his current position. 'But while we're still negotiating, we need to keep a low profile.' She reached for a cliché he would feel comfortable with. 'I don't have to tell you, of all people, that there's no point in the sheep legislating for vegetarianism, if the wolves are against it.' She heard the faintest of snickers from Jim Pinkus and hurried on. 'At the moment, you're laying yourself open to charges of trying to stifle the competition.'

'Competition?' Yancey widened his eyes, clenched his jaw. 'I never said I didn't want competition. When did I ever say that? I don't like losing—'

'Who the hell does?' Seigel put in.

'—but I welcome competition. That's the whole point about this proposed merger with Tomorrow

103

Technologies Inc. It's about combining complementary strengths. They have the product, we have the financing and marketing skills. By going ahead with it, we'll be increasing the capacity for competition, not reducing it.'

'As the deal stands at the moment, the unions are going to fight it hard,' Ruth said. 'It'll mean some of their people will have to go.' The way they looked at her and nodded in agreement reinforced her sense of self. She felt at home here; she was in control. And best of all, she could forget Josie for a little while. 'And some of yours,' she added.

'You make an omelette, you break some eggs.' Yancey smoothed his well-groomed silver hair. 'I'm not going to pretend that there won't be some short-term job loss and redundancy, in order to maximize efficiency. But the way we see it, we're *building* the potential for good jobs, not tearing it down.'

'Five years down the road,' said Seigel, 'TTI and Merchants' will both be in a much stronger market position. And that means more jobs, not fewer.'

Again Yancey banged on the table. 'I sympathize with the unions, but I won't be bullied. Nor will I let my emotions get in the way of what looks to be an advantageous deal. The merger will be good for everyone, no question of that. Ourselves, our shareholders, our employees.'

'Hell,' said Seigel, 'it'll be good for the *country*.'

'Our job', said Ruth, 'is to get that across. It won't be easy: patriotism's not going to mean a whole lot to a guy who's just been made redundant.' She looked at her watch – they were one minute ahead of schedule – and stood up. 'Thank you, gentlemen. We'll move ahead, then. Indications are that most of the negotiations should go through without a hitch. I'll instruct my

104

associates to set up a meeting with the union people most closely involved. COBRA law means we'll have to look carefully at their continued medical insurance coverage. But I think a good outplacement scheme, together with an attractive buyout package, will help to bring them on side. We should have word for you within the next two weeks.'

As they filed out of the room, she wondered why it was that she could not run her home life as efficiently as she managed her office business.

Back at her desk, the telephone buzzed. 'Mrs Connelly?' It was a warm male voice she did not recognize.

'Yes.'

'It's Rob Farrow here. From Harvard?' When she remained silent, he added: 'I'm a – I *was* a friend of Josie's.'

She did not answer.

'I wanted to tell you how really sorry I am. About what happened.'

'Thank you,' she said, tight-lipped. Why was he calling her at the office? There was no place for Josie here. This was her sanctuary, her Josie-free zone.

'I guess they still haven't found her,' the voice continued.

'No.'

'That's so terrible. For all of you.'

Ruth put down the receiver. She was shaking as she bent over her papers.

For Thanksgiving, the three Connellys flew to California to stay with Paul's brother in La Jolla. Luke, a wildlife photographer, had recently split up with his long-time partner and, like them, needed family around him. For the Connellys, the laid-back Californian lifestyle, the sunshine and mild temperatures, were as far from Boston as they could find. Without acknowledging it, all three adults spent the vacation trying to build new memories, giving Will – and themselves – a fresh book of experiences. Starting over. They did things with him that they had never done with Josie. They ate seafood at Antony's and toured Universal Studios. One day they drove over the border to Tijuana where, in a small back street, Will bought Ruth a silver ring with money he had been given for his birthday and Ruth found Paul a leather belt with a turquoise as big as a golf ball set in the buckle. They visited the San Diego Zoo, marveled at the size of the elephants, exclaimed at the pinkness of the flamingo flock, tried to catch a glimpse of a koala bear. They drove up to Carmel, round Seventeen Mile Drive, listened to seals bark offshore at Point Lobos. At Pebble Beach, they drank coffee and watched the sun make rainbows in the sea spray.

But however much she tried, nothing soothed the raw edges of Ruth's damaged heart. She smiled for Will's sake, played long games of Monopoly, sang along to the car radio, but all the time the absence of Josie throbbed inside her like an abscess waiting to burst.

'You guys should move out here,' Luke said. 'God's own country and all that.'

'I've tried to talk Ruth into it many a time, but she's a real New England girl,' said Paul.

'Mom can't take too much sunshine,' Will explained quickly to his uncle.

'As your brother well knew when he married me.'

'Hoped I'd change your mind, darlin'.'

'Fat chance.'

'I like winters.' Will looked from one parent to the

106

other as though afraid to antagonize either one. 'I mean, California's cool, but so is back east. Right, Mom?'

'You said it, kid.'

'But it's really great to get some sun,' Will said.

On their last afternoon, Ruth and Will decided to loaf around the communal pool attached to Luke's apartment block, while the brothers drove up the coast. The two men parked on a piece of blacktop overlooking the coastal estuary, a salt-marsh preserve full of wildlife. They walked in single file along a narrow path running between stands of pickleweed and bulrush and rustling reeds. Standing on the edge of the mudflats, they breathed in lungfuls of air medicinally scented by the nearby eucalyptus groves.

'What's wrong?' Luke asked.

'Wrong?'

'You and Ruth. It's like there's nothing between you anymore. Or rather, there *is* something, but it's so darned edgy. You guys used to be one of those couples who gave marriage a good name. You were so . . . what's the word? So connected. So all this . . . is it just Josie, losing her the way you did?'

'Just isn't quite the word.'

'Don't fence with me, Paul. You know what I mean. Is it the two of you still struggling to come to terms with something utterly devastating? Or is there a real rift between you? Because that's sure as hell how it seems to this particular outsider. And, I suspect, to Will.'

'Why d'you say that?'

'Haven't you noticed how anxious he gets if he thinks you two are about to fight? Like that perfectly innocent conversation at Pebble Beach, about you two moving out here? It's as if he feels he's got to play umpire all the time.'

'I don't know exactly what's wrong.' Paul stooped and picked up a piece of shell. 'I honestly don't know. Ruth's just not – it's as if she's gone somewhere else, somewhere I can't go with her.'

'And it's splitting the two of you apart.'

'That's what it feels like.'

'Have you thought of, like, maybe a trial separation? Something like that?'

'I don't want to be separated from Ruth.'

'Listen, man, from where I'm standing it looks like you already are, whether you like it or not.'

'Jesus, Luke. You've no idea. I know it only happened a few months ago, and she needs time to get over it – we all do – but it's like living with a damned wind-up toy at the moment. She comes, she goes, she does what she has to do, but it's not Ruth anymore, it's a machine.'

'Have you tried talking to her?'

'Of course. Jesus, I *need* to talk to her. But she just vanishes into whatever hole she's dug for herself and pulls the lid over her. I think she still holds me responsible for – for what happened in the summer.'

'Do you think she's right?'

'I've gone over and over the accident. A hundred times. A thousand. We were unlucky. The squall just came boiling up out of nowhere, and if we'd headed out to sea, ridden it out, I don't think we'd have had a problem. I've talked to several people who were sailing at the same time, and that's what they did. It's just Ruth's always been terrified of the sea, and I respect her – always have – for even stepping on board a boat because every time she does, it's a real struggle for her. And she wanted to get the hell off the water.'

'What are you saying? That it was her fault?'

'*No*. I was juggling too many things, I guess, her fear,

our safety, the best thing to do. Trying to make split-second decisions. And the engine going out like that didn't help. By the time I'd called for help, it was already too late.' Paul stared at his brother. 'I have to blame myself, Luke. Like I said, I can rationalize it all, say that we just ran out of luck that afternoon, but when push comes to shove, I can't offload the responsibility on anyone else.' He bowed his head, plucked a grass stem and rolled it between his fingers. His shoulders began to shake. 'Oh Luke, what am I going to do? In the end it's always going to be me I blame. I can't forget that. I'm the one who let my daughter drown.'

Luke put his arm across Paul's shoulder. 'Hey,' he said softly. 'Hey, now.'

'And the worst thing is, not being able to talk it through with Ruth. With my wife. Every time I try, she just . . . removes herself. Goes to that other place she's got inside her head. I tell you, the silence is killing me.' A wrenching groan broke from Paul's mouth. And another. 'Oh Jesus. It's all so terrible. And it's never going to get better. Not until I'm dead myself.' He began to sob, head bent, curled against his brother's shoulder.

In the distance, the sea rolled toward them, small curved breakers of a brilliant green. A flight of cinnamon teal swung into the air, freckled against the blue of the sky. A snowy egret was fishing in the shallows, a grebe paddled energetically across a stretch of brackish water.

'Look,' Luke said, after a while. 'A brown pelican.'

Paul wiped his eyes on his arm. Sniffed. Put his field glasses to his eyes and saw, half a mile away, a heavy-bodied bird plunging itself beak-first into the breakers, emerging a few moments later with a fish wriggling in its bill. It flapped clumsily away, stretching its neck until the fish disappeared into its pouch.

'So what are you going to do about it?' asked Luke.

'If it wasn't for Will, I think I'd leave,' Paul said miserably.

'Would that help?'

'I don't know. I don't want to, but I can't see what else is left. Luckily – God, who'd have thought I'd think it lucky! – next month she's going to England for a few weeks. Maybe that'll give us both time to think. Come to our senses.'

'How does Will feel about his mother taking off like that?'

'It might be easier on him.' Paul bit his lip. 'That poor kid. Losing his sister's bad enough. To have two parents who don't seem to be living on the same planet as each other must be damned scary.'

'What about sex?'

'Non-existent, if you really want to know. Ruth and I share the same bed, but that's as far as it goes. I've tried, but she doesn't want to know.'

'It was good before, between you two, wasn't it?'

'Very. Always. Right from the beginning. I'm not being some kind of macho jock about it, either. I mean, obviously there were times when one of us wanted to and the other didn't – that's bound to happen in any marriage – but it was genuinely good for both of us, and getting better all the time. But since Josie's death, there's been nothing.'

'Is she seeing someone else?'

'She says not.'

'Are you?'

'Why would I? I want Ruth. She's my wife. I love her.'

7

Will came into the kitchen where Ruth sat staring into a cup of coffee. 'Are we going up to Carter's House for Christmas?' he said.

'I don't think that'll be possible.' Ruth kept her expression steady.

'Why not?'

'Because . . . because I'm not up to it.'

'I want to, Mom.' His voice twanged with emotion. 'I *need* to.'

'Why?'

'I just need to . . . to go back.'

'You've *been* back. You and Dad. Making that bench.'

'Not into the house.'

'It might be more than you can handle, Will.'

'Jesus, Mom. I'm fourteen. Not a kid anymore.'

You are, she wanted to tell him. Just a kid. My precious kid. And I can't give you what you want, because it would destroy me to return to the place where we once were happy. 'I know that. You'll just have to trust me.'

He sounded mutinous. 'I *like* it up there. We always go up there.'

Used to, she wanted to say. *Used* to. Once upon a storybook time. But that is all over now. 'Discuss it with your father when he gets in,' she said.

'Aw, Mom. What a cop-out.'

When Paul came in, Will tried again. 'Dad, are we going up to Maine for Christmas?'

Ruth could see that the thought had never crossed Paul's mind. 'To Carter's House?' He looked at his wife. 'I don't think so.'

'Why not?'

'I think you can imagine why, pal.'

'I can't.' Will's freckles stood out sharply against his face.

'Then try,' Paul said shortly.

'Please, Mom?'

Ruth wondered how much of Will really wanted to go back. If it was simply a question of coming to terms with the loss of his sister, he would have to wait. The image of Carter's House floated in her mind, beautiful and poisoned. She shook her head. 'No,' she said.

Will stared at her expressionlessly. 'I don't understand why we can't go,' he repeated. Recently, he had begun to avoid her attempts to embrace him, just as Josie had once done, otherwise she might have been tempted to stroke his cheek, put an arm round him. What would he say if she told him that he was the only thing which made her life worth living at the moment? That she existed only because of him?

'If you really can't,' Paul said, 'that would tell me you were not very sensitive to other people, Will. And I don't want to believe that about you.'

'I want to go with you two. Like a family.'

A family? Ruth almost laughed. That was far beyond them now. 'No,' she said again. She was undoubtedly blocking something that was important to Will. Nonetheless, the thought of opening the doors upon the ghosts in Maine was more than she was currently able to face.

'Why can't we go and live up there permanently?'

'We've already had this discussion, more than once,' Ruth said. 'We live in the city because that's where we work.'

'It's where we earn our living,' said Paul. 'Maine is a depressed area. How do you think we could afford to keep you in the comfort to which you've been accustomed all your life if we had to try to find work up there?'

'We could cut down. Live more simply.' Will glanced at his mother with an expression which knifed her heart. For a moment, it was as though Josie had come back. 'We don't *need* all the crap we've got. We've got enough stuff to last us for the rest of our lives.'

'I do not want to discuss this any further,' she said.

'You never want to discuss *anything*,' Will said. 'Never. You just shut me out. And Dad.' His eyes were stormy as he slammed off to his room.

'It's the only way I can cope,' Ruth said helplessly.

'He needs to talk, Ruth. Both of us do. All three of us. Maybe we should find some proper help, see a professional, a grief counselor or something.'

'No.' The thought was too alarming. A professional would require her to dredge up her grief, to remove her armor. 'I'm not ready for that.'

'I don't think we can go on like this for much longer.'

'Like what?'

'Living this kind of lie. Not talking about what all of us are thinking about.' Paul came over to stand behind her. 'It's not healthy, Ruth. It's not healing us.'

She picked up her coffee cup. Because Josie's body had never been found, the reality of her death would always remain clouded. Even when she was an old woman, Ruth suspected that she would still cling to the possibility that somewhere a tangible Josie still existed. 'Do you ever think that she might still be alive?' she asked suddenly.

'No.'

'Never?'

'Will's asked me that.' Paul came round the table and took the chair opposite Ruth. 'Of course she's not alive. What kind of damned stupid speculation is that?'

'I only wonder sometimes if by any chance she could have—'

'Stop it, Ruth. Stop deluding yourself.'

'I only said I sometimes *thought* about it.'

'She's *dead*. You have to face it. We all have to. To think anything else is halfway down the road to madness.'

Later, he came and sat down next to Ruth on the sofa in the living room. 'I'm sorry,' he said. 'I shouldn't have reacted like that.'

'That's okay.'

'Don't you think we should find some room in our schedules for ourselves?' He put his arm round her. Squeezed her shoulder.

She remembered the first time they had made love. She had never slept with anyone before. She smiled at him, vaguely. 'We're together all the time, except for work.'

'*Proper* time,' he said. 'Quality time.'

She had been so nervous. His hand on her breast. Not really sure what it was all about, what she was supposed to feel. He had kissed her nipples. It had been pretty much of a non-event for her, though she had never said so.

'We've been through an unbearably stressful time,' he said. 'It's been nearly six months.'

'Six months is nothing.' Ruth could think only of her daughter, lost at sea, rolling with the tides. 'It'll be with us for ever.'

'I think we – you and me – need to find each other again.'

'We still have each other. The way we always have.' It was not true, but Ruth did not want to discuss it with him now. Or ever. She looked over at the table where her papers for tomorrow were spread, and started to get up. 'I've got work to do.'

Paul held her back. 'Leave the damn work, Ruth.' He tried to kiss her but she turned her face away.

'Don't,' she said.

'Why not? We haven't made love since . . .'

'Sex: is that all you can think about?'

'Life doesn't stop. Life goes on. It has to. I need you, Ruth. I need your love. I need the intimacy of sharing. There's nothing wrong with that.'

'I don't want to,' she said, her voice sharp. 'I can't bear to, not after what happened.' She looked down at her hands, and noted how thin they looked, almost bony, the knuckles standing out. She spread them on her lap and moved the wedding ring up and down her finger. She had thought he was such a good person, in their college days. So committed, so inspiring. He had ideas about the world which she had never heard articulated before; he moved with a crowd which was not prepared to swallow the pap which they were fed by their teachers or the government, who marched in protest for their principles, who believed in things. And it had all ended up like this.

He took her chin in his hand and forced her face

round to his. 'Ruth,' he murmured. 'I'm your husband and I want to make love with you. I need to feel that life is going on, that it hasn't come to a stop.'

Once this man could move her. Once, the words he spoke would have made her soft and damp. She would have fitted herself to him, moved under him in the expert way of a loved and happy wife, waiting to ease him into herself and enjoy him in the ways which had become familiar from long usage. Now she shifted away from him, keeping her body tight. Making love with Paul would seem like a betrayal.

'What are you doing to us, Ruth?' he asked, his face set. 'Don't you feel anything for me anymore?'

'Of course I do.'

'For the past months you've been so . . . closed.'

'How else do you expect me to behave? I'm hurting, Paul. I'm dying inside.'

'We all are.'

'Ever since . . . the accident, it's been as much as I can do to get out of bed in the morning. Even at work, away from the . . . the memories, I can barely function.'

'I understand that, Ruth. But it's not just me who needs you, it's Will, too.'

'You know I try to make time for Will.'

'Oh yes. I bet it's even on your schedule: one hour with Will, in between the appointments and the papers and the lunches.'

His words pierced her. She stared at him, her mouth trembling. 'That's bullshit.'

'I can't imagine having to . . .' his voice was heavy with sarcasm, '*make time* for my son.'

'You know what I mean. No one can say I'm a neglectful mother.'

'How about a neglectful wife?'

116

'Excuse me?'

'You heard.' His gaze was hard. 'Why don't you show some emotion, for God's sake?'

'I already said: I can't afford to.' The remembrance of Josie lay tightly coiled inside her. 'I'm terrified, Paul. I honestly think that if I allow myself to give in to my feelings, I'll disintegrate.'

'You make time for your son. Ever think about making time for your husband?'

She shook her head. 'You're an adult. You have to work things out for yourself.'

He tried again. He took her hands and forced her to face him. 'We're married, Ruth. We're supposed to be a team. Don't you think I have needs? Just as Will has?'

'I also have needs,' she said sadly. 'And for the moment, this is the only way I can handle them.'

Despite William's continued pleas that they spend Christmas in Maine, the three of them flew down to Florida to visit Ruth's parents. Though they all pretended to be enjoying themselves, there was something manic behind the silences which frequently fell. They were all suffering; they all knew that if they were to allow the thoughts of Josie to emerge, they might degenerate into total meltdown.

Eventually Ruth's mother could hold it in no longer. As she and Ruth prepared food in the kitchen, while Will walked on the beach with his grandfather and Paul was down at the supermarket with a list of last-minute supplies, Betty Carter said: 'Why?'

'Why what, Mom?'

'Why Josie? Why did it have to happen? I can't understand why it— Was there anything either of you could have done to—'

'Nothing.' Ruth shook her head, trying to banish the resurrected image of Josie's face in the curious purple-black stormlight, the earrings under water, the dark space of her mouth, her terror, her . . . 'Nothing, Mom, okay? I really don't want to talk about it.'

'But I do. I need to, Ruthie. She was my grand-daughter. Don't you realize your father and I have suffered, too? And still are?'

But nothing like I am, thought Ruth. Nothing. The pain gapes inside me, the edges raw and fierce, tortur-ing me. 'I know that. But talking about it doesn't do any good. It just revives the memories.' She had thought they might have softened a little, but they had not. They surged back into her mind, as sharp, as horrific, as when the events first took place.

'That's what I'm afraid of, dear. That I'll lose the memories and then she'll be gone. You both seem to take it . . . what happened . . . so well but your father and I, well, it's devastated us.'

Ruth was seized with a swell of rage. 'How did you *want* us to take it?' she demanded. 'How else *could* we take it? Don't you think we're devastated too, all three of us? Our lives will never be the same. But what good does it do to scream and howl and bang our heads against the wall?'

'It's a natural thing to do,' her mother said mildly.

'Well, it's not the way Paul and I are dealing with it.'

'I admire the way you've both gotten on with things. I don't think I'd have had the kind of strength you have.'

'I didn't think I did, either.'

Suddenly, her mother began to sob. 'It was so terrible, Ruth. So terrible.'

'I know.'

'We were so . . . I remember the night she was born

118

. . . funny little baby . . . still got the first picture she . . . six years old . . . so pretty . . . that hair . . . like you when you were . . . so *lovely* . . .'

'Mom . . .'

'And talented . . . her painting . . . your father always thought she could . . .' Betty blew her nose, tried to pull herself back into coherence. 'She was going to be someone, we knew it from the first time we saw her, staring up at us, big serious eyes. Your dad said to me, there's a little go-getter, if ever I saw one.'

'Don't, Mom. Please.' Ruth's eyes were wet.

'You were so hard on her, though.'

'*Hard* on her?'

'Whatever she did . . . nothing seemed to please you . . .'

'*What?*'

Ruth's mother wiped her eyes. 'Poor baby. She tried her best but whatever she did, it never seemed good enough.'

'That's a terrible thing to say.'

'But it's true. Your dad and I used to think . . .' Betty quailed before the look Ruth gave her. 'You were always kind of tough on her, Ruth. I know you wanted her to be the very best she could be but sometimes . . .'

'Sometimes what?' Ruth demanded fiercely.

'You could have let things go. Praised her a bit more, criticized her a bit less.'

'I can't believe I'm hearing this.'

'You were always so much more relaxed with Will, that's all I'm saying.' Betty broke open the head of an iceberg lettuce and tore it into pieces.

Ruth was amazed at how much the accusations hurt. Was her mother right? *Had* she been harder on Josie than on Will? The way she saw it, Will was just easier to handle, always had been, right from the start. And yes, she had always wanted Josie to fulfill her potential, and if that meant pushing a bit, was that so very wrong? She was pierced by her own last words to her daughter, and by the way she had refused to take Josie's concerns seriously. She remembered her in the kitchen at Carter's House, staring at her with uncertain gray eyes. She looked out at the palm trees, the exotic plantings round her parents' tenth-floor condo, the brilliant sea. Eternal sunshine was too undemanding for her nature: she could not imagine herself ever retiring to a place like this, where everything was made easy and there were no challenges. Anxiety overwhelmed her. A friend of Ruth's had once described how her sister's unruly fifteen-year-old son had been carted away in the middle of the night, in handcuffs and chains, and dispatched to some isolated place in Jamaica. Surely Josie had not believed Ruth would pull something like that.

'What about Will?' her mother asked, breaking into Ruth's mood of self-condemnation.

'What about him?'

'Is he really as adjusted to it all as he seems?'

'What can I say? I just hope so.'

Back in Boston, Will came down with a chest infection that kept him off school for several days. Frantically, Ruth juggled her schedules so as to be home earlier and leave later, all the while fearful that she might be damaging her career prospects. She was leading a team handling a complicated bank merger against a background of dissent from a coalition of consumer-rights groups who argued that the big banks were abusing federal protection laws to increase their profits. In addition to the hearings scheduled on this issue, she was trying to find time to submerge herself in the complex details of the McLennan merger plans, preparing for the restraint-of-trade case scheduled to be heard in the British courts in the next few weeks.

Though worried about Will, she was conscious of a feeling of irritation. Why did he have to get sick now, of all times? Repeatedly she reminded herself that he was only a child who needed love and time in order to heal from the loss of his sister. Love, that was all. And time. The first she could give him but – with so much going on at the office – not enough of the second.

'The antibiotics don't seem to be doing him much good,' she said to Paul.

'I guess that's because they're only masking the symptoms, not providing a cure.'

'You think this infection is a psychosomatic reaction to . . . what happened?'

'Don't you? He's hardly had a sick day in his life until now.'

Ruth massaged her temples wearily. 'I know it sounds really unsympathetic, but this couldn't have happened at a worse time.'

Paul looked at her with disgust. 'Right now he needs support, not more guilt.'

'I know, I know.' She felt panicky. 'But I'm in a pretty severe time crunch right now. I've *piles* of paperwork to get through, and frankly, if Will doesn't get better soon, my position at LKM's going to be up for grabs. There're thousands of hopefuls out there, just dying for a chance to score.'

'Is that all you care about these days? Your career?'

'It's about the only certainty I've got left.'

'What about me and Will?'

'After the . . . after what happened, I have this constant

121

feeling that nothing's going to last. I know there's still the three of us, but deep down, I kind of expect it all to crumble.' She looked at her husband wistfully, longing for him to understand. 'Do you know what I mean?'

'No.'

She cringed inwardly at the indifference in his voice. 'I feel all the time as if I'm walking on a tightrope across a bottomless pit and if I'm not very careful, I'm going to fall in. If I put a foot wrong, I'll lose you and Will as well as . . . as well as her.'

'For God's sake,' he said impatiently. 'You're being totally irrational.'

'Am I?'

Paul reached for the TV's remote control. 'Nobody ever said any of this would be easy.'

'I guess not,' she said bleakly.

The night before she left for England, she said: 'You're sure about this, aren't you? Me leaving you and Will?'

'Absolutely,' said Paul. Avoiding her eye, he said, 'Actually, it couldn't have come at a better time.'

'What's that supposed to mean?'

'I've been thinking for a while that we need some space.'

The word filled her with dread. 'Space?'

'The time away from each other will do us both good.'

'What are you saying?'

'For God's sake, Ruth.' Impatiently he shook his head. 'Even *you* must have noticed that things aren't right between us.'

'How could you expect anything to be right?'

'They could be better than they are. With you gone, at least we'll both have a chance to think things through.'

'What things?'

'Us.'

'You mean our marriage?'

'That too.'

She was silent. 'Paul,' she said after a while, and despised the way her voice wavered. She did not want to appear desperate. 'I couldn't bear it if I lost you. I just couldn't bear it.'

He avoided her gaze. 'We aren't connecting anymore. Sometimes I wonder if we ever did, even before the accident.'

'How can you say that?' she said. 'Something like that, something so dreadful, was bound to throw us off course. We had a good marriage. We still can have.' Even as she spoke the words, she was not sure that they were true.

'I don't know who you are anymore,' Paul said wearily.

'I'm the same as I always was.'

'Oh no. No, you're not.'

Tears gathered at the back of her throat. If she gave in to them she might drown. Instead, she stiffened her shoulders. 'What are you saying exactly? That you want a trial separation or something?'

'Sounds good to me,' he said.

'Thank you, Paul. That is so exactly what I needed right now.'

'I'm sorry.' He did not sound it. 'I know my feelings aren't of much concern to you, but it seemed better to get it out in the open, before you left.'

She did not answer him. There was nothing she could say.

8

The McLennan Corporation had provided Ruth with a two-bedroom company apartment in Chelsea. It was luxurious but unexciting; it required none of her attention, did not demand that she admire or dislike or in any other way become involved with it. A woman came in a couple of times a week to clean, run errands and buy the few groceries that Ruth required.

There was a small balcony overlooking the Thames, and she sat here sometimes, bundled up against the cold of a London January, watching the play of light on the water, drinking her coffee before setting off for the McLennan Corporation's London offices. The river was always busy. Big barges drifted past on the tide, tourist boats chugged up toward Greenwich, smaller craft hurried by. She put Paul's last words out of her mind. If she was to carry out the task she had been sent here to do, she could not afford to indulge in worries about her relationship with her husband. Instead she found that, away from Boston, she could begin to let her memories unclench. To allow her thoughts to stray to Sweetharbor and Carter's House. And to Josie, a little girl falling from a boulder, in the Beetle Cat with her brother, opening her stocking on

Christmas morning with her face alight with wonder.

Ruth had been afraid she would be lonely in England. Instead she found that she was simply on her own. This she enjoyed. It occurred to her that, for twenty years or more, she had never been alone. England was virgin territory. In Boston, at the end of the day, she had to become Paul's wife again, Will's mother. Here, she was simply Ruth Connelly, judged only by her performance. She found it liberating. As the days unfolded, one after the other, she began to see that Paul was right: this intermission was exactly what they had needed. The McLennan case had already generated a ton of paperwork. Despite that, Ruth made one rule. The case could have her for the rest of the week, but Sundays were hers. Although the weather was wet and cold, she took buses from London out to Cambridge, to Oxford, to Canterbury. She stood beneath Gothic roofs, walked through ancient cloisters, and marveled. She had never seen anything like this before. She was moved by the sense of history which flowed past her in a constant stream. It was a world away from the life she was used to. It moved her but did not make her yearn to be part of it. She looked forward to being home again, taking up her life once more.

Her evenings were spent catching up with all the ramifications of what was an exceedingly complex piece of litigation, involving McLennan subsidiaries not only in England but also in France, Spain and Germany. Two weeks after her arrival, following extensive meetings with the European teams, the London lawyers retained by Dave McLennan, the Office of Fair Trading and representatives from the Competition Commission, they seemed to be making no headway at all.

Ruth telephoned Dave McLennan on his private

number in Boston. 'The Germans think we should opt to settle,' she told him.

'Fuck that.'

'I agree. So far there's been no abuse of market power, and I can't see that there ever will be. The CC doesn't have a leg to stand on. We ought to win easily. Wish you were here, though, so you could tell them yourself. It's too important a case for us to compromise on.'

'Tell you what. I was going to Frankfurt at the end of the week. I'll come a day early, via London. Set up a meeting, will you?'

'Fine.'

'Thursday, eight o'clock British time, at the Holborn offices.'

'Eight? In the morning?'

'Of course.'

'The French team is going to love that,' said Ruth.

'In that case, make it seven thirty.'

'Dave!'

'So?'

'They're supposed to be on your side. You don't want to antagonize them.'

'Don't I? Anyway, why do the bastards think I employ them? To be there when I want them there, that's why. I'll set it up with my people this end, soon as we stop talking.' There was a supercharged pause, then McLennan said, in a different tone: 'So, Ruth, how's it going?'

'Fine, thanks. Just fine.'

'Good.' The phone was replaced.

Thursday morning, Ruth found herself seated at the handsome circular zebra-wood table which dominated the boardroom of McLennan (London) Corporation.

126

The entire cast of lawyers and advisers was also there, some of them looking a little less than wide awake. Dave McLennan stared pugnaciously round at them.

'I understand there's disagreement about how best to proceed. Some of you are urging a settlement.' He paused, sticking out his chin. 'I want you to know, right up front, that I'm opposed to that. I think we should tough it out. Ruth, perhaps you'd give us your views on the matter.'

Ruth had already made her views very plain, but was happy to do so again. 'I . . . that is, we – Landers Keech Millsom – believe that it's premature at this point to settle. Quite apart from the question of establishing precedent, we think we stand an excellent chance of prevailing, if we go the distance.'

Nick Pargeter, the English lawyer, nodded. 'So do we. Frankly, I can't understand what the problem is.' He was the most elegant man Ruth had ever met: his suits were beautifully cut, he had the kind of English hair she associated with gentlemen's clubs.

'But what happens if we lose?' said one of the gray-haired, gray-suited Germans.

'This is the problem.' One of the French nodded. 'In such a case, we could be looking at a disaster.'

'We aren't *going* to lose,' said Pargeter. He cast his eyes up to heaven, not bothering to conceal his exasperation. They had been over this, or very similar, ground numerous times in the past week.

'I don't need to tell you, gentlemen,' said Ruth, 'that there are basically two ways to fight any case. When the facts are on your side, plead the facts. When they aren't, plead the law. In this case, the facts are our best ally.'

'What do you mean?' It was the gray German again. She had already explained to him a number of times

127

how the facts worked in their favor. Hiding her impatience, she kept her hands lightly curled on the table in front of her. 'Herr Jacob, as I've said before, in order to prosecute us successfully in an anti-trust action, the Commission must show there has been an abuse of market power. In other words, that competition has suffered or will suffer. We believe the present market is simply too volatile for that claim to stand up to the scrutiny of the court.'

'As we've repeated from the very beginning,' said Pargeter.

'Then why are they bringing this case in the first instance?' demanded the Frenchman.

'Nick, do you want to explain?' said Ruth.

Pargeter gave an exaggerated sigh. 'Ms Connelly has told you that the market is volatile. That's because new players are coming in every day, including the Japanese, and the Germans. Your own compatriots, Herr Jacob. So no one can claim a controlling share, because no one knows for sure how big the market actually is.'

'That might change in eighteen months, two years,' Ruth put in. 'But as matters stand at present, the prosecution is whistling in the dark.'

'Whistling in the dark?' The Frenchman frowned.

'Flying a kite. Um . . . haven't got a leg to stand on,' said Pargeter. Ruth saw his mouth curl as he tried to suppress laughter.

'It is all very well', said the gray German, 'for you, Frau Connelly, and you, Herr Pargeter, to be so carefree. But the consequences if we lost this case . . .' He shook his head. 'You will not be around to pick up the pieces, but we shall.'

'So shall I,' said McLennan. 'And I don't want to lose this case anymore than you do. If I thought there was

128

the slightest chance of losing it, I'd go along with you guys, press for a settlement. But Miz Connelly here disagrees with you, and that's plenty good enough for me.'

'I assure you', Ruth said, 'that LKM doesn't offer its advice lightly. Perhaps you recall Texaco *v.* Pennzoil?'

The French team shook their heads.

'Remind them,' said McLennan, impatiently.

'Some years back, lawyers from Texaco's investment bankers gave them poor advice, which caused them to be sued for breach of contract. The loss literally bankrupted them, they had to file for Chapter Eleven, and begin all over again. The investment bankers still haven't recovered their credibility.'

'I remember this now.' The Frenchman threw up his hands in despair. 'And you are asking us to see this as a reassuring example?'

'Not in the slightest. I merely mention it to demonstrate that we're very aware of your liability if things go wrong – and ours! But Mr McLennan is paying us a high six-figure retainer every year to give him the best advice we can. And personally, I think he – and you – would be foolish to ignore it.'

The Europeans grumbled, conferring with their associates, shuffling through their papers. Nick Pargeter drummed his fingers on the table, staring at the ceiling. Catching Ruth's eye, McLennan winked. 'I've ordered a continental breakfast to be brought in,' he said to the company at large. 'Coffee, croissants, fruit. And some cheese for you, Herr Jacob.'

The gray German permitted himself a small gray smile. 'Thank you.'

'Shall we have it now?'

Paul had reorganized his teaching schedule so that

during Ruth's absence he could spend most of his time in Boston, in order to be around for Will. For the first time, he wondered if he had ever really given his son the time he needed. His own father had always been busy, out on the road, pushing some new line for whatever company he was currently working for. The most Paul ever saw of him was a weekend here and there, when he would sit, prematurely gray, stubble-chinned, watching football on TV until it was time to take off again, his big sample case sitting on the back seat of his car. Paul could not remember a single conversation he or his brother had ever held with their father. When he died, unexpectedly, in Pensacola, his passing made scarcely a ripple in the fabric of their family life. Paul had always determined that he would be a better father when he had children of his own.

Ruth's absence had panned out conveniently. Even before Bob Landers' offer, he had arranged a sabbatical semester in order to make a final push on his book. With any luck, he would be able to deliver it to his publishers by the end of the month.

On the way back from seeing Ruth off at the airport, he and Will had a serious discussion about mealtimes. 'I'm warning you,' Paul said, 'I'm not intending to live off vegetarian glop for the next few weeks.'

'Who said anything about glop?' said Will. 'Some vegetarian food is real gourmet stuff.'

'Prove it.'

'Okay, I will. Bet by the time Mom comes back you'll refuse to eat anything else.'

'I don't think so.'

'I do. But hey, I'm not gonna end up on kitchen duty every night. That wouldn't be fair. I mean, I've got stuff to do. The band. The team.'

130

'How about some studying?'

'That too.'

'Okay. Turn about's fair play. I'll be chef one night, you the next. But you ought to eat meat every other night, if I've got to eat veggie.'

'Dad, trust me. After tasting my stuff, you'll never touch meat again.'

The two spent a lot of time shopping together in the Farmers' Market, dreaming up elaborate menus for each other, cooking, eating together, enjoying each other's company. Without Ruth's wounded presence casting a blight over the apartment, Paul found himself regaining some of the former joie de vivre which had vanished with the death of his daughter. It was not that he wanted to play down her loss, simply a recognition that life had to continue without her, and given that fact, then there was enjoyment to be squeezed from it. He put his relationship with Ruth on hold: it was, he decided, the best way to handle it.

One night, as he watched the late movie, he heard Will moaning in his bedroom. Quietly opening his door, Paul saw that the boy was asleep but tossing restlessly, the sheets kicked down, his pillows on the floor. As he watched, Will moaned again, flinging out an arm as though pushing something away.

'Will.' Paul put a hand on the boy's shoulder. 'Wake up, son.'

Will groaned a few indistinguishable words.

'It's okay,' Paul said reassuringly. 'I'm here. You're all right.'

Slowly, Will opened his eyes, stared up at his father, the shreds of the nightmare still clinging to his expression.

'What was it?' Paul demanded. 'What were you dreaming about?'

'It was awful. I dreamed I was—' He broke off. 'That we were all—'

'All what?'

'All drowning.' Will grabbed Paul's hand so tightly that the bones cracked. 'We were out in the boat and the sea came . . . and we were all drowned.'

'Sssh.' Paul sat down and put his arm round Will's shoulders. 'It was just a dream.'

'She swam away,' Will said painfully. 'She said if it wasn't for me, my birthday, none of this would have – would have happened. And then she vanished under the water. I could see her, Dad, her face disappearing under the sea, all white, and she was saying it was my fault she was drowning.'

'That's nonsense, Will,' Paul said, shaking the boy's shoulders. 'I've told you that before. So has your mom.'

'No. It's true. I was the one who wanted to go to Bertlemy's, so we did, and then the accident happened. If we'd stayed home . . .'

'How could it possibly be your fault? You weren't responsible for the storm. Or for anything else that happened that day.'

'I *was*. It was because of me wanting that stupid picnic on Bertlemy's. If I hadn't done that . . .'

'An accident like that, any accident, can happen any-time. And most of the time it's absolutely nobody's fault.' Paul could see the luminous hand of Will's bed-side clock. 'Look, Will, it's nearly two in the morning. Want to come and keep me company in bed, the way you used to when you were little?'

'I'll be okay, Dad.'

'Are you sure?'

'Sure.'

Paul bent to shake up his son's pillow and as he did

so, something fell onto the floor. He picked it up and put it beside Will's head. A cuddly bear with a spotted bow tie and big brown eyes of glass. He frowned. 'Isn't that – wasn't that Josie's?'

'Hardy, yeah. Uncle Luke brought it back from England.'

'Where did you get it?'

'From Carter's House. After the accident.'

'Will . . . It's not going to be easy, to get over losing Josie. It'll take time, you know that, don't you?'

'That's what the guy at school said.'

'Which guy?'

'The school shrink. I – I went in to see him the other day, talk to him.'

'Did you?' Paul hoped his voice sounded sufficiently casual, though he could feel the thump of his heart. 'Did someone suggest it would be a good idea?'

'No. It's just, he told me a while back that if I ever needed to talk to him, to go right on in. So I did.'

A bubble of guilt and sorrow filled Paul's chest. Was his son so unhappy that he voluntarily went in to see the school counselor? Oh Will, Paul thought. What can we do to help you?

When Ruth next called from London and asked how Will was, Paul said forthrightly: 'Not good.'

'What is it?' she demanded. 'What's wrong?'

'He's not sleeping well. Having nightmares.'

'What about?'

'Would you believe death? By drowning?'

'Oh, no.'

'Not just his own, but all of us.'

'I guess I hoped that after all this time . . .'

'I know. He doesn't talk much about what happened. I suppose he's over-internalized all that grief and turmoil and it's coming out this way.'

'Maybe he needs to talk it through with someone more objective than his parents, like the school psychiatrist.'

'He already has, a couple of times. It was his own decision.'

'Oh no. The poor baby. He must be feeling terribly lost.'

'I spoke to the guy myself, and he said we had to be prepared to accept that it would take a very long time for him to get over the trauma of bereavement. If he ever did. Things might get worse before they get better, he said. Even told me that these chest infections Will gets could be down to that.'

'He still blames himself.'

'That's what he said last night. He'd been dreaming that . . .' Ruth had for so long refused to use her daughter's name that now Paul too found it hard to do so, 'his sister was accusing him of being responsible for her death.'

'That's terrible. And whatever we say, he'll go on believing it.'

'Did you know that he sleeps with . . . with her teddy bear?'

'What was he called – Harvey? No, Hardy. I thought he'd been left at Carter's House.' There was a pause. 'Paul, should I . . .' He could hear Ruth's reluctance in her hesitation. '. . . come back? I can, if you think it would be best. I mean, it would be really difficult but—'

'I can't see the point.' Frankly, Paul was happier to be alone in the apartment with Will. Ruth's absence made things easier all round. At least for now. 'It's not as if we can do much to help Will.'

'So we just go on showing that we love him.'

'I do that,' Paul said sharply. 'All the time.'

'Me, too.'

Paul did not respond.

Ruth called to say she would come home for the following weekend. 'Oh, damn,' Paul said.

'Well, thanks a lot.'

'I don't mean we don't want to see you. It's just that we've already set some things up.'

'Can't I join in?' she said, chilled that he was not more enthusiastic about her visit. Would they still have a marriage when she got back? 'What sort of things?'

'Well, Will was planning to go off somewhere with Ed, so I've arranged to go up to Brunswick, hold a couple of seminars, that kind of thing.'

'Are you . . .' She hardly dared ask the question.

'Am I what?'

'Is there someone you're seeing?'

'No, Ruth, there is not. But the way you've been lately, it would hardly be surprising, would it?'

Ruth did not push it. After all, she was the one who had chosen to move three thousand miles away; she could hardly blame them for making plans which did not involve her. 'How about the weekend of the spring break?' she said. 'You could both come over, travel a bit. I can't be around the whole time, but there's no reason why you two shouldn't have fun. And we could go to Stratford-upon-Avon. Will's studying *Macbeth* in his English class, isn't he?'

'Could do, I guess,' Paul said.

'You don't sound too keen on the idea.'

'It's a lot of trouble and expense for just a couple of days or so. And frankly, I'm kind of worried about Will. He's not eating well.'

'He can't afford to lose his appetite, Paul. Not on a vegetarian diet.'

'Hey, tell me about it.'

'I wish he'd give up this vegetarian kick. You're making sure he takes those vitamin supplements, aren't you?'

'Yes.'

'How about the nightmares? Is he still having them?'

'Sometimes. He's doing such a lot at school at the moment that some days he gets really tired. But that's adolescence for you. He's got an iron supplement to take: they thought he might be anemic. I've arranged for him to take a blood test.'

She tried to ignore the unspoken criticism in his tone. 'It's most likely trauma-induced, isn't it?'

'That's what the school shrink suggested. It's not been easy for him, these past months. Of course, if you were *really* worried, you'd come on home.'

She refused to be irritated by the implication that she could – or would – so lightly abandon the work she was involved in. 'As I said, that would be difficult. I have to be on call all day, every day.'

'Of course you do.'

His sardonic tone flustered her. 'No one else knows as much about the case overall as I do. That's why they asked me to come here in the first place.'

'Right.'

'Paul, it'd be virtually impossible to find someone to take over from me at this late stage.'

'When is it likely to end?'

Ruth did not tell him that there was a possibility the case might overrun its original schedule. Dammit: they had discussed Bob Landers' proposition together; together they had reached the decision that she should accept it. If his college had wanted him to go overseas for a semester, she would have encouraged him to do so and accepted the consequences. 'A week or two more,' she said, deliberately vague. This was not the moment to talk about the sense of acceptance which was seeping into her bones as she watched the river traffic from her balcony, as she busied herself with matters which contained no emotion.

Nonetheless, she felt both guilt and worry about her son. Sometimes she wondered whether she should face up to the scorn of the senior partners and tell Bob Landers she had to come back to Boston. Rationalizing, she told herself that if she did go back, there was little she could do to help Will through this period of delayed mourning. He would have nightmares whether she were there or not. And remembering his words on that last evening, she knew it was better to give Paul the space he had said he needed.

Which she needed, too.

'Want to go up to Maine for the weekend?' Paul said.

'Cool.'

'We could take off in the afternoon, be there by supper.'

'Don't guess we get to stay at Carter's House, do we?'

'Not this time, pal. I'll book us in at the Cabot Lodge. I thought we might go for a hike, get some air in our city lungs, check up on our bench.'

'It'll be cold.'

'According to the weatherman, *damn* cold.'

'I can handle that.'

'Me too.'

It was almost dark by the time they reached Sweetharbor. They took their bags up to the room they were sharing, then walked down Old Port Street to stand on the harbor quay. Snow was falling. Yellow dusklight was reflected in the ice which hemmed the harbor waters. The lobster boats lay still on the dark water, rusty and battered. There were fewer of them than Paul remembered; in the course of researching his book, he had heard too many stories of layoff and bankruptcy not to realize how fast the fishing industry was declining, year by year. Beyond the harbor, the stony shores were bleak, the trees and rocks powdered with snow. The wind rammed across the gray water, tugging at the boats at their moorings. Chains rattled. Lines thrashed and snapped.

'Aren't you glad you're not a fisherman?' Paul said, his breath pluming into the freezing air. Even through layers of winter-proof clothing he could feel the bite of the cold.

'One winter, Josie went out fishing with Ben Cotton,' Will said. 'She told me it was the coldest she'd ever been in her life. Took them thirty minutes just to get through the ice to the mooring.'

Paul shivered. 'No wonder your grandad moved to Florida.'

That evening they took in a movie playing at the little local cinema before turning in. The next day, after a big breakfast, they drove up to Carter's House and parked in front of the barn then struck up through the trees toward Caleb's Point. The going was tough. Snow lay beneath the trees, obscuring the trail, making it easy to blunder into crevices, to trip over concealed roots and creepers.

'Still want to move up here permanently?' Paul asked, taking a breather. He leaned against a treetrunk and clapped his arms several times around himself. 'Jeez, it's cold.'

'You got to admit, Dad, it's kinda gutsy living up here.'

'Guess I'm happier being a coward down in the city.'

'Think about the Cottons and Hechsts,' said Will. 'And all the other year-rounders.'

'I do think about them,' Paul said. 'Which is exactly why I don't want to be up here in winter, thanks very much. There's only so much the human spirit can endure.'

'We've endured, haven't we?' Will looked very small beneath his layers of wool and flannel. Under his woollen cap, his face was pale. Paul was moved by his son's expression. And by his words. There was so much left unsaid. 'Yes,' he said quietly. 'We have.'

When they finally reached the bluff, they sat for a moment or two on the bench they had made together. It looked as if it had sat there for ever, as much part of the scene as the snow-flecked grass and the boulder with its now-withered little garden. The wind roared at them, burning their cheeks with minute slivers of ice, burrowing inside their clothes, goosebumping their flesh.

'I'm cold,' Will said. He stood and stroked the carved heart on the back of the bench with his gloved hand. 'Josie,' he said softly. 'She loved it up here.'

'Josie,' echoed Paul. He took his son's hand.

'We had some good times here, didn't we, Dad?'

'We sure did. And will do again.'

'Except Mom doesn't want to come back.'

'One of these days . . .' Paul said vaguely, able to promise nothing. The house belonged to Ruth; he had no say over when they might return. He remembered her white face when the Coast Guard had arrived with Josie's lifevest, and her vehement voice: *I will never come here again. Never ever.*

139

As they came down the trail, Ben Cotton's pickup eased round to the back of the house. The back of it was piled high with frost-covered logs. He waited until they reached him then got out stiffly and shook Paul's hand, enveloped Will in a bear hug. 'How ya doin'?' he said. His breath hung in the frozen air. His eyebrows were stiff and gray with cold. Years of Maine winters had grizzled his complexion to the texture of leather.

'Fine. And you, Ben?'

'Good. Good. Things is kinda slow, though.'

'Always the same, this time of year.'

'Don't know that it's been this bad before.' The old man let out a long breath. 'Heard you was back, so I brung you some wood. The log pile's gettin' kinda low.'

'That's good of you, Ben.' Paul moved his shoulders around, searching for warmth, then unzipped his jacket and reached a hand inside.

Ben stepped back, holding up thick-mittened hands. 'No,' he said. 'Don't want payin'.'

'But Ben . . .'

'Old Doc Carter was good to us. Looked after Marietta real kindly. Never asked for one red cent. Besides, what's a load of wood?'

'It's time, Ben. And money. You could sell it elsewhere. And we're not staying.'

'No?'

'Not this time.'

'You wuzzn't here at Christmas, neither.'

'Maybe next year.'

Ben smiled at Will, wrinkles fanning across his face like feathers. 'Been up to the Point, have you?'

'Ayuh.' Will grinned back.

'Gorry but it's cold up there – least you're all garbed up.' The old man touched Will's shoulder. 'That's

140

some elegant seat up there. Made it yourself, I heard.'

'Me and my dad,' Will said proudly.

'And how is Miss Cotton?' asked Paul.

'Thank you kindly for askin', Marietta's middlin' good. Missin' Josie, though. Used to come visitin' whenever she could, cheered her up. She was some good girl, your Josie.'

'She was that,' Paul agreed. Here, in the deep-down cold of winter, in the place where Josie had belonged, he found it easy to talk of his daughter. How different it was from the stifled unspoken grief of the Boston apartment. He was unexpectedly glad that Ruth was not with them.

The old man turned away. 'See you some time.' Raising a hand in farewell, he climbed back into his pickup.

Back in Sweetharbor, Paul and Will dropped by to see Mrs Dee. She shook hands warmly. 'We don't often see you summer people up here at this time of year.'

'We thought it would do us good to get out of the city.'

'How do you like this weather?'

'It's wonderful,' Paul said. 'I'm really enjoying freezing to death. Stay here much longer and if I'm really lucky, my toes'll drop off.'

She laughed. 'With regard to the house, there's been a problem with the septic system, nothing serious. I had it fixed.'

'Good.'

'And a shutter came adrift, but I got a carpenter in – it's been sorted out.'

'Sam Hechst, I bet,' Will said.

'That's right. A real good worker.' Mrs Dee checked her papers. 'I ought to warn you that some of the empty cottages have been broken into. We do our best to keep a lookout but . . .' She shrugged.

'There's not much to be done. According to my wife, it happens every winter.'

'How *is* Mrs Connelly?'

'She's in England, on business.'

'Ah.' Mrs Dee shifted the files on her desk. 'She asked me not to forward the mail, so I've left it at the house.'

'That's fine. We'll pick it up some time.'

'Why not today?' Will said.

'Yes, why not?' Mrs Dee put her head to one side.

'I think my wife would prefer it if we didn't,' Paul said.

'She said you wouldn't be coming back this summer: any change on that?'

'No.'

'It's stupid,' Will said loudly. 'I don't see why we can't come back.'

'Your mom doesn't want to,' said Paul. He knew he was passing the buck, blaming Ruth when on this one he agreed with her: he too was not ready yet to step inside the house and see signs of Josie everywhere.

'Will and I went up to Carter's House,' Paul said, telephoning from Boston one evening.

'Oh?' Ruth closed her mind. She did not want to hear about it.

'Didn't go in, of course. Just looked around outside, made sure everything was shipshape. Mrs Dee's had a shutter fixed and cleared some problem with the septic system.'

'Good.'

'We went up to the Point, too. Checked out the bench Will and I made.'

142

'Did you?' Ruth was seized by a sudden sense of loss and rejection. Her husband and her son had formed a unit of two, while she was here on her own. 'How's it surviving the winter?'

'Just fine. By the way, Mrs Dee says there's mail in the house.'

'I told her not to forward it,' Ruth said quickly. It would be letters of condolence for the most part. She was still not ready to read the polite regrets of other people.

'That's what she said.'

Ruth changed the subject. 'How's the book coming?'

'Fine. The publishers had a few queries and one chapter's going to have to be rewritten, but otherwise they're pleased with it.'

'I'm so proud of you, Paul. I'll be able to tell people I'm the wife of a published author.'

'That'll be almost as good as having a wife who's a partner in a prestigious law firm.'

His tone was cool, but Ruth let it pass. 'When do they plan to publish?'

'Next year, probably, in time for the fall semester. But you can't count on it. These academic presses work to a schedule that bears no relation to normal life. Might not appear for five years, might be out next week. Who knows?'

She felt a sudden need to break through his distance to the warm reservoir of his love. 'Paul, I—'

'Here's Will.'

'Paul . . .' But he was gone.

'Hi, Mom.'

'Hi, honey.' Hearing her son's voice, Ruth was overwhelmed with regret. 'How're you doing?'

'Fine.'

'Fine fine, or *really* fine?'

'Really fine, Mom.'

'You sound tired.'

'You'd be tired too, if you had an English teacher like I've got. What a ball-breaker.'

'That's no way to talk about Miss Carling, William.'

'That's Marling, Mom. If you'd made it to the Parents' Night last semester, you'd have met her and you'd know what I mean.'

'Sorry.' Why had she missed the evening? Ruth tried to remember – a meeting that had run over time, as far as she could recall, and then Bob Landers had asked her to take the client to dinner. 'So it's nothing but the mountains of homework that are taking it out of you, is it?' Ruth kept her voice light, trying not to appear over-anxious. Will really did sound exhausted. She trusted Paul, but she knew that it was she who should be supervising her son's life. That's what mommies were supposed to do.

'You betcha.'

'I'll be back soon, hon,' she told him. 'Very soon. Promise. I really miss you.' Her voice skipped a beat, broke.

'Hey,' said Will, awkward. 'Don't go all weepy on me.'

She tried to laugh but could not. 'Weepy? *Moi?*'

'I'm being a good boy and drinking up my milk.' As always, he tried to lighten the atmosphere, scared by the intensity of adult emotions. 'And I promise to quit smoking, cut down on the booze, stop gambling and flush my stash down the john, okay?'

This time she managed to laugh. 'Okay.'

Putting down the receiver, she thought she had never been lonelier.

Two days later, she sat at the apartment's dining table, her papers spread across it. She was going over them one last time before sitting in on a meeting tomorrow between Nick Pargeter and the Commission people. Although the well-briefed Pargeter had all the facts necessary to put his case to the bureaucrats, he had nonetheless requested that she be present, in case questions about McLennan Corporation's dealing came up which he could not answer.

From the intercom attached to the wall beside the door she heard a squawk. When she went to the speaker, she was astonished to hear Chris Kauffman's voice asking if he could come up.

'Third floor,' she said. She pressed the buzzer and opened the door. 'Chris!' she exclaimed as he appeared on her landing. 'What are you doing here?'

'I'm in town for a couple of days,' he said, giving her his almost-smile. 'I ran into Bob Landers a couple of weeks ago, and he said you were in London. I thought I'd look you up.' He handed her a sheaf of freesias. The faint sweet fragrance pierced Ruth's heart.

She poured Chris a drink. He had put on weight since she last saw him, though his suit was expensive enough to cover it. She asked after Aileen. How work was going, what the kids were up to. They chatted inconsequentially, and all the while she wondered why he had come, what he wanted. As Chris psyched himself up, she realized with dismay that he was going to say something about Josie – it was clear in the shift of his eyes, the set of his mouth. She tried to keep talking, but eventually he put his glass down. He was not going to be deflected.

'Ruth,' he said, leaning toward her. 'I haven't seen you since the memorial service for Josie. I guess

145

you know how I – how all of us – felt about that.'

'Yes, Chris. I do.'

'It was just a terrible thing to happen. Terrible.'

'We'll never get over it.' Stop, she wanted to shout. Don't. But he went on.

'Sixteen.' He shook his head. 'So young. And she was such a pretty girl.'

Don't!

'She looked so like you,' he said. 'I always thought that.'

Stop!

But it was too late. Her defences had been breached. Grief, long-dammed, poured through her. 'We loved her so much,' she whispered. 'So very much.' Helplessly, she began to cry. 'Chris,' she said. 'Oh, Chris.'

He took her hand.

'You can't – you simply cannot imagine the pain I feel. The pain . . . That last afternoon, Paul and I were – I can't forgive myself. I can't stop wondering if she remembered it as she was . . . was dying, whether the last memory she had was of me screaming at her.' Tears streamed from her eyes. 'It haunts me. And she was so . . . so hostile that last summer.'

She remembered, suddenly, that last day, Josie's voice, contemptuous. Could she possibly have known about their short-lived affair? If so, what kind of opinion could she have had of her mother? Ruth's face burned.

Chris was holding her. 'Kids her age are like that.'

His shirt was wet under her cheek. 'I never – I never told her how much I loved her, Chris. I can't stop hoping that she knew – and being afraid that she didn't.'

'I think all our kids know we love them,' Chris said.

'She was full of some kind of pain, that summer, and I was too busy to find out what was causing it,' said

146

Ruth. She could feel a skin peeling from around her heart. The protective covering she had wrapped round it had been torn by Chris's questions and she was vulnerable again in a way she had refused to be ever since it happened. 'I want her back,' she sobbed. 'I want it all to be different. I miss her so. I want my daughter back again.' Her tears seemed to well up from some inexhaustible spring, as though they had waited all this time for release. She pressed her fists against her wet face. 'She asked me if I would give up my life for her and she didn't believe me when I said yes. But I would. I would have done, Chris. Gladly.' She fell against the back of the sofa and opened her mouth wider to let out the groans of pain. 'Oh. Oh, Josie. My child. Oh, God. I can't bear it.'

'Don't, Ruth. Don't.' Chris put his arms around her and they rocked together.

'It can never be put right,' Ruth said. 'That's the very worst thing of all. She's gone and I'll never ever see her again.'

'Have you talked to someone? There are people trained to help. Counselors.'

'I've got to work it out for myself.'

'Ruth, Ruth.' Chris tilted her face up to his. 'You may not be able to. There are some things we need help with. This could be one.' He leaned forward to kiss her lightly on the cheek but Ruth turned her head so that his lips met her mouth.

'Make love to me,' she whispered urgently.

'Ruthie . . .'

'Please, Chris.' Suddenly she understood what Paul had meant when he said that making love was an affirmation that life continued after even the darkest tragedy. 'Please.'

147

'Honey, I don't think this is what you really want.'

'It is. Oh, Chris. It's exactly what I want.' She kissed him again, thrusting her tongue into his mouth.

He pulled her roughly against him. 'Christ, Ruth. I didn't come here for this, I swear.'

'I know.' She began to undo his shirt, pulled at his tie. He put his hand inside her blouse and down into her bra. As he held her breast, brushed her nipple with his finger, excitement flowed through her body like electricity. She tore at her clothes. 'Oh Chris,' she moaned. 'Quick. Come inside me. Deep deep inside. Quick. Fuck me, Chris. Fuck me the way you used to.'

In the bedroom, she fell back onto the bed and opened her legs to him. When had she last made love with Paul? Somewhere in the distant past. She remembered what he had said that last night: '*I don't know who you are anymore,*' and her reply, '*I'm the same as I always was.*' Then Chris was pushing into her and the old familiar fire raced through her, blotting out her pain, blotting out her loss.

9

A few days later, Nick Pargeter called her. 'They've given in!' he said, his tone exultant. 'We are talking total capitulation.'

'What?' Ruth had gone to bed around two, after working the entire evening on one of the clauses that the OFT seemed to find particularly difficult to accept. And it was now – she glanced at the alarm clock beside her bed – barely seven o'clock. 'Who's capitulated?'

'The Commission, blast their eyes,' said Nick. 'I had a formal letter this morning. They've agreed that there's no case to answer and that we're off the hook.'

'That's *great*!'

'Just a couple of days to sort out the nitty-gritty, and after that, we can all go home.'

Energy seeped back into her body. Total capitulation: it sounded so good. 'Hey, Nick, do we make a great team or what?'

'Unbeatable. You and me, I'm talking about, of course. Not that frightful German shower.'

'If Herr Jacob had said "I vish to be qvite clear vere ve stand on zis" one more time, I was going to scream!'

'I think I *did* scream, on more than one occasion.'

'But he had a very nice line in pearl-gray ties, don't you think?'

'Pearl-gray ties to match his pearl-gray personality,' said Nick. 'No, it was that blasted Frog who got me down.'

'Do I detect a hint of xenophobia?'

'We're all Europeans now, so I wouldn't admit for a single moment that I was anything but the most fervent admirer of all things French—'

'Of course.'

'—but, let's face it, the man's aftershave was an abomination. Bring back the guillotine, I say.'

Replacing the phone, Ruth felt light-headed with euphoria. She could not remember when she had last felt so good. They had won! Or, rather, they had presented such a tight defense that their opponents had realized there was no case to answer. Dave McLennan would be delighted. Her colleagues at Landers Keech Millsom even more so.

Paul greeted the news that Ruth was coming home with mixed feelings. 'That's wonderful,' he managed to say. He wished he meant it.

'As soon as I've dealt with a few outstanding matters, I'll be back. The end of the week, probably. Friday.' The excitement in her voice confused him. For so long she had shut down; now it sounded as though she was opening up again.

'I – I can't wait to see you,' he said.

'You don't sound very convinced.'

'Of course I am. We've missed you.'

'Have you—' she dreaded his answer, 'had any more thoughts about us?'

'Plenty.'

'And?'

'Let's talk about it when you're back.'

Apprehension seized her. 'Paul, please . . .'

'When you're home,' he said firmly.

When Will came in from school, Paul told him the news.

'Oh no!' Will said.

'What's up? Don't you want to see your mom again?'

'It's not that.' Will looked round the apartment. 'We better do something about this place.'

'Looks okay to me.'

'To me, too. But it won't to Mom. Especially with Bess being away sick the last two weeks. Look at your trainers out there in the hall, and that yucky sweatshirt you wore down to the gym. It's been lying in the corner of the bathroom for days.'

'So I missed the laundry basket.' Paul grimaced. 'But I guess you're right, kid.'

'The kitchen's kinda disgusting, too. I burned that thing I made last night, and I can't get it off the bottom of the pan.'

Paul ran his finger across the coffee table and held it up for Will's inspection. 'Are we slobs, or what?'

'Superslobs.'

'Something must be done.'

'And you, Dad, are just the guy to do it. I've got a history project to get on with.'

'Oh, *right*. When the going gets tough, huh?'

'You got it.'

Ruth's absence had crystallized one thing for Paul: he could no longer live with the barriers she had built between them. He had talked about needing space: space was all there was now. The only thing they shared was Will. Even their grief over Josie was separate and individual. When Ruth got back, he would move out. Not for ever, maybe, but for a while. He had already looked at an apartment near the Boston campus, a one-bedroom bachelor apartment he could lease for six months.

He was not proud of himself. What would Will think of him? Could he just walk out on his son? He had longed to be able to talk to someone about it, but his brother was away on an assignment in South America and he did not want to distress his mother. There was nobody else to whom he felt he could entrust his doubts and despair.

A couple of evenings later, as he walked across the campus parking lot, he ran into Carole Barwick, from the Philosophy Department. Seeing her, he remembered she had taken the last semester off, though he could not remember what she had intended to do in the time, if he had ever known.

'Hi, Paul,' she had said, holding an armful of books, trying to fit her key into the lock of her car. 'Good to see you again.'

'Welcome back,' he said. 'Enjoy your sabbatical?'

'Very much. I got a lot of work done.' A couple of files slid from the pile in her arm and he bent to pick them up, standing in front of her, thinking he had not realized how attractive she was, thinking maybe the time off had done her good. 'You're on one now, aren't you?'

'That's right.'

'Finishing a book?'

'Not just a book, but *the* book.'

She surveyed him critically. 'You're looking pretty down. Anything in particular that's wrong? Or is it life in general?' Her voice was soft and sympathetic, reminding Paul of how much he longed for a bit of kindness. He tried to remember if there was a husband, a family.

'Do you have time for a coffee?' he asked, hoping he did not sound desperate. 'A beer? A bottle of wine?'

'Make it a glass, and I'll say yes.'

They ended up at a nearby wine cellar, squeezed together on a padded bench under a low whitewashed ceiling. The music was loud and defiantly Sixties, the clientèle mostly student, the choice of wines surprisingly good. Carole was persuaded after all to share a bottle of wine; talking together, Paul found her quiet voice as soothing as warm oil. If only Ruth had been like this over the past months. If only the two of them had been able to talk about Josie, instead of sealing themselves inside their separate griefs. Three glasses of wine in and he found himself pouring out his problems, to the insistent beat of the Stones. 'I'm thinking of moving out,' he concluded. Said like that, it sounded stark and uncaring.

Carole listened attentively, her kind face concerned. 'Shouldn't you talk to Ruth before you leave?'

'Talk? Ruth doesn't talk. Not to me, at any rate. That's part of the trouble. She used to, but since we lost Josie—'

Lightly she touched his hand and withdrew again. 'I felt so deeply for you.'

He remembered a note she had sent, one of many from colleagues he had scarcely known. 'Ever since then I haven't been able to get through to her at all. And now she's coming home after working on a case in England, and somehow I just can't face it. Moving out seems the best of a series of bad options. I don't know what else to do. Or how else to do it.'

'You've been living on your own?'

'My son's with me, so not alone in the sense you mean. Just wifeless. And it's been good, just the two of us, without—' Paul stopped, ashamed of what he had almost said.

'Do you want a divorce?'

He shook his head. 'I still love my wife – I *think*. At least, I love the Ruth she used to be.'

'You sound like you blame her for this breakdown in communication.'

'Some of it's down to me, I know that. But I do feel as if I've been trying against all the odds to hold things together, whereas she's simply opted out.'

'What's it going to do to her if you leave?'

Paul laughed a little bitterly. 'On recent form, she probably won't even notice.'

'Are you sure?'

'She's plenty strong enough to handle it.'

The music changed. The Grateful Dead. Reminding him that all those years ago, he too had been young. Looking at the youthful faces all round them, Paul wished he still possessed their absolute confidence that things would turn out well.

'More importantly,' Carole said, 'what will it do to your son? How's he going to cope with you leaving?'

Her eyes were a curious green-brown color which reminded Paul of a forest pool. Beyond her, he could see two of his students leaning toward each other across a table, heads pressed together at the forehead while they stared sideways at him. Probably wondering if there was a thing going between him and Ms Barwick.

'He's the one I worry about. He's already pretty screwed up by the accident. For a while there, he

154

seemed okay, but it's all coming out now. Nightmares, infections, withdrawal.'

'Is he seeing anyone about it?'

'Just the school counselor. If there was anything I could do to help him out of it, I'd do it. But the way things are right now, I don't see that there is.'

'So you're going to walk out on him.'

'Put like that, it sounds irresponsible of me.'

'Isn't that what it is?'

Crammed against her in the vaulted space, he could smell her perfume and, under it, the faint acrid smell of her sweat. 'Don't think I don't know that I'm acting like a shit. But what else is there to do?' On second thoughts, it might be kind of fun to have people wondering about him and Carole Barwick.

'Stay. Tough it out.'

'I've tried that, and it didn't work. It's not exactly an ideal family situation for Will, is it? Two parents locked into a Cold War situation? I keep telling myself I'll be a better father to him if I'm happier myself.'

'Sounds like the usual hypocritical bullshit men your age come up with when they're trying to justify their decision to abandon their responsibilities.' Carole lowered her eyes. 'It's what my husband said before he left me for somebody else. "Think of it as creating two happy homes for the children," he told me, "rather than one unhappy one." If I hadn't been so glad to see the back of him, I'd have hit him.'

'But I'm not moving out because I'm looking for something or somebody new. It's just, I can't go back to the situation we were in before Ruth went to England. The coldness. The distance.'

'She's lost a child, Paul. The thing that every parent dreads most. How do you expect her to be?'

155

'I feel like I can't talk to her about anything. At least, nothing that matters to me. Maybe one of these days we can start over, but for now, I've just got to get out.'

'That's the coward's way,' she said crisply.

'Is it?'

'Yes.'

Walking her back to her car, Paul found himself wanting to ask if they could do this again sometime. And might have done so if he had believed there was the slightest chance she would say yes.

'Ruth, have dinner with me tonight,' Pargeter said. 'To celebrate the successful conclusion of our joint undertaking.'

'I ought to be packing. I fly out tomorrow and there's still masses to clear up in the apartment.'

'Leave it. We've been working all the hours God gave on this case. A decent meal and a bottle of bubbly is more than our due. We'll charge it to McLennan's.'

Ruth thought of the mess back at the Chelsea flat. And then of how much she would like to have dinner with Nick Pargeter. 'All right,' she said. 'On one condition.'

'Name it.'

'You don't invite Herr Jacob along too.'

He laughed. 'I may be an uptight Englishman, but I do have some notion of what constitutes a good time. And it does *not* include Herr Jacob.'

Later, over excellent food, they talked about everything except the case. That was finished. For each of them, the next project already loomed. But first, there was time for this interlude. 'I'm going to miss you,' Nick said regretfully. He raised his glass. 'Not many lady lawyers are both as sharp and as funny as you. It's an exhilarating combination.'

'Thank you.'

'And beautiful with it.' He surveyed her from under half-closed lids. 'Why did you become a lawyer?' he asked suddenly.

'There's a question.' Thoughtfully she sipped her wine. 'Why does anyone do anything?'

'There's an evasion.'

She sighed. 'I guess I wanted to change the world. Don't we all, when we're young?'

'I can't remember that far back.'

'I did, though. And instead I took the easy path, went into corporate law when the chance came. It wasn't the money that tempted me, it was the prestige, the chance to show that I was as good as, if not better than, most.'

Pargeter poured her another glass of wine and she raised it to her mouth, thinking back to college, to the plans she and Paul had made, her determination that somehow she would make a difference. 'Yes, I decided on law because I wanted to right wrongs, work miracles. I wanted to make the world a better place for the little people. I remember . . .' It was coming back to her in a warm rush of nostalgia, 'I remember being appalled, in school, at the way the law could be subverted, how there seemed to be one law for the rich and another for the poor.'

'It's the same in this country.'

Ruth's face was flushed with an emotion she had almost forgotten. 'And how unfair life could be, and how the law was supposed to be there to protect the innocent but so often it wound up protecting the guilty.' She laughed. 'My daughter was just the same. She used to get all fired up about the unfairness of things.' It was the first time she had thought of Josie without pain. 'She

157

was sixteen . . .' The words slipped out before she could stop them.

'Was?'

'She . . . died. Last year.'

'My dear, how perfectly awful for you.' He put a hand over hers. 'How dreadful.'

'It was. It still is. It will always be. I haven't handled it well, I think. I felt that the only way I could cope with something so terrible was to block it out. I've been using my work as an excuse not to deal with it.'

'What happened?'

'It was a sailing accident.' The sound of the wind in the sails and the crash of the waves came back to her with a vividness that was almost unbearable.

'Was anyone to blame?'

'Blame?' She stared at him, her eyes suddenly filling. 'Blame?'

'Ruth, I'm sorry, I shouldn't have asked . . .'

'We were caught in a squall,' she said painfully. 'My husband wanted to ride it out, but because I was frightened I wouldn't agree, I wanted to get home. We drifted onto the rocks . . .' It was something she had never admitted before. 'I guess if anyone is to blame for my daughter's death, I am.' She could feel his emotional withdrawal. He had expected a mild flirtation with a colleague over a bottle of claret and instead he had been drawn into something private and desperate. She looked at her watch, said lightly: 'My God, is that the time? I still have so much to do. Would you mind, Nick, if we broke this up now?'

Paul met Ruth at the airport. Despite the heavy work-load of the past weeks, her time on her own had smoothed away some of the lines of stress which had begun to gather round her eyes and mouth. She looked younger and more carefree than she had for some time, and consequently – to his distress – smaller and more vulnerable. No longer the competent, ambitious lawyer, but someone much closer to the girl he had fallen in love with.

Oh, hell. How well he remembered that little duck of the head when she saw him, as though her pleasure at being with him again would blind him with its brightness if she did not deflect it. He recalled other meetings, other comings together after separation, when he would sweep her into his arms, call her name, feel his heart soar with the sheer joy of seeing her once more. He put his arms round her.

'Where's Will?' she said.

'He had to stay after school. Basketball practice.'

'I can't wait to see him again.'

'He's looking good. He's shaken off that cold at last. Eating everything in sight. I'm making trips to the supermarket three or four times a day, to keep him from chewing up the furniture.'

'I'm glad he's got his appetite back. From what you told me, I was seriously worried about him.'

'Not *that* worried,' Paul said.

'Excuse me?'

'Or you'd have come home earlier than this.'

'That's unfair.'

'Is it?'

Ruth felt her gut clench with anger. 'Yes, it damn well is. And you know it.'

'If you want to know what I think—'

'I don't. And I'm not going to argue about it now: I'm far too tired.'

They walked together to the parking lot, the silence

thick and awkward between them as Paul backed the car out and made his way onto the freeway. After a while, he asked about the wind-up of the McLennan case and she told him some of the details. Finally, she said: 'I'm bushed.'

'Why don't you close your eyes now,' Paul said. He gripped the steering wheel, willing her to agree. 'We can talk later.'

He turned his head and smiled at her. Jesus: what a rat he could be. But driving along the freeway was not the optimum location for telling your wife you were leaving her. To his relief, she yawned and leaned her head against the back of the seat.

He felt sick. What would she say when he told her? He glanced at her and noted the familiar line of her jaw, the little chocolate mole just below her left ear. She had once been so dear to him. So familiar. And now? He didn't really know. There was a void where love used to be. Although he had gone over the arguments a hundred times during her absence, he still found himself debating his decision. Was he doing the right thing? What about Will?

They traveled up in the elevator without speaking, avoiding each other's gaze. When he let her into the apartment, she looked around appreciatively. The place gleamed. The furniture was polished, the rugs vacuumed, there was a vase of white freesias on the coffee table. Even the windows sparkled. 'Wow! You must have paid Bess extra, to get it looking like this,' she said.

'Bess is off sick.'

'Are you telling me *you* did this?'

'I would – if I thought you'd believe me,' Paul said. 'No, I found someone in the Yellow Pages. They came

160

in and scrubbed the place down. For a price, of course.'

'It looks great. Wonderful.'

'Will and I decided it was that or jumping out the window before you saw what it looked like without you in charge.'

'Bess won't have to clean house for six months,' she said lightly.

Paul went into the kitchen. 'Coffee?' he called. His hands were damp with sweat.

'I have to take a shower before I do anything else.'

In the shower, she closed her eyes as the water fell over her shoulders. Despite the spat at the airport, there was still so much between them. It had been a long time since they made love, far too long. It was her fault, she knew that. She was ready to acknowledge how wrong she had been. The separation had made her realize how much he meant to her. Above all, she wanted to tell him that it was not his fault that Josie had died.

She came out of the shower with a towel wrapped round her and said, without preamble: 'Let's go to bed.'

'What?'

'I want to make love with my husband again, Paul. Let's do it, before Will comes home.'

'Ruth, I . . .'

'It's so good to be back with you,' she said. 'I've missed you so much.'

'Me too.' Slowly he came toward her, put his arms round her. 'You're dripping water on the carpet.'

She stood on tiptoe and kissed him, pressed closer to him. 'Paul,' she murmured. She undid his shirt and let the towel slip. Slid her hands over his body. Felt again the silky skin that she had not caressed for so many months. His tweed jacket was rough against her

161

body. She ran a finger along the hard line of his ribs, touched the jutting bones of his hips, the firm flesh of his thighs. When she moved down his stomach to the wiry hair of his crotch, she expected to feel his erection, hot and strong, ready to take her quickly and fiercely. But . . .

'Paul,' she whispered. 'What's wrong?'

'I don't know,' he said.

'Don't you want to?'

'I do, but . . .'

She stepped back. 'But what?'

'Not now.'

'Then when?'

He looked at her hard and she could see the shine of tears in his eyes. 'I don't know.'

She turned away. 'I feel like such a fool,' she said.

'Don't. It's my fault, not yours.'

In silence, she bent to pick up the towel, covered her nakedness, went into the bedroom. When she came back, fully dressed, he was in the kitchen, drinking coffee, staring at the table. 'Okay,' she said. 'Let's talk.'

He drew a deep breath into his lungs. 'I'm . . . I'm moving out, Ruth.'

'You mean, leaving us?'

'Not Will. Just you. You, the way you are.'

'You don't want to give us a second chance?'

He shrugged.

'Is it because I went to London?'

'No. It's more than—'

'It wasn't just my decision.'

'It's *not* that. I told you before you went: we just don't seem to have anything in common anymore.'

'That's a pretty poor reason. Especially after nearly twenty years together.'

162

'It's the main one I have.'

'Is this all because of the . . . what happened?'

'Let's face it, Ruth. Things weren't going right before that.'

'Nowhere near wrong enough for you just to pick up and go.'

'You don't begin to understand my feelings. Maybe that's what was wrong with us in the first place: an inability to see the other's point of view.'

'We didn't start out like that.'

'Perhaps we changed too much somewhere along the way. When you joined LKM, you became a different person, someone I didn't know. Your work always seemed to be more important than we were.'

'I always tried to do my best for everyone.'

'Especially for Ruth Connelly.'

'That's so unfair,' Ruth said furiously. 'I *had* to work. In all the time we've been married, you still haven't been able to put together a tenure-track post.'

Paul sighed. 'I wondered how long it'd be before you brought that up.'

'It's the truth.'

'You know as well as I do why I couldn't get tenure when I first hit the job market. Nobody could – there just weren't any positions going. And since then, there've been more and more cutbacks.'

'You've always resented the fact that I earned more than you did.'

'Most men would. I did my best. Nobody could say I didn't work hard – and still do. Commuting between Boston and Brunswick, assistant prof one place, part-time lecturer at the other, writing the book. Whatever I did, I was never going to match your salary.'

'But I didn't see it as *my* salary – it was *ours*.'

'Right. But you controlled how we spent it. And made me feel pretty worthless while you did so.'

'That's not *true*. It was always *us*, as far as I was concerned, never just me.'

'Look,' Paul said. 'I know you think I'm a shit—'

'I don't.' She buried her face in her hands. 'Even now, when you're behaving like one, I don't think that.'

'—but I can't take your constant disapproval anymore.'

'I *don't* disapprove of you.'

'That's not how it looks from where I'm standing. You've put such a distance between us that I don't see how we can ever cross it.'

'Don't say that, Paul,' she begged. 'Please don't.'

'We've been apart for – what, nearly four weeks? And I'm afraid I've enjoyed it, being on my own with Will. It's been such a relief not to be shut out by the person I'm supposed to be closest to.'

'I've changed. The time away helped me to see things so much clearer.'

He shook his head. 'I've changed too. I loved you once. Maybe I still do. But every time I think about us, all I can remember is you ignoring me, keeping me at arm's length.'

'You're right. I know that. But I realize it now and I didn't before. Oh, Paul . . .' She was crying. 'Don't go. Please don't.'

'We want different things now,' he said quietly.

'No, it's not true.' *If I put a foot wrong*, she had said, *I'll fall into the abyss.* And here she was, falling, falling.

'I feel as though your job gives you more satisfaction than I do.'

'Again, not true.'

'I just don't seem to figure in your life anymore.'

164

Ruth wiped the tears from her face with the back of her hand and picked up her coffee mug. Anger had begun to build where only minutes ago there had been anguish. He was going to walk out on them, just like that. He had been planning it all the time she was away. 'You've made up your mind, haven't you?'

'That's right.'

'If you want to leave, then you should go.' She looked down at her wedding band. She was frightened suddenly. She had hoped that they could start again and instead they were breaking up completely. 'I suppose there's another woman?'

He tried to speak but she rushed on. 'What is she, one of your students? Some young creature who props up your ego, and makes you feel like a stud? Stares up at you with big adoring eyes every time you speak? Well, believe me, Paul, that won't last. You've seen it happen on campus a dozen times. Ten years down the road, you'll be in the same situation with her as you think you are with me, except you'll be supporting two families, not just one, and you'll be ten years older.' Ruth pushed back from the table. 'You're crazy if you think—'

'Ruth.' He reached over and put a hand over hers. 'There isn't anyone else.'

'Then – why?'

'If you'd only talked to me, instead of burying yourself in your work.'

'My fault again.'

He spoke very deliberately: 'I need to talk about Josie.'

She flinched. 'I can't, Paul. Not here, where she . . . Not just yet. Soon, maybe, but not now.'

'That's why I have to go.'

'Have to?'

'You don't know how many times, since Josie died, I've reached out in the night for you, and you've pushed me away.'

'So this whole thing comes down to me. It's all my fault.'

He did not answer.

'Does Will know?' she asked.

'It seemed only fair to wait until you got back.'

'Fair? Did you say *fair*?'

He seized her hand again, held it tight. 'When I first met you, I thought your eyes could see right into my heart. The first time we . . . when I felt your naked breasts against me, I thought: this is someone I want to know, I want to spend the rest of my life learning.'

For a moment she was on the verge of flinging herself into his arms, once more begging him to change his mind. Then she remembered how he had looked when she stood naked in front of him. How he had turned away. 'Very touching,' she said.

'Oh, Ruth.' He shook his head. 'Perhaps it's my fault you've become what you are now.'

'Someone you don't want . . .'

'Someone so hard that you'd need a digger to find the person underneath.' Paul stood up. 'I don't want to be doing this. We've walked together down a road we thought would lead us somewhere—'

'And found it's a dead end.'

'But the truth is . . .' He hesitated. 'The truth is, I'm more comfortable when you're not here. I can cope better on my own.'

She gazed at him in disbelief. 'How can you . . .? That is such a hurtful thing to say.'

'If you'd just allow yourself to show some emotion. If you would only talk to me . . .'

166

'How many times do I have to tell you I've changed? The time in England was just what you said: it gave me space to think. But since you've made your mind up, what is there to say?' Tears began to roll again down her cheeks.

'If you'd just tell me you still loved me, then I'd stay.' He stared at her challengingly: 'Tell me, Ruth.'

For a long moment, she hesitated, then she looked away. 'If you're leaving, better do it before Will gets back,' she said.

10

He left before Will came home from school. His bags had been packed and stowed in the back of his car. Sitting in the driver seat, he leaned over and popped open the glove compartment where he kept a photograph of Ruth. She gazed at the camera, laughing, eyes squinched up against the sun. Clear gray eyes, just like Josie's. Every time he looked at her, he saw his daughter again. God, they were so alike. Not Ruth now, but Ruth as she was when he first met her, eighteen years old, walking across College Green in a blue cotton skirt, her blond hair pony-tailed. Ruth, kissing him for the first time, never been kissed before, she said, except once there had been a boy at a party, a sophomore from Brown, who had shoved his tongue down her throat.

Suddenly, he was weeping. A grown man sitting in his car, sobbing. What would people think if they saw him? What did he care what they thought? All that mattered was whether he was doing the right thing. It was hard to know. He smudged the tears away and stared into the bleak concrete space of the underground parking lot. If she came down now, if the door of the elevator opened and she came toward him across the oil-stained concrete, asked him to stay, he knew he would.

He turned the key in the ignition, floored the accelerator, gunned out of the parking space and up to street level, just missed hitting a messenger on a bike. He slammed on the brakes. Stupid bastard shouldn't have been on the sidewalk in the first place. His hands trembled. Across town, the sterile new apartment waited for him. He looked right and then left, wondering where to go, whether just to take off and drive forever, right across America to California where he was born, leave the mess of his personal life behind. On the other side of the street, the guy in the barbershop was staring at him through the window. He burned rubber, cutting across one taxicab to get into the stream of traffic, almost rear-ending another. Christ! If he wasn't careful he'd end up in the ER.

He hadn't smoked since the kids were born; now the desire for the rush of nicotine into his bloodstream was almost unendurable. There was sweat on his forehead and his upper lip; maybe he was running a fever. At the lights, he flipped the indicator, ready to turn, ready to go back. Ruth, he thought. I think I love you. But if he changed his mind, the situation would simply revert to what it had been before. She had said things were different now but he did not really believe her. 'Tell me, Ruth,' he'd said. Meaning, tell me you love me. But, for whatever reason, she hadn't been able to do it. At the last minute, as the lights blinked from red to green, he pulled straight ahead, and listened to the indignant horn-blasts of the drivers who had piled up behind him.

After so many weeks in the anonymity of Chelsea, Ruth had looked forward to being among her own things again, sitting in familiar chairs, eating off plates which she had chosen herself, picking books out of the bookcases, cooking in her own kitchen. Instead, she moved about the big apartment in a daze. Jetlag made her brain feel sluggish; she could scarcely keep her eyes open. Objectively she noticed that the bedrooms needed repainting, that the bathroom she had shared with Paul for so many years had a faintly musty smell and there was – despite the hired cleaners – mold on some of the caulking.

Paul. The thought of him quivered in her heart. There had never been anyone else but Paul, not really. Chris Kauffman, briefly. Nobody else. She sat down on one of the two broad window-seats and stared unseeing at the traffic in the street below. When she was first pregnant with Josie, they had decided they should buy rather than go on renting, and although this roomy, slightly shabby apartment had been way beyond their means at the time, both of them had felt at once that here was where they wanted to live.

'What seems like a fortune in monthly payments now will be peanuts in five years' time,' Paul said bravely, looking up from the depressing figures their budget made, whichever way they worked them.

Nothing had mattered back then except being together. Building together. 'We'll swing it,' Ruth had said, holding her stomach, reassuring the baby inside.

'Only if we walk everywhere, reduce our alcohol consumption and cut food out entirely,' said Paul.

'As long as we can pay for a diaper service, we're okay,' Ruth said, 'because I'm not washing them by hand.' And they had both laughed a little shakily, well aware of the financial risk they were taking. Josie had been born here, and later Will. And if they ever tired of the city streets, the explosive blend of fumes and noise and crime, there was always Carter's House waiting for them up in Maine. But now, all Ruth could think of was that Paul was gone. In the days ahead she would probably learn to paper over the wounds, but for now there was only an agonizing sense of loss.

Much later, she heard Will's key in the lock. 'Mom!' he said, his face alight. 'You're back.'

'Did you think I wouldn't be?'

'Of course not.' But she could see that at times he had been afraid.

She hugged him, held him tight. When she finally let him go and looked at him properly for the first time, she was suddenly alarmed. What was going on here? In the few weeks she had been away, he had changed. He looked ill. Exhausted.

Sitting with a coffee in the kitchen, while he drank most of a half-litre of milk straight from the carton, she said carefully: 'Your father has moved out.'

He wiped his mouth with the back of his hand. 'Where to?'

'I don't know.' Paul had tried to tell her but she had found it impossible to stay in the same room with him. Before he left, he had said something about writing down his new address and leaving it on the pinboard in the kitchen but she had not yet looked at it.

Will's eyes widened. 'You mean, like, moved *out*?'

'Yes.'

'I don't get it. Has he gone to live with somebody else?'

She herself could not comprehend it, so why should he? 'He says not.'

'Are you upset?'

'We've been married for nearly twenty years.' She got up and hugged him again, trying to hide her tears. 'Honey, I'm sorry. I'm really sorry.'

'It's not your fault.'

'I sort of think it is. Or *he* does, which comes down to the same thing.'

Will scratched at the waxed surface of the milk carton. 'Do you still love him?'

'Of course I do.'

He bit his lip. She watched him trying to be brave, trying to pretend it did not matter. Her chest ached with the realization that he did not want her see how upset he was. 'I don't see why he's all of a sudden got to go,' he said.

'After me being away so long, I think he's realized he's happier living on his own.'

'What about me?' His chin trembled. 'I'm his *son*.'

She started to weep. 'Ah, Will. Sweetheart.'

'We had some good times together while you were in England,' he said. 'I thought he loved me.'

'He does. He does. His leaving has nothing to do with you. It's not your fault, I swear it. You must always believe that, Will.'

'First Josie, now Dad,' he said unsteadily. 'Why does shit like this happen? What did we do?' He began to sob. 'What else is going to happen to us, Mom?'

'Nothing, Will, I promise you. This is as bad as it gets. From here on in, it'll start getting better.' She put her arms round him and held him close. 'And maybe, after a while, Dad'll realize it's more fun living with us than on his own.'

'He said we'd rebuild the *Lucky Duck*,' Will said. His body shook with repressed sobs. 'Him and me, we were going to . . . He said it'd be our spring project.'

'It still will be. Just because he's – he's living somewhere else doesn't mean he's stopped being your dad.' How could Paul want to rebuild the boat

172

in which his daughter had drowned? It made no sense.

The two of them swayed together, mother and son, until Will jerked himself upright, wiped his face on his sleeve. 'Don't cry, Mom.' He put his hand up and curved it round the line of her jaw in an oddly adult gesture. 'We'll be okay.'

'Will we?'

'Paul's gone, Dad.'

'How do you mean, he's gone?' Ruth's father sounded as if she had just woken him up. She could hear the television in the background.

'He's left us. Moved out.'

There was a silence, then Jonathan Carter said: 'Oh, dear God. Oh honey, I'm so sorry.'

'Dad, I . . .' She could hear her father calling his wife, telling her to switch the damn TV off, and her mother's sudden alarmed response as she snatched the phone away from him.

'Ruthie. Darling. What's happened? What's wrong? Did Dad get hold of the wrong end of the stick? These days his hearing's not all it—'

'He heard okay.'

'Paul's gone?'

'Yes.'

'*Left* you?'

'Yes.'

'Why? Why?' Betty Carter's voice rose. 'Why'd he do that? I don't understand. You two were always so . . .'

'I know we were.'

'Was it because you went to England? I was afraid this would happen, I always wondered if it was wise, leaving him on his own. Men are kind of—'

'There isn't anyone else, no other woman,' Ruth said. 'Or so he says.'

'Ruthie. Oh, Ruthie. Are you all right?' Her mother began to weep. 'Of course you're not, how could you be? This is just terrible, I can't believe it.'

'Nor me, Mom.'

'What about Will?'

'Poor baby. Poor kid. He's being so brave about it. Oh Mom . . .'

'Want us to fly up and be with you?'

'Not just yet. Not till I've . . .' Pulled myself together, Ruth wanted to say, then wondered how long that would take.

'We love you, hon.' Her father came back on the line. 'Remember that, Ruth. You'll always be our darling girl.' His voice fogged with emotion. 'Ruth, I'm so sorry . . .'

'Dad, Dad. I don't know what to do.' Ruth broke down. She rested her head against the wall beside the telephone and let herself cry, open-mouthed, the way she used to as a child, when she knew that whatever went wrong, her parents could put it right. Dimly she could hear her father's tears, and, behind him, her mother's inarticulate cries of distress. They were there for her now, as they had always been. The way she had not been for Josie. 'Oh, Dad, what am I going to do?'

Suddenly there was such a rush of work that she barely had time to scramble through the days. Coming home exhausted at night, she would find messages from Paul on her answering machine. She did not return the calls. She was running on autopilot, juggling home and work, aware that home was coming off second best. Paul's departure meant that her self-confidence was at its

174

lowest ebb, but at the office she was treated with a respect which helped to fill some of the hollows in her heart. The successful outcome of the McLennan Corporation's anti-trust case was seen as a triumph for her; word had spread and people began to seek her opinions, drop by her desk to ask for her advice. Bob Landers suggested they should move her to a bigger office; he hinted at further promotion.

Her initial concern about Will's health abated somewhat. She put his paleness down to the fact that he was growing too fast. He seemed to be getting taller by the day: his clothes appeared to have shrunk, sleeves halfway up his arms, pants way above his ankles. Each night, before she went to bed, she would stand at the doorway of his room, checking whether he lay awake, whether his sleep was disturbed. At least the nightmares Paul had spoken of seemed to have stopped. Looking at his face on the pillow, hearing the steady sound of his breathing, she was able to believe that the alterations in his behaviour were simply his way of coping with the stresses to which he had been subjected.

Almost overnight, he had become difficult and uncooperative. His response to her grew increasingly hostile. She tried to adjust to life without Paul, make things easier for him, but he offered her no help.

'How did it work when I was away?' she asked him. 'You guys had some kind of routine for running the place, didn't you?'

'What's your point?' he said rudely.

'Dad told me on the phone that you were taking turns cooking. Want to go on with that?'

'You're back now. Anyway, I won't have time – my workload this semester is unreal.' He sounded like his father.

175

'We'll just have to eat out more, then, or call stuff in, because I'm also up to my—'

'I don't eat junk food.'

'Takeout's not junk.'

'Stuff cooked at home's much better for you.' He gazed at her resentfully. 'Anyway, cooking's what moms are supposed to do, isn't it?'

'Fine,' she said. 'But if you think you're going to get haute cuisine, kiddo, think again.' He was punishing her. For going to England. For Paul's departure. She tried to be patient. 'And listen, with Bess still off sick, you're going to have to help more around the place. I haven't time to find anyone else to cover for her.'

'Ever heard of the Yellow Pages?'

'Thanks for the advice,' she said, keeping it light, determined not to let him rile her. 'But until I have more time, you could start by not leaving wet towels all over the bathroom.'

'What difference does it make?'

'I don't like it, William. So don't do it.'

'Anyone would think this was a friggin' showhouse or something.'

'If it was, you certainly wouldn't be allowed to leave your room looking like a nuclear disaster zone.'

'I like it like that.'

'I don't.' She clenched her teeth, not wanting to shout at him. 'So pick it up, please.'

'It may look like a mess to you—'

'It most definitely does.'

'—but I know where everything is.'

'Clean it up, Will.'

'But then I won't be able to *find* anything.'

'And don't *argue* all the time.' He sounded just the way Josie used to.

176

She came home after work one day to find him watching a rerun of *Star Trek* instead of doing his homework. Buttered popcorn was spilled all over the scatter rugs. Her patience had worn very thin indeed. She had spent the afternoon with the entire board of a Texan company whose executive had seemed incapable of grasping even the most basic procedures of corporate taxing. On top of that, three of them had smoked cigars throughout the meeting, despite the notice displayed on the boardroom wall, so that now her head throbbed and her throat was raw.

'Will,' she snapped. 'What the hell's all this mess?'

'What?' He looked about him.

'Greasy popcorn all over the place.' Now she would have to hire someone to clean the rugs. She picked up a silk-covered cushion. 'Look at this: it's ruined.'

'Guess I must have knocked the pan over.'

'Well, clean it up right this minute. And turn off the set. You know the house rules: no TV until your homework's done.'

'This is educational,' he said.

'Don't be ridiculous, Will.' She picked up the remote control and snapped off the set.

'Don't *do* that,' he shouted.

'Don't try to kid me that Mr Spock is educational.'

'But it is. It's the one where they go back in time to the Twenties.'

'So?'

'So we're studying the Twenties in school.'

'You can learn a lot more from books than from watching some stupid sci-fi show.'

He grabbed the remote and flicked on the TV again. '*Star Trek*'s not stupid.'

'Will,' she said. 'Turn it off.'

'I want to watch it.'

'You heard me. I said no.' She dropped her bags on the table. 'Besides, I've got a terrible headache.'

'You don't care about anything except yourself, do you?'

'Don't talk to me like that.' Frustration made her peremptory.

'No wonder Dad left,' he muttered.

'That's enough,' she said, her voice rising.

He stood up and strode menacingly toward her. 'Well, it's true.'

She stepped back, her heart beating in doublequick time. What was going on here? Will had always been so equable, so sweet, so biddable. 'I'm not going to argue with you,' she said, trying to stay calm.

'That's because you know I'm fucking right.'

'I don't care what you do at school, but don't use that kind of language round here,' Ruth said curtly. She bent and pulled the plug for the TV out of the socket. 'And get on with your homework.'

She went into the kitchen to start preparing supper. Chopping vegetables, she took several deep breaths, trying to calm herself. For a moment there, she had almost thought he was going to attack her.

One afternoon she arranged to meet him downtown after school, in order to go clothes shopping. Standing outside the school gates, she watched him come through the doors with Ed Stein and Dan Baxter, the three of them laughing, fooling about, being guys. It was reassuring to see that he did not look very different from either of his friends: pale, spotty, too young for his body.

As soon as he saw her, he stopped laughing. His face

changed, grew sullen. He broke away from the others and came over. 'I can buy my own clothes,' he said.

The other two had followed him. 'Hi, Mrs Connelly,' Ed said.

'Ed, Dan. How are you two doing? You haven't been round to the house for a while.'

'We're trying to get the band going,' Ed said.

'My dad thinks he might get us a gig,' Dan said. 'The Kiwanis or something.'

'You never know where it'll lead, do you?' Ruth said, wondering why Will had not mentioned it. 'Great oaks from little acorns grow and all that.'

Behind her, Will made an impatient snorting sound.

'That's what my dad said.' Dan smiled at her. 'Guess I'd better get on home or my mother will freak out.'

'Me, too,' said Ed. 'Nice talking to you, Mrs Connelly.'

'See you, guys.'

'Jesus,' Will said, as soon as they had gone. 'Embarrassing or what?'

'What is?'

'You.' He raised his voice an octave. '*Great oaks from little acorns* ... what do you think, they're retards?'

'Knock it off, William,' she ordered. 'Now let's go find some clothes you can get into.'

'Why d'you have to come with me?'

'Because someone has to pay.'

'Why can't I have an allowance? Ed Stein does.'

'Ed's a year older than you are.'

'*Nobody* goes clothes shopping with their mom,' he said disgustedly.

'William Carter Connelly does.'

'Why can't I have my own credit card, like Josie did?'

179

'She was nearly seventeen. And a darn sight more mature than you appear to be.'

'Fuckin' A.'

She grabbed his arm and squeezed it hard, half-dragging him toward the car. 'Watch your tongue,' she said furiously. 'I *will* not be spoken to like that.' Looking at his sulky, belligerent face, she felt as though her life was falling into ruin.

When they got home, he slouched grumpily off to his room and emerged only when she knocked at the door to say supper was ready.

Slumped in his chair, he stared at the roasted vegetable lasagne she had prepared and pushed his plate away.

'Aren't you hungry?' she asked, concerned.

'Starving. But that looks disgusting.' He reached for the bread basket and lavishly buttered a roll before cramming it into his mouth.

She could feel herself splitting into a thousand small pieces of fury. 'Pull yourself together,' she said. 'It's vegetarian, which is what you've asked for. It took me ages to make it last night, when I had plenty of other stuff to do for the office. I may not be the best gourmet cook in the world but you know as well as I do that it tastes good. Now eat.'

'I'll throw up.'

'Eat it,' she shouted. 'Eat it, Will, or I'll damn well take a spoon and feed you myself.'

He stared at her. 'What did you say?'

'I said I'd feed you, Will, just like I did when you were a baby. And I mean it. I'm sick and tired of your behavior. Have some consideration for me, will you? I know you miss your father, I know all that. But you're not the only one suffering. It's sad for me too. Whatever you're feeling, I'm feeling the same. We've had a terrible terrible year, what with . . . with your sister and the accident, and now your dad.'

'It's not *my* fault he went.'

She had been here before. She had seen that same look of hostility in Josie. She had felt the same dislike flowering between them. She was not going to let it happen again. She shut her eyes and counted to ten, then said as calmly as she could: 'I can't go on like this, Will. I just can't cope with your rudeness and surliness and the way you act as though you can hardly bear to be in the same room as me.'

'Maybe I can't.'

'Then perhaps you'd better go live with your dad.'

He threw his knife down on the table. 'Everything fuckin' *sucks*!' he shouted. '*Everything*.'

'Tell me about it.'

Reaching for another roll, he glared at her.

'I've got feelings too, dammit,' Ruth said. Her hands shook as she tried to lift her water glass and drink from it. 'I'm hurting inside, just like you are. I understand how you feel, William. I honestly do.' She drew in a deep ragged breath and covered her face with her hands. She began to weep. 'I d-don't think I can c-carry on like this for much longer.'

Will seemed bewildered by her outburst. 'Hey, calm down, will you?'

'Please, please stop taking everything out on me. *Please.*'

'Look, I'm sorry . . .'

'I'm doing my best. You may not believe it, you may not like it, but I'm really trying to do my best,' she said, sniffing.

'Okay. I'm sorry.' He reached for the baking dish on

the table and took a large helping. 'All right?' He dug his fork into the pasta and began to eat it.

After a while, she peeked through her fingers. 'You're right,' she said.

'What about?'

'It does look disgusting, doesn't it?' She tried to laugh.

'Kinda. See, what you did, Mom, was you didn't make a cheese sauce and pour it between the layers.'

'Didn't I?'

'No. That's why none of it's sticking together.'

'I'm sorry, darling.'

'Tastes okay, though,' Will conceded. He drank half a diet Pepsi, then said, not looking at her: 'Maybe I could do some cooking over the weekend or something. Show you a few things.'

'I'd really like that,' she said humbly.

'I asked you to take the laundry out of the machine and fold it,' Ruth said one evening, about a week later. The two of them were living in an uneasy partnership. Explosion was never very far from the surface, but Will was obviously trying to be less surly and Ruth made an effort to hide her irritation at the listless way he dragged himself about the apartment.

'I know you did.' He was lying on the couch in the sitting room.

'So why is it still scrunched up in the dryer, which means now it'll have to be ironed?'

'I was too tired when I came back from school.'

'You were too tired last night to put the dishes in the dishwasher, so I had to do it,' she said. 'Have you done your homework?'

'Not yet.'

'Why not?'

'Because I'm fucking pooped, that's why.'

'You weren't too tired to go up to Sweetharbor with your father last weekend.'

'We didn't go in the end. We stayed in his apartment instead, took it kind of easy. Went to the movies. Watched football on TV.'

'At your age, you shouldn't be tired.'

'What do you expect, with all my schoolwork to do. Plus team practices all the time. And the band's taking up all my slack.'

'Maybe you should drop the band for the moment.'

He stared at her. 'No.'

'Is it just that you're trying to do too much? Or is there something else wrong that you're not telling me?'

He did not answer for a while. Then he said reluctantly: 'I haven't been feeling real good lately. I keep throwing up. And I get these pains in my joints.'

'We'll have to go to the clinic, get you looked at.'

'Maybe all I need is a couple of days off school.'

'You've never had a day off school in your life.'

'All the more reason to have one now.'

Frowning, Ruth got up and stood over him. 'What's this?' There were a couple of angry yellow-tipped boils on his neck and another halfway up his arm.

He ducked away from her. 'Nothing.'

'Are there any more of these on you?'

'One or two.'

She tilted the lamp. 'Are you sleeping okay? You've got terrible shadows under your eyes.' Her heart began to beat faster with anxiety. Was he doing drugs?

'Don't fuss. I'm just tired, that's all.'

'You still hanging out with Ed and Dan?'

'Course I am. They're my friends. Shouldn't I be?'

'I heard that Dan had a problem.'

'Dan Baxter *is* a problem,' Will said. He grinned at her. His gums were pale, overfull of teeth. There was a group of red pus-filled spots near one corner of his mouth.

'I meant a drug problem,' Ruth said.

'So what if he has?'

'Are you involved with anything like that?'

'No.'

'Everybody experiments with these things. I did myself.'

'Didn't realize they even knew about drugs when you were a kid.'

'William, I promise I won't be angry if you tell me you've been trying stuff out.'

'I haven't.'

'Would you tell me if you were?'

'But I'm *not*.'

She shook her head at him. 'I have no way of knowing whether you're telling me the truth or not. But you're looking terrible. You don't eat. I can't see when you get your studying done. If you're in trouble, let me help you.'

'I'm not *in* trouble, for chrissakes.'

'I hope you realize how helpless I am. I can only ask you and hope you'll be honest with me.' Tears sprang to her eyes and she turned to blink them away. There was too much pressure on her at the moment. She was overloading. No longer in control.

'Read my lips, Mom.' He closed his eyes wearily. 'I do not have a drug problem, okay? Dad says I'm growing too fast, that's all, and he was just the same.'

It would have to do for the moment. Exhausted, Ruth went back to the papers she was preparing for the next day's work.

The following morning, she went into Will's room to hurry him along for school, and found him still under the covers. That was all she needed. She looked impatiently at her watch: they were always rushed in the mornings and by the time she had chivvied him into his clothes and supervised his breakfast, she would barely have time to drop him off at school without being late for work herself.

'Come on, Will,' she said briskly. 'Up, up, up. We're running late.'

'I don't think I can get out of bed,' he said, his voice rasping. It sounded like he was coming down with yet another cold.

'We all feel like that sometimes,' she said.

'I mean I *can't.*'

'Can't what?'

'Get up.'

She laughed. 'If this is a way of skipping the math test, forget it,' she said, pulling at his covers. 'Come on, guy. I'll be late if you don't get a move on.'

'Mom, I mean it. I just can't seem to . . . I feel too weak.'

'Weak?'

'Yeah.'

'Too weak to get out of bed?'

'Mmm.'

He seemed serious. Ruth felt his forehead. 'You don't have a fever,' she said. She made some quick calculations. The only really urgent thing was her ten o'clock meeting. If she could rearrange the rest of her schedule a little, maybe she could get Will up and running. She tried not to sound impatient. 'Look, I'll go and call the office. Tell them I won't be in until later.'

'Sorry, Mom. Honest. It's not the math test.'

185

'I believe you.'

'I . . . I don't know what it is.' His eyes were suddenly frightened.

Ruth looked at him, biting her lip. Dare she leave him alone? She could rush into the office, cancel her lunch date, get back at noon. But if he really could not get out of bed . . . she headed for the phone. This was exactly why her firm was so leery of promoting women: when there was a family emergency, they always put the family before the job. Despite paying lip service to equal opportunity and political correctness, several of the partners made no secret of their doubts about giving women senior positions. Only a few weeks earlier, one of Ruth's associates had called in to say she could not make an important client-conference because her husband was off work with the flu. 'You women talk about equality,' Jack Finley had said angrily, searching for papers the associate was dealing with. 'How can you consider yourselves equal when you drop everything because of some minor family crisis? You fight your way into a position of power and then the minute one of the kids gets the sniffles, you drop everything and stay home.'

Ruth knew he was one of those who had opposed her own promotion. 'What would you do if your wife went off to her office and left your sick child on his own?' she had retorted. 'Would *you* stay home instead?'

'My job is more important than hers.'

'Bullshit, Jack. She may not be earning as much as you, but Nancy's certainly in as powerful a position at her agency. And how would you feel if you yourself were recovering from an operation or something, and she just walked out the door, saying she had to get to work and she'd call at lunchtime to see if you were okay?'

186

It was obvious that he wanted to make some smart-ass remark about that being exactly what Nancy would do, until he saw how it would weaken his original argument.

Now, Ruth called her assistant: 'I'm going to be late, Marcy.'

'Nothing serious, I hope,' Marcy said.

'My son's not well. Get hold of Jim Pinkus, will you? Tell him I'm delayed, see if he can reschedule my ten o'clock appointment for eleven. Better still, eleven thirty.'

'What about your lunch date with Baker Industrial?'

'I can't imagine I won't be in the office by eleven.' Ruth thought about it a moment. 'Might not be a bad idea to call Petrinelli's assistant, though, just in case. Warn her there could be a problem. Maybe reschedule. Make up some excuse.' But Baker Industrial was a potential new client. 'On second thoughts, don't reschedule until I call back and update you.'

She called the Health Maintenance Organization clinic and explained that Will had no fever, but seemed weak. The receptionist put her through to a nurse-practitioner. Ruth went through it again. She was asked when Will had last had a blood test and said that as far as she remembered, it had been just after Christmas, when he had been tested for anemia.

'You say he's feeling weak. In what way?'

'He says he's too weak to get out of bed.'

'And he's fourteen?'

'Yes.'

'Mmm.' A pause. 'Can you get him down here so we can take a look?'

When she went back into Will's room, Ruth was fighting panic. Seeing him lying there, trying to smile,

187

his face almost as white as the pillow, it was hard to disguise her fear.

'Anything you want, darling?' She would have fetched him the moon if he had asked for it, but he shook his head.

'The bathroom?'

He looked embarrassed. 'I do sort of need to go,' he said.

'Here. Let me help you up.' She slid an arm around his shoulders and tugged him into a sitting position. She had not realized how thin he was. She swung his legs sideways so that by pulling him forward, he was standing on the floor. He stood, knees trembling like a new-born foal's, already a head taller than she was. 'Come on, now. Put your arm round my waist.' She grabbed hold of his other hand, holding it firmly against her body, and together they tottered toward the bathroom. He smelled as he always did, of boy-sweat and cigarettes – she had guessed for some time that he was smoking – and slept-in sheets.

'I can manage now, Mom,' he said. 'Thanks.'

'Are you sure?'

'Really. Perhaps I just kind of got locked into position or something.'

'Call me if you need help.'

She heard the flushing of the toilet, then Will called from the bathroom door. He sounded stronger already. 'Maybe I'll take a shower.'

Relief filled her. She went out into the passage and looked at him leaning against the bathroom doorpost. 'Do you feel like eating something?'

'Not really.'

'Sure?'

He smiled at her and nodded. She had the absurd

notion that he was reassuring her. But that ought to be her role, not his. Hot tears stung her eyes. There could not be anything seriously wrong with him. A wave of fear swept through her and passed, leaving her weak. How could it be anything serious? 'I think you ought to try to get something down you. And then . . .'

'Then what?'

'I'm going to run you to the clinic.'

'Aw, Mom.'

'We need to get this dealt with,' she said firmly. 'Whatever it is.'

While he showered, she called Paul's number. He did not always have classes in the morning. That day he apparently did. Keeping her voice calm, she left a message on his machine, asking him to call her, adding that it was about Will. She did not want to admit it to herself, but she was afraid that if he thought she was calling on her own behalf, he might not call back. On second thought, she telephoned his office. Melda, the department secretary, answered. 'Miz Connelly,' she said. 'It's good to hear your voice.'

'Hi, Melda.' Did she know that Paul had moved out? 'Is my husband there?'

'Professor Connelly has classes right now. But I can get him to call you, soon as he comes back. Should be here mid-morning.'

'Please do, Melda. Tell him it's important.'

'Not somethin' serious, I hope, Miz Connelly.'

Oh, God, so do I, Ruth thought. 'Just say it's about Will.'

'How is that boy?' Melda asked. 'Las' time the professor brought him in, while you was over there in Europe, he didn't look good to me, not at all.'

'He's . . . he's . . .' Ruth tried not to burst into tears.

189

'I'm taking him down to the clinic right now. Just tell my husband to call me,' she said, and broke the connection.

Why had the nurse-practitioner wanted him to come in? What did they suspect? She felt ignorant and helpless. They had never had any serious illness in the family, beyond the usual childhood diseases. Dread lay heavy in her chest.

Water was still running in the bathroom. She went into Will's room. It looked pretty much as it had when he was ten. Or even six. His skateboard leaned against the wall. His roller blades lay in a corner. On the bookshelves above his desk was a baseball glove cupped round a baseball. One of his two guitars lay across the end of his bed. *Make Way For Ducklings* was sitting next to his computer. She riffled through the pages, smiling at the old-fashioned illustrations, remembering the many times she and Paul had taken the children to the Public Garden, and how they always hoped they would see Jack and Lack and the rest of them, marching in line down Beacon Street behind Mrs Mallard.

She began pulling Will's dirty sheets off the bed. By the time she had finished making it up with fresh ones, Will was shuffling back into the room, a towel round his waist. So like his father, she thought. The shoulder blades were the same, and so was the way his back muscles lengthened into his waist. He was a boy still, but the man he would become was plain to see. Already there was a pattern of dark hair on his stomach, veeing down toward his crotch.

She wanted to kiss him, tell him how much she loved him. When had she last done that except in the most mechanical way? There were bruises on his body, by the elbows, at his shoulder. More of the boils flared on his back, red and angry. Drops of water lay across the line of his collar bone and on top of his shoulders. She had laid out clean clothes for him.

'Are you okay to get dressed by yourself?'

'Think so. I feel a bit better.' He sat down on the edge of the bed and closed his eyes. 'Sort of, anyway.'

'Sure about breakfast?' She did not want to alarm him by rushing him out of the apartment. 'There's cereal? Eggs? Waffles? Or blueberry pancakes, I could easily do some for you.' Eat something, she wanted to beg him. Eat, and assuage some of my guilt.

'I'm not real hungry, Mom.' He reached for the shirt she had put out and began to pull it on. The bones of his arms pushed against the transparent skin, almost fleshless.

Ruth had not seen him naked for years. My God, she thought, can he be anorexic? Is that what is wrong with him? It was supposed to be a disease which mainly afflicted girls, but she had read that boys suffered from it too.

'Wrap up warm,' she said. 'Put your down jacket on. It's sub-zero outside.'

'Okay.'

'I'll help you down to the lobby. You can wait there while I get the car.' She hoped she sounded calm, businesslike. But searching for her keys in the kitchen, she held on to the edge of the counter and bowed her head for a second or two, breathing in through her mouth, deep calming breaths which she hoped would still the fevered clamor of her brain. Anorexia would explain the weakness, the loss of appetite, the tiredness. Maybe even the pains in his joints which he had complained of recently. But it could be cured. Kids did die of it, she knew that, but only a few. Not children like

191

Will. Anorexia: if he had to have a disease, let it be that. Because otherwise, it could be something much much worse.

Driving across town to the clinic, it seemed as if every light turned red as she approached it, every driver was drunk, every bus in town had deliberately stopped in front of her car to slow her down. Breath plumed from the pedestrians on the sidewalks, not one of them aware of her need to get where she was going as soon as she could. Yesterday, she had been just as careless of the predicaments of others. This morning was different. Will was collapsed in the back seat. His breath crackled in his chest. Her own breath was coming quick and short. Her thoughts churned, panicky, terrified.

Anemia. Anorexia. Anemia. Anorexia. They were not life-threatening diseases. Hang on to that. What can't be cured must be endured. She would dump the job. Call Bob Landers tomorrow. She would do anything, as long as Will was all right. Anemia. Anorexia. One or the other. Will was ill, but he was going to be all right. He was. He would be all right.

She pulled up untidily in front of the building. The air glittered with frost particles as she ran in and told the receptionist who she was. Someone followed her out and helped transfer Will from the car to a wheelchair, then took him inside and waited while she parked the car. She pushed him down the polished corridors, the way she used to when he was still in a stroller. Will. If anything happened to him . . . the thought was not to be pursued.

Greg Turner, the pediatrician, was waiting for them. She watched his expression change as it fell on Will. He checked the boy's mouth. Pushed up a sleeve and examined the skin of his arm. Asked if he had any pain.

When Will mentioned his stomach, the doctor's fingers probed gently, withdrawing when Will winced. He picked up the phone on his desk and spoke discreetly into it.

Then he looked at Ruth. 'I want him to go down to the hospital,' he said. 'Right now.'

'But why? What's the matter with him?'

'I want him to have some tests done.' He made no attempt to soothe, or to play down the gravity in his voice.

'What is it?' Her heart was revving up like the engine of a racing car. Sweat was breaking out under her arms. She stepped closer to the pediatrician and spoke quietly so that Will would not hear. 'Is it something serious?'

'Ruth.' Greg took her hands in his. 'I wouldn't presume to make any kind of diagnosis without proper tests.'

'It *is* serious, isn't it?'

'You can't possibly expect me to say without much more information. Now, I've called an ambulance—'

'Ambulance?'

'—to take him in. You can ride along with them. They'll tell you what to do.'

Ruth looked at her son. He gave her a ghostly grin. ''S okay, Mom. Chill out.'

Was she looking that agitated? As they passed through the office, she caught sight of herself in the mirror on the wall. Her face looked as white as Will's, the lines deeply scored, as though someone had re-defined them with a stick of charcoal.

More than anything else, she wanted Paul.

11

'Said it was important, Professor.' Melda passed Paul a Post-it note. 'She's taking your boy to the clinic. Wanted you to call her.'

'The HMO clinic?'

'That's what she said.'

'When was this?' Paul could hear student laughter down the corridor, the hum of voices, trainers squeaking across rubberized floors. A door opened, letting out the sound of a lone voice talking, and then closed again.

'Almost an hour ago.'

'Did she say what it was about?'

'No, sir.'

'Nothing at all?'

Melda shook her head.

Paul picked up the handset and dialed the number of the apartment. All he got was the clipped efficient voice of Ruth's answering service. He called her office number but Marcy could only tell him that Ruth had not yet shown up. Taking out his wallet, he searched through it for the small plastic card with the HMO's phone number. When the switchboard answered, he asked for the pediatrician. 'Which one?' he was asked.

'Greg,' he said, desperately trying to remember the

doctor's last name. 'Uh . . . Greg Turner.' What was this all about? Ruth would not have called him at school unless it were something really serious. Why wasn't she at work? Had Will been in an accident?

'Hello?'

'Dr Turner,' Paul said. 'It's Professor Connelly. Will Connelly's father? I got a message to call my wife but she's not—'

'I sent her down to the hospital, along with William.'

'But why? What the hell is wrong?'

'I can't be sure, Professor.' Turner's voice was remote, impersonal. 'As I said to your wife, I'm not going to make any kind of diagnosis just off the top of my head. I suggest you join her down there.'

Paul replaced the handset. He stared at Melda, at the familiar office, without really seeing either. Nearby, a phone kept on and on ringing. Two men whose voices he did not recognize were walking along the passage outside, discussing a late batch of student essays. Something important, Ruth had told Melda . . .

'Cancel my classes for the rest of the day,' he said.

Driving through midday traffic, Paul could feel the anxiety fizzing through his body. An accident. It had to be some kind of accident. Not serious. Not *too* serious, or she would have had him pulled out of class. Or was it . . . Will had been not exactly sick, but not completely well, for months now: last weekend he had commented on it, wondered if he'd been doing drugs, eating badly, then, since Will was obviously uncomfortable talking about it, put it down to understandable emotional stress. Suppose it was something more concrete than that?

He got to the hospital just before noon. He had never been here before, never had cause to. He was directed to the Hematology Department, where he found Ruth alone in a waiting area, cut off from the busy passages by a half-wall full of house plants. She was sitting with a magazine on her lap and her eyes closed. He took a moment to watch her. She was much too thin, the cheekbones aggressive, her body angular under her fashionable short-skirted suit. She looked so frail. The flesh seemed to have vanished from her bones. Was all this the result of a summer storm eight months ago? That was how it sometimes seemed. Before then, surely things had been good, when they were still that dull and unusual thing, a happy family. A fairly happy family, at any rate. He recalled blue skies over the pond, the children jumping from the wooden dock, birdsong.

How could he have walked out on her? On Will? He called her name and she opened her eyes with a jerk of the head, rising to her feet. When he spread his arms, she stepped inside them and leaned against his chest. Just for a moment, he allowed himself to think that this was the way it was, instead of the way it used to be.

'I'm scared,' she said.

'What the hell is going on, Ruth?'

'I can't . . . I can't really t-take it all in. They're running all s-sorts of tests, Paul. It's something . . . something bad.' Out in the peach-colored passage beyond the planter, a woman walked by holding the hand of a kid who looked to be around eight or nine years old. The kid wore baggy jeans and a T-shirt. Its eyes were hollow, its skull naked except for a fringe of pale hair at the nape of the neck. It was impossible to tell whether it was a boy or a girl.

'What kind of bad?'

For answer, she began to sob. 'I can't bear it, Paul. They're talking about . . . they've done some blood tests and I overheard one of the technicians saying it could be—' She seemed to be too frightened to pronounce the word.

'What, Ruth?' He shook her impatiently.

'Cancer. Leukemia.' The word barely made it through her lips.

'Oh, my God.'

'It's not definite. But that's what this guy said.'

'You sure they were talking about Will?'

'I – I don't know.' Her arms hung down at her side, the hands open and slightly curved. 'Paul,' she said, as though she did not realize he was there with her. 'Help me, Paul.' Tears filled her eyes but did not fall.

He drew her down to sit beside him. 'Leukemia? Oh God.' He took her hand, squeezed it, hoping to tap into her strength. The word had no meaning, and yet it spelled a horror he felt too drained to contemplate. He had seen a TV documentary on it not long ago. Leukemia was for other people. Leukemia meant blood drives and donor appeals and television documentaries. Leukemia meant pain and the ravaging of a body. And little kids dying.

How could any of that have relevance for Will?

Ruth shivered, as though she were in the winter chill of outdoors instead of an overheated hospital wing. 'I should have seen it, Paul. I was just too fucking busy, getting on with my stupid job, ignoring all the signs. I knew he didn't look good, he didn't look right, he was so tired all the time, but I was too wrapped up in my work to do anything about it. You told me, even Melda said so.'

'Melda? When did she—'

'I spoke to her this morning.' It seemed a lifetime ago now, in another, safer world. 'Even Melda said he didn't look good. Your own secretary, Paul, but his mother, me, I was too fucking involved with my stupid shitty *job*!' Ruth screamed out the last word. She tore herself out of Paul's half-embrace. Picking up the magazine from the floor where it had fallen, she threw it violently against the wall. 'Because I'm a lousy, godawful mother who never deserved to have children in the first place.'

He shook her, then slapped her face. 'Stop it. Stop, Ruth. We don't even know for sure what's wrong with him. Maybe Greg Turner was just playing safe, sending you down here.' He was talking for his own sake as much as for hers. 'Besides, if . . . *if*, God forbid, it *is* . . . leukemia, it's nothing you or I've done that's caused it, nothing we could have done to prevent it. Blaming yourself isn't going to achieve anything.' He pressed shaky fingers against his forehead.

Someone joined them. They both looked up at him. A doctor. *The* doctor? He carried a clipboard. Under his white coat, he wore a button-down Oxford cloth shirt and a paisley tie. He nodded at Paul. 'Hi. You must be Professor Connelly. I'm Mike Gearin. Staff hematologist. Sorry to keep you waiting.'

'What's . . .' Ruth swallowed. 'What's wrong with my son?'

The doctor tried to smile. 'Obviously you're anxious to know what's happening. But I'd prefer not to discuss it further until we can give you a clear diagnosis.'

'Something,' Paul said. 'Surely you can tell us something?'

'Well.' The doctor looked down at the notes in his hand. 'At this stage it does look as though your son has a serious blood disorder.'

'Oh God,' whispered Ruth.

'What blood disorder?' Paul said.

'He's currently being checked out by a team of experts.' The doctor ticked them off. 'A hematologist. An oncologist. A urologist. A neurologist.' He looked up and curved his mouth into the shape of a smile although it was like no smile Paul had ever seen. 'Nothing but the very best. And not much is going to get past those guys, believe me. We've done the blood work, but now we have to wait for the results of the other tests. If there's something there to find, we'll find it.' But his eyes said more than his mouth. Paul felt cold. Those eyes said he knew already that something had been found.

When he had gone, they sat in silence for an immeasurable space of time, the minutes dragging as they might have done before an execution.

It was almost six o'clock when Gearin reappeared. This time he asked them to follow him to a small side room which held a low couch and two chrome upright chairs. One of them was already occupied by an older doctor who was examining the contents of a blue folder.

He stood up and held out a hand. 'Good to meet you both,' he said. 'I'm Dr Caldbeck, Chief of Hematology.'

'I wish that sounded more reassuring,' said Paul.

Gearin took the other upright chair. 'Right,' he said. He had a very direct gaze; his bright brown eyes gave him an eager and hopeful air. Useful, Ruth thought, if you were going to be the bringer of bad news. 'William.' He looked sideways at his colleague. Laced his fingers together. Unlaced them. Took in a short sharp breath and expelled it, like an athlete preparing for a sudden burst of activity. 'Yes,' he said. 'Well, there's no point trying to soften the blow for you. As we suspected, William is seriously ill.'

'What is it?' Paul was the one who asked. Ruth's hands trembled in her lap. She could not have put the question. She felt as though she were suspended by a fraying rope over a deep ravine. There was no ground under her feet, only black chill space.

'Looks like ALL,' Gearin said. His prominent Adam's apple bulged. 'Acute lymphoblastic leukemia.'

'But leukemia's almost incurable, isn't it?' Ruth began to shiver.

'By no means. ALL is extremely responsive to therapy. We – researchers in the field, that is – are constantly expanding our understanding of the disease, which means that the chances of recovery keep on improving as we discover more effective treatments.'

'Does that mean something, or is it just medibabble?' Paul said.

Dr Caldbeck intervened. 'Not at all. These days, we look for cures in as high as eighty per cent of the cases presenting.'

'Are you absolutely certain of the diagnosis?' Paul asked.

'As sure as we can be, I'm afraid.' Gearin spoke to the silent Ruth, rather than to Paul. 'The blood work we've done seems fairly conclusive, though we'll have to perform a bone marrow aspiration to come up with a precise diagnosis. After we've seen the results of that, and have determined the extent of the disease, we can begin the treatment. Now, how much – if anything – do you know about leukemia?'

'It's cancer of the blood cells, isn't it?' Again it was Paul who spoke. Ruth had shrunk inside herself, not wanting to hear any of this, even though she knew she should be listening, taking it in, that every word he spoke was vitally important.

'That's right. The blood is made up of three types of cells, white and red blood cells and platelets. The white blood cells – leukocytes – are the ones which fight infections; what happens with leukemia is that the body begins to produce large numbers of abnormal white blood cells, which don't function properly. The disease starts in the bone marrow, which is essentially a mechanism for producing blood cells. If one of these cells mutates, it multiplies at a rapid rate, overwhelming the other healthy tissues. Looking at Will's medical history over the past few weeks, he's been subject to chest infections, poor appetite, fatigue, joint pain. All of them are classic symptoms of the disease.'

'We thought it was psychosomatic,' said Ruth. 'Because of the . . . the accident.'

'Accident?'

She could not tell him about Josie. Not at this moment. 'If we'd had the slightest idea that there was something seriously wrong . . .'

'He had a blood test only a few weeks ago,' Paul said. 'Why wasn't this picked up sooner?'

'He wasn't given a broad spectrum blood count,' Gearin said. 'According to his file, they were looking for anemia, not leukemia.' He gazed at them, his eyes wide and shiny. Incongruously, Ruth was reminded of Josie's toy bear: had Will also noticed how like Hardy's the doctor's eyes were? 'Because some of the symptoms are similar, it's possible that the one masked the other. On the other hand, he might not even have developed the disease at that stage.' He swallowed, his Adam's apple bulging as he did so. 'It can occur very suddenly.'

Caldbeck nodded in agreement. 'We could give tests on one day which showed there was nothing wrong, and twenty-four hours later, do the same tests and find he's got the disease.'

'That quickly?'

'I'm afraid so.'

Ruth felt as though she had blundered into someone else's nightmare. Her head seemed to be full of drifting clouds through which she could dimly perceive Will, floating away from her until he was no more than a speck in the distance.

'What are his chances?' Paul asked. 'That's the only thing we can take in right now.'

'We can't really say at this point,' Dr Caldbeck said. 'So much depends on the patient himself and his response to treatment. I can only repeat what Dr Gearin told you, that ALL is very sensitive to chemotherapy treatment, and these days we look to an eighty per cent cure rate.'

'It's worth remembering that many malignant diseases which once proved fatal are now curable,' added Gearin. 'And even in the less responsive cases, there's every hope that some of the newest treatments will eventually extend to cures. But, of course, we can't draw up a treatment plan until we have all the information about the type and extent of the disease.'

'Why on earth not?'

'Professor Connelly, I'm sure you can see that I can't give you exact answers to your questions at this stage. Bodies subjected to chemical attack don't work on a precise schedule. Only when we have all the individual information can we choose the correct course of treatment for Will, our aim being to achieve as prompt a remission of the disease as we can.'

'How would you do that?' Shivering, Ruth told herself that Gearin was not responsible for what had happened to Will, that the doctor was doing his best under difficult circumstances. Having to tell parents even once that their child had a potentially fatal illness would be pretty draining. To do it, as he had to do, on an almost daily basis, must be completely soul-destroying. And he was being patient with them, as well as efficient. It seemed reasonable to assume that one way doctors had found to deal with the effects of the mortal blows they had to deliver was to withdraw a little from the people on whom they were inflicting them.

Gearin began to outline the treatment choices available. 'There's chemotherapy, which uses drugs to kill the rogue cancer cells. Or radiation therapy, where high-energy rays are employed to zap the cancer cells and inhibit their growth. Sometimes we choose a combination treatment, depending on which looks right for the patient.'

The patient. Will. It sounded so cold, so distant from the boy who waited for them somewhere in a hospital room.

'There's a downside to all this, isn't there?' Paul said.

'The use of high-dose chemotherapy to kill the cells destroys the bone marrow,' Gearin said quietly. 'If the loss of bone marrow becomes critical, we have to find a healthy donor and infuse bone marrow from him or her into the patient. In other words, replace Will's own bone marrow with that taken from the donor.'

Ruth heard what he was saying, but could not take it in. 'I'm cold,' she said. Shock and stress had set up a reaction in her own body. 'I'm so cold.'

She felt as though she was shut up in a deep freeze. *My blood ran cold. His feet had turned to ice.* They were phrases so often read that they had ceased to have meaning. Until now. Her jaw trembled. *My teeth chattered*. She stared dry-eyed at the two doctors, their words running round her head, each one shadowed by terror. Bone marrow transplant . . . White cells . . . Radiotherapy . . . How did any of it connect with Will, funny Will, whom she had known deep down was not well, but for whom she had simply not found the time? What kind of a mother did that make her that she could have neglected him to such an extent? She began to hyperventilate, panting like a puppy, shivering, goosebumps standing out on her arms.

She might lose her son. What would her career matter then? Once it had been all-important, the driving force in her life. Now, it seemed meaningless, compared to the enormity of Will's illness. When he was little, his tears when he hurt himself could be kissed away, his pain could be eased by the comfort of her arms. Now, he was on his own. She could not follow him into the places where he would be taken, only be there waiting when he got back. The chill surrounded her heart. She felt infinitely small, utterly helpless.

Gearin lifted a phone and pressed in some numbers. 'Could we have some coffee in here?' he said. 'As soon as possible.' He gazed at Ruth with concern.

'Take my coat.' Paul removed his jacket and draped it round her shoulders.

'Thank you.' The jacket carried the heat of his body and this calmed Ruth. Her shivers subsided. Warmth began to creep back. She leaned against him and felt his hands strong on her shoulders. She reached up and grasped them.

'Will's going to be all right,' Paul said. He squeezed her shoulders. 'You heard what the man said. Eighty per cent of cases are cured.'

'Which means twenty per cent aren't.'

'Don't talk like that,' said Paul angrily. 'Don't even think it.'

'I should have noticed. I should have brought him in sooner.'

'Don't blame yourselves,' Caldbeck said. 'That's always the first reaction parents have when they hear a diagnosis like this – that somehow it's their fault.'

She did not believe him. It *was* her fault. She *was* to blame.

As though he could read her thoughts, Caldbeck shook his head at her, offered a half-smile. 'You must have faith in the fact that it's not due to anything you could have prevented. At the moment we have very few clues as to the causes of leukemia. We know that more males than females get it, that it occurs more often in Caucasians than in other ethnic groups. But very little beyond that.'

They went through a few more details, but Ruth could not concentrate. Will was all she could think of. Her boy. Her son. She had been so blind. If she had not gone to England, maybe this would not have happened. She started to sob, covering her face with her hands.

Gearin gave them papers to sign, to allow the surgery involved in taking blood marrow samples from Will to be performed. 'He won't be able to leave for a while,' he told them.

'Can we stay with him?' Ruth asked.

'If you wish.'

'Of course I wish.' Her voice rose. 'He's my son, my child, why would I want to leave him alone in a strange place, he's probably terrified. I must stay with him, of course I must, he's my—'

'Ruth,' Paul said firmly, and she realized that she had

been babbling, that hysteria lay very close to the surface.

'There are daybeds in some of the rooms, and others have chairs which convert to cots,' Caldbeck told them. 'But first . . .'

A call for Dr Caldbeck came over the intercom, and he got up. 'I'm sorry,' he said again. 'I'm truly sorry. There is no news worse for a parent than to learn that their child has cancer. But we have every hope that between us we can beat it – and I assure you that you won't find a better or more dedicated team than the one we have here.' Once more he held out his hand. 'Unfortunately, I'll be seeing you again. Meantime, just stay strong, for your son's sake.'

When he had gone, Dr Gearin led them through the benefits and disadvantages of chemotherapy. There would be unpleasant side effects, but most of them would be transitory, and meanwhile, healthy new cells would be developing.

'What sort of side effects?' Paul asked.

'Hair loss, ulcerated inflammation of the mouth and throat, nausea and vomiting, a change in food preferences, that sort of thing. Uncomfortable while they last, but, like I said, they're usually temporary.'

'Usually?'

'Nearly always. And not all patients in chemotherapy will experience all the adverse side effects.'

Gearin's mouth opened and shut. Words. Pouring out of him. Telling her things she did not want to hear. Nausea. Hair loss. Ulcers. My poor Will, Ruth thought. My poor boy. She wanted to be anywhere else but here, with her child nearby lying on a bed, deathly sick, among other sick children. The thought of the clear air of Caleb's Point came back to her. Brightness of sun on sea. Clearness of wind. Sound of the pine trees murmuring at her back. Where had it all gone, the treasures that she once had owned: children, husband, home? What fool's gold had she traded them for?

'You must feel free to come and go as you please,' the doctor said.

If she never heard his voice again, it would be too soon. At the same time, she knew that inevitably, over the coming weeks and months, she would be forced into developing a relationship with him. They were tied together. Handcuffed. Sharing the same kind of unequal partnership as existed between kidnapper and victim, master and slave. Jailer and captive.

As soon as Ruth could get to a phone, she called Bob Landers at home.

'Ruth!' he said. 'I heard you didn't come in this morning. Don't worry: Jim Pinkus handled the Phillipson meeting just fine. Jake's kicking up his usual—'

'I'm resigning, Bob.'

'You're what?'

'From the job, from the partnership.'

'Resigning? For God's sake, why?'

'I'm phoning from the hospital.'

'Hospital? Which hospital?'

'Will has just been diagnosed with leukemia.'

'Oh, my God. Ruth, how appalling. Oh, I'm so very sorry.'

'Yes.'

'Leukemia: how dreadful. Oh Ruth: how does one get through something like that?'

'I'll have to find out, Bob. At the moment, it's going to be one day at a time. That's the best I can hope for.'

'Ruth, I'm devastated for you.' Landers expelled a deep breath. 'But I'd urge you not to do anything drastic at this initial stage. Especially not to resign.'

'I have no choice.'

'We'll grant you an extended leave of absence instead.' She could almost hear the whirr of his brain as he calculated the pros and cons of letting her go. The temporary loss of one expensive partner who might or might not come back to them, versus the difficulty of finding and then training someone to take her place. 'Quite apart from anything else, there's the health insurance benefits. You may find you need them.'

'I hadn't even thought of that.' The future stretched ahead, bleak and cold.

'Don't resign, Ruth. Not yet. That way, if and when—'

'There may not be any ifs or whens, Bob. Will is seriously ill. He may . . .' Her voice trembled. She could not say the word. Eighty per cent survive; twenty per cent do not. The figures pulsed like neon signs in her brain. One in five does not survive, one in five does not survive . . .

'This is truly awful news, Ruth. I'm just – I don't know what to—'

Ruth cut in. Time had shrunk. She did not want to waste it on words when what was important were the sentiments they attempted to express. 'Believe me, I'm grateful for your thoughts, Bob. By the way, don't worry about the Phillipson negotiations. There's not a lot we can do until the comfort letter arrives from Washington. Meanwhile, Jim'll handle everything: he's sat in on all my meetings with Jake. He knows where all the files are and what our strategy over the next few weeks was going to be.'

'As if any of that matters now.'

'Not for me, Bob. But it does for you.' She put down the phone.

Much much harder were the phone calls which had to be made to Paul's mother, to Luke in California. Their shock and grief only served to emphasize what Paul and Ruth themselves were undergoing.

She called her own parents. 'Mom, it's me. I'm calling—'

Her mother cut in, instantly aware that something dreadful had happened. 'What's wrong? What is it, Ruth?'

Ruth explained and listened to her mother's harsh sobs on the other end of the line. Her father took the phone and she explained again. She could feel his bewilderment.

'Why?' he said. 'Why you?'

'Why not?'

'So many cruel blows . . . Josephine, then Paul going, now William. Why?'

'If I knew that, Dad . . .' Ruth felt stronger and calmer than she had for months. It was as if the knowledge of Will's illness had cut away all weakness. If he was to survive, then she must be strong, not just for him but for herself, for her parents.

'We'll come up at once,' her father said heavily. 'Take an apartment nearby, stay as long as we can be useful. If we can get a flight, we could leave tomorrow – there's nothing pressing to keep us down here.'

'It's good of you to offer,' Ruth said gently. 'But for the moment, there's no need. You stay and take care of Mom.'

'But, Ruthie, we want to help.' Her mother came back on the line, her voice distorted by her tears. 'We want to be with you. And poor little Will. Cancer . . . oh, my *God*. And Florida's so far away.'

'There's nothing you can do for now.'

'Will you tell us when there is?' Jonathan Carter had taken the phone from his wife.

'I promise, Dad.'

'You absolutely will?'

'I absolutely will.'

'What about money?'

'We have health plans, insurance. Both of us. For the moment, that's not going to be an issue.'

'Just remember, girl, that we want to help. That we *need* to help. Will is our only grandchild. And you're our child, our daughter. We've always been so proud of you, so . . .' His voice wavered, bringing Ruth to the edge of breaking down.

'I know that, Dad. And I'm so grateful to both of you,' she said. 'Not just for now but for . . .' Her throat jammed. Why had she never told them before how much she loved them, how much she appreciated what they had done for her, throughout her life? Always there, always strong. '. . . for everything.'

Her father seemed to understand what she wanted them to know. 'We love you, hon.'

Tears slid down her cheeks. She had never been good at saying it, but now she did: 'I love you too, both of you, far more than you can imagine.'

At last they were allowed in to see Will. He was in a glass-fronted room off the corridor leading from the nurses' station. More of the peach-colored paint in here, some pictures on the walls, a daybed in an alcove, a clothes locker. He was lying on a bed, wearing a loose green hospital gown over his boxers. An IV drip led from a plastic bag of clear liquid attached to a pole beside his bed into the vein inside his elbow. Behind him was a tall table holding a tangle of transparent tubing and a box which looked like part of a stereo system. A monitor stood on top of it, lines of electronic green marching erratically across its screen.

Will looked exhausted, ancient, as though his boy's body had been invaded by an old man. His shirt, jeans and sweat shirt lay neatly folded on the locker beside him, his L. L. Bean boots set side by side underneath. The unusual orderliness of the clothes only emphasized the chaos that was threatening to engulf them.

Seeing them, Will smiled, trying, as always, to break the tension with a joke. 'Hey, what kept you? I was beginning to think you folks had gone on vacation.'

'Oh, honey . . .' Ruth took his hand and Will winced.

'Careful, Mom. I've had so many needles stuck in me I don't dare have a drink in case it all leaks out onto the floor. Bet I look just like a pincushion.'

'You look fine,' Ruth said. 'Just fine.'

The lost look on her face sent a shiver of pain and remorse through Paul's heart. He could feel her fear; he knew she wanted to say more, much more. Knew that, like him, she wanted to smooth Will's hair, bend over him, look into his blue eyes and say, yes, you look fine, you are my beloved son, my special Will, and you have never *ever* looked so fine as in this moment when you must know there is something terribly wrong with you and you try to reassure your parents, when it is they who should be reassuring you.

He cleared his throat. 'Like the outfit.' His voice shook slightly. Not cancer. Please God. Not Will. How were they going to get through this? He sat down suddenly on the edge of the bed, his legs too weak to hold him upright. Not Will.

'Hope none of the guys from school comes by. Anyone sees me dressed like this, that's my rep gone.'

'Tell 'em it's what the hip dudes are wearing.'

'Like, they're gonna believe me.' He looked from Paul to Ruth. 'Are we going home soon?'

'Not just yet,' Ruth said. 'They still have some tests to do.'

'I'd really really like to go home,' Will said, his eyes sliding away from them. 'I don't want any more needles.' His mouth began to quiver.

'Hey,' Paul said gently. 'Hey, there.' He held his son's hand tight.

'They've pushed the darn things in everywhere,' Will said. His eyes filled. 'It hurts.'

'It's not for much longer. Just till they – till they find out what's wrong and how they're going to cure it.'

Will stared at them both. 'I'm really sick, aren't I?'

Paul knew they had a choice. They could fudge, pretend, distance themselves from Will by dishonesty. Or they could tell the truth. He bit his lip, then said: 'Kind of looks like it.'

'Am I gonna die?'

'Not if we have anything to do with it.' Like Paul, Ruth forced strength and vigor into her voice.

'Hey, you guys.' Will tightened his mouth at one side. He spoke to both but looked at his mother. 'Thanks for being here. You know?'

'You're the only one who matters,' said Paul. 'The hell with the damn students.'

'Ungrateful sonsa bitches,' said Will.

'Man, you said it.'

Paul wanted to get out of this room. He wanted a

drink. Instead of having to be strong for Ruth and Will, he wanted someone who would listen and understand, someone who would be strong for him. He felt an almost overpowering need to give up, to break down and howl his grief and despair.

'Have I got cancer?' Will's matter-of-fact voice broke into Paul's thoughts. He glanced across at Ruth. Her face white and drawn, she nodded fractionally at him.

Paul took his son's hand. 'Yes.'

'Can I be cured?'

'We don't know yet, son. We certainly hope so.'

'They told us most cases are cured,' Ruth said.

'How long do I have to stay in here?'

'A little while longer,' said Paul. 'But one of us will stay with you. I promise.'

'I wish I had my Walkman.'

'I'll drive back home a bit later,' Ruth said. 'Anything else you want?'

'Books, maybe.' Will looked fretful. 'Miss Marling's gonna have a fit. I'm supposed to hand in a paper tomorrow.'

'I'll call her.'

'Just make sure she knows I'm not trying to cut classes.'

'I'm sure she'll understand.'

'You don't know her,' Will said darkly. He sighed. 'Guess you'd better bring in my school tapes, too. I'm supposed to be studying the beginning of the Civil Rights movement. And I gotta read *The Crucible*, too.'

'One of those plays whose sum is greater than its parts.' Paul adopted his solemn professorial face. 'A comment, if you will, on our contemporary culture which adds a whole new perspective to—'

'Knock it off, Dad. Gimme a break, just for once, will you?'

'Don't blame me if you fail your college boards.' With the remark, Paul felt a certain optimism push its way into his head. In spite of the doctor's diagnosis, it was unthinkable that Will would not eventually be well enough to attend college.

Will's eyes drooped. 'I promise.'

That first night, both Ruth and Paul stayed in the room with Will, listening to the sound of his breathing. Nurses came and went, taking notes, staring at the monitor, adjusting the IV bag, checking Will's pulse and temperature. Neither of them was able to sleep, though they took it in turns to lie on the daybed, open-eyed in the half-dark. The electronic lines and figures on the monitor threw an eerie glow over Will's bed. A small red bulb winked in the casing below the screen. Light seeped through the blinds which had been let down to cover the window onto the corridor outside.

Throughout the long hours of darkness, Ruth alternated between shivering cold and feverish heat. Terror flowed like an ocean through her body, sometimes receding, other times threatening to drown her. Hearing the whiffle of Will's breath, his occasional grunts and sleep-sighs, she felt bonded with him in a way she had not done since the weeks after his birth. When Paul left home, she had promised Will that, from here on in, things would get better, that this was as bad as it got. Once again she had let him down. If he were not cured, if they could not combat the disease, then he would die.

And if he did, then so would she.

12

'We're proposing six more sessions of in-hospital chemotherapy,' Dr Gearin told Paul. 'Each treatment will mean several days here. In between, Will can go home, under certain conditions and providing certain rules are observed, in order to give his blood time to recover.'

Paul was angry. Bitterness crept along his veins, corroding his ability to function. Aggression bristled under his clothes. He told himself that none of this was down to the doctor; Gearin was trying to do his best for Will. His anger was fueled by his own impotence. The sight of Will imprisoned between the metal sides of a hospital bed was bad enough. Far worse was watching the vitality drain out of him, knowing that all day, every day, the plastic tubes from the drip were delivering a massive dose of drugs into his son's weakened body. And pushing this once active, healthy, sport-loving boy down the rubber corridors in a wheelchair, while the drugs flowed from the attached IV drip, set up an endless silent scream inside him. 'How long will that take?' he asked.

'We can never be entirely certain,' the doctor said. 'Many weeks, probably. Blood recovers at its own speed, and the time it takes varies with each patient.'

'How will we know if it's worked?'

'The results of treatment will vary; no two patients are going to react in exactly the same way. What we're hoping is that the drugs will do their job and send the disease into quick remission.'

Paul forced himself to relax, breathing in deeply through his nose, letting his shoulders sag, and his head. He smoothed his face into less aggressive lines. Forced a modicum of courtesy into his voice. 'And how will we know when we've done that?'

'Blood tests will show that the cancerous cells have been eliminated and only healthy ones are being produced. Once that happens, we cross our fingers and hope that the disease doesn't recur.'

'Remission isn't the same as cure?'

'Call it a temporary cure. That's as far as we dare go. Recurrence is always going to be a possibility.'

'You'd think somebody would have come up with a way to beat this by now.'

'Part of the problem is that the century itself is a root cause of the disease, for instance via pollution or exposure to radiation. There are genetic factors, too, but for the moment, we can only hypothesize. And keep on trying to find out what the causes are, so we can work on prevention and treatment.'

Paul looked down at his hands. The anger fizzed inside him. 'Have you got children, Doctor?'

'Yes.'

'Then you'll understand how frustrated I feel over all this.'

'I'd be exactly the same, in your place. The children in my care make me feel so humble. A few days on the ward and you begin to realize that true courage isn't about fighting wars and slaying dragons, it's about facing the longest of odds with dignity and pride.'

'I appreciate that, Dr Gearin. But my concern is not your other patients. It's Will. My concern is not diluted, it's not split between a couple of dozen others, the way yours has to be. My concern is one hundred per cent concentrated on my son.'

'Of course it is.'

'Can you imagine how I feel, as a parent, having to stand aside while my child, my innocent child who deserves none of this, is suffering?'

'Believe me, I—'

'Watching him, those damn needles, the drugs, knowing that there isn't anything I can do for him – can you imagine how it shames me to have let him down? You're supposed to protect your children, and I haven't, I haven't. Not Will, not his sister.' Paul's voice broke and his eyes filled.

'Professor Connelly. You are not to blame.'

'Why Will?' Paul said helplessly.

'Why not?'

Paul lifted his head and met the doctor's stare. 'What did you say?'

'I asked: Why *not* you? Why *not* Will? It's unfair, we both know that. But if it wasn't Will, it would be someone else, who might be asking the same question.'

'I guess.' Paul sighed. 'I'd give my life if it would help him.'

'But it wouldn't.'

'What makes it even worse is that he just . . . he just takes it all.'

'Which is why we can only go on doing what we're doing.'

Paul smeared his hands over his face. 'What happens if the disease does recur?'

'Then we try again. Either with more chemo, or with radiotherapy or a bone marrow transplant. Though the latter depends on a match being found.'

'Great.' Paul stood up abruptly. 'That is just great. What a lot we have to look forward to.'

'Do you mean for yourself, Professor Connelly? Or for Will?'

The chemo treatments left Will too weak and disoriented to do much for himself. When he came home, Ruth found herself having to care for him in the same intimate fashion as she had when he was still a baby in diapers. He who had grown into self-reliance was forced to revert to dependency. She could only guess how much he hated the physical weakness which resulted from the drugs. Having been so active, to find that he needed help even to turn over in bed was for him almost the worst aspect of his illness.

He found it acutely embarrassing to have his personal privacy invaded. They had never been the kind of family who wandered around their home naked; though Paul and Will had occasionally showered together, he was at a sensitive stage of development and did not want his mother to see his burgeoning man's body.

As well as the drugs needed to fight the disease, he was taking medication designed to combat infection, which often made him nauseous. His skin broke out into rashes and boils. He developed serious ulcers in his mouth and throat, making swallowing even liquid extremely painful. Ruth knew that along with all this was the fear he must be feeling. He was too old, too intelligent, not to be aware that the discomfort

218

he was enduring would not necessarily cure him.

Her grief at seeing him so weak and incapacitated was profound. As a young mother, she had always thought herself the equal of any danger which might threaten her children. She could have fought anyone, anything, to keep them safe. Since then, all her assumptions about her ability to protect them had proven false. First for Josie, now for Will. His heavy eyes, his lethargy, his wounded skin, wrenched her. She had to clap her hands over her ears to hide the sound of his retching. She, so desperate to help, was powerless. Oh, if I could only take away some of this pain from you, she would think. Her heart felt as if it were slowly being flayed.

Going back to the hospital was traumatic for both Ruth and Will. It was not just the treatments, the hospital smells, the prospect of pain. There was no way to avoid seeing the ghostly army of hairless children, whose treatments were further advanced than Will's, whose naked white skulls gave them the appearance of creatures from outer space.

'They look like aliens,' Will said once.

'I know.' The deep shadowed eyes, the gaunt faces, haunted Ruth's dreams.

'Am I going to lose *my* hair? I don't – I don't want to look like that.'

'If by any chance you do, it'll grow back.'

Ruth had read that most parents given a diagnosis of cancer in their child believe that death will occur very soon. She did not. Even after the treatment had commenced, she managed to convince herself that Will would pull through. She told herself that the only connection between him and the other children at the hospital was a single word. Cancer. In all other

219

respects, he was not part of this innocent group of sad humanity.

Or was he? Sitting beside his hospital bed, she watched his attempts to remain cheerful in spite of the drips attached to his body, the needles inserted between the knobs of his spine, the fluid drained from him, the blood withdrawn, the samples taken, and marveled. Like the other children there, he was so brave. God, how brave they *all* were, even though many of them did not have any concept of how seriously sick they were. And the parents: how did they manage to play with their children, read to them, bring in toys, decorate their rooms with cards and pictures, all the time behaving as though it were perfectly natural that a little girl should be eaten away almost to nothing by her illness, that a six-year-old boy should have eyes that seemed to see back to before the Creation?

What made the return visits even worse was Will's dislike, bordering on phobia, of needles. The pain made him scream aloud. Sometimes his arm swelled up like a balloon. Yet there was no way to avoid them. After one particularly harrowing session, he wept.

'I don't want any more treatment.'

'Hold on, honey. It's not for much longer,' Ruth said. She pressed a hand to her leaping heart. Even worse than the sight of his pain was her inability to stop it. It should be *me*, she wanted to shriek at the nurses. Let *me* suffer, not him. Not him.

'I'd rather die now than have to go through that again.' Tears rolled slowly down his white face. His bloodless lips quivered.

'Well, I'm not going to let you,' Ruth said. 'Who'd I have to nag at, if you weren't around?'

He was usually quick to respond to even the feeblest

joke, as though he felt that laughter was the only way they would survive all this. Now, the effort to move his lips into a smile seemed too much for him.

When he had fallen into a frowning doze, Ruth went into the hospital washroom and stared at herself in the mirror over the handbasins. Doubts trampled through her mind. Was she doing the right thing? Should she be inflicting this physical suffering on him? Would he be cured, and if not, would it not be better just to let him go in peace?

One of the other mothers came in. Ruth had noticed her before, a too-thin bubbly blonde who always looked as if she was dressed up for a night out on the town. She smiled at Ruth's reflection. 'You're Mrs Donnelly, aren't you?'

'Connelly, yes. Ruth. And you're Michelle's mom.' Eight-year-old Michelle was on her third course of chemo treatment and it was known on the ward that she was not likely to survive for very much longer.

'Lynda Petievich.' For a moment the woman's face crumpled. 'I wish I could be as brave as you are.'

'Brave? Me?' Was she putting on such a good front that someone actually believed that she, Ruth Connelly, was being *brave*?

'You seem so *strong*.' Lynda gulped, and her eyes filled with tears. 'Will is a lovely kid. So patient. He spends hours playing silly games with my Michelle, even though she's so much younger. Most boys his age wouldn't be bothered with a little girl.'

'She's such a pretty child.'

'Shoulda seen her when she still had her hair,' Lynda said. 'Your boy's okay that way.'

'So far.'

'And knock on wood. It would be real hard for you if anything . . . if he . . .'

221

'He won't.' Ruth's doubts vanished. 'He *won't*.'

'I wish I could say that.' The other woman's face melted like wax and anguish darkened her eyes.

Ruth reached out and took her hand. 'I'm not brave,' she said. 'Nor strong. Not in the least. I'm terrified. Every minute of every day. I see you, and Jamie, and Michelle and all the moms and dads, and I feel truly humbled.' She glanced down at her creased jeans. 'And you always look so glamorous, too.'

'That's for Michelle's sake,' Lynda said. 'Before she got sick, I used to slob around like we all do, but I want her to know what a special person she is to me, that she's worth taking some trouble over. So now I always dress good. I don't know if it helps her, but it sure helps me.'

'Of course it helps her. We've all seen the way she lights up when you appear – it's like having a movie star visit.'

'C'mon!' Lynda laughed. 'But thanks anyway for saying it.'

'I mean it. I never thought about it before. I should take more trouble myself. I always assumed Will would know I think he's special.'

'He is, he really is.' Lynda's eyes were again full of tears and she laughed shakily. 'Look at me. It's kind of strange, isn't it, that I can get emotional over your boy but I just don't dare over Michelle.'

'Perhaps I should cry for Michelle, and let you cry for my boy,' Ruth said. Her own eyes filled. 'Then we needn't bother about being brave because we're crying for someone else's kid, not our own.'

'That's a real . . . that is *such* a great idea.' For a moment, Lynda almost shone.

'It is, isn't it?' Ruth smiled too.

'I just never dare give way – it upsets my husband so much. Michelle was – *is* – the apple of his eye and he just refuses to give up on her. He's been unemployed for the longest time, you see, but now he has something to work for. You wouldn't believe how hard he's worked since she got ill, setting up bone marrow drives and fund-raisers, traveling all over, helping cancer charities. So even when I'm at home, I have to bottle it all up. But if I can cry for your William, and know you're crying for my Michelle, why that's just . . . *thank* you.' She put her arms round Ruth and the two women stood for a moment in a silent embrace before pulling away.

As Ruth was going out the door, Lynda said: 'You won't forget to cry for her, will you?'

'I promise you I won't.'

He was driving dangerously fast. This far north, winter still maintained its icy grip. Snow was piled up on either side of the deserted roads, dirty now with the muddy spray from the pulp-trucks and the semis beating their way up to the border. The sky was as black as the hard-top which stretched away into the distance. Bleak green forests spread all around him, mile upon mile of them, powdered with snow, silent under the burden of winter.

The anger beat like a pulse in his throat, threatening to choke him. Will . . . his boy. They had been going to rebuild the *Lucky Duck*. That last weekend before he went into the hospital, they'd planned to drive up to Sweetharbor and assess the damage, and then at the last minute Will had said, Sorry, Dad, I'm bushed, I can't face the drive.

I should have known right then, Paul thought. I should have seen. Will was never too tired for anything. And three days later, he was diagnosed with cancer.

Leukemia. My God. Oh, my *God*. The tears rose again. In all the rest of his life put together, he hadn't cried as much as he'd cried these past few weeks. There'd been a song . . . 'Big Girls Don't Cry' – and that went for big boys, too. Only more so. Big boys don't cry. But he did. For his son, and for himself.

Will. William Carter Connelly. He remembered the leap in his body, like an electric shock passing through him, when they told him he had a son. He adored Josie, but having a son had grabbed him in a purely atavistic way. The solidity of it. Passing on the name. Continuation of family. All that male bonding: ball games and sailing, rock-climbing, things girls didn't want to do. Out on the water, wind in the sails, wind in their hair. Racing on weekends, coming up from behind, rounding the marker buoys, standing in the yacht club afterwards, showered and changed, a drink in his hand and his son by his side. Or even just watching the big game on TV, rooting for their team, popcorn and root beer, yelling their heads off. Or the bench they'd made together for Josie. Working with Will in the barn, smoothing down the planks of wood, planing, watching the heap of shavings grow on the floor, seeing the bench take shape.

My son.

Deep and thick as vomit, the rage gnawed at him. My *son*. He had no idea where he was. The tires hissed on roads leading nowhere. Trees crowded to the edge of the road, menacing in the fading light. His headlights caught sparkles from the grimy snow. An illuminated sign indicated that there was a coffee shop up ahead and he realized that he needed to eat something. He had gone to see Will at the hospital that afternoon, sit with him, hold his hand. When Ruth came to take over, he

224

had gone down to the parking lot and cried. Got into his car. Sat there while the anger built up again, snapping through his body like whipcracks. The need to get away from it all, somewhere, anywhere, had been overpowering and in the end he'd just taken off. It wasn't for a couple of hours that he recognized he was headed up toward Maine. Toward Sweetharbor and Carter's House.

He pulled into the parking lot in front of the coffee shop, got out, pushed through the doors into warm, candy-scented air. Most of the tables were full, though there were a couple empty over by the back wall.

A waitress came over. 'How ya doin'?' she said.

He smiled wearily. 'You don't want to know.'

'Like that, is it?'

'Sure is.' He ordered a double cheeseburger, with extra French fries and a side order of onion rings. Comfort food.

'Where you headed?' the waitress asked, when she brought his food to the table.

He didn't really know. Wasn't certain how he'd come to be here in the first place. 'Hartsfield way.'

'Sure is pretty up there in the summer,' she said.

'I know.'

'Live up there?'

'Just visiting,' he said.

The coffee was hot enough to burn his mouth. He sipped it quickly, taking in the other customers. Men mostly, in plaid flannel shirts, staring down at their food, not talking, just stoking up. He'd talked to so many like them, in the course of writing his book. Heard the same stories over and over, heard the same fears about a way of life gradually eroding. Josie used to come with him sometimes when he was

225

interviewing. She was good at it. Occasionally he let her take over, drawing out from them information which he never could have done himself.

He picked up his cheeseburger and bit into it. Flavors of cheese and raw onion and the red juice of charcoal-grilled meat. It tasted good. He picked up a fry and dipped it into the fluted paper cup of dressing on the side of his plate.

One of the men at the next table looked up from his food and caught his eye. He nodded at him, and the other guy nodded back. Sort of. Moved his head a fraction of an inch. They didn't overdo things up here.

He shouldn't have taken off like that. He had no business running away when Will was down there, tubes all over him, needle marks everywhere. The boy looked so sick. And Ruth wasn't much better. Tired. Must be even worse for a mother than for a father. She'd lost Josie and now it looked like she might lose Will. What was she feeling?

For the first time since Josie had died, he was able to understand how Ruth had found that denial was the only way to cope. It was the same with him and Will. He didn't want to talk about it. Not even to Luke. He'd shared everything with his brother, all their lives, especially after their father had died. But his feelings about Will being sick were too painful to discuss. Ruth wanted to verbalize it, to describe symptoms, treat-ments, all that. Often he wanted to scream at her to shut up. It was bad enough that Will was ill, without having to hear all the details.

When he paid the bill, the waitress said: 'Have a nice one.'

'No chance of that.'

'Can't be that bad.'

'It can.'

As the doors swung to behind him, he braced himself for the cold before making a dash to his car. He'd drive back down to Brunswick, stay there for the night, give Ruth a call. He had a lecture to deliver on Monday, faculty meetings to attend, a couple of make-up exams. He needed to get a grip on himself. His students had been complaining about the number of tests he'd flung at them in the past few weeks, but he told them it was good for them. 'It's not fair,' one of them had said last week, and he'd wanted to strangle her. 'Whoever said life was fair?' he'd asked savagely.

Monday evening he'd drive to Boston, back to his empty apartment, back to the hospital. To Will.

Ruth found herself talking to the parents of other sick children as though they were old friends. Hollow-eyed women. Men whose nerves had stretched their faces tighter than the skin of a balloon. She wondered whether she was capable of being as strong as they were. Pretense. It was all about pretense. Like the other ravaged parents, Ruth found herself striving to establish a normalcy in Will's hospital room, bringing in posters and books, setting up cards from friends in his class, covering his bed with a yellow wool throw which his grandmother had crocheted for him, with his name picked out in blue baseballs. Despite her best efforts, everything she did seemed only to emphasize the room's alienation from ordinariness.

'Ruth . . . it's Paul.' He hated talking to the machine but ploughed ahead. 'I'd like to come round tonight, see Will, if—'

She picked up. 'Hi, it's me.'

227

'Can I come round later?'

'I'll tell Will, he'll be glad to see you.'

'It'd be nice to see you too,' he said awkwardly. 'Maybe we could have a drink or something. I'll bring a bottle with me, if that's okay with you.'

He felt absurd, being so hesitant about it. She was still his wife, after all. There was nothing strange about the two of them sharing a glass of wine. She liked Chardonnay: he bought a bottle of Stag's Leap, wondering if she'd remember the time they'd driven up to wine-taste in the Napa Valley, years ago, before the children came, and bought half a dozen bottles from the winery. He'd gotten disgustingly drunk, and she'd had to drive back down to San Francisco while he snored on the back seat.

At the door, he gave her a hug and handed her the bottle and a package.

'What's this?' She fingered the pretty gift-wrap.

'Well,' he said. 'You have two choices: either you stand there all night feeling it through the paper and guessing. Or you open it and see. Ninety-nine per cent of people polled favored the latter option.'

Inside was a wad of tissue paper, tied with thin gold ribbon. Inside that was a necklet. Four little wooden hearts strung on a leather lace. Her face lit up. 'How lovely, Paul. Where did you find them?'

'Would you believe I made them?'

'As a matter of fact . . .' She smiled at him. 'Yes, I would.'

'Since Will and I made that bench for . . . for—'

'Josie,' she said calmly. 'You can use her name round me, Paul. It's okay.'

'Ever since then, I've gone back to working with wood. Brought some tools down from Carter's House:

a colleague's been letting me use the shed in his back yard.' He hoped she did not see the loneliness behind his words. After school was over for the day, however much committee work he took on, there were still a lot of hours to fill. There was something therapeutic and heart-easing about the smell of wood, the feel of it.

'They're lovely,' Ruth said. 'Unusual.' She laid the hearts in a line on the coffee table. Ran a finger over the delicate carving. 'Thank you so much.'

Paul drew the cork and poured them each a glass of wine. 'May I say, Mrs Connelly, you're looking particularly good tonight.'

'Thank you.'

'You've put back a couple of pounds. It suits you.'

'You're not looking bad yourself.'

'Where's Will?'

'In bed. It hasn't been a good day for him – a lot of nausea and cramping.'

'I'll go and visit with him a while.'

Carrying his wine glass, he went down the passage to his son's room, thinking: she didn't pick up the necklace again. Didn't put it round her neck. Probably thought it wasn't sophisticated enough for that dress she was wearing. He wondered where she'd been earlier, to be all gussied up like that. Who she had been with. Not that it was any of his business. Four hearts. One for each member of the family they used to be.

He knocked at Will's door. 'Can I come in?'

'Hi, Dad.'

Paul pushed open the door and went in. 'How're ya doin', son?'

Will lay back against his pillows, his face pale and weary. 'Okay, I guess.'

'I brought you a new tape,' Paul said, feeling the

anger burn like acid. Will was a fourteen-year-old kid, for God's sake. 'Nobody I ever heard of but they're supposed to be good.'

'Barenaked Ladies. Neat.' Will picked it up, looked at it, tried to produce enthusiasm. 'Ed hasn't got this one yet.'

'Anything I can do for you, son?'

'Actually, Dad . . .'

'What?'

'I'm feeling kinda tired.'

'Too tired to talk?'

'Almost.'

'Want me to go?'

'No. But . . .'

'But what?'

'I'd kind of like it if you – if you'd read to me? You know? Like you used to when I was a kid?'

'Be my pleasure.'

'I really wanted to read, but my eyes gave up on me.'

'You can get tapes of books, you know,' Paul said. His throat ached with unshed tears. 'I'll bring some in next time I come by. I use them a lot when I've got a long trip in the car.'

'Great.' Will lay back against his pillows, closed his eyes.

'Nothing nicer than being read to, is there?' said Paul gently. He took his son's hand.

'Nope.'

'What shall I read? Grownup stuff? Kid stuff? Poetry, drama, history, geography, philosophy, religion, anything in this wide world, provided it's in this apartment.'

Will pointed to the nightstand. 'Actually, I'm halfway through this vampire book.'

'Vampires? Give me a break.'

'It's neat, Dad. All about this handsome young vampire who's fallen in love with this beautiful girl whose brother was murdered by a—'

Paul groaned. 'I just remembered there's something else I'm supposed to be doing.'

Will laughed, a quiet, weary sound so unlike his normal laugh that Paul almost burst into tears. 'I'm on page fifty-seven,' Will said. 'You'll love it, when you get into it.'

Will was back in the hospital for the next in his series of treatments. Arriving to spend time with him, Ruth heard voices through the open door of his room. Peeking through the half-drawn blinds which covered the window, she saw Michelle sitting on the edge of the bed. The little girl had Will's hand on her knee and was painting his nails with different colored polishes. Her face was very serious as she surveyed the most recent nail. 'It's gonna look so pretty, like a rainbow,' she said. 'You just wait and see.'

'Hey, Michelle.'

'What?'

'You know guys don't usually wear nail polish, don't you?' Will said.

''Course I do, silly.' Michelle screwed the cap back onto a tiny bottle of bronze polish and picked up another. 'This one's called Inca Gold. My mom wears this one for special, like when she and my dad go out dancing.'

'Do they do that a lot?'

'Every Friday. My mom's got these gowns she wears, all covered in sparkly stuff. She made them herself. She made me one, and Kelly, too.'

'I'll bet you both look really good.'

'My dad says we're the prettiest girls in the world.'

'What color is Kelly's gown?'

'Kind of shiny bluey. My mom chose it to match her eyes. And mine's pink.'

'To match *your* eyes?'

'Nobody has pink eyes,' said Michelle sternly. 'It's pink 'cause that's my favorite color. My mom mostly wears green 'cause that's what she was wearing when my dad fell in love with her. Where did your mom and dad fall in love?'

We were walking across College Green, Ruth thought. Buds just breaking, blue sky, the hint of spring in the air, the promise of hope. That's where we fell in love. She had almost forgotten the feel of Paul's hand brushing against hers, the certainty she had that this was going to lead somewhere, that this was the man she wanted to be with for always.

'I don't know,' Will said. 'Maybe at our house in Maine. It's called Carter's House.'

'Why?'

'Because it was built by somebody called Carter. My great-great-great-grandfather, I think. Or maybe it's my great-great- great-great-grandfather.'

'What's it like?'

'It's painted white and it's got black shutters, and there's trees all round and the sea in front,' Will said. 'It's perfect. All the rooms smell of pine trees and salt. And everybody's happy there.'

Ruth felt a knife twist in her heart. They should have spent last Christmas up there, as he had begged to do. But even as she thought this, she could feel her own fear at the possibility of pain. Josie was up there. What was left of her. The Boston apartment had been rendered bearable by clearing out her room, having it repainted, the furniture shifted around. But Carter's House was just as it had been that sunny afternoon, when Josie had left it for the last time.

'The sun always shines up there, and the birds sing,' Will said.

'All the time?'

'All the time.'

'Even at night?'

'Specially at night.'

Michelle put her head on one side and regarded with satisfaction the golden nail she had just painted. Her tiny fingers clasped Will's rough boy's hand. 'I bet you never had a manicure in your whole life, did you?'

'Boys don't have manicures.'

'My brothers do. And my dad. But that's 'cause Kelly's practicing on them.'

'You tell Kelly she can practice on me any time she likes.'

'Okay. She gives me manicures, too,' said Michelle.

'She's kinda pretty, isn't she?'

'She's *real* pretty,' corrected Michelle. 'She's going to work in a beauty parlor when she grows up.' She picked up a brilliant green polish and took off the cap. 'Go on about the birds singing at night. Don't they keep you awake?'

'There's this special cap I wear,' Will said. 'I pull it down over my ears if I want to sleep.'

Michelle touched the pink gingham mob-cap she was wearing to hide her naked skull. 'My sister made this for me.'

'It's real cute,' said Will. 'Think she'd make one for me?'

'No, 'cause you'd look *stoopid*,' Michelle said. 'Now, what shall we do for the last nail?'

'How about purple?'

'Okay. Pink's my favorite, but purple's good too. What else do you do up there in your house by the sea?'

'I go out in my boat. Catch lobsters and crabs.'

'I never ate a lobster. I like French fries and Pop Tarts best.'

'Lobsters are kind of hard work,' said Will. 'You have to smash them to pieces and then dig the meat out with these special forks and things. But they're worth it in the end.'

'What else do you do in your boat?'

'I just mooch around,' said Will. Ruth could hear the longing in his voice. 'Just look at the rocks and the trees. Smell the air.'

'Can I come and see your house when I'm better?'

'Sure. I'll take you out in my boat.'

'I can't swim.'

'I'll teach you. And Kelly too, if she wants to come along.'

'She'll be afraid of mussing up her hair,' said Michelle. 'She's kinda fussy about her hair.'

Will looked up and saw his mother on the other side of the glass. He smiled at her and she raised her hand, not wanting to interrupt, but he called out, 'Mom! Come in.'

Ruth walked into the room. 'Looks like somebody's been getting the beauty treatment.'

Will splayed his hands girlishly across his T-shirt. 'Hey, whaddya think?'

'Truly gorgeous,' Ruth said.

'I feel like a drag queen.'

'What's a drag queen?' asked the little girl.

'You don't want to go there,' Will said.

'Hi, Mrs Connelly,' said Michelle.

'How are you today, honey?'

'Very well, thank you.'

The little girl's cheeks were unnaturally swollen, puffed out with the drugs she was taking. Her face was chalky white, except for around her eyes, which were set deep into their sockets. She looked very frail. 'I love your hat,' Ruth said. God, how difficult it was to behave normally, faced with such sadness.

'My sister made it. Will wants her to make him one, too, but I think he'd look *stoopid*.'

'I don't know . . .' Ruth smiled as the little girl began to pack her nail polishes into a pretty bag patterned with bluebells. 'Are you going to stay and visit for a bit?'

'I gotta go see Billy,' Michelle said. 'He's feeling bad today.'

Ruth stood at the door of Will's room and watched the child walk away down the corridor. From behind, she looked like any other little girl, skipping occasionally to catch up with herself.

Bob Landers called her at home one evening. After asking how Will was, he said: 'Ruth, I need a favor from you.'

'What's that?'

'Jake Phillipson's acting up.'

'So what else is new?'

'You said it. He called me yesterday. Said they don't want to proceed without you on board.'

'Did you tell them they don't have much choice?'

'Sure did. Explained the circumstances. Jake brushed all that aside. Guess what he said.'

Remembering Phillipson's wrecking-ball attitude and limited perspective, Ruth said: 'Bet he came right back and told you he didn't get where he was today by taking no for an answer.' There was a strange comfort in the thought that while her personal life had turned upside down, the office scene continued unchanged.

Bob laughed. 'On the nose. Said we had to get you back, so I said I'd try.'

'No dice, Bob.'

'Not full-time, of course not.'

'Not even half-time.'

'I was thinking a couple of days a week. At your convenience, not Phillipson's.'

'I'm fully committed to Will,' Ruth said.

'I know that. I told Jake that. He said, Goddamit, if I was a kid, I wouldn't want my momma on my back the whole darn time, however sick I was. So . . .'

'So, Bob?'

'So I wondered if Will might be feeling something like that.'

'I haven't asked him.'

'Let's face it, Mrs Connelly, it would keep your hand in. You may be spending all your time running between home and hospital at the moment, but Will's not going to be sick forever, is he? One of these days he's going to get better, and there you'll be, looking for a job again.'

Even if it was manipulative, the certainty in his voice was cheering. She reflected that after all, she had been made a partner because she was *good*: with detail, with people, with ideas. And she had worked hard to get to where she had been. Even if Will was sick, that had not changed. 'Two days a week, you said?'

'Entirely at your discretion. Flexibility being the name of the game.'

236

'You wouldn't by any chance be wearing your Good Samaritan hat, would you?'

'I got rid of that old thing years ago,' Bob said. 'Looked like hell on me. No, tell the truth, I don't find that many good corporate lawyers, and almost never do I find a brilliant one. So when I do, I try to hang on to them. Besides, as you know, the customer is always right, even if it's Jake Phillipson, so we do our best to please. And if he wants you back, we'll try to get you back.'

It was true that in each week there were many hours a day when Ruth found herself with little or nothing to do. Caring for William did not occupy her full-time; she would find it rewarding if she had work to fill the spaces between his sessions with the doctors. During the hours he spent hooked up to drips or just dozing, there was not much for her to do and as a result she found herself bored and unstretched. Bob's offer could not have come at a better time. 'Let me think about it,' she said.

She was sitting in the hospital cafeteria one morning when Lynda approached her table, carrying a coffee. 'Mind if I sit down?' She looked thinner and more attenuated than ever.

'Please do.'

'We're taking Michelle to Disney World, week after next,' said Lynda. 'I think she'll enjoy that. It's through the Make-A-Wish scheme, you know?'

'I've heard of it.' Ruth took the other woman's hand. Once, she had found these gestures of common humanity almost impossible to make. In the past painful weeks, she had learned the comfort of reaching out to another human being. Of being part of the family of man. 'Michelle will love it there,' she said. 'We took our children one vacation and they had a ball.'

Lynda was surprised. 'I didn't realize you had any other children.'

'I don't.'

'But you just said . . .'

Ruth took a deep breath. It was time. She would say it. 'Josie.' She said it again, her voice a little stronger. 'Josie. My daughter was called Josie. But she died.'

'How terrible. You poor thing. Especially now that . . .' There was no need to complete the sentence.

'It's nearly a year since it happened.'

'That doesn't make it any better, does it?'

'Not in the least.' Ruth half-smiled. 'I kind of thought it would. They're always telling you time is a great healer and that sort of thing. And some of the time, I do actually forget about it. But as you say, it doesn't make it any better.'

'Would it help to talk about it?'

I could not have done so once, Ruth thought. Especially to someone I know as little as I know this woman. 'She drowned,' she said. She pressed her lips together for a moment. 'We were out sailing, up in Maine, and there was an accident and Josie was swept away.'

'My God, Ruth. How old was she?'

'Sixteen.' Ruth's voice broke. 'Nearly seventeen.' The conversation could have stopped there, but for the first time Ruth wanted to go on. 'And you know the worst thing, Lynda, the very worst?'

'No.' Lynda's eyes were huge.

'They never found her body.'

'That's terrible. So you've never really said goodbye.'

'That's right. Never properly grieved.' Nor bought

238

white freesias for her. Nor even sat on her bench. Josie's bench, made by her father and her brother, overlooking the sea. 'And you know what else? Because of that, I've never really been able to let her go. A little bit of me still thinks she's out there somewhere, just waiting for me to find her.' Why was she telling Lynda something she had scarcely even allowed herself to think?

'Maybe she is.'

Ruth stared at her. 'How do you mean?'

'Like, maybe she's still waiting for you to say goodbye. Her spirit, I mean. Waiting up there, where it happened.' Lynda grasped both Ruth's wrists and stroked them with her thumbs. 'Losing her at sixteen? That's so sad, Ruth. Kelly, my eldest, is just seventeen. They're funny at that age, aren't they? Up one minute, down the next. And so rude. I want to slap her sometimes, I really do.'

'That's just how it was with Josie. That last summer before she . . . died, it was as if she hated me.'

'She probably did,' Lynda laughed. 'I know my Kelly hates me, because she's always saying so. Except she doesn't really. Not underneath. Anymore than your Josie did.' She leaned over. 'Got a photo of her?'

'No.'

'No?' Lynda began to dig in her purse. 'Well, I'll show you one of Kelly, if you like. The original doting momma, that's me – oughta been Jewish, I guess. I never go anywhere without my pictures, so I can bore people to death with them. I'll show you Kelly's brothers, too – I've got four kids, Michelle's my youngest.'

'I think Will's really smitten with Kelly. He never stops talking about her. Maybe she could stop by and see him some time.'

'She already does.' Lynda rolled her eyes at Ruth then leaned across. 'Look, this is my Mikey . . .'

Lynda's family was an attractive one. Ruth looked at photos of Lynda's husband, the two sons, the family dog, thin blond Kelly. 'What a beautiful bunch.'

'They are, aren't they.' Lynda gazed for a long time at a photograph of Michelle in a long white dress with a pink sash round the waist. 'That's when she was a flower-girl at my cousin's wedding, back last spring.' Her expression began to falter. She looked up at Ruth with desperate eyes. 'I cried for Will a whole lot last week,' she said quietly.

'Thank you,' Ruth said gently. She knew that Michelle had been diagnosed with further cancers and had little time left. The visit to Disney World was likely to be the last trip she took before she died, her last breath of non-purified air, her last glimpse of blue sky and sparkling sunshine.

'She's going to die,' Lynda said. 'I've faced that. It's Mikey who can't. He wants to go on and on trying. Every time he reads about a new miracle cure or whatever, he wants us to hop on the next plane to England, or Australia or Sweden. Wherever. I had to say no. Enough is enough. We can't do this to Michelle.'

'Oh God, Lynda. I'm so sorry. I don't know what I'd do if we reached that stage with Will.'

'He's bigger than Michelle. Stronger. He'll pull through. I'm sure he will.'

Tears filled Ruth's eyes. 'Suppose he doesn't.'

'I'll stop by his room next time I'm passing and tell him he has to. Better still, send Kelly.'

'For Michelle's sake.'

'Yeah. For Michelle.'

13

Ruth's father telephoned one evening. 'I was talking to Rick Henderson the other day – remember him?'

'Vaguely.' Rick had been a colleague of her father's up in Maine.

'He tells me that Rick Jr is going on vacation for a couple weeks, and his apartment will be empty. It's right around the corner from you. So your mom and I thought it would be a good idea if we came up. Get a chance to see you, see Will.' There was a pause while her father audibly swallowed.

'That'd be great, Dad, but it really isn't—'

'Help out a little, Ruth. Give you a break.'

'I'm okay.'

'Give us a chance to do something.' Jonathan Carter's tone was full of entreaty. 'Lord, you don't have any idea how useless we feel down here. Your mother just sits and cries.'

He was asking for something she could not refuse him. 'That would be wonderful, Dad. I'd really appreciate it.'

'We'll be up at the end of the week. Don't worry about meeting us: we'll take a cab from the airport.'

'Will will be so happy to see you. Me too.'

'How's he doing?'

'All right. The doctors seem pleased with his progress.'

'But it's still too early to tell.'

'Too early to start hoping,' said Ruth quietly.

Having her parents near at hand made it both harder for Ruth, and easier. Harder, because the pain they were so visibly experiencing only exacerbated her own, and meant that she had to be brave for their sakes as well as for Will's; easier, because occasionally she was able to break down and admit that she despaired. They belonged to a generation which did not easily express emotion but now the three of them would sometimes sit in a stranger's living room and weep together.

Her father worried endlessly about the finances involved in paying for the treatment. 'There was this kid with cancer in Daytona Beach,' he said. 'Parents got stiffed by their insurance company so badly that they couldn't pay for treatment, and he died.'

'It's not like that with us,' Ruth told him. 'We're covered, I promise you. We'll be all right. Money's the least of our problems. The very least.'

'Will's looking better than I expected,' Jonathan Carter said.

'But not good.'

'No, not good.'

'He's so weak. So ill.' It was a relief to be able to voice her fears.

'Last time I visited,' her father said, 'I spoke with the physician – Dr Gearin. He told me Will was responding well – they're feeling pretty optimistic.'

'He's going to get better. I promise you, darling,' her mother said.

'Yeah.' Ruth dared not allow hope to creep into the tight hold she forced herself to maintain over her feelings. Better to believe the worst until she was sure. Nonetheless, even if Ruth could not accept them, the words were comforting to hear. Left unspoken in all their minds was the thought that if he did not recover, no family could have been more unlucky.

Ruth took her parents to the hospital to have a blood sample taken. Dr Gearin was reassuring. 'We hope this procedure will be entirely unnecessary,' he said. 'Will's doing well. We're very hopeful of beating the cancer.'

'Right. But since we're in town . . .' Dr Carter said, unrolling his shirt sleeve.

Gearin swabbed the inside of the older man's elbow with alcohol. 'As you know, we took blood from Professor and Mrs Connelly some months back, just in case. And from the professor's brother. Unfortunately without any success.'

'I thought the immediate family provided the best hope of coming up with a match for Will,' Ruth's mother said.

'Even so, there's still a less than one in three chance.' Gearin picked up a disposable syringe and tore off the wrapping. 'It's a question of finding someone with the same combination of proteins as Will.' Carefully sliding the needle into the popped vein on Dr Carter's arm, he added: 'With any luck, a bone marrow aspiration won't be necessary, but if it is, then at least we'll know where to look.'

'Or where not to look,' said Betty Carter.

'I don't know how I'd cope,' Ruth said one evening toward the end of their stay in the city. She twisted her

243

wedding band around on her finger. 'If anything happens to Will, I'll die myself.'

'Hush, honey,' her mother soothed. 'Don't talk like that. That's not an option.' She held her daughter close and patted her back the way she had done when Ruth was a baby.

The safety of her mother's arms was something Ruth had long ago forgotten. 'He looks so sick,' she said. 'So desperately sick.'

'I know,' said her father. 'But you have to remind yourself that part of that's the medication.'

'Anybody'd be sick,' her mother said, 'the stuff they pour into those poor kids.' She looked older and much more tired than last time Ruth had seen her. The strain of the last few months had not been Ruth's alone.

Will was not in his hospital room. Frowning, Paul went in search of him. Anxiety thumped inside his ribcage but he tried to ignore it. Nothing had happened. Nothing *could* have happened. He'd spoken to Ruth just that morning. The shiny corridors seemed endless: he hated the peach-colored paint everywhere. Why didn't they use something less anodyne, something with more life in it?

At the nurses' station he asked where Will was, trying to sound unconcerned but knowing he did not.

'He's just fine, Professor Connelly,' one of them said. Lucille. She had a plastic badge pinned on her white uniform.

'Only he's not in his room and I thought . . . I wondered . . .' His mouth wasn't working properly. 'I was afraid . . .' If they told him Will's condition had worsened, he would simply start screaming, banging his fists on the counter. The stress of the past weeks was getting to him in a big way.

'Don't you worry,' Lucille soothed. 'He's with Michelle.'

'Michelle?'

'He's in her room, been reading her a story. You've got a real nice boy there, Professor. Takes a lot of trouble with the younger kids in here.'

'Th-thank you.' Reprieve made him stutter. 'Wh-where are th-they?'

'Just go down the corridor a ways. Michelle's room's on the right-hand side.'

'Th-thanks.'

Paul hurried along the passage, his head spinning with relief. He heard a weak burst of laughter, the breathy short-lived kind that he often heard in here, as drug-assaulted lungs struggled for air. Then a wheelchair containing a little girl negotiated the doorway of one of the rooms and turned into the passage toward him. Paul stopped. Will was pushing the child, talking to her. She lay back with her eyes closed, her face almost transparent. She wore a pink gingham mob-cap over her naked skull. Unselfconsciously, Will wore a similar one perched on top of his hair.

Paul gulped. 'Hello, son,' he said softly.

'Hi, Dad.'

'I guess this must be Michelle.'

'That's right.' Will bent over the chair. 'Can you say hi to my dad, Michelle?' he asked tenderly.

With enormous effort, the child opened her eyes. 'Hi,' she said, and closed them again.

'I'm taking her for a walk,' Will said. 'She's too tired to play today.'

'Can I come along?' Paul said, his voice unsteady.

'Sure.'

Side by side, Paul and his son walked along the

corridor. 'The hat suits you, Will,' he said.

'Kelly made it for me. That's Michelle's sister.'

'Looks good.'

'Looks *stoopi . . .*' Michelle said, scarcely audible. ''S like mine . . .'

'I can see that. You look real pretty in pink.'

''S my favorite co . . .' The sentence drifted away, unfinished.

'You ever see that movie, Michelle?' Will said. '*Pretty in Pink*? Ever see it?' There was something desperate in his voice.

The little girl nodded infinitesimally.

'It was a good one,' said Will. 'I enjoyed that. Not as good as *Home Alone*, though. That was fun.' Wearing a funny hat to please a little girl, he pushed the wheelchair along, talking, talking, while Michelle leaned her head back, her eyes shut. Her mouth drooped open a little, the lips bloodless, the eyelids as delicate as silk.

Between treatments, when Will was back in the apartment but still unable to attend school, his friends often came by, bringing school assignments for him to complete. Overhearing their conversations, Ruth knew that they were all under the spell of Miss Marling, the English teacher, the one they called Witchy Woman. When Miss Marling herself appeared one afternoon at the door of the apartment, shortly after Ed Stein had shown up, Ruth could see why they were in awe of her. Her accent was straight out of *Gone With the Wind*, her short black hair was only millimeters longer than a West Point crew cut, and her pale blue eyes might have belonged to a piranha. She was dressed entirely in black: leather trousers, a cashmere turtleneck, a metal-studded leather jacket. She seemed to operate within a forcefield of barely harnessed energy.

'Now, I don't want you to think I don't sympathize with you, Miz Connelly,' she said briskly, over a cup of coffee. 'But my brother, Dean Jr, he had leukemia when he was about the same age as William, and I tell you, my mom was not about to let his grades slip. So she just kept him right at his studies all through his sickness. She used to say, he may be sick but he's gotta give it one hundred per cent. And how right she was.'

'Was she?'

'Sure was. Because when Dean Jr was cured, he was right up there getting straight As, in spite of all the time he had to take off studying. And now he's pre-med and still giving it one hundred per cent.' Miss Marling's laserlike glance swept around the kitchen, while small objects cowered on the counters.

'Good,' Ruth said meaninglessly. What could have brought a woman with such looks and such crackling determination to Boston? She should be down in Washington, running the country.

'It's terrible that William's sick too, and I understand how sometimes he doesn't feel like completing those assignments, but you just got to keep at him because if you don't, he's going to miss out.' Miss Marling pushed back her chair and paced across the kitchen floor, picking up objects and putting them down as she moved. 'He's a bright boy, and he can do it.'

'Sometimes he's in such pain,' said Ruth. 'I haven't the heart to force him.'

'Oh, shoot,' said the teacher. She straightened a picture on the wall, stepped back, examined it and minutely adjusted the angle at which it hung. 'You don't want to take any notice of him. Boys are all the same, do anything to get out of working at their books. As I'm sure you're aware, Miz Connelly, at this age girls outstrip boys in all the aptitude tests we throw at them. But that's purely because girls want to do well and boys don't really care.' She came back and sat down on her chair, moved her coffee cup to a different position, returned it to its original place.

'I'm sure you're right.'

'I *know* I'm right. And I always say my classes are equal opportunity, I don't want to see the girls outshining the boys, I want every one of those boys getting down to it and working, Miz Connelly. Giving it one hundred per cent.' She banged the table with her hand, making Ruth jump. 'Especially the bright ones like William and Edward Stein. So what I'm going to do, I'm going to come by and see William, those occasions when he can't make it into school, and I'm going to give him extra tutoring so he's got no excuse to fall behind.'

'That's very—'

'I'm not going to allow him to use his illness as an excuse not to work.' Witchy Woman looked up suddenly and called out, 'Right, William?'

Ruth heard some shuffling and giggling out in the passage and realized that Will and Ed had both been listening in on the conversation. 'Right, Miss Marling,' an unseen Will said.

'Edward?'

'Right, Miss Marling.'

'Looks like they're lucky to have you,' Ruth said, as she escorted the teacher to the door.

'They are, ma'am,' Miss Marling said. 'They surely are.'

Ruth telephoned Paul. 'Now Will's back home again, it

would be good if you'd plan to sleep over every now and then,' she told him. 'I think he'd find it easier if you were around more.'

The thought of returning to their apartment made Paul's heart sink. He was often lonely in his one-bedroom place, but at least it was of his own choosing, and not forced on him. Could anything be worse than sitting in the same room as your wife and being lonely? Doubt made him sound hostile. 'Why?'

'I don't think you're behaving well over this,' she said, her tone unfriendly. 'I've got a hell of a job to do, with Will so sick. Not that I grudge him a minute, a second, of my time or my love. But you should be helping too. For his sake, as much as for mine.'

'I know that,' he said. 'I – I just don't want to go back to where we were before.'

'Not a chance, believe me.'

'I'm looking at a hectic schedule this semester. It'd be good if our routines could've been put on hold while Will was sick, but life doesn't work that way.'

'You can change things around if you want to. That's your problem. All I want is what's best for our son. And at the moment his life is difficult enough, without adding to the embarrassment of the physical care he needs.'

'What kind of physical care?'

'If you were a fourteen-year-old kid, imagine how you'd feel if you were throwing up all the time. If you were so sick that you needed someone to clean you up after a crap. If your shit had to be examined for signs of bleeding before it was flushed. Imagine having no physical privacy anymore. Imagine being unable to control your body and think how you'd have hated it.'

The picture she painted made him uncomfortable.

Perhaps he hadn't been doing as much as he should. Even though he often dropped by to see Will, drove him to the hospital, spent time with him – hours, even – took him out when he felt well enough, it was not the down-to-earth, nitty-gritty stuff she was talking about. Stuff he'd tried not to think about. 'Okay.' Paul sighed inwardly. If Will needed him, then he must do whatever was best. 'I'll work out some kind of a schedule so I spend more time with you.'

'Not with me, Paul, with Will. If you prefer, I can make arrangements to be out of the apartment while you're there.'

'Ruth . . .' He hesitated. 'Just tell me what you want me to do.'

'I'd like you to spend at least three nights a week here in the apartment, until this course of chemotherapy's been completed and evaluated. There's no need for us to overlap—'

'Ruth . . .'

'—I can go stay with the Steins.'

'. . . that won't be necessary, for God's sake. Unless you want to.'

'Of course I don't.'

'When would you like me to start?'

'Today's Thursday.' He wished she did not sound so impersonal. 'Let's say after the weekend. How about next Tuesday?'

He turned the pages of his diary. 'That looks fine.'

'We're talking maybe months of this, Paul,' Ruth warned. 'Not just days or weeks.'

'I know that.' Paul cleared his throat. 'Uh, Ruth . . .'

'What?'

He wished he had not started the sentence. 'Are you . . . are you seeing anyone else?'

250

Her voice could have formed ice-cubes in a heat wave. 'You've forfeited any right to ask that kind of question.'

'That means you are,' he said. The thought of Ruth with another man made him desolate.

'Why should you give a damn?'

'I'm still your husband, goddammit. You're the mother of my son. I still . . . care about you both.'

'Even though you chose to walk out?'

'I told you why.'

'And walking out's so much easier than staying and trying to sort out the problems, isn't it?'

Jesus, what was happening to them? 'You just didn't want to know.'

'Are *you* seeing someone else?' she said, as though she could care less.

'There's someone I see occasionally, since you ask,' he said deliberately, though it was not really true. A drink with Carole Barwick from time to time; dinner with a female colleague. 'Nothing serious.'

'I'll assume you'll be unaccompanied when you come round,' she said coldly.

'I'm not a complete jerk.'

Almost in a whisper, he heard her say: 'I never thought you were.'

Ruth was in the kitchen, reading the paper and drinking a mug of coffee when Will got up on Monday morning and went along to the bathroom. Listening from the kitchen to his slow, old-man's step along the passage, she closed her eyes. She heard the swish of the shower curtain along the chrome rail, the sound of water splashing against Will's body. Ordinary noises. Soothing sounds. Suddenly, Will screamed, his voice raised in

inarticulate distress. Terrified, Ruth ran to the bathroom and rapped at the door.

'Will! Honey! What's the matter?'

'Nothing.' His voice was muffled. Anguished.

'Something is.'

'Mom,' he moaned. 'Oh, Mom.'

'Can I come in?'

He did not answer and she pushed open the door.
The water in the shower was still running, but Will
stood naked in front of the full-length mirror on one
wall, gazing at his reflection, so appalled that he did not
even reach for a towel with which to cover himself
when she came in.

'My God.' Ruth stepped into the bathroom, aghast.
Apart from a few wisps of hair, Will's skull gleamed
white, startlingly naked above his bony face. For the
first time, he looked like the other children at the
hospital. The sight was truly shocking. Much of his
body hair had also gone. Reaching for the shower
faucets, she saw most of it lying in the bath tub, clogged
around the plughole.

'I was soaping myself,' he said, 'the shampoo . . .' He
choked, inarticulate, and turned toward her, face
screwed up in despair, eyes full of self-disgust. 'Mom,
look at me.'

It was difficult to look anywhere else.

Anticipating this moment, dreading it, she had
rehearsed what she would say when it came. Now the
words stuck in her throat. The nausea, the vomiting,
the mouth ulcers, these he could handle. To lose his hair,
his looks . . . Eventually she managed to say: 'It worked
wonders for Kojak.'

'Kojak's dead,' Will shouted. 'And I wish I was, too.'
He began to cough and weep at the same time.

'Oh Will, don't say that.' She grabbed a towel and handed it to him. 'Don't ever say it.'

'Why not? It's – it's true.' He stared at his reflection again with horrified fascination, while behind him she sniffed back the tears, helpless, unable to do anything to comfort him.

'Dr Gearin told us this might happen. It's normal. You've seen the kids down at the hospital,' she told him.

'I didn't think . . .' Will swallowed hard, tears standing in his eyes. 'I just hoped it wouldn't happen to me.'

'Honey, I promise you it'll all come back. It's temporary, just temporary.'

'It's fucking shitty, that's what it is. This whole thing is shitty.' He began to cry again, his expression utterly miserable. 'Look at me, Mom,' he gulped. 'I look like some weird space monster. And . . . and I feel lousy.' He clutched at his stomach suddenly and heaved. 'I'm gonna throw up.'

'You don't look *that* bad,' Ruth said, and he tried to laugh before he vomited into the bath.

Later, when she had cleaned him up and the bathroom, she went into his bedroom. 'Don't those Southie homeboys tie scarves round their heads?' she said.

'You have to be black,' he said sulkily.

'Skateboarders, then. Even joggers.'

'Oh, *Mom*.' He swallowed hard. There was a handmirror on his desk into which he kept staring, tears rolling down his cheeks.

'Then if you're feeling okay tomorrow, why don't we go down town and buy you a hat?'

'A *hat*? Only geeks wear hats.'

'Actually, I wasn't thinking of buying a geeky hat.' It was difficult to keep on being cheerful but Ruth made an effort. 'What about a watch-cap? Or a Russian cossack's hat. Or one of those borsalino type things.'

'You mean like pimps wear?' He brightened. 'Hey, that'd be cool. One of those black ones with a wide brim and a really jazzy snakeskin band?'

'Why not? You've got the height. You could carry it off.'

'I could get a Day-Glo pink zoot suit to go with it. And you could have the car customized in fake leopard fur.'

'I could not.'

'And I could get me a string of gorgeous girls.' He was trying hard. 'Maybe I could put Witchy Wom— Miss Marling out to work.'

'I don't think we need to overdo things here.' She looked away, not wanting to mortify him further. 'Of course, we could go for a wig.'

'A *wig*? For me? No way.'

'Why not?'

'Suppose it fell off? Anyway . . .' His eyes filled again. 'Whatever we do, nothing's gonna hide the fact that I'm as bald as a . . . as . . .'

'An egg?'

'A bowling ball.'

'A turnip? A vulture?' She got him to smile at that one. She wanted to tell him he did not look nearly as bad as he thought he did. She wanted to say how the lack of hair made his face stronger, more adult. She wanted to kiss him and tell him she loved him, but was afraid that if she did so, he would think she was only saying it because she thought he looked so terrible.

After school, Ed Stein came round with an assignment Miss Marling had given the class. Before Ruth could warn him to be tactful, he was knocking on the door of Will's

254

room at the same time as he pushed it open. There was a moment's stupefied silence. Then Ruth heard him say: 'Hey, *dude*. You look really cool.'

'Fuck off,' Will said.

'No, man, I mean it. You look – jeez, I've been trying to get my mom to let me shave my head for months now.'

'I didn't fucking shave it,' Will said.

'You mean, your mom did?'

'It fell out, asshole.'

'Fell – oh, you mean your medication and stuff? Man. You look wicked.'

'Think so?'

Ruth guessed Will was looking into his hand-mirror again, reviewing his image in the light of Ed's envious tone.

'You bet I do. Wait till I tell the others. You could oil it, make it really shine. Hey, you know what you need?'

'What's that?'

'One of those ear studs. Diamond. That'd be *sooo* cool. Think your mom'd go for it?'

'It's not Mom I'd be worried about, it's Miss Marling.' Will sounded almost normal again, an ordinary schoolkid.

'Darling Marling. Hey, would she have a stroke or what?'

'She'd go ballistic.'

'*Ooh, ooh, Witchy Woman, see how high she fli-i-ies . . .*' the two of them sang together then Ed said: 'Will-ee-yum, each an' ever' day-uh, y'all hev gotta give it one hunnerd puh cent.'

It was a pretty good imitation of the teacher's voice, and hearing Will laugh, Ruth thought: Thank you, Ed. Oh, thank you.

Later, when Ed was leaving, she called him into the kitchen. 'I'm so grateful to you,' she said.

'What for?'

'Telling Will he looked okay. He wouldn't believe me.'

'Hey, I meant it,' Ed said. He was nearly a year older than Will, just as tall but filling out, already broader than Will was ever likely to be.

'Ed – tell me what I can do for him. What I can buy to help him take his mind off . . . all this. I know he likes playing his guitar but at the moment, with his platelet count right down, he can't do that.'

'Why not?'

'It sometimes makes his fingers bleed. His skin is very thin at the moment.' She explained that the platelets, which help with blood clotting, are destroyed by chemotherapy, so that even the smallest cut will bleed excessively. 'And when that happens, there's an increased risk of infection.'

'How about something else then, just till he's better? The sax wouldn't be too difficult for him. Or, hey – how about drums? A set of drums. You know about the band . . .'

'Yes.'

'We're all okay on guitars, and Stu's cool on the sax. And I've been doing trombone at school. But if we had a drum set, we could really take off.'

'Will's been hinting about having a set for his birthday, but I already told him no. Because of the noise. There are people above and below us.'

'My dad freaked out too,' Ed said. He shook his head. 'But, oh boy, Will'd really like a drum kit.'

'Could he manage it? He gets tired so easily.'

'So? When he's tired, he stops.'

256

'I guess if he did it during the day, most people would be out,' Ruth said slowly.

'Sure. Or you could, like, soundproof his bedroom or something.'

'I'll talk to the super. And the neighbors. Explain he's ill. I want to give him anything that'll give him some pleasure, and the hell with anyone else. Anything that would make him happy.' Because there was damn little happiness going begging right now. Tears filled her eyes. Reaching for a tissue, she said: 'I'm sorry, Eddie. Mothers aren't supposed to cry.'

'Hey, that's okay, Mrs Connelly. My mom cries all the time.'

That made her laugh. 'Knowing Carmel, I find that hard to believe, but thank you for saying it.'

'No, I mean it. Over the stupidest things. Like I mean, last week, right? My dad's out of town, right, and she makes this kind of pasta sauce with all green stuff in it – pesto or something – and my sister's like, "Eeugh, this tastes like pig shit," and my mom says how does she know, since she's never eaten pig shit in her life, and Mamie's going, I sure have, because that's all we ever get to eat in this house, and Mom's really mad, saying if that's how she feels, she can make her own supper in future, and Mamie's like, she'd be glad to, if that's what it takes to get something decent round here to eat, so then Mom bursts out crying.'

'I'm not surprised.' Ruth was fascinated by this glimpse into Carmel Stein's life which from the outside always seemed so shinily perfect.

'I mean, can you imagine anyone letting a creep like Mamie get to them? My sister is the pits, believe me.'

Dabbing her eyes, Ruth wondered if this unusually long-winded story was as artless as it sounded, or whether Ed had launched into it so as to give her time to recover. If so, she had to admire his social skills.

'Uh, Mrs Connelly, could I ask you something?'

'Go right ahead.'

'Will is pretty sick, isn't he?'

'About as sick as he can be.'

'Is he going to – you know. Is he going to die?'

She ought to deny it, but she could not. She was crying again. 'I don't know, Ed. And that's the truth. I just don't know.'

Paul was staying the following night for the first time since his departure. Ruth found herself taking extra trouble with her appearance, opening a bottle of expensive wine she had picked up at the supermarket, getting the ingredients together for a green pepper steak, which she knew he liked.

'Will went to bed early,' Ruth said, kissing his cheek. She led the way into the sitting room. 'You look like you caught the sun. Nice tan.'

'One of my colleagues at Bowdoin has a son with a boat,' Paul said. 'We went sailing last weekend.'

'I see.' What had she hoped from his presence here overnight? Nothing, really. Nothing at all. It was over between them. Nonetheless, the ease with which he brought the colleague – the someone he had been seeing, right? – into the conversation, the casual way he spoke of 'we', caused Ruth more pain than she could have believed. Although he had not yet brought up the subject of a divorce, she was sure that some day soon he would. When that happened, only Will would be left as a reminder of the happiness they had once shared.

When Will had first been diagnosed with cancer, there had been a certain rapprochement between them.

258

Since then, Paul seemed to be growing more distant. Looking at his tanned face, his blue eyes, she remembered how he used to wait for her after classes, how they had talked over beers in the student bars, shared cheap pasta dishes in the Italian restaurant just off campus, gone hiking in Montana one vacation with a group of friends, held hands at the movies. She had played hard to get, it was what girls did back in those days, with the feminist movement in one of its quiescent phases. To show any eagerness was somehow considered improper; men were supposed to do the pursuing and women had to pretend to be pursued. She had never wanted to do that: from the first moment she had seen Paul, she had been drawn to him.

'I've got steaks,' she said. 'Salad. A baked potato.'

He looked stricken. 'Oh, no. Sorry, I didn't realize you – I already ate. I was at a friend's and we made salmon steaks with hollandaise sauce.'

'A female friend's?' Ruth asked, before she could stop herself. As if she gave a damn.

'As it happens, yes.'

Well, isn't that just peachy, thought Ruth, determined not to let him see how disappointed she was. 'That's okay. They'll keep.'

'A drink would be good,' Paul said. 'I'll just look in on Will first.'

'Don't wake him. He's sleeping very badly at the moment.'

When he came back, she handed him a glass of wine. 'He looks . . . exhausted,' he said.

'He is. The chemo . . . it's very draining. And he frets about the fact he can't do much, even on the good days.'

'Is he going to get through this?'

'I think so. My dad spoke to Gearin, doctor to

259

doctor, you know? They seem optimistic.'

'That's good.'

They sat together without speaking until Ruth, for something to say, said: 'Are you going up to Sweetharbor any time soon?'

'Maybe next weekend.'

'Sailing again? With your colleague?'

'Not this time,' he said evenly. 'Why do you ask?'

'The agent rang. She thinks someone's been in the house again.'

'I don't know what I could do about it that she can't.'

'I think she wanted to check that nothing's been stolen.'

'She's got the inventory: she probably knows more about it than I do.' He leaned over and refilled his glass, offered her the bottle.

She shook her head. Sitting together like this, the way they had so many evenings before, was a painful reminder of what they had lost. That she should be trying to make conversation with her own husband cast a shadow on her heart. 'I think I'll go to bed,' she said. 'You're all clear on Will, right? What to do if he wakes?'

'I think so.'

She stood awkwardly, wondering if she ought to kiss him, thinking how absurd this was, the two of them in the home they had bought together, had shared for most of twenty years, and she did not know whether she should kiss him goodnight. In the end, she smiled briefly and went.

Had he detected a hint of jealousy in Ruth's voice when he mentioned eating with a friend? He should have added that it was the wife of one of his colleagues, to whom he had promised to deliver some papers. When he showed up at the door she had explained that she was alone that night, her husband had been called unexpectedly to visit his mother in her nursing home: would Paul like to have supper with her? The alternative being a microwave meal from the supermarket, he'd agreed with pleasure.

It had not occurred to him that Ruth might want to eat with him. Cook for him.

He wished she had at least put her arms round him before she went to bed. He switched on the TV, surfed the channels, settled down to watch an *Inspector Morse* he'd seen at least four times before. What a miserable guy the British policeman was. Never cracked a smile. No wonder he never had any luck with women.

He was dozing to the staccato theme music at the end of the show when he heard Will's voice. 'Dad . . .'

Paul jumped up, disoriented, wondering for a moment where he was. Will was standing at the door of the sitting room.

'Will. Hi, son.' It was the first time he'd seen Will since the hair loss and he did his best not to look surprised.

Will came in and sat down on the sofa beside his father. 'What're you watching?'

'Some British thing. *Inspector Morse.* Ever seen it?'

'A couple of times.'

'What do you watch these days?'

'*Simpsons. South Park. The X-Files.*'

'*NYPD Blue?*'

'That's good, yeah. And I like all those nature programs. Condors. Beavers changing the environment. There was a real neat one about whales the other day.'

'I saw that.' Paul faked a double take. 'Hey, love the haircut.'

'Thanks for pretending you didn't notice.'

'And did you know you've got a diamond stuck in your ear?'

'It's fake,' Will said. 'Mom and I went out the other day and had it done. I thought I'd have to spend a couple years persuading her, but she just said okay. So we went right ahead. What do you think?'

'Cool.'

'And we bought a hat, too. But you can still tell I'm bald.'

'Have to say it's kind of startling, first glance. For a moment there, thought I was watching Kojak, not Inspector Morse at all. Ever thought of a wig?'

'Sure.'

'And?'

'Stopped thinking right after I started,' Will said.

'Oh.'

'Hey, Dad. How can you tell if a toupee is a cheap one?'

'I don't know. How can you?'

'When it comes with a chin-strap.'

Paul laughed immoderately, at the same time marveling at his son's matter-of-fact courage. Would he himself be able to joke, in similar circumstances? He thought not.

'Aren't there any other famous bald guys than Kojak?' Will asked.

'Got to be. Just give me a moment and I'll come up with someone. How about Shakespeare?'

'Doesn't count. He had hair on the sides.'

'Michael Jordan. Magic Johnson.' They ran through the names of some other athletes. Some rappers. Male models.

'And a guy who's a bit before your time,' Paul said.

'Yul Brynner — he starred in a film called *The King and I*.'

'I've seen that.'

'*Shall we dance*, da da dum,' Paul sang. '*On a bright cloud of music? Shall we fly?* da da dum. *Shall we then*—'

'Dad,' Will said.

'What?'

'I've got enough troubles without you singing.'

'You don't like my voice?'

'Nothing wrong with the voice. It's the singing I can't handle. Don't forget I'm sick.'

The two of them burst out laughing. Paul spread his arm across the top of the sofa, and Will snuggled in close. He picked up the remote and pressed it. 'Hey, look. Clint Eastwood, in *Unforgiven*. Ever seen it, Dad?'

'Of course. It's one of those films whose sum is greater than its parts,' Paul intoned solemnly. 'A comment, if you like, on our contemporary culture which manages to—'

'Cut it out, will you, Dad? Let's just enjoy the movie.'

They sat together in companionable silence, Will held close by his father's arm.

From the bedroom, Ruth, sleepless, heard them talking, laughing. She wanted to be invited into the circle of two. She wished she was in there with them, sharing, a family again, not out here in the dark. She wished she was not so alone.

14

In early May, Will returned to the hospital for his final dose of chemotherapy. As Ruth pushed him down the corridor, they had both automatically glanced into Michelle's room, only to see that there was another child lying on the bed, that the two adults with her were strangers.

'Gone home for a couple of days, probably.' Ruth kept her voice light though a weight of anxiety was tying a knot in her chest. Michelle was far too ill to go home.

'Let's ask.' Will grabbed her hand. 'Oh Mom, I hope she hasn't . . . isn't . . .'

'So do I, darling.'

Ruth found one of the nurses and asked where the little girl was. There was no need for an answer: the expression on the woman's face was enough. Will began sobbing, his thin shoulders heaving. 'No, oh no,' he said. 'No. Please no.'

'Will . . .' Ruth put her hand on her son's shoulder. There was nothing she could say. 'When?' she said softly to the nurse.

'Two days ago.'

'Michelle,' Will said. 'Oh no.'

Ruth covered her face with her hands. Poor Lynda. Poor, poor Will. He was going to take it hard. *After the first death, there is no other* – she had read that at college. Tears seeped through her fingers at the thought of the brave little girl who had died. No fourteen-year-old should have to know what death meant.

'It was very quiet,' said the nurse. 'We all knew it was coming.'

'That doesn't make it any better when it happens.'

'I know. But it helps some, if you're prepared.'

Ruth raised her head and stared at the woman. 'Can anyone really be prepared for the death of an eight-year-old?'

The nurse looked away uneasily. 'Her mom and dad were there, and grandparents. And her big sister. She just kind of smiled at them all and closed her eyes, and didn't open them again.'

'It's not fair,' Will said, his voice breaking. 'She was only a little kid.'

'Why should these innocents have to suffer?' Ruth demanded.

'God has his reasons.' The nurse fingered the crucifix pinned to the neck of her uniform.

'I would *really* like to know what they are.' Ruth could think of nothing to say that would comfort Will. As they walked on down the passage toward the room waiting for him, she said: 'Michelle loved being with you, Will. You helped her such a lot.'

'She helped *me.*' Will dug into the bag resting on his knees and fetched out the pink gingham mob-cap Kelly had made for him. He sat in the chair, clutching it, trembling.

When he had been settled in his room and Dr Gearin had arrived to examine him, Ruth walked away to the bank of phones and called Lynda's house. 'It's Ruth Connelly,' she said to the answering machine. 'Will's mom. I'm so very very sorry. Please, Lynda, get in touch.' She left her phone number.

Since Will had first been diagnosed, she had tried hard not to consider his death, though the specter was ever present. Now, thinking of Michelle, eight years old, her life over before it had really started, she found herself again rejecting the bleak possibility of losing him as well as Josie.

It was not going to happen.

Lynda called back. Michelle's funeral – only it was not really a funeral – was to take place the following afternoon and she hoped Ruth would attend. They had known she was dying, she said. They had had time to come to terms with it. Which did not help, or make it any the more bearable. 'Does William know?' she asked.

'First thing he asked when he came in this morning,' Ruth said. 'He's so upset.'

'I hope it won't make things worse for him.'

'He's due for treatment this afternoon. Means he won't be able to come to the funeral.'

'Perhaps that's a good thing,' Lynda said.

'Maybe. I don't want to depress him just when the chemo seems to be working. His blood counts are up again. The doctors are very hopeful.'

'I'm so glad.'

Next day, Ruth spent some time deciding what to wear to say goodbye to Michelle. Somber colors seemed wrong to mark the death of a child: in the end, she chose a daffodil-yellow suit in a fine wool, with a green silk scarf tucked into the neckline, the colors of spring, the colors of hope. She drove to the address Lynda had given her and was surprised to find that it was neither a funeral parlor, nor a church, but instead seemed to be a hall attached to the back of a restaurant called The Old Warsaw. The place was packed with people and noise and laughter. Some were wearing clothes she recognized as native costume – full black skirts, white blouses with green and red decorations, headbands embroidered with flower motifs. Many of the men were in black suits and white shirts buttoned at the neck without a tie. For the first time, she absorbed the fact that Lynda's ethnic roots were Polish. There was a long table covered in platters of food, and another stacked with bottles of wine and vodka. Someone handed her a glass and she pushed her way through the crowd toward Lynda, who stood at the end of the room, flanked by her husband, and the three children Ruth recognized from the photographs she had been shown. A large portrait of Michelle stood on a table, draped in long curling strands of pink and white gift ribbon and surrounded by soft toys and dolls. Rainbow-colored balloons hung from the walls and ceiling and vases of tight pink rosebuds stood all around the room.

'We're having a party to celebrate her,' Lynda said, hugging Ruth. She wore a dress the color of strawberry ice-cream. 'Not a funeral to mourn her.' She dabbed at her eyes. 'I'm not crying for her, I'm really not.'

'She would have loved it,' said Ruth, looking around. 'Such beautiful roses.'

'Pink was her favorite color.'

Lynda introduced her husband, a big man in a bright blue suit, who seized Ruth's hand and pressed it against his chest. 'Thank you for coming,' he said. His eyes were red with weeping, but he smiled. 'Lynda has told me about your boy.'

'I'm so sorry,' whispered Ruth. 'Michelle was such a lovely child.'

'An angel,' her father said simply. 'A little angel.'

'Yes, she was.'

Ruth walked round the room. Michelle's pediatrician was there, holding a plateful of food; recognizing Ruth, he waved. She identified several other parents from the hospital: one of the fathers said to Ruth: 'You belong to a special club now.'

She knew his six-year-old son was ill with an inoperable tumor and that the prognosis was very poor. 'It's not one I'd have asked to join.'

His eyes were haunted. 'Nor any of us. But we have to make the best of it.'

'Yes.' Ruth touched his shirt sleeve, felt the living warmth underneath. 'We do.'

A man in baggy black trousers and a grey felt jacket fastened with silver buckles stepped forward. An accordion hung on an embroidered strap round his neck. He squeezed off a few chords and the crowd fell silent. Lynda took her husband's hand and addressed them all. 'You know why we're here,' she said. 'To say goodbye to Michelle.'

Behind Ruth someone sobbed quietly. There were several shapeless older women in white headscarves, who sat on chairs at the edge of the room, weeping. Grandmothers. Great-aunts. The vital underpinnings of an extended immigrant family.

'We said our own private farewells to her at the church this morning,' Lynda continued. 'But Michelle always planned to have a party when she was better – and this is the party she would have had. If you want to cry, go right ahead, but remember that she was just a little girl, the bravest in the world, and she didn't cry much in her short life, so we shouldn't either. She was a real special little girl and we're so glad that we had her for eight years.' Tears tumbled down Lynda's cheeks but she kept on smiling. 'Some people might think that it's been a waste, losing her so young, but it hasn't been. We've had the privilege of knowing her. And because of her, my husband, Mike, has done such a lot to make sure other little kids don't have to suffer like she did. I'm so proud of him, and Michelle would be too.'

Everybody clapped and, beside her, the plump husband pressed his lips together, his chest heaving with sobs. Both his sons were weeping too but, like their parents, trying to smile.

Lynda continued: 'Kelly – Michelle's big sister – is going to read you something now, and then we'll all sing one of Michelle's favorite songs.'

We did not do this for Josie, our daughter, our sister, Ruth thought. Instead, we bottled it up, kept it inside. How unlike this the service up in Maine had been, how sterile, with the autumn leaves falling and the Arctic wind scything through our bones.

Kelly stood very straight. She was wearing a pink top over a black microskirt and had tied her blond hair back with a pink ribbon.

'This was Michelle's favorite poem,' she announced. She stared around the room with sad eyes. 'I read it to her lots when she was sick. She used to make me mad sometimes, taking my makeup and messing with my clothes, but I loved her so much and I'm – I'm going to miss her all the rest of my life.' She opened the book she held.

Listening as Kelly read a poem for her dead sister,

grief and guilt overwhelmed Ruth. Josie had been allowed to go from their lives without any of this celebration. And it was *her* fault. She was the one who had refused to allow her family to mourn.

When Kelly had finished, the man with the accordion began to play a song Ruth's own mother used to sing to her. '*Hush, little baby, don't say a word, Momma's gonna buy you a mocking bird.*' Softly people around the room began to join in, everyone in tears, holding on to each other, sobbing. *And if that mocking bird won't sing, Momma's gonna buy you a diamond ring . . .* And yet, Ruth thought, overcome herself, despite the occasion, the atmosphere is so happy, so . . . festive.

The music switched. A man stepped forward and, with one hand outstretched to the listeners, began to sing in some foreign language, a song so full of quavers and minor tones, a song so sad that a moan rose from the older people on the sidelines. 'He sings about exile from the homeland,' an elderly man next to Ruth said. 'A very sad song.' He lifted a glass of wine to his lips and shook his head. 'We are always happy to hear this song.'

When the singer finished, people clapped. Three men sprang forward, laid their arms along each other's shoulders, and, with the accordion accompanying them, broke into what appeared to be a merry drinking chorus, clicking their heels against the floor, miming drunkenness. A young woman stepped forward and recited something, and was clapped in her turn. Four older women in shawls and flowered skirts held hands and paced back and forth in a stately dance, plump hips shaking from side to side as they dipped and swayed.

The accordion was passed to the elder of Lynda's sons and he began to play something, his face solemn, lower lip held by his teeth as he concentrated on getting it right. 'Michelle loved to sing this song,' Lynda announced. 'Her great-grandfather taught it to her when she was just a baby.' Everyone looked to the side of the room, where an ancient man nodded and smiled. The elders sang softly in their native tongue, while the boy accompanied them. When he had finished, Michelle's father shouted: 'To little Michelle.' Everyone lifted their glasses.

The mood changed again. People were talking now, eating, drinking. Dancing began. The temperature rose, the food disappeared, the bottles emptied. Ruth was pulled into the throng, dancing with pale-haired, lantern-jawed youths, with toothless old men, with the pediatrician, with Lynda herself. 'You're wonderful,' Ruth managed to gasp. 'Michelle would have loved this.'

'Wouldn't she, though?' Clasping each other, the two women whirled round the room.

'Please let's keep in touch.'

Red-faced, Lynda shook her head. 'If William gets better, I don't reckon you'll want to be reminded of these sad times.'

Where did a woman like this, barely educated by Ruth's own standards, gain so much wisdom? How did she learn to look with such clarity into the human heart? Driving back to the apartment, Ruth was ashamed of her own inadequacies.

Though classes were over, there was still a lot of college paperwork to deal with. That evening, Paul planned to review his departmental evaluations and produce his textbook orders for the fall semester. He was hoping to be done in time to watch the game on TV. He made himself a gin and tonic and had just taken the first sip when the telephone bleeped. He picked up. 'Yes?'

'Paul?' The voice was so faint he hardly recognized it.

'Ruth? Is that you? What's wrong?'

'It's Will,' she managed.

'What? What about Will?' She stayed silent. 'Tell me, Ruth.' He could feel the disorienting fog of panic creeping along his veins. 'What's happened?'

'I don't know. I came home to find a message from Dr Gearin. He wants me to call him as soon as I can and – and the thing is . . . Paul . . . I – I don't think I can face any more bad news on my own.'

'I'm on my way,' Paul said.

Was Ruth worrying unnecessarily? Will had seemed so well recently, despite his continuing reactions to the cocktail of drugs he was taking. Paul switched on the car radio and pressed buttons, looking for music, segued from Michael Jackson to Alison Kraus to Mahler; they all sounded exactly the same, disconnected notes beating into the foggy mush of his brain. Will had to be all right. He was going to be all right. Definitely. No question.

He parked and ran into their apartment building, nodded at the doorman, saw the elevator was on the fourth floor and did not bother waiting for it to descend, took the stairs two at a time. He plunged his key into the lock and opened the front door.

Ruth was waiting for him in the lobby. How pale she was. He put his arms tightly about her and they stood locked together in silence. After a while, he stepped away from her and took her hand. 'Come on,' he said. 'There's two of us now.'

He dialed the number Gearin had left, while Ruth watched him, her eyes wide with apprehension. Behind

272

the doctor's voice he could hear the noises of the hospital: people talking, the squelch of rubber soles on polished floors, a baby crying. Nearer at hand, two desk nurses were arguing over some missing case notes. 'It's Professor Connelly,' Paul said. 'You asked us to call you.'

'Yes. Absolutely.' Gearin's voice shifted a notch or two, from exhaustion to elation. 'Yes, I wanted you to know the good news as soon as possible.'

Paul hardly dared hope. He kept his voice unemotional. 'Does that mean what I think it means?'

'The leukemia's in remission. The last tests we did showed no traces of the disease. The cancer cells have gone. He's cleared. For the present, Will is cancer-free.'

'Oh God.'

'We hope the disease won't recur but of course we'll be keeping a close eye on him over the months to come. He'll have to continue taking medication, come in for regular checks, blood tests, that sort of thing. We can never be completely sure that the cancer will stay in remission. We just have to keep praying that it will. And there are many cases where it has. Many, many cases.'

In other words, it's gone away, Paul thought, but maybe only for the moment. We shall never be able to sleep easily again. He did not say this aloud. Ruth had carried a heavy burden over the past months and he was not about to add to it by being less than enthusiastic. 'I can't tell you how grateful we are for everything you've done,' he said.

'It's almost as wonderful for us when this happens as it is for the parents,' Gearin said.

'Thank you, Mike. Thank you so very very much.' Paul slammed down the phone and turned to Ruth. He gave her a two-hundred-watt smile and held her tightly against him.

'It's okay,' he said. 'It's okay!'

Ruth held a hand to her mouth, scarcely able to believe him.

'They found no trace of the cancer in his last tests – the chemotherapy's worked. He's beaten it, Ruth! The cancer's gone.'

'He's going to be okay.' She collapsed onto the sofa and began to cry. 'I can't believe it,' she said numbly. 'I just can't.'

'Nor me.' He leaned over her, seized her face between his two hands and kissed her wet cheeks, her closed eyes, her mouth. 'Is there any champagne in the fridge?'

'Sure is. I'll get some glasses.'

They sat on the sofa together. She leaned against him, her head on his shoulder. 'I tried to believe that he would be cured, but I was still terrified he wouldn't. All these months – looking at him, wondering how much more suffering he had to go through, seeing other kids on the ward who didn't make it and feeling absolutely desperate about Will. And now . . . he's cured.'

'Cured . . .' Paul pressed her against his side, refusing to remember Gearin's qualified approval of the term. 'It's a strong word.'

'It's a good word,' Ruth said. 'The *best* word.'

Paul leaned toward her, took the glass from her hand and set it down on the table. 'The very best,' he said softly.

'Oh, Paul . . .' Joy leaked from Ruth's eyes, from her mouth. Joy made her hair seem almost incandescent, and lent a golden glow to her skin. She put her hand on his chest, above the heart, slid a finger between the buttons of his shirt, stroked his skin. She looked up at him with her luminous gaze and he remembered the first time, how she had looked at him with absolute trust.

She shook her head and drew away from him. She kissed the corner of his mouth. 'Will is waiting. Let's go and tell him.'

Driving to the hospital with her beside him, he was consumed with the sense of something infinitely precious which had been wantonly discarded. Gently, he put his hand over hers.

15

As Will picked up his life again, gradually going back full time to school for the last days of the semester, Ruth was able to return to the office. Surveying the crowded city streets, waiting at the WALK/DON'T WALK crossovers, smelling the fume-laden, salt-tinged air, noticing as though for the first time the clothes in the store windows, the flowers in the public gardens, she realized how narrow her existence had grown over the past months.

As long as Will stayed well, they could look forward to the future. Yet she knew that she would watch him, listen out for him, worry about him every second of every day. One cough and she would flinch. One bruise and she would know the cancer had come back. One sleepless night, and she would, in imagination, see his death.

When she asked him what he wanted for his fifteenth birthday, he did not hesitate. 'A drum kit.'

'We already talked about this darn drum kit. Isn't there anything else you'd like?'

'Not really.'

'Where would you practice?'

'In my room.'

'That's going to be really disturbing,' Ruth said. 'I mean, I often have to work in the evenings.'

'You could wear earplugs.'

'Get real, Will. I do not intend to sit in my own home wearing earplugs. And what about the neighbors? I already spoke to the building super and he's not too thrilled.'

'Is that a definite no?'

'It's a definite I very much doubt it.'

'Gee, Mom. Me and the guys were really hoping you'd . . .' His face fell.

She hated to disappoint him. 'Let's be practical about this. Is there somewhere else you could keep the damn thing? Someone's garage or something?'

'Stu's the only one with a garage. And his dad said no way, he didn't pay like, zillions of dollars for a Merc in order to leave it out in the driveway.'

'Very sensible.' She smiled at him. 'We'll see. It's not until the tail end of the summer. If it works out, could you go with Ed and get what you need?'

'Oh, Mom . . .'

'I didn't say yes, yet.'

'But almost.' Will's eyes sparkled. 'We could all go. The band, I mean. We'd probably have to take a cab home, though. There'd be a lot of stuff to bring back.'

'That's fine. Take one going, too. It doesn't matter what it costs, I really don't care what anything costs, just as long as . . . as you . . .'

He hugged her tightly. 'You're a star.'

'I'm going to worry about the noise, Will.'

'If we lived up in Sweetharbor, I could—'

'But we don't. Now, another question, where would you like to go for your birthday?'

'I'd like to go up to Carter's House,' he said, brightening. 'We haven't been there for ages.'

'Oh, Will . . .'

'What?'

'I . . . I can't.'

'Why not?'

'Because ever since . . . since . . .'

'Since Josie died.'

'Yes, ever since then I've been afraid that if I go up there, I'll see . . . *her* everywhere.'

Suddenly Will exploded. 'Josie, Mom. Her name's Josie. *Josephine*. Why can't you ever *say* it? Just because she's dead doesn't mean she never existed. She's got a perfect right to be remembered and talked about and be a part of our family. You've just shut her out of our lives and it's not fair to her or us. That's why Dad left, because he couldn't stand the way you keep pretending that she never was, when I'll just bet that we all, all three of us, think about her every day and miss her and want her back and . . . and . . .' He was crying now, harsh boyish sobs which erupted from his thin chest with the force of cannon-fire. 'She was my *sister*. Your daughter. Why can't we accept it and talk about it, instead of this weird shit you've got us all doing, acting like we're fucking normal and nothing ever happened? Because it *did* happen, Mom.'

'Yes. I—'

'Josie drowned, and she's gone and we *aren't* normal.' He wept harder, dragging his arm across his face to mop up the tears. 'We *can't* be normal ever again. Why do you always try to act like we *are*?'

'I guess . . .' She paused, trying to put it in terms he could understand. 'I guess I saw it as a sign of strength that we'd carried on as before.'

278

'But *why*? What's strong about it?'

'That we refused to give in to our grief. It would have been so easy to drown in it – God, the days I've wanted to cave in . . .'

'Maybe it'd have been better if you had.' Will sobbed harder. 'I know it would have been for me. I want to talk about her, about Josie, but you've made it impossible. I wanted to talk about Dad leaving, too, but . . .' He rested his forehead against the wall and shook his head. 'I even went and had a Coke with that dorky boyfriend of Josie's, when he asked me, just so I could talk about her.'

'Rob Fowler?'

'Rob, Bob, whatever the fuck his stupid name is.' Will glared at his mother accusingly. 'At least he *listened*, didn't cut me off every time I mentioned my own sister.'

'You make it sound like a bad thing that we've managed to continue when surely it's quite the opposite.' When he left the room, she said aloud: 'Isn't it?'

A couple of weeks after the summer vacation had begun, she came home from work to find Ed Stein in the kitchen. 'Hi, Mrs Connelly,' he said.

'Hello, Ed. How're your mom and dad?'

'Just fine.' He glanced across at Will. 'By the way, we're leaving tomorrow for Maine and they wanted to know whether Will could come up, spend some time with us.'

'I wonder what on earth could have put that notion into their heads.' Ruth glanced sharply at Will.

'I did, Mrs Connelly.' Ed's gaze was one of limpid innocence. 'It'd be really great for me if Will could join us this summer.'

'I don't think so,' Ruth said brusquely.

'Why *not*?' demanded Will.

'We've been through this already, Will. And I said no.'

'Any particular reason, Mrs Connelly?' Ed was polite, but determined. Primed by Will, Ruth thought. 'I mean, we'd love to have him with us. I mean, my parents are really excited about him coming along. And let's face it, he's summered up there all his life. Why change things now?'

'Ed, last year we went through . . . I think the place will be full of memories for Will. I don't think he realizes how painful it could be for him.'

'Jeez, let me handle my own life, will you?' Will said.

'I think he can cope with it, Mrs Connelly. I really do. I know he's younger than me, but that doesn't mean he can't deal with . . . with bad stuff.'

Bad stuff? Was that what the whole circumstance of Josie's death was reduced to: bad stuff? 'Also,' she said, 'don't forget Will's still recovering from a serious illness. He's got to take things easy.'

'Where would be easier than up at Sweetharbor, Mrs Connelly? No homework, no classes, no freaks on the streets. No pollution.'

'Is this a prepared speech or just off the top of your head?' Ruth laughed. 'Though you do have a point.'

'Hey, what's with you two?' said Will crossly. 'I'm not a baby. I can make my own decisions.'

'I'll think about it,' Ruth said.

'Well, I'm *going*.' Will shouldered out of the kitchen, followed by Ed, who turned at the door and smiled. 'Don't worry about it, Mrs Connelly. The only thing Will needs to worry about in Maine is my sister Mamie. She's a real pain.'

280

'Is that right?'

'Honest, I think he'd be okay.'

That evening, Carmel Stein rang.

'Let me guess why you're calling,' Ruth said. 'You want Will to join you in Maine for a few weeks.'

'How did you—'

'Ed already asked', Ruth said, 'and I told him I didn't think so. The truth is, I don't like the thought of Will being so far away from the hospital.'

'From you, you mean.'

'No, I—'

'Ruth Connelly, you're going to turn Will into a momma's boy if you're not careful. A real Caspar Milquetoast. You never let the poor kid out of your sight.'

'That's bullshit, Carmel.'

'Is it really?'

'His whole system is vulnerable,' Ruth said. 'I'm still worried sick about him.' In the silence which followed, she added: 'Okay, maybe I'm a tad over-protective. But you can understand why.'

'I can understand. I'm not sure I can go along with it. You've got him virtually imprisoned in that apartment. The only time you let him out is to go to school, or when you can go with him.'

'But he's been so ill.'

'All the more reason to give him some freedom now that he's in remission. Call Will's physicians, Ruth, see what they say. You can't wrap him up in tissue-paper and lock him away in a drawer forever. You've got to let him go. He's a big boy, and an intelligent one. He knows that he has to take care. And just think how much better it'll be for him to be breathing that clean sea air downeast than the Boston traffic fumes.'

'I'm also worried about how he'll feel about his sister when he gets there.'

'He won't know until he finds out, will he? And Ed's a good kid,' said Carmel. 'He'll keep an eye on him. And it goes without saying that Franklin and I will.'

'I don't know . . .'

'Trust me, Ruthie. Let him go.'

'Can you cope with his dietary needs?'

'With Mamie in the house, I've learned to handle just about anything.'

'Will'd enjoy it,' Ruth said thoughtfully. 'And he does love it up there.'

'So you'll let him come?'

Ruth saw that Will was moving away from her. She had to recognize that the choice was not hers, but his. She took a deep breath. 'Yes,' she said.

'Good. That's great. Mamie's bringing a friend up and poor Ed would find himself completely at their mercy if he was left without reinforcements.' Carmel laughed. 'Mercy? What am I saying? I don't think teenage girls know the meaning of the word, do they?' Realizing too late what she had said, aware of Ruth's refusal to talk about her daughter, Carmel hurried on: 'What about you, Ruth? Why don't you come up and visit too?'

'I . . . I can't, that's why.'

'Why not?'

'You know why not. Because of what . . . happened.'

Carmel hesitated. 'Honey, maybe I never put it into words, but you don't know how we've felt for you over the past twelve months.'

'At least Will has come through. I hardly dared hope that he would, but the doctors say he's completely okay now. If I let him come up to Maine, you'd call me

282

instantly if there was the slightest thing wrong, wouldn't you?'

'Trust me.'

'And make sure he slathers on the sunscreen, Carmel. It's vital, even when the weather seems cloudy. The drugs from his therapy make him really susceptible to burning. Make him wear a cap whenever he's outside, even in the shade.'

'I'll do everything I can. He'll probably take it better from me than from you.' There was a sudden exclamation. 'Hey, Ruth! Will's birthday.'

'What about it?'

'Why don't you celebrate it up here? There's no need to go to your cottage if you don't want to. You can stay with us. It would do you good after these past months.'

'I'll think about it, Carmel. I'm not just saying that, I really will.'

'Let's fix it right now.'

'I'm not sure I—'

'Get your calendar, Ruth Connelly. If not before, I definitely want to see you up in Maine for Will's birthday.'

'I'm still not clear on this letter from the FTC, Ruth.' Jake Phillipson set both his hands on the table and leaned forward. With his head of thick white hair and small black eyes, he looked more like a polar bear than the head of a powerful electronics corporation.

'What don't you understand?' Behind his head, the city burned in the summer heat. The parched urban landscape was coated with a metallic sheen as sunlight bounced off brown reflective glass in the surrounding buildings. Ruth thought of Will. At least he was out of this, safe in Sweetharbor.

'What legal force does it have? What if the Washington people change their minds?'

'Jake, we already explained that it's the Federal Trade Commission's way of saying that they'll waive the formal process of scheduling an exemption hearing.'

Jim Pinkus set the edges of his palms squarely on the table. 'It means you're home free – you can go ahead with your acquisition.'

Ruth nodded. The dust and heat of the city was unbearable. Even in the air-conditioned boardroom, she was sweating lightly. Sharply she remembered the clear air of Maine, the pine woods and the fresh sea-scent. And the memories.

'I'm not sure I'm comfortable with that,' Phillipson said. 'Is it binding? After all, it's only a letter.'

'Stop worrying. Even though it seems a mite informal, the FTC considers applications very seriously and hardly ever reneges. Isn't that right, Jim?'

Pinkus nodded vigorously. 'Absolutely. As a matter of fact, a few years ago the FTC did pursue a hearing after issuing one of these comfort letters and really got screwed. The company took them to court.'

'Right,' said Ruth. 'And the Federal Court of Appeals ruled that such letters have the force of law.'

'Believe me, the FTC hasn't tried *that* one again,' Pinkus said.

Jake Phillipson turned his head toward him and narrowed his small eyes until they were hardly visible. 'Don't take me wrong on this, kid, but you seem awful young to me.' He looked at Ruth. 'He knows what he's talking about, does he?'

'Don't let those boyish good looks deceive you,' Ruth said reassuringly. 'Jim's already argued four cases before the Massachusetts Supreme Court, and won them all.'

'Hey.' Pinkus spread his hands and looked modest. 'What can I tell you?'

'Okay, I'm convinced. But I want a letter from LKM – from you personally, Ruth – stating that in your professional opinion, we are legally justified in going ahead. I need to satisfy my Board before we can make any kind of a move.'

'I'll have it Fedexed to you this afternoon,' said Ruth. They were twelve floors up, with the windows shut, but she could still hear the clamor of a police car, and the insistent honks as frustrated drivers leaned on their horns. Sweat beaded her forehead. She pushed her fingers through her hair and smiled at Phillipson. 'It's all going very smoothly, Jake. Don't worry.'

'I try not to.' Phillipson pushed back his chair and stood up. The other members of his team began packing up their briefcases and shutting down their laptops. His pale ice floe face showed concern as he came close enough for her to smell the breath mints he favored. He touched her shoulder. 'How's that boy of yours doing, Ruth?'

A smile lit up her face. 'He's in remission, Jake. He's so well, in fact, that I've let him go up to Maine for the summer.' She glanced at her watch. 'I'll be heading there myself in a few weeks. It'll soon be his fifteenth birthday.'

He shook his broad head. 'How about that? I'm really pleased for you, Ruth. And so will Verna be when I tell her. We had a nephew . . . well, I told you.'

'Yes.' Ruth put a hand on his jacket sleeve. 'You did. And I'm so sorry. I'm well aware that I'm one of the lucky ones.'

Will had telephoned his father from the Steins' house,

suggesting he come up and visit. 'We could get in some sailing,' he said.

'Sounds good,' Paul said. 'Sounds *wonderful*.'

'We always made a good team, didn't we, Dad?'

'Sure did, son. Pity we won't have the *Lucky Duck*.'

'Mr Stein'll let us use one of his boats. Ed can come along too, can't he?'

'Listen—' Paul wanted to say Will could bring the entire State Assembly along if he wished. To hear his son's voice bubbling and eager again was like being given back his own life. 'Yes, Ed can come. Hey, William . . .'

'What?'

'Did you check this with the Steins? Maybe they don't want to see me, what with the way your mother and I—'

'Course I did. You don't think it was *my* idea to have you come busting in on my vacation, do you?'

'So young, and yet so cruel,' Paul said.

He took the I-95 up as far as Brunswick, then turned off onto the back roads. He was not a native Mainer, like Ruth, but he was more than happy to be an adopted son, to enjoy it with the particular relish of one with proprietary rights. The smell of balsam sap filled the car, and lilac; for once, the sky was clear and blue. With each glimpse of shingled siding, each breath of pine and kelp, each sighting of the flat-calm sea, his exhilaration grew. Eventually, he stopped the car under some pines beside the road and got out, too euphoric to sit still. Summer in Maine. And Will well again.

He remembered how he and Josie used to be out on the water together all through the summer. He'd taught her the rudiments of sailing when she was only five or six, first in the Beetle Cat and later in the *Lucky Duck*.

He remembered light dancing on the brasswork, Carter's House set on its bluff, birds wheeling overhead, the salty air, water slapping against the side of the boat. Josie never seemed to have the slightest sense of danger. The harder it blew, the more she enjoyed it, wind stirring the sea into a chop, lee rail a foot under white water, the two of them hanging horizontal to keep a balance. And then Will started to come along with them, and that was good too, a father and his children, handling a boat, being a family. Except that after a while, Josie seemed to take against sailing, seemed so much less eager to come out with him. That last summer – Paul walked further in among the trees. That last summer, she didn't sail with him and Will once. He hadn't thought about it before but now it bothered him. She'd sail with Will, but not with him. Did she feel that he had preferred Will to her? Was she jealous of the closeness between her father and her brother? Had she felt excluded?

His mood dampened a little, he drove on to the Steins' house. Franklin and Carmel were sitting out under sun-umbrellas. There was lemonade on the low table between them, and magazines, a book, a copy of the *Wall Street Journal*, lying on the grass at their feet.

'You two look really busy,' he said.

'We are.' Carmel waved a languid hand at him. 'Busy doing nothing.'

Franklin made a half-hearted attempt to get out of his chair and abandoned it. 'Paul. Good to see you.'

'And you.' He bent down to kiss Carmel.

'You're looking pale,' she said.

'That's what living in the city does for you. How long do you think it'll take to burn off the fish-belly look?'

'Don't overdo it, will you?'

287

Paul cocked his head. 'I don't hear the merry sound of boys at play.'

'They're down at the yacht club. Sailing, I think, but maybe playing tennis with the girls.'

'I'll see if I can find them before I settle into sluggard mode,' said Paul.

'Lunch at one,' Carmel called after him.

The yacht club looked much as it had done since his first visits there as Ruth Carter's fiancé. There were rockers on the porch, half of them occupied by ancient ladies knitting, chatting, dozing. They were the mothers and grandmothers and great-aunts of people who'd been coming here since they were children, who had themselves spent their summers here, sixty, seventy years ago.

A few boats still lay tied up to the dock built out into the little deep-water harbor; the rest were out on the water. From the courts next door came the thud of tennis balls on racquets and the calls of the players. Laughter floated on the air.

Inside the club, the shaded rooms were empty. He walked across the sanded pine floor and stood looking out at the water, remembering the countless times he'd come here over the years. So much had changed.

'Professor Connelly?'

He turned. Two teenaged girls in Sweetharbor Yacht Club T-shirts were standing side by side under the slowly whirring electric fan. 'Hi,' the older of the two said. 'I'm Amy Prescott. This is my sister Lizzie.'

'Prescott? You must be Sue Prescott's girls.'

'Yes, sir. That's right.' Amy smiled politely. 'I guess you're looking for Will. But he and Ed are off racing this morning.'

'Won't be back until much later,' Lizzie said, showing a mouth full of ironwork.

'That's a shame.'

'He's looking real good, Professor Connelly,' Amy Prescott said earnestly.

Beside her, Lizzie nodded. 'Couple of years ago, our cousin CJ got sick with the same thing.'

'And now he's doing just fine,' said Amy.

'Like Will is,' Lizzie said. She glanced sideways at her sister. 'He's a real hunk, isn't he, Amy?'

Color burned its way up Amy's face. 'He's okay,' she said, glaring at her sister.

'Okay?' said Lizzie. 'Is that all?'

'Listen, you little—'

'Thank you, girls.' Paul smiled at them and went out again, trying not to laugh. He liked that. The girls beginning to sit up and take notice of Will. That was good. As a matter of fact, it was more than good. It was fantastic. At the bar, he bought a beer and sipped it, wondered if Will was taking notice back.

A month after Will had left for Maine, Carmel Stein rang Ruth at her office. 'Now, you're not to panic, Ruth.'

'Cue for instant hysteria,' Ruth said lightly, striving to remain calm.

'It's Will. He's been running a fever.'

'No.'

'Not a very high one, Ruth.'

'No,' moaned Ruth. 'Please . . .' Blackness filled her. 'I couldn't *bear* it if—'

'We took him straight down to the hospital in Hartsfield, but they didn't seem too worried. Paul said—'

'Paul?'

'He was here. He said—'

289

'Paul was staying with you?'

'He's come up a couple of times to visit Will, yes.'

Ruth was silent.

'Don't be like that,' Carmel said. 'We love you both. You're both our friends. We don't want to lose either of you.'

'I understand,' Ruth said. 'Of course I do.' She hesitated, wanting to say more. Carmel was right, but that did not prevent her from feeling somehow let down.

'Will's back with us now,' Carmel said. 'Everything's fine and Paul said I shouldn't worry you about it but I thought you should know.'

'Thank you,' Ruth said. Guilt consumed her. Paul had already been up to visit Will twice while she had not yet been up once. 'Shall I come up and get him?'

'There's no reason why you should. Like I said, they seemed to think he was fine.'

'I'll get his doctor at the hospital to give them a call,' Ruth said, fighting terror, fighting despair. She had read so much about Will's illness over the past months. She had thought it was seared into her brain, that she would remember the fearful details and possibilities until the day she died. Now, not a word of it remained in her head. Running a fever: was that significant? The truth was, anything had been significant when he was sick and prone to infections. But he was not sick, he was better. In remission.

'He's eating well,' Carmel said, 'running around with Ed all the time, just a normal kid, enjoying the summer vacation. He's absolutely fine, Ruth. I wouldn't even have bothered to call you if it wasn't for his medical history. And because I promised you I would.'

Despite her friend's reassurances, Ruth felt nauseous. 'Thanks, Carmel. I'll get back to you.'

Not again. Please, not again.

She called the HMO clinic, which promised to contact the Hartsfield hospital. She telephoned the hospital in Boston and was told the same thing. There was no answer from Paul's apartment. She went to a meeting with one client, had lunch with another, attended a conference of partners when she got back. Though she took notes, made points, none of what was discussed really penetrated her brain. Will was the only thing she could concentrate on. This anxiety was something she would be living with for years, until so much time had elapsed that it would be almost safe to assume that Will had escaped the threat of terminal illness. She rang the clinic again, spoke to the nurse-practitioner and was informed that Greg Turner, the pediatrician who had originally sent William to the hospital, was unavailable. She called the Boston hospital again, but they could not find Dr Gearin, and Dr Caldbeck was on vacation.

She drove back to the apartment, more anxious now than when Carmel had first telephoned. There was no one she could talk to. No one to calm her down. There was still no answer from Paul's apartment. She did not want to ring her parents, for fear of worrying them needlessly. Most of her close women friends, the ones who could be relied on for comfort or simply a sympathetic ear, were out of town with their families. In the end, she lifted the phone and punched in Lynda's number.

As soon as she heard Ruth's voice, Lynda was apprehensive. 'What's happened?' she said.

Ruth explained.

'It's probably nothing,' said Lynda, sighing with relief.

'Are you sure?'

'Hey, I'm not a doctor,' Lynda said. 'But a fever? Could be nothing more than too much sun.'

'You're probably right.'

'I'd like to tell you not to worry, but whatever I say, you will. For years you'll worry. That's what being a parent is about. Even when they're not sick, you worry. What're they doing? Who's she with? Why are they late? You know how it is.'

'It's the price you pay,' Ruth said. 'I never thought about it like that before. The price for creating a life. It means you never stop worrying, never stop praying that they won't get hurt. It's like a scream, waiting at the back of your throat.' She remembered that last summer up in Maine. If only it were possible to return to the innocent days before the accident. If only . . . 'You're right.'

'I'm always right,' said Lynda. 'At least, that's what Kelly tells me.'

'How is she? I really appreciated the way she used to drop in on Will when she was visiting Michelle.'

'Fine. Missing her little sister, of course. We all are. I think your boy sent her a postcard from up there in Maine, by the way. Told her to come up and visit him anytime she wanted.'

'He was always sweet on her.'

The two women talked quietly of Michelle. Of Will. Of how Lynda's boys were coping with the loss of their sister. 'They had time to understand what was going to happen,' Lynda said. 'And time to appreciate her. I always think that the worst thing of all must be to lose someone without ever having told them how much you loved them.'

Like I did with Josie, Ruth thought.

'On the other hand,' continued Lynda, as though she

292

understood exactly what Ruth was thinking, 'we wouldn't be human if we lived every moment as though it was the last, would we?'

'I suppose not.'

'You just have to do your best.'

'Yes.' Ruth would never be able to rid herself of the feeling that with regard to Josie, whatever she had done, it had not been her best.

'Don't worry, Ruth.'

'How can I not?'

The waves grabbed at her. She tried to get out of their reach, but found she could not move. The water glittered cruelly, sharp as razor blades, receding as though to reassure her then lunging back again when she least expected it. Terrified, she watched it lap at her knees, her waist, her breasts, her throat, cold as the polar oceans, icier than the frozen Arctic waters. It's the sea, the sea, someone said above her head as one roaring green wave detached itself from the rest and slammed against her, covering, devouring her. This was the end. All her life she had feared death by water and now it was here. After this long choking moment of terror, there would be nothing. Only oblivion.

She woke sweaty, buried under a tangle of sheets, with the taste of salt on her tongue. Gasping, she pushed herself up against the headboard, tried to force herself awake. The nightmare clung to her brain, the panic refusing to let go even when she flicked on the light, went into the kitchen for a glass of water, found a book.

It was futile to try and reinvent the past. Nothing would bring Josie back, nothing would return any of them to where they had once been, to that shining summer which had ended so abruptly. She had been heedless of life's lavish prodigality then. Sitting at the kitchen table, she shivered, although the trapped heat of the day still hung heavily in the air. Of all the abundance she had once possessed, Will was the only thing left.

She dressed quickly, flung some things into a bag, found her car keys. Out in the street, the darkened city was empty, though cars whooshed in the distance and she could hear the thump of electronic music. Somewhere a gull screamed. The night air was almost cool.

She was able to make good time up the Maine Turnpike. She drove with the windows open, relishing the damp air which flowed past her. Normally she would have avoided Route 1, but at this time of night hers was almost the only car on the road. Memories flooded her. Of journeys up here with her parents, back when everything was still fresh and full of hope. Of her grandparents, small, courteous, a galaxy away from her, filtered by the space which hung like a curtain between the generations. What did they know of her life? Or she of theirs? And yet the cottage, the summer vacations, the fading photographs on the walls of the staircase, linked her to them, so that she was always aware of time stretching back from the two of them to an unimaginable past and, at the same time, the string of the future leading onward into the unknown.

Carmel Stein was surprised to see her. 'You should have telephoned.'

'It was a sudden decision,' Ruth said. 'I woke in the night and started worrying.'

'Will's fine. I told you that.'

'It just seemed easier to drive up and reassure myself

that he was okay. And it's so beautiful up here. So peaceful.' Through the trees which surrounded the Stein house, the waters of the Sound glittered. 'Coming up here is like a massage, it soothes all the aches and pains right out of my system.'

'Then come up more often. Come up for the summer, the way you used to. It's too late this year, of course, but there are plenty more summers to come.'

'I'll go down later and talk to Mrs Dee,' Ruth said, prevaricating.

'She'll be glad. We met her at a dinner party the other night and she was saying how sad it was that your house is still shut up.'

'Where's Will?'

'Down at the Yacht Club. With Ed.'

'I'll drive down, see if I can find him.'

'With Ed, Ruth. And with Paul.'

'Paul?'

'Paul came up again.'

'I see.' Ruth stared down at her sandalled feet. 'Maybe I'll drive down to Sweetharbor and have a coffee there. And then . . . I thought I'd take Will back to the city with me.'

'What about his birthday?' Carmel frowned. 'I already invited people. Ordered a cake and everything.'

'I need to have him where I can keep an eye on him.'

'He's okay, Ruth.' Carmel put her arm round her friend's shoulders. 'You have to believe that he's fine. After what he's been through, you should let him have these precious summer days up here. This is where he's happiest.'

Parking the car behind the little convenience store in Sweetharbor, she sat for a moment, hands loosely grasping the wheel, eyes unseeing, as the past came flooding in on her. Only two days before the accident, she had hiked down from the house with Josie: they had sat on high stools at the counter of the donut shop, she with a coffee, Josie with the shop's specialty, a cinnamon-apple donut. She remembered the powdered sugar on Josie's upper lip, white against her tan, and how she had laughed, reached out a finger to wipe it off, saying Josie looked like an old man who had forgotten to shave. It was one of the few moments that summer when Josie had behaved like an untroubled teenager.

She walked down busy Main Street: Josie's presence was everywhere, woven inextricably into the fabric of the place. Much had changed since Ruth and Paul first brought her here, but the memories remained. She probed them gingerly, like an aching tooth: the little art gallery, the sidewalk where Josie had once tripped and twisted her ankle, the Cabot Inn where they used to eat on special occasions, the all-season Christmas shop where every year the children had been allowed to buy something new to dangle on the tree they would pick out in the woods when Christmas came around. It was easier than she had expected: time had stroked smooth the edges of her loss.

Down on the quayside, where the water lapped against wooden pilings and the lobster boats bobbed on the swell, she stopped to watch a merganser paddle by, trailing a string of babies. In the year since she had last been here, the little town had grown shabbier. Even though this was the height of the tourist season, many of the shopfronts were boarded up. She moved on to look in the window of the little craft shop cum art gallery. The window display featured driftwood draped with swatches of batiked silk in brilliant colors. Set against the fabric were carved wooden artefacts: bowls, dishes, salad servers, photograph frames.

'Mrs Connelly?' The voice was deep and warming.

She looked up to see a tall, bearded man who was vaguely familiar, though she could not immediately remember why.

'Sam Hechst,' he said. He held out a hand and she took it. Warm fingers, rough at the tips. A wide smile showing strong square teeth. Eyes dark enough to be almost black. 'You're Dieter's nephew,' she said. Incongruously, with summer all about her, she thought of Christmas, the rich and promising comforts of eggnog or mulled wine. Something she had heard about returning to Maine came back to her. *A gift from a true love* . . .

'That's right.' He wore jeans and a denim shirt with the sleeves rolled up. 'Are you all up here?'

There was no reason why he should know that Paul had left them and she was not well enough acquainted with him to explain. 'I'm just visiting my son – he's vacationing with friends up here.'

'You're not staying at Carter's House?'

'No.' Ruth swallowed, knowing that the words had to be spoken. 'Josie – my daughter – I'm sure you heard that she drowned last summer. Our cottage is too . . . I can't bear to be there, knowing that she'll never be there again herself.'

He glanced at her, indicated the Cabot Inn across the way. 'Would you – do you have time for coffee?'

'That would be nice,' she said.

In the dining room of the inn, they found a table by the window which gave on to Old Port Street. When the waitress came over, Sam asked for coffee while Ruth ordered breakfast, the full works: hash browns, and two eggs, bacon, a stack of pancakes, coffee. She was suddenly ravenous, having left Boston without eating.

'You said you were visiting your son.'

She looked down at her plate then back at the man sitting opposite her. 'He's – he's been very sick with leukemia.'

'I'm so sorry. I didn't know.'

'No reason why you should.'

'Except that up here everyone knows everyone else's business. Is he better?'

'For the moment. With any luck, for good.'

She braced herself for some knee-jerk expression of sympathy but instead, he said: 'But you're not opening up Carter's House?'

'No, I . . . I'm not here for long. And as I said, I haven't felt like staying there. Too many ghosts. Too many memories.'

'Of Josephine?'

'Of . . . happiness.'

'Mrs Connelly. Ruth. If memories are all you have, then you should glory in them, not ignore them.' His dark eyes moved over her, soft as molasses. 'You should go back to your house. I'm sure that the memories you have of your daughter are good ones.'

She nodded. 'Yes. Most of them.' She drew in a breath. 'There was something on her mind that last summer. She seemed to turn against me. One of the worst things about her death is that we never had the chance to put right whatever it was that bothered her.'

'Perhaps you should try to forget that, just think of all the good things. For instance, she was a remarkably talented painter. As I'm sure you were aware.'

'Yes.' He was the kind of man to whom, had she wished to, Ruth could have said straight out: No, I was not. I looked at her paintings and said meaningless things, but I did not really see them. She felt instinctively that he would not have been judgemental.

He smiled. 'I was able to give her some help. Not that she needed much. Josephine was extraordinarily sensitive. Some of her insights into what artists were trying to achieve in their work . . . I just wish I'd had the privilege of teaching someone with her gifts.' He broke off. Smiled. Said: 'She also had a very strong personality.'

'Yes, indeed.'

'But she had a sorrowful soul.'

A new Josie was forming in Ruth's mind. Not a daughter, but a person. 'Sometimes I think I never really knew her,' she said simply. 'Do you have any idea why she was troubled?'

'Don't you think that creative people suffer more than most? I've come to the conclusion – though I'm by no means the first or the most qualified to do so – that they're all born a couple of skins short. They feel more, so they suffer more. Fear more. The compensation, of course, is that they also delight more.'

'In what?'

'Everything,' he said simply. 'Higher highs, lower lows. It goes with the territory.'

'Are you creative too?'

'I'm a competent craftsman, nothing more than that. But Josephine: she had the makings of the real thing.'

Ruth looked out at the busy street. 'Which makes her death even more of a waste.'

'Nothing is ever wasted. Who knows what will come out of the experiences you've undergone. Press forward, Ruth. There was a song they used to sing in the war: *Keep right on to the end of the road.* I remember my uncle singing that to me when I was a child.

That's what we all have to do. Keep right on to the end.'

'I'm not sure I agree with the sentiment.'

'What else is there to do?'

'If my son had died of leukemia, I'd certainly have killed myself.' Spoken over the banalities of maple syrup and fried bacon, the matter-of-fact words seemed overly dramatic but she did not mind, certain that he understood.

'Then that would have been the end for you,' he said calmly.

'Would you call that giving up halfway?'

'That would depend.'

She glanced out at the street. 'What do you do, Sam?'

'Whatever is needed.'

'You said you were a craftsman.'

'Yes, I work in wood. But I can turn my hand to anything, from house painting to carpentry. Up here, you have to. Lobstering isn't enough.'

She looked surprised and he laughed. 'I've had a string of lobster traps since I was a child. Many of the native Mainers do. I love it out there on the sea. Maybe you'd like to come out with me sometime.'

'Thank you, but I don't think so.' Though she refused his invitation, the prospect of getting into a small boat again was not as frightening as she might have thought. With Sam Hechst around, the sea would keep its distance. Josie had talked about going lobstering: had it been with this man? She glanced at her watch. Across the road, a queue had formed outside the donut shop. She turned her direct gaze on him. 'I must get on.'

As they stepped into the street, he turned to her. 'Your son is cured?'

'Yes.'

'Definitely?'

Her mouth moved in a wry smile. 'As definitely as it's possible to be with this kind of disease.'

'That's good.' He laid his hand over hers. 'That is so good to hear.'

She watched him walk away from her, then turned into the offices of Dee's Realty. Mrs Dee stood up behind her desk and smiled. 'Mrs Connelly! Great to see you again!'

Although she did not resemble her in the least, Belle Dee reminded Ruth of Miss Marling, the English teacher. 'Hi,' she said. 'I wanted to—'

'We've looked after Carter's House for the past year, and it's *such* a lovely home. Beautiful. Full of warmth and atmosphere. Of course, my refurbishment team goes in regularly and takes care of the immediates, but in the long term it's not good for a house to be left alone.'

'You can surely understand why I find it difficult to return.'

'You poor thing, of course I do. But think how you'd feel if it was you, loved all your life long and then suddenly abandoned.'

Hey, lady, Ruth wanted to say. *Tell* me about it.

'Are you opening it up this summer?'

Ruth shook her head.

'Then you should make up your mind to let it,' said Mrs Dee. 'I can supply you with any number of extremely suitable clients, all with the highest of references.' Belle Dee cleared her throat. 'Please don't think I'm suggesting you put tenants in because I want to make a commission – though that's never bad, is it? It's only because I feel for that house.' She leaned forward. 'And there's the problem of break-ins.'

301

'You've mentioned that on the phone. Have you found any damage?'

'It's only a matter of time before there's theft or breakage. In my opinion, so far you've been very lucky.'

'I hear what you're saying.'

'There's mail waiting, too. Has been, ever since you shut the place up. We'd have sent it on to you in the city but your husband said you didn't want us to, so it's been left in the house.'

'I'll pick it up soon.' Feeling slightly steamrollered, Ruth walked slowly back to her car. Belle Dee was right: it was wrong to neglect a house that had been so much part of the family for so many generations. She ought to go up and look at it. Instead, she walked down to the little harbor and looked across toward the channel which led to the open sea. Gulls fighting over something in the water. Breath of tar and fish on the wind. A lobster shack with a steaming cauldron of water beside it. Smoke from a barbecue grill. It was all so familiar, and so dear. These had always been the places of her heart. Her spirits soared as they used to. When they were still together. When they were still a family.

A gift from a true love . . . Paul had read the words to her one summer afternoon, as the two of them sat under a shade tree in a rare moment of shared peace. The children were swimming in the pond with friends; on the grass the shadows were black where the sun nailed them to the ground. Katydids chirped. Paul looked up from his reading: 'Listen to what E. B. White wrote about returning to Maine after being away from it . . . *I do not ordinarily spy a partridge in a pear-tree, or three French hens, but I do have the sensation of having received a gift from a true love.*'

She had laughed. 'I like that. I know just what he

means: it's almost exactly how I feel sometimes, when we come out of the trees and see the house for the first time each summer.'

He had smiled at her. Reached for her hand. 'We're lucky, Ruth. Luckier than most.'

Back then, she had thought it was true.

Driving back to the Steins' cottage, she passed the turnoff which led to Carter's House. Slowing down, she peered between the treetrunks. Wild flowers nodded along the sandy track which ran toward the meadow in front of the house. Butter-yellow sunshine glowed where the trees broadened out. Would she ever drive down it again? Maybe. But not yet.

Will and Ed were sitting on the porch of the Steins' house, waiting for her. The dogs lay at their side, panting in the heat, tongues lolling. Both boys were in Bermudas and sea-stained Topsiders, looking so normal, so quintessentially boylike, that Ruth laughed aloud. The air was scented with salt-tang and seaweed and the pine trees which crowded up to the very edges of the cottage.

She got out of her car and ran toward Will.

'Mom!' He jumped up. 'Good to see you.'

'Darling, you look great!' In the weeks he had been up here, his pale face had acquired a light sea-tan. Now that his ulcerated digestive tract had been given a chance to heal, he was obviously able to eat properly and had put on some weight.

'You look pretty good yourself, Mrs Connelly.' Ed spoke from the top step.

'Why, thank you, Ed.'

'You changed your hairstyle, didn't you?'

'Good of you to notice.'

'I always notice stuff like that.'

'You're going to be a big success with the girls, Ed.'

'What's with this "going to" bit?' said Will. 'He already is.'

'Can't keep their hands off me,' Ed said mournfully.

'Where's . . . where's your father?' Ruth asked Will. 'I thought he was up here.'

'He went off with Sam Hechst,' said Will.

'But I'm sure if he'd known you were here, Mrs Connelly . . .' added Ed.

'Sure,' Ruth said, hoping Will did not notice the relief in her voice.

'Mom, look at this.' He took off his baseball cap. His scalp was lightly tanned and covered with a fine fuzz of hair.

'What about it?'

'Think I should shave it?'

'That's got to be up to you, hon.'

'I kind of like the image,' he said seriously. 'Especially since people think I did it on purpose, you know?'

'It's dramatic, I'll give you that.'

'And my ear stud . . . it's not gonna look the same with hair.'

'You should go with what feels good,' Ed said.

'I agree. Let the hair grow and if you don't like it, you can really shave it this time.'

'That's cool,' Will said. A choice, after so many months without one, clearly appealed to him. It was all Ruth could do not to tell him to paint his head green if that was what he wanted, that the question of hair versus no hair was immaterial compared with his health and strength, now so obviously restored.

Will looked apologetic. 'Sorry, Mom, but we gotta get back down to the yacht club. We'll see you later, okay?'

'Guess you're going to meet up with some of those nice girls,' Carmel said, rolling her eyes.

'*Some* girls?' Ed punched Will's shoulders. '*A* girl, don't you mean? A girl beginning with *A*? Am I right?'

'Get outta here,' said Will.

As the boys charged off, Ruth turned to her friend. 'Thank you,' she said quietly. 'Will looks absolutely great.'

'Doesn't he, though?'

'I can't hardly believe it.'

'I had to lay down the law about the sunscreen.'

'It's obviously worked.'

Carmel laughed. 'What I did was, I told Ed I'd hold him responsible if Will got burned, because Will's his guest. Ever since, he's been fussing round that kid like a mother hen.'

Will and Ed returned, again without Paul. 'I thought I should take you back to the city with me,' Ruth said, trying it out, knowing he would not agree, not even sure it was the right thing but feeling she should say it nonetheless.

'What, *now*?'

'What's wrong with now?'

Will looked mutinous. 'I don't want to go home yet, Mom.'

'You had a fever the other day,' Ruth said. She could not stop looking at him, the fresh growth of hair, the clear blue eyes, the tanned face. His body had filled out, there were new muscles under his T-shirt. He looked so well. So damned *good*. Nobody could tell he had ever been sick.

'*Everyone* had a fever that day,' said Will. 'The temperature was practically in the hundreds. Even Cool Hand Ed here had a fever.'

'It's true, Mrs Connelly. Sweat poured off me. Thought I'd melt into a little wet pool.' Ed looked at his friend. 'I think you should leave young William here where I can keep my eye on him.'

'Yeah,' said Will. 'One day he'll make someone a very good mother.'

'Get outta here,' Ed said.

'I still think you should come home with me,' said Ruth. 'After all, the summer's nearly ended.'

'Which is why it'd be *mean* to make me go back to the city before I have to. And there's my *birthday*. You promised I could have it up here. And you have to admit I look really well, don't I? It's *good* for me to be up here.'

'Really, Mrs Connelly,' Ed said gravely. 'I think he ought to stay here.'

Ruth held up both hands in mock surrender. 'Okay, okay. You convinced me.'

'Yo!' The two boys gave each other a high five and jigged around the room.

Ruth laughed. 'So I'll see you again soon, darling.' She smiled at her son. 'Oh Will, I can't tell you how much it means to see you looking so good.'

'Right, Mom.' Will looked embarrassed. 'Come on, I'll walk you out to the car.'

Saying goodbye, she held him close, tighter than usual, not wanting to let go of him. He let her for a moment then broke free. 'Mom,' he said. 'Don't worry about me. I'm okay. We licked it, between us, didn't we?'

'We did,' she said, elated. 'Yes. We really did.'

16

'I'm going up to Sweetharbor for Will's birthday,' she told him on the telephone.

'Oh.' Paul's heart dropped. Even though they seldom seemed to meet, now that Will was better, he nonetheless gained a measure of satisfaction from knowing that she lived in the same city as he did, breathed the same air. There was an excitement in wondering whether he would bump into her somewhere, whether he would go to a party and see her across the room.

Can I come too? The phrase screamed inside his skull. Can I belong again? He was silent, remembering Will's last birthday. It seemed both far longer than twelve months since Josie had died, and no more than a few days ago. The memory of his daughter was never far away. 'How's he doing?'

'According to Carmel, you'd hardly know he'd ever been sick. She says she doesn't see a lot of the boys – they're out sailing most days or down at the Yacht Club or playing tennis. Will gets tired more easily than Ed, but that doesn't seem to have stopped him much.'

'He's making up for lost time. How long will you be gone?'

'Only a couple of days.'

'Will you open up the house?'

There was a long silence. Then she said quietly: 'Not this time.'

'You'll have to eventually, Ruth.'

'You're probably right. When it first . . . after we lost Josie, I thought I could never go up there again, but I can see now that I shall have to, if only for Will's sake. He's really anxious to be back there.'

He cleared his throat. 'If you want some moral support for the celebrations, I'm willing to volunteer.'

He could hear her smile. 'That's good of you, Paul.'

Thanks a lot, but no thanks, in other words. 'Ruth,' he said. 'I've been thinking about things.'

'So have I.'

'I said some things which were unfair. A lot of things.'

'So did I.'

He wanted her to reassure him but she wasn't going to. 'Maybe . . . maybe we could have dinner when you get back.'

'I'd like that.'

Her inclination had been to push on up Route 1 until she reached Sweetharbor, but she knew she had to get out of the habit of hovering over Will, checking him constantly for the tiny indications which presaged a further bout of infection. Instead she had made arrangements to stop overnight in Brunswick to visit an elderly cousin of her mother's and, doing so, was soothed by the old wooden house and its quality of time having stood still. Almost nothing had changed since her first visit to this ordered home, over thirty years before. The same plates, the same food, the same conversation, gentle and undemanding. The bedroom was exactly as she remembered it, with a white cotton coverlet on the brass bed, white sheets and lace-edged pillowslips, silver-and-tortoiseshell brushes on the cherrywood chest. Cousin Thalia spoke of Josephine's death and William's illness with a detached air which Ruth realized did not stem from indifference but from acceptance. Death and illness, she seemed to imply, were as much a part of life as the weddings, the births, the celebrations. Ruth remembered that there had been brothers lost in the Second World War, a son killed in Vietnam, a lonely widowhood since the death of her theology professor husband. Perhaps, after all, time *did* heal, if only because it wove a recognizable pattern from the past.

The next morning, before driving on, she strolled across Bowdoin Quad, recalling walks here in the fall with Paul, with Cousin Thalia's husband, the dropping leaves so thick in places that they reached way above her shoes, the noisy frat houses, the carefully maintained historic buildings. She walked across the brick-laid forecourt of the Walker Art Building and in between the lions, to wander through the upstairs galleries, admiring the portraits of people long dead, musing on the impermanence of man's short span. Maybe what really mattered, in the end, was not that someone had died, but that they had lived.

The children had long since gone about their own affairs, and the three adults were able to linger over dinner. A warm breeze blew in off the sea, a sense of ease. 'Last time I was up here, I ran into Sam Hechst,' Ruth said idly.

'Hechst? The carpenter? He put in a new parquet floor in the living room for us last winter,' said Carmel.

Franklin nodded. 'What a craftsman. He did the

309

whole thing by eye.' He drank vigorously from his wine glass. 'Interesting guy. Used to teach art history at a private girls' school down in Connecticut. Gave it all up to come back here. Told us he'd try doing what his forefathers had always done, working with wood. Not just carpentry, but sculpture too.'

Carmel passed round a platter of local lobster, set out bowls of home-made mayonnaise and melted butter. 'I bought a piece of his only the other day. Absolutely exquisite.' Candles stood on the wooden table, smoking in the wind from the invisible sea.

Ruth picked up her wine glass. 'He told me he used to help Josie with her painting. He said she had a sorrowful soul. She was certainly upset about something last summer. I wish I knew what it was. I guess although kids today seem so much more in control than we were at the same age, they aren't really.'

'That's right,' agreed Carmel. 'They still find themselves in situations where they're way out of their depth.'

'A sorrowful soul,' repeated Ruth.

Carmel laughed. 'According to Mamie, all women have sorrowful souls. And it's all down to men.'

'Spare me the feminist bullshit,' groaned Franklin. His strong teeth gleamed as he forked lobster flesh into his mouth. 'I get enough of that in the office. These days, you daren't even tell your personal assistant she's looking good in case she slaps a harassment suit on you.' Butter glistened on his chin. 'But hey, what do I know? I'm just an overworked executive busting my ass to put bread on the table for my ungrateful wife and kids.'

'Oh, you . . .' Carmel said fondly.

*   *   *

Later, in her bedroom, Ruth leaned out of the window and stared into the night. The dark was absolute. There was no moon, no sea to cast back the silver reflection of the sky. She breathed in the rich fragrance of the junipers which surrounded the Steins' house, heard the deep breathing of the earth.

What had been troubling Josie so much last summer? Had she found herself trying to cope with a situation too complex for her? I do not even know if she was a virgin, Ruth thought. I did not know my own daughter. Those summer vacations they ran free, the two kids, they could have gone anywhere, done anything, and I would not have been aware.

She thought of Paul. Where was he tonight? Did he stare into the darkness, as she did, and wish they were still together?

She slipped out of the Steins' house early the next morning. The sky was gray, heavy with clouds. Between treetrunks the sea gleamed like pewter. Taking the path toward the road, she found it hard to believe that twelve months had passed since Will's last birthday. In that time, the family she had once thought so solid had disintegrated, fractured by grief. By loss. By death.

Today was Will's fifteenth birthday. And the anniversary of Josie's death. For the rest of their lives, the two events would be irreversibly linked. Her daughter's voice sounded in her head: *Would you love me no matter what? Would you give your life for me?* Why had Josie asked such questions? What had been bothering her? Could she have had some foretaste of her own death?

Under her heart lay an ache like a bruise. Walking along the familiar lanes, she wondered if she was expecting too much. She wanted simply to be grateful that Will had gone into remission. It ought to be enough. But it was not. It would never be. The loss of Josie sat inside her like a gaping wound, always there, incurable.

By the time she reached the path between the junipers and hemlocks which led toward the rough pasture in front of Carter's House, the cloud layer was breaking up. The air was warm and pine-scented. Clouds of no-see-ums danced in the shadows. The space beneath the trees on either side of her was filled with slanting lemon-green light.

She had said she would never set foot here again, but, nonetheless, here she was. The desperate woman who had made the vow had long since become something different. Something stronger.

She thought of the many times she had emerged from between the trees and driven up the track to park beside the red-painted barn, already knowing that here, in this beloved place, she would be able to prize off the shell of stress which accumulated in the city. This was where the ghost of the girl she had once been still walked. Now, the phantom of her lost daughter floated noiselessly across the broad pine boards, ran up the curved staircase, lingered in the kitchen with oil paint on her fingers. Perhaps, Ruth thought, she would one day find sufficient strength to enter the house but it would take more than she presently possessed to search for the key hidden under the side porch, and turn it in the lock of the front door.

The house looked weathered. One part of her mind detached itself from melancholy and noted that the woodwork needed painting again: the winters in Maine were hard, the salt air as potent as acid, able to eat through anything. It was over a year since it had last been done: like a dagger thrust, she remembered Josie complaining that the fresh paint ruined the look of the house.

She took the trail up behind the house, walking between the slim treetrunks, across the bridge over the culvert, past the boulder where Josie – '*I'm the Queen of the Castle!*' – had fallen and gashed open her forehead, until the view widened again and she found herself on the point overlooking the Sound. The teak bench was anchored there, solid and significant. She ran her hand over the carved heart. When she sat down, the slats were warm and smooth under her thighs. It seemed bitterly ironic that once she had sat on the warm grass and thought about having a bench put here.

She touched the brass plaque with her daughter's name and dates on it. Green, now, with verdigris. Josephine Carter Connelly. She gazed out at the glittering waters of the Sound. Trees, water, rocks, sunshine. Elemental things. In the dip of the boulder, the pixie garden flourished and, for a moment, a skipper hovered above it. She had expected to feel disturbance but, strangely, she felt peace.

Josie had gone. Josie would not be coming back. She would always be part of her but Ruth was slowly learning that she had to push on through life without her.

In honor of Will's birthday, the Steins threw a lunch party. Most of the guests were old friends, people she had not seen since the previous summer. Smiling, chatting, Ruth could feel burdens lifting from her shoulders. Order was at last being restored. Josie was gone, and the grief of that would be with her always, but, as Paul had said, life went on.

Finding herself next to Chris Kauffman, she said quietly: 'Forgive me, Chris.'

'What the hell for?' He put a big arm round her shoulder.

'London – that evening you came round. I put you in a difficult position and I'm—'

'London?' he said. He smiled his lopsided smile. 'I don't know what you're talking about.'

'Thanks, Chris.'

Ted Trotman came toward her. 'Ruth: it's good to see you. You're looking great.'

'You too, Ted.'

'Hey, listen, Ruth. When we all get back to the city, I'd like to set up a lunch date.'

'You have my number. Anything in particular you want to talk about?'

'Yes.' Trotman looked around as though afraid of being overheard. The trees overhead cast black shadows across his face. 'I don't want this generally known, Ruth, but I'm thinking of transferring a big percentage of my business away from the guys currently handling my affairs.'

'Why's that?'

'Various reasons. Eggs in baskets, for one thing. Always a mistake. And we've had a couple of minor hiccups working with those guys. Think LKM could take us on?'

'I'm absolutely sure they could,' Ruth said. She had been trying for years to get Ted Trotman's business. Bob Landers would be ecstatic if she could bring him on board.

'What I hear, you're doing well, Ruth. The McLennan thing. I was talking to Jake Phillipson at the health club a couple of weeks back. Said you were the smartest guy in the firm.'

'It's true, Ted. All of it's true.'

He put a hand on her shoulder. 'Wanted to say, Ruth, how bad I felt about your kid. Josie. She had guts, I'll say that for her. Always taking me on. I was able to put her right on a couple of things.' He chuckled. 'Boy, now there's a kid who'd have made a good lawyer.'

'You think so?' Was that what Josie had wanted? To be a lawyer like her mother? It seemed unlikely.

'And your boy – William, is that his name?'

'That's right, Ted.'

'I'm real glad to know he's better. Must have been pretty bad for you, this past year.'

'You could say that.'

Raising a hand, he moved away, leaving her standing alone. Light fell between the branches of the junipers. Caught between the trees, the air was thick, warm. Her body felt honeyed with contentment. She had never thought she would feel happy again.

That evening they ate dinner at the yacht club. Will sat at the head of the table, laughing, kidding around with Ed. She sat beside him, not saying much, just glad to see him strong and shining again. Somewhere inside her, a remembrance of her lost daughter stirred. When she got back to the house, she would call Paul and allow the tears to fall, but for now she must celebrate, not mourn.

Franklin offered a toast to the birthday boy and they all raised their glasses. One of the white-jacketed waiters began to lead a chorus of 'Happy Birthday To You' and the rest of the diners joined in. Several of them, knowing of Will's illness, came over and stood at the table.

When they were eating the birthday cake Ruth had ordered earlier, Will leaned toward her. 'Thanks for being here, Mom,' he said quietly.

'You don't think I'd miss your birthday, do you?'

'Except it's not just my birthday, it's also the day that . . . that . . .'

'That Josie died,' she said steadily.

He looked down at his plate. Pushed the cake around with his fork. 'All day long I've been thinking about her. Remembering.'

There were so many things she could have said. In the end, she sighed. 'Me too, Will. Josie's part of us, part of up here. She always will be. It's taken me far too long to accept what you said: that she has a *right* to be remembered.'

Both of them were silent for a moment. Then Will said: 'Sorry I haven't spent more time with you while you've been visiting, Mom.'

'That's okay.'

'It's just it's summer and there's such a lot to do up here, and I—'

'Listen to me, Will.' She picked up his rough boy's hand and squeezed it. 'I am so very, *very* happy at this moment. Seeing you well again, it's like a miracle. You don't have to apologize to me for anything, ever.'

'*Ever?*' He cocked an eyebrow at her.

'I may need to revise that statement. But for the moment, it's more than I could have asked for just to see you here, where I know you're happy, just . . . *being*. Okay?'

'Okay, Mom.' Awkwardly, he put an arm around her shoulders and hugged her, crushing her up against his chest. She smelled his sun-warmed skin and thought: one of these days there'll be another woman in his arms. It won't be me. And that is good. That is so wonderfully, unexpectedly good.

316

17

The fall semester began. Although Will had to work hard to catch up on his missed schooling, he managed to play hard as well. Most of his spare time was spent with Ed, Stu and Dan.

'It's the band, Mom,' he said, when Ruth told him not to overtire himself. 'This gig that Stu's father fixed up for us.' He threw spinach leaves into a bowl and shook the skillet in which he was roasting pine nuts.

'The Kiwanis dance thing?'

'Yeah. It's the week after Thanksgiving and people are *paying* to hear us, so we gotta be good.' In the skillet, the pine nuts danced and spun, slowly turning brown.

'Can I come?'

'*You?*' His expression was horrified.

'Yes, William. Me, your mother.'

Will sighed. 'Why do parents always want to come to things?' He emptied the pine nuts into the salad bowl and began to shave fresh Parmesan cheese.

Watching him, marveling at him, Ruth savored her martini. 'I seem to remember you getting annoyed because I *didn't* come to things.'

'This is different.'

'In what way?'

Will scraped at a blackened pan of roasted vegetables, a melange of tomatoes, eggplants, zucchini and onion, which he'd removed from the oven earlier. He lifted a piece on a fork and tasted it. 'Mmm, that's good.' He held the fork toward her. 'Try that.' Chewing, he surveyed his mother. 'It's just – you'll be kind of old.'

'Thank you very much, William. What's the average age of a Kiwani, I wonder?'

'They're putting this dance on for disabled kids, not adults. Anyway, you'd hate it. We don't play your kind of music.'

'How do you know what my kind of music is?'

Will rolled his eyes heavenward. He crushed garlic cloves with the flat of a knife. 'Okay. I guess you can come if you really want to. Ed's mom will be there. And Stu's dad.'

'Now you tell me.'

'Jeez.' Will shook his head. 'Just don't do anything that'll destroy my rep, okay?'

'Like what? Dance naked on a table?'

'Like . . . *kiss* me or something stupid like that.' Deftly, Will used a fork to mix oil, mustard and raspberry vinegar with the garlic.

Ruth laughed. 'I promise.'

'She's pretty smashed up,' Paul said. Hands tucked inside their jackets and caps pulled down over their ears, he and Will walked one last time round the *Lucky Duck*. Fog hung over the boatyard, salt and wet, burrowing into their throats, thickening their lungs. The autumn storms had begun and the winds were beating down the coast, whistling round the masts of the boats tied up to the boatyard's dock. Halyards drummed against aluminum masts; gulls screamed overhead, the turbulent air tossing them in and out of the fog like balls of paper. 'What do you think?'

'I bet it could be mended.' Will's nose was red and his eyes were tearing up with cold. He ran a hand over the boat's wooden hull. Smashed timbers surrounded the gaping hole in her side. Where the mast had snapped, there was a splintered stump. 'Lotta work, though.'

'The inside's not so bad, it's the hull which really took a beating.' This was the first time Paul had truly comprehended the strength of the storm which had overtaken them. 'Maybe we should ask someone like Sam Hechst to give us a hand. He knows lots more about this sort of work than I do.'

'And then we – you and me – could do the cabin?'

'Work on the hull too, if you like.'

'Sounds good to me.'

'What I'd like', Paul said wistfully, 'is if we could get her ready for next season. So we can get some racing in, soon as we get out on the water again.'

'Can't see why not.'

'It'd mean coming up here most weekends before the winter sets in.'

'Don't know about that,' Will said. He was almost as tall as his father now. 'There's the band. I gotta be ready for our gig.'

'When's that?'

'Week after Thanksgiving. Can't do anything at weekends until after that.' Will looked round the boat-yard, at the boats shrouded for winter, at the heavy lifting-gear and the half-formed skeletons of the wooden boats that were built here. 'How about we get them to move the *Duck* up to Carter's House?'

'What for?'

'If we, you and me, cleared out the barn a bit, the *Duck* could go in there. At least until her mast's replaced. That way, once Thanksgiving's over, we could work on her right through the winter.'

'Hey, good idea.' Paul clapped his son on the shoulder. *You and me*: he loved it when Will said that. 'We've got kerosene heaters in there already. It'll cost us to have her moved, though.'

'C'mon, Dad. It'll be worth it. And it'll be cheaper than a new boat.'

'Guess you're right.' Paul brushed at the cold pearls of moisture on the front of his jacket and hastily put his ungloved hand back in his pocket. 'All these years and I never knew your mom and I had produced a genius.'

'It's not as if I didn't keep telling you.'

They began to walk toward the iron gates of the yard. Paul said: 'Want something to eat?'

'You bet. I'm starving.'

They drove toward the nearest eatery, fog thick against the windscreen. With the first frosts, the grass which lined the rutted sandy lanes round Sweetharbor had turned yellow and brittle. Barberry and rowan gleamed crimson under the trees, each berry dripping with moisture; in the meadows, the dead seedpods of lupines hung from slippery black stems. Sumac leaves, brilliantly scarlet, hung along the roadsides. Although they could not see it, behind the fog, the steel-blue sea heaved and tossed.

Biting into an overfilled crab roll, Will said indistinctly: 'I *love* it up here.'

'Me too.'

'I wish we could live here forever.'

'Yeah.' Unlikely, Paul thought. Ruth would never agree to them leaving the city . . . then he remembered that he and Ruth now led separate lives.

As though following his thoughts, Will asked casually: 'You coming by the apartment for Thanksgiving?'

'Your mom hasn't asked me.'

'Would you if she did?'

'I guess I would,' Paul said, trying not to sound plaintive. 'If she did.' Now that Will was recovered, Ruth and he appeared to be drifting further apart. He could scarcely remember when they had last spoken on the phone.

'Next time we come up, Dad, we should go visit the Cottons. See how Marietta's arthritis is doing.'

'Okay.'

'Take some candies with us – she likes Reese's peanut butter cups.' As they walked back to the car, Will added: 'That's what Josie used to do. Take her candies. You know?'

'I didn't.'

'Can Dad come for Thanksgiving?' Will said.

'Dad?'

'You know, Mom: the man you're married to. My father. Can he come over for dinner on Thanksgiving?'

'What makes you think he'd want to?'

'I asked him, that's what. He said he'd come if he was invited.'

'It'll be sort of . . . awkward.'

'Thanksgiving is a time for everyone to be sweet to everyone else,' Will said. 'For families to get together. And even if you and Dad don't live together, you're still my family.'

'Well . . .'

'You don't hate him or anything, do you?' Will's eyes were wide with the need for her to say no.

'Of course not,' Ruth said.

'So will you ask him?'

'All right.'

'Cool.'

'But I don't really—'

'Do it, Mom.'

Since Will's recovery, Paul had withdrawn from her and she had been happy to let him do so. Only occasionally did she think of how it had been, the four of them together, the life they had led. 'I'll call him this evening.'

Much later that night, Ruth was awakened by some sound. She lay under the covers, still half-asleep, and heard Will retching in the bathroom. Instantly she was wide awake, swinging her legs out of bed, reaching for her robe. She stumbled out into the passage. Will had left the door open and she could see him hunched over the pedestal.

'What's wrong?' she said. Her face felt stiff, sodden with sleep. Inside her ribcage, her heart thumped with rediscovered fear.

Will flapped an arm at her, wanting her to go away but she stayed leaning against the wall until he had finished.

'What's wrong?' she said again, when he had rinsed out his mouth and washed his face.

'Nothing, Mom.' He grinned shamefacedly. 'I went out with the guys after school, pigged out on fries and a toasted cheese sandwich. Plus a couple of Cokes. Guess they didn't mix too well.'

'Are you sure that's all it was?'

He shrugged. ''Course.'

In the morning he seemed fine, though Ruth examined his face minutely, looking for – for what, exactly? Boils, shadows under his eyes, unexplained bruises? There were none: he looked well, the last of the summer's tan still warm on his face. She tried not to worry: kids threw up all the time, especially if they ate too much junk food. It was nothing.

A couple of weeks later, she came back from the office to find Will asleep on the sofa in the living room. Ed was sitting next to him, watching TV with the sound turned right down.

'What's going on, Ed?' she said quietly, dumping her bag and papers on the table. With her head, she motioned him into the kitchen, where they could talk without disturbing Will.

'I came back with him, Mrs Connelly. Miss Marling asked me to.'

'Why? What happened?' Bubbles of alarm popped along her veins: momentarily she felt dizzy with terror.

'He was throwing up this afternoon.'

'Oh, Ed . . .'

'Don't worry, Mrs Connelly. We had to eat this really gross fish thing at lunch: I bet it was that. A couple of the other kids were barfing their guts out too, but Miss Marling said I was to come home with Will in a cab and wait for you, because of Will's being sick earlier.'

'Thanks, Ed. You're a star.' Both of them knew she was thanking him for more than his company on a cab ride.

'So's Will.'

'I know that.'

When Ed had gone, Ruth went into the living room and looked down at her son's sleeping face. Devoured it. Try as she might, she could see no sign at all that he was sick. A little pale, perhaps, but that was understandable.

She clasped her hands together and raised them to her mouth, pressing back dread.

Her parents arrived at the beginning of the next week. Ruth's father held his grandson by the upper arms, appraised him, let him go. 'Hey, boy. You're looking wonderful,' he said. 'Really good.'

'Hope you brought some warm clothes, Grandad,' Will said.

'Listen, I lived up here for most of my life. I know to bring warm clothes,' Jonathan Carter said.

'Oh, sweetheart.' Betty Carter hugged Will. 'Don't you just look great?'

'Still vegetarian?' Jonathan asked.

'Only way to go, Grandad.'

'Do we get to eat turkey on Thursday?' Will's grandfather wondered plaintively. 'That veggie stuff does my digestive system no good at all. At my age I need to sink what's left of my teeth into something good and solid.'

'I could make you a good solid nutburger,' said Will.

'I'd like to see you try,' said Ruth's mother. 'Your grandad would sooner eat stewed muskrat.'

'Much sooner,' said Jonathan.

'What a coincidence,' Will said. 'Mom made a stewed muskrat casserole just last night, didn't you, Mom?'

'Certainly did. And there's a nice roadkill pâté first.'

'Just so long as we get turkey on Thursday,' said Jonathan.

Later, Ruth said: 'What do you think, Dad?'

'About our boy?'

'Yes.'

'He looks fine.'

'He's thrown up a couple of times in the last week or two.'

324

'Could be anything. Any of those bruises?'

'Not as far as I can tell. He doesn't want me to see him naked and I have to respect that, but I'm sure he'd say, wouldn't he?'

'I hope so.'

'Ruthie, I can't tell you . . .' Betty put down her magazine. 'I just can't tell you how marvelous it is to see him better again. After those terrible months when we thought . . . we thought he wasn't going to make it . . .'

'I know, Mom. I know.' Ruth sat down beside her mother and hugged her. 'By the way, Paul's coming round for Thanksgiving lunch.' She had invited him with a certain reluctance, had sensed the reluctance with which he accepted. Both of them had agreed, over-eagerly, that they were doing this for Will.

'Paul?' Her parents glanced at each other. Betty took a big breath, her face determined. 'We haven't asked you before, but we never did understand what happened, why he left you.'

'I don't know why, either,' said Ruth. She twisted her hands together. 'No. That's not quite true. I *do* know. At least, I think I do. There was a lot of resentment simmering away between us. I – I guess I wasn't always as tactful as I might have been about the fact that, almost from the beginning, I earned more than Paul. It bothered him. And maybe I was kind of high-handed about it.' Ruth bent her head. 'It wasn't just the differential in our earning power. Josie dying – I couldn't cope. I shut it out. Didn't want to admit it. Paul needed to talk, and I wouldn't. In the end, maybe it was easier for him to go.'

Ruth's mother reached over and touched her daughter's hand.

* * *

On Thanksgiving Day, Will complained of an earache. His summer tan had faded, and he was looking very pale. Fiercely questioned by Ruth, he admitted that he had been feeling tired lately, that he'd thrown up a couple more times recently.

'Why didn't you *say*?' Ruth tried to cram the panic back inside her but it refused to stay put. 'I wish you'd told me.'

'It's stupid. I feel like I'm making a fuss.'

'Of course you're not. You've been *ill*. We'll need to keep tabs on you for a while yet.'

'I'm okay. Just this earache.'

'I'll give you a painkiller for the moment,' Ruth said.

She walked down the passage to her parents' room. 'Will's got an earache,' she told them flatly.

She saw her own anxieties reflected in her father's eyes. 'Anything else?' he asked.

'He's been feeling tired. He's thrown up again.'

'But when we arrived, he looked great,' her mother said. 'He was fine.'

'Oh God,' her father said heavily. He sat down on the side of the bed and leaned forward, staring at his shoes.

'Are we overreacting, Dad?' asked Ruth.

'I don't know.'

'Do you think I should take him down to the hospital right now?'

'Better continue as planned,' her father said. 'Another twenty-four hours won't make much difference either way.' He moved his head slowly from side to side, his expression despairing.

When Paul arrived, Ruth did not tell him about Will's earache. He had made a cherrywood bowl for her mother, and as he showed it to Will, as he poured wine for her parents, Ruth thought how easy it would be for a stranger to conclude that this was a normal happy family. But watching her son picking at the elaborate vegetables she had prepared for him – sweet potatoes baked in molasses, a purée of root vegetables, potatoes roasted with onions, sprouts, green beans sautéed with garlic, the big mixed salad, all things he would normally have devoured – Ruth realized she would have to face the truth.

While Paul and her parents stacked the dishwasher in worried silence, she went into Will's room. He was lying on his bed, looking exhausted. 'Show me your arms,' she commanded. 'Your legs.'

There were bruises around his elbow joints, purple blotches behind his knees. The telltale petechiae were sprinkled under his skin. Watching her face, he said defeatedly: 'It's come back, hasn't it?'

'Don't be ridiculous, Will,' she said, more confidently than she felt. 'We won't know anything until we've had you checked out. It's probably nothing more than a minor infection.'

'It's back.' He turned his face to the wall. 'I've been feeling bad for a while now.'

'Why didn't you tell me?'

'Don't know.'

But she knew that he did. He had kept silent from fear. 'It could be anything,' she said, keeping her voice calm. 'The treatment you had – the chemo – all those drugs are bound to undermine you.'

'I was fine during the summer.'

'And you'll be fine again.' She hoped she sounded strong and knowledgeable, the way a parent is supposed to be.

'Will I?'

If it's back, Ruth thought, if the mutant cells are once

327

again ravaging my child's body, there is help at hand. Chemo. Radiotherapy. A bone marrow transplant. We have options, we have chances, this means nothing, these bruises, he will be *okay*. 'This could just be some delayed reaction to all those drugs.'

'Yeah. Right,' Will said bleakly.

'We'll have the doctors look at you.' She sat down on the bed and cradled his head against her chest. 'Oh Will,' she said. 'I love you. You do know that, don't you?'

He nodded, his head moving against her.

She held him tight. 'Will, don't despair. My darling, my . . . love.' She had never been a woman given to easy endearments; her use of one now was sufficient indication of her state of mind. 'Don't despair.'

'I can't stand it, Mom,' Will said. 'I mean it. I'm not going through all that again. The needles. Aching all over. Wanting to throw up all the time.'

'You're giving up before we even know.'

'*I* know.'

'You don't.'

'And even if I do have more treatment, it'll all be for nothing in the end.'

Ruth put her arm around his shoulders. 'You're wrong. Life is good, Will. You have to go on believing that.'

'Not for me. Not if I'm sick again. I'd rather die.'

'Don't.' Savagely she pulled his face toward her, ignoring his cry of pain. 'Don't *say* that, William. Not ever.'

'Why not? It's the truth.'

'You're going to live. You *will* live.' She produced a shaky laugh. 'Listen to us! We don't even know for sure that there's anything wrong.'

328

He stared into her face and the territory behind his eyes was the bleakest of landscapes. 'Don't we?'

As soon as she came back into the room, Paul knew. He'd been aware of tensions from the moment he'd arrived. Mom and Dad Carter had been wound up about something, but at first he'd assumed it was because they were disconcerted at seeing him again, not knowing quite how to behave around their daughter's estranged husband. Will had seemed okay, too. Until they sat down to eat.

Now Ruth's face said it all. He got up and put his arms round her. She rested her head against his shoulder and he held her tight, neither of them speaking. Behind him, he heard Ruth's mother begin to cry.

'We'll take him to the hospital tomorrow,' he whispered into Ruth's hair. 'I'll be there for you.' And yet, even as he spoke, he wondered how true that was. Could he go through the horror of it all again? Could Will?

Alienation. Distance. Uninvolvement. Last time round it had seemed like the only way he could handle it all. If the cancer had come back – and he felt sure it had – this time it would be even worse. It would mean – wouldn't it? – that Will's chances were much slimmer than before.

He squeezed his eyes shut, pushing the images of Will to the back of his mind: My son . . . my son. Wind in our hair. Ball games. The *Lucky Duck* . . . The future receded, contracted.

They waited in a small room with a low ceiling. There were two armchairs upholstered in brown corduroy, separated by a square wooden coffee table. To one side

329

was a love seat upholstered in contrasting beige. There was a picture on the wall of mountains covered in snow. Through high windows, she could see the sky. This was not the room which had become so familiar during Will's previous illness; Ruth wondered if it had been chosen in order to avoid dredging up memories.

Doctors Caldbeck and Gearin came in, looking subdued. 'Professor Connelly. Mrs Connelly.' They shook hands before sitting down together on the love-seat and opening the files they carried.

'We're very disappointed,' Dr Caldbeck said, after a few moments. 'After such a prompt remission, we had hoped for better results than this.'

'Did you stop the treatment too soon?' Ruth asked bluntly. The confusion and fear she had felt the first time round had temporarily vanished. She was not going to give in, nor allow Will to do so.

'I don't think so. His blood was clear, the disease had gone.'

'We certainly wouldn't want to be feeding such high doses of powerful drugs to a healthy body,' Gearin said. 'And that's what Will had.'

'What are his chances?' Paul asked. 'Last time you told us eighty per cent of cases like Will's end in a cure. What's the percentage now the disease has recurred?'

Gearin answered. 'Somewhat lower than eighty. I can't pretend otherwise. But we have every hope that we'll be able to combat the disease again.'

'You told us before that you were confident Will would be cured,' said Ruth.

'Yes. As indeed he—'

'You were wrong last time.'

'Not wrong.' Gearin held up a hand. Today his brown eyes were half-concealed behind gold-rimmed glasses. They made him seem much older. 'He went into remission.'

'And now he's ill again. How can I believe anything you say?'

'You can't,' Caldbeck said. He pulled at the knot of his tie as though it had suddenly tightened round his neck. 'You just have to do what *we* do, which is to go on hoping that we'll find the successful combination of treatments.'

Ruth said combatively: 'How can I hope? More importantly, how can *he* hope? He went through all that horror for *nothing*.'

'Not for nothing. You have to believe us,' Caldbeck said.

'It's only a few months since you told us he was cured,' Paul said. 'And here he is, back in hospital, sicker than ever.'

'Let's talk about that,' said Gearin. He glanced down at his folder. 'Since Will's form of the disease is proving resistant to the standard drugs, we think we should move to the next level of therapy and this time combine chemo with radiotherapy.'

'He hates those needles.'

Caldbeck nodded, looking at a spot on the wall behind her. 'Radiotherapy isn't as painful as chemo, in terms of actual treatment. But the side effects are very much the same: nausea, vomiting and so on. Joints aching. Luckily, as with chemo, they're mostly temporary.'

Ruth held the sides of her chair. If it was like this for her, what must it be like for Will? 'We're doing the right thing, aren't we?' she said, suddenly doubting her convictions.

'We are, Ruth.' Gearin nodded his head, touched the

gold frame of his glasses. 'I have to believe that.'

'The maintenance of life is what we dedicated our-selves to when we became pediatricians,' said Caldbeck. He too nodded.

'Whatever the cost?'

'I have to believe that,' Gearin repeated.

'Neither of you sound very convinced.'

Caldbeck stepped in. 'When one of our patients comes back, like Richard who came in last week, clear of the disease, healthy, leading a normal life, to tell us he's getting married next month, then I *know* that we're right. And hard though it is to believe, there's an increasing number of people like him walking around. Survivors. People we can point to and say: see, it may be hard, but it works.'

'In the last few days, Will's just sunk deeper and deeper into depression,' Paul said. 'How psychologically pre-pared is he for another course of treatment?'

'We'll arrange for him to see the family psychologist. That might help. And you should talk to her, too, both of you. This is equally hard on the parents.'

'Worse, Mike. Much much worse.' Ruth had intended to be strong, to fight, but suddenly she was weeping. She buried her head in her hands and felt the tears flow. 'I can't bear it,' she said. 'I don't know how I'm . . . what I'm going to do if . . . if . . .'

Gearin got up and came round the desk to put a hand on her shoulder. 'Let it out, Ruth. It's better that way.'

'Have you told Will what you've found?' asked Paul.

'Not yet.'

'He knows,' said Ruth harshly. 'He's known for days. He didn't want to admit it, that's all.'

'What now?' Paul said.

'We begin the treatment as soon as we can. Like today. We've done all the preliminary tests.'

'How much of the time can we be with him?'

'Like last time: as often as you want. You can accompany him for some of the radiotherapy treatments, for instance.' Gearin's teddy-bear eyes clouded over. 'Though I should warn you that it can be very upsetting.'

Five days later, Will was given his first dose of radiotherapy. The room in which the treatment was conducted was bad enough: the dim lighting and the brooding shapes of the equipment produced a malevolent atmosphere made all the worse by the silence. Despite the determined cheerfulness of the technicians, Ruth knew there was little to be cheerful about. She held Will's hand as he was lifted onto a vinyl-covered table and then stepped back as they began to wrap him in sheeting, almost like a mummy. Packs of lead-shielding designed to prevent unnecessary incidental radiation were placed round him; they leaned against his unresisting body like ramparts against the cancer-destroying lights. Even his face was covered. Just before the cloth was placed over his head, his eyes met hers, and she saw in them the same look she had seen, months before, in the eyes of other children.

The table slid slowly into the dark cavern of the machine. A sob rose in her throat and she backed into a corner, pressing her hands to her mouth, trying to hold it in. Come back. Come back. Oh, William, my son, my little boy . . . What was he thinking about, inside that steel casing, alone, afraid, hurting?

One of the technicians approached her, brushing at her green scrubs. 'It looks worse than it really is,' she said. 'Honestly it does. They don't feel anything, and it doesn't last too long.' She glanced across at the sinister glow inside the machine, and added: 'Poor kid.'

Because his immune system was still low after the previous series of treatments, Will had to spend more than two weeks in hospital. His needle phobia made each jab an ordeal. Standing by and watching while the nursing staff dug needles into his flesh, trying to find a place where there was enough blood to draw a sample, became almost as painful for Ruth as it was for him. That is my son's body, she wanted to shout. Leave him alone. Don't let him be hurt anymore. Hurt me instead. I cannot bear the agony of helplessness.

She wanted to tell him not to try to be brave, but she recognized that maybe his pride was the only thing he felt he had left. She took refuge in aggression.

'Should he be mingling with the other children?' she asked sharply, standing at the nurses' station, quietly beating her clenched fist on the counter.

'That's how we—'

'He's susceptible to infection. He ought to be kept in isolation.'

'The doctors know what they're—'

'Do they? They told me my son was cured last time and he wasn't.'

'Mrs Connelly, I don't think you can put that down to—'

Her fist thumped. 'My boy needs every chance he can get if he's going to beat this thing.'

'It's not hospital policy.'

'Maybe it ought to be. Maybe I should speak to the hospital administrator.'

'He would agree with us, Mrs Connelly,' an older

334

nurse said quietly, looking up from some notes she was reading.

'Well . . .' Ruth beat another restless tattoo on the counter and moved away. She was behaving badly, she knew that. The mother from hell. But last time she had allowed the hospital to dictate to her. She had trusted the doctors, and they had let her down. She still wondered whether Will had been sent home too soon. This time round, maybe she should be more proactive.

She looked at Will through the glass window giving onto the passage. He saw her and waved, beckoned her into the room. She stood at the door. 'I don't think I should come in,' she said.

'Why not?'

'I'm worried about infection.'

'You know what, Mom?'

'What?'

'You sound like you've lost it.'

She stared at him. Lost it? Lost *you* . . .

The ache of future devastation set up a fine trembling in her limbs. 'No,' she said quietly. 'I'm simply trying to do the best that I can.'

'Nearly Christmas,' Ruth said to Will. 'Got any ideas about it?'

'Plenty. Or . . . just one, really. But you won't go along with it.'

'Try me.'

'I want to go up to Carter's House.' Small spots of color stood out on Will's cheekbones, emphasizing the bony contours of his face. 'We always used to spend Christmas up there when we were little kids, until . . .'

Until there were office parties Ruth had to attend, and meetings and important lunches with clients.

Things which made it impossible for her to arrange the kind of festivities she wanted the family to have.

'I know we did, but . . .' Her whole being rebelled at the thought of entering the house. Especially at Christmas.

He turned his head away and her heart clenched as she saw the shiny scalp under his thinning hair. Was he going to lose it all again?

'Funny, isn't it?' he said, his voice scarcely above a whisper, as though his strength was running out. 'I've heard you telling Dr Gearin that you'd give anything in the world if it would save my life . . .'

'And I would, baby, you know I would.'

'Then why can't you give me what I want most?'

She was cut to the quick by the truth of what he said. 'It'll be darn cold up there at this time of year.'

'It's heated. And we can have open fires. There's masses of wood stacked under the porch and in the barn. Ed and I were over there a couple of times during the summer.'

'And suppose we get snowed in? Suppose you get sick and I can't get you to a doctor?'

'It'd be a good place to be, in that case,' he said simply.

'Let me think about it,' she said.

She found Mike Gearin in his office. 'What do you think?' she said. 'Will wants to go up to Maine for Christmas.'

'Sounds like fun.' Dr Gearin took off his glasses and rubbed the top of his nose. He looked exhausted.

'But is he going to be okay to travel?'

'I can't see why not.'

'Even though he'll be away from his support systems? You, the hospital . . .'

'Ruth, I'm sure you're aware that one of the best treatments of all for any kind of cancer is a positive attitude. If Will's going to be happy spending Christmas in Maine, then let him do so.'

'Are you sure?'

'If you decide to go, what I can do is call the hospital in – it's Hartsfield, isn't it? – to check that if an emergency arose, they could care for him there.'

'All right,' she said doubtfully.

In spite of Will's pleas, the more she considered it, the more Ruth knew she could not go back to the cottage. She circled round the problem, seeking a compromise, seeking to give Will what he wanted so much while at the same time trying to avoid the pain of the empty house where they had once been happy.

And then it came to her. The next day she said to Will: 'Suppose we had Christmas up in Sweetharbor . . .'

'Oh *great*! That's really—'

'. . . but not', Ruth said, 'at the cottage.'

Will's face drooped with disappointment. 'What would be the point of that?'

'Suppose we all stayed at the Cabot Inn?'

'A hotel? For Christmas? No, thanks.'

'We've done it before – remember when the furnace broke down and we went there for Christmas dinner?'

He looked at the wall behind her. 'It wouldn't be the same.'

'William.' She stepped toward him and gently stroked his hair. 'I want to make you happy, truly I do. I know how you want to go back to Carter's House, but I'm simply not ready yet.' She pressed a finger against her lips. 'When I came up to visit you at the Steins' in

337

the summer, I went up to the Point, sat on Josie's bench. I thought it was going to be fine, I could go back to the house. But when it comes to the crunch, I have to be honest with you, Will. To go back will take more strength than I currently have.'

His eyes were huge, luminous with suffering. He gave an immense shrugging sigh and stared at her, flexing his mouth. 'I suppose if we went to the Cabot Inn, it'd be better for Grandad and Grandma.'

Ruth wanted to say that her parents would gladly spend Christmas in an igloo if it would make their grandson happy. She recognized that Will too was compromising. 'That's true,' she said. 'So what do you think?'

'Guess it wouldn't be too bad.'

'Really?'

'Not as good as going to Carter's House, but okay.'

'Shall we call them, ask what they think?'

'If you like.'

Ruth picked up her mobile and pressed her parents' phone number. 'Mom! Hi, it's me.'

'What's wrong?' her mother instantly demanded. 'What's happened?'

'Nothing, except – Will and I decided that it'd be kind of nice to spend Christmas up in Maine.'

'At Carter's House? But it's always so cold in winter.'

'Thought we'd book some rooms at the Cabot Inn. We hoped you might join us.'

'You know we'd do anything, go anywhere, for the chance to be with you two.'

'I know. So provided there's room at the inn . . .' she heard Will snort at her little joke, '. . . can we expect you?'

'With bells on, darling.'

338

Ruth telephoned the inn and spoke to Tyler Reed, the manager.

'Mrs Connelly.' His voice was warm. 'How nice to hear from you again.'

'It's been a long time for all of us, Mr Reed. I'm coming up with my parents—'

'Dr and Mrs Carter – it'll be good to see them again.'

'—and my son. He's . . . I don't know if you've heard but he's been very sick and he'd really like to spend Christmas in Sweetharbor. Trouble is, we can't face opening up the house.' It was no more than a slanted take on the truth. 'Will you have rooms for us all? And, if so, could we bring some of our own things? Decorations, a tree, that kind of thing? I want to make it as much like home for my son as possible.'

'How about if you took a couple of our two-room suites? You could do what you liked then.'

'That sounds perfect.'

'I'll book you in and we look forward to seeing you, Mrs Connelly.' Reed hesitated. 'Dr Carter delivered my two daughters – I don't know if he remembers, but one of them was real difficult. We've always been grateful to him, he sat with my wife right through it all.'

'Will your daughter be around at Christmas?'

'They're coming up from Norfolk. And the grand-children.'

'That'll make it extra special.'

When she put down the phone, Will said: 'What about Dad?'

'*What* about Dad?'

'Is he coming too?'

'If he wants to,' she said lightly.

Will was finally allowed home. He was much weaker

than he had been before. Watching him struggle against nausea, listening as he vomited up even the blandest of foods, seeing the defeated stoop of his shoulders, Ruth sometimes wondered whether it would not be kinder to let him do as he wished, and simply let nature take its course. She had persuaded him that this time it would be easier, but it was not. His reaction to each stage of treatment was more intense: darker bruises from the insertion of needles, deeper depression from the drugs given to combat infection, greater pain from the ulcers which inevitably accompanied the treatment. His emotional withdrawal, too, was greater than before: daily she watched him growing further away from her.

'Why should I have to do all this?' Will asked fretfully. He was lying on the big couch in the living room. His eyes were closed, the lids so fragile that she fancied she could almost see the blueness of the irises beneath. 'It's pointless.'

'It's not,' she said quietly. She sat at the dining table, her papers spread before her, but pushed them away, put down her pen, so that he could see she was listening with her full attention.

'I mean, even if they manage to catch the cancer this time, I'm never going to be able to live a normal life.'

'That's not true.'

'I read about it, Mom. I might not be able to . . . to have kids.'

'Some people could see that as a blessing,' she said, trying to make a joke of it.

'You don't mean that.' She got up and went over to perch on the arm of the couch, trying not to touch him. She had forced herself to acknowledge that Paul was right, the nurses were right, he should be hugged; the reason for avoiding contact now was because it was so easy to bring up a bruise on his pale tenderized skin. 'Last time I was at the hospital, Dr Gearin told me about one of his patients who's getting married in the summer.'

'So?'

'He had leukemia when he was thirteen, same sort of age as you did – and it took two doses of chemo before they got rid of it. And look at him now. So don't start giving up just yet.'

'I'm doing this, aren't I?'

'I didn't mean to sound as if I thought you were wimping out,' Ruth said quickly. 'Quite the opposite. You're being so . . . you're just as brave as you can be, Will. I don't know if I would be, in your position. I mean that.'

He did not say anything. His thin hands were clasped across his chest, the knuckles pushing at the flimsy bloodless skin, larger than they ought to be. There was a big purple contusion on the back of his left hand, spreading beneath the surface like spilled grape juice. He looked so frail. Almost transparent.

When he had gone to bed, in despair she called Lynda. 'It's Ruth Connelly.'

'Ruth! How are you? How's Will?'

Fighting to hold back her terrors, Ruth did not respond, and Lynda said, on a downward note: 'He's sick again.'

For answer, Ruth began to sob. She could hear the way the telephone amplified the sound of her pain and the breathing of her friend, steady as a heartbeat. Neither woman spoke, while Ruth, her heart shredding like paper, wept.

'I can't help you,' Lynda said finally. 'There is nothing I can . . . It was like this with Michelle. You have to

341

believe that it will be okay, Ruth. You have to go on believing that right to the end.'

'I can't do it. I know he's going to die.'

'That's not fair to him,' Lynda said sharply.

'Lynda, he's so sick. So sick. And I can't do anything for him, I can't take the pain away from him, I feel so . . . so completely useless.'

'You're not, Ruth. You've got to be strong because he can't be. Whatever you feel inside, you *must* be.'

'I know all that.' Ruth wiped the tears away with her fingers. 'But it doesn't make any difference. He's my son, my child, and he's dying and I can't do a single thing about it.'

'Except be there. Be strong. Not let him see your doubts.'

'Oh, Lynda.'

'It's all right, Ruth, it's all right.' Lynda's voice on the end of the line murmured and soothed.

But when she finally replaced the receiver, Ruth knew it was not all right. It was not.

He hardly ever saw her now. They passed each other in the hospital corridor, bumped into each other briefly in the parking lot. That was it. Nothing deliberate about it, just the way things were. They were both suffering and it seemed easier to suffer alone than together. Last time he'd seen her, she had looked dreadful, too thin, eyes over-bright, skin stretched to splitting point across her cheekbones. Always with a frown. When she looked at him, he wasn't even sure she saw him.

He nerved himself to pick up the phone and call her. 'Want me to come by, give you a break?' he asked.

'It's up to you.'

'If it would help . . .'

'It would help Will, I guess. At this stage, that's more important than either of us.'

'You're important too, Ruth,' he said quietly.

Her tone softened. 'Thank you, Paul.'

'What are your Christmas plans?'

'My parents are coming up from Florida.'

'Will mentioned you were going up to Maine.'

'Yes.'

'Staying at the Cabot Inn.'

'That's right.' She waited a fraction too long then said: 'What about you? What will you be doing?'

'Nothing in particular,' he said.

'Luke?'

'He'll be in Prague.'

'Will you be on your own?'

'Probably.'

There was another long pause then Ruth said unwillingly: 'I'm not sure about this, but Will would like it, so why don't you join us up in Sweetharbor?'

'Gee, you really know how to make a guy welcome.'

'A guy who walked out on us, Paul.'

'A guy who made a mistake he bitterly regrets,' he said. He bit his lip. 'I wish we could go back.'

'Back where?'

'To where we were.'

She made an inarticulate noise. 'Shit happens. It's happened to us. We can never go back.'

'We chose each other years ago and you're still the one I want to be with,' he said doggedly, almost sure it was still the truth. 'You and Will.'

'Too bad you didn't think of that before you left.'

I wish we were working things out together, instead of apart, he wanted to say. I wish we could share our

343

pain. But he was the one who had walked out and he had to accept her hostility. He even understood it. Will was what mattered, not her, not him. 'You haven't let me help with Will, this time round.'

'You haven't asked to.'

'I'm asking now.'

There was another long pause. Then she sighed. 'Why don't you join us for Christmas, Paul.'

18

Ruth found herself growing obsessed with the determination to ensure that this Christmas was as good as it could possibly be. Although there were boxes of decorations in the basement storage room, she frenetically shopped for more, hundreds of them. Strings of lights. Baubles and candles and glittery chains. Glass icicles, frosted silver balls, glossy red apples, candy-canes. Instead of just one, she bought several Christmas trees – one for the hall, one for the living room, a smaller one for the kitchen – and, with Will's help, loaded the branches down with golden stars and silver bells, iridescent ornaments, trails of silver glitter. She purchased armfuls of greenery from the flower shop, covering mantelpieces and furniture surfaces with pine and holly and eucalyptus leaves until the apartment smelled like a forest. She sat up at night stringing cranberries and popcorn, she purchased seasonal tablecloths and table napkins, played CDs of massed choirs singing carols.

This was going to be a good Christmas. The *best* Christmas. The very best she could make it. Because always, at the back of her mind, was a possibility she could scarcely bear to contemplate.

'What're you doing now?' Will asked one evening, as

she busily assembled sultanas and glacé cherries, pecans, almonds, candied orange peel, brandy. Ever since it had been agreed that they would go to Sweetharbor over the holiday, Ruth had watched him will himself to grow stronger again, to ignore the side effects of the cocktail of drugs he was taking to combat nausea, infection, ulceration.

'I'm making mince pies,' she said. 'Remember how you kids used to chop the goodies for me?'

'Remember how we needed a chisel to break through your pastry when they were done?'

'You're so mean.'

'Just teasing, Mom. But you have to admit you're not the world's best pastrymaker.'

'And you are, I suppose?'

'Better than you. Grandma showed me how.' He watched her awhile. 'Mom! Honestly.'

'*What?*'

'You can't squidge the stuff together like that. You're supposed to let the air get to it. Look, how about I make the pastry and you chop the stuff, okay?'

He came round the table. A medicinal smell emanated from his clothes, from his skin, his hair. His fingertips were white, his chalky nails edged in blue. She almost asked if he could manage but was able to bite the words back. 'Okay,' she said and turned away so he would not see the anguish in her face.

Ruth's parents arranged to fly up to Boston a few days before Christmas then pick up a hire car and drive the rest of the way to Sweetharbor.

'Want us to take Will up with us, hon?' her father asked. 'It'd leave you free to do last minute stuff if you need to.'

'Good idea. And it'd give you a chance to visit with him.'

'That's what we thought.'

'We could pick him up in Brunswick if you like, since you're spending a couple of days with Cousin Thalia.'

'Let's do that.' Jonathan Carter coughed. 'How's he doing?'

'Not good, Dad. Not too good.' Ruth let her shoulders slump: keeping up an appearance of cheerfulness was tiring. 'But he's really thrilled about being up there in Maine.'

'We are too. This is going to be the bes . . . a really *wonderful* Christmas,' her father said enthusiastically, but the words had a hollow ring, and Ruth remembered, with pain, how much he had loved the festive celebrations and how, as the preparations hotted up, he would rub his hands together and say: 'This is going to be the best Christmas ever.'

Paul picked Ruth up from the apartment and they drove up to Brunswick, hardly talking. Though the invitation to join them had originally been prompted by Will, she had felt a rush of compassion at the thought of Paul alone and unhappy, buying a tiny tree and some sad little decorations, throwing a TV dinner into the microwave, opening a bottle of wine and getting maudlin drunk. Now he seemed to find the situation as awkward to handle as she did. Stopping in Portland to buy coffee, they drank it quickly, standing by the car, stamping their feet, shoulders hunched against the cold, avoiding each other's gaze.

When they reached Cousin Thalia's gracious old house on Federal Street, Will was watching out for them, already dressed against the chill. He came running out to the car and hugged Ruth, his cheeks glowing. 'Come on, guys. Let's get moving,' he said. 'I can't wait to get there. It's gonna be *cool*.' He looked so happy that for the first time since the recurrence of his cancer, Ruth dared to allow herself just the smallest renewal of hope.

As they headed north on Route 1, the harsh reality of a Maine winter drew them in and enclosed them. On either side of the road the land lay leaden under thick steel-gray clouds. Trees crowded the edge of the road, so dark a green they were almost black, bent under the weight of the last snowfall. Fog pressed down on them and although the roads were clear between the piled-up banks of snow, visibility was low. The snow tires thrummed against the damp road.

For most of the drive, Paul sat in back with Will; every time Ruth glanced in the rearview mirror they both seemed to be asleep. But as they approached Sweetharbor, Will sat up. Ruth turned off the highway and began to negotiate the narrow lanes. As they passed the snowy turn down to the Hechsts' house, he said, 'Can we stop at Carter's House, Mom?'

'Will, I don't think I—'

'Let's at least go look at it. Please?'

'Good idea,' Paul said. 'Check the place out.'

She felt his finger lightly brush her cheek. Did he understand how she felt? 'Just look, no more than that,' Ruth said, and was surprised at how unsteady her voice was. Even though she had gone to the house last summer, walked up to Caleb's Point, found a measure of healing there, to come here at this special time of year, with her estranged husband and her sick son, was an experience she shrank from. 'Just look.'

'That's all,' Will promised.

She reached the turnoff to the house. Snow had drifted up against the trees and the sagging stone wall which someone had built years ago and which had been quietly collapsing ever since. The wooden house sign above the postbox was faded, almost unreadable, the letters obliterated by wind and weather. The track was covered in snow, but the overhanging trees had provided some protection so that they were able to bump along until they came out of the pine woods.

'Oh,' breathed Will. 'Look at that, will you?'

The house and barn glowed in the last of the winter daylight. The sun hung low in the misty sky, indistinct and hazy as though submerged in dry ice. The flat pasture was a thick pale blue, and beyond it the spired spruces stood black and cold.

William sighed with pleasure. He squeezed his mother's hand. 'It looks just great.'

'Just the way I remember it,' said Paul. He leaned forward and Ruth felt his breath against her neck. 'It's so good to be back.'

We're *not* back, Ruth thought. We're here, but we're not *back*. We can never be back.

'Can I get out?' Will asked.

'If you want,' she said. 'Just make sure you've got your—' but he had already opened the door and jumped into the snow. They watched him struggle toward the house, whooping faintly with joy, tumbling into the snow and dragging himself up again. His breath hung in the icy air.

'Will he be okay?' asked Paul.

'Tomorrow he'll be bruised and his joints'll ache, but the hell with that. It's so good to see him happy again.'

'He looks like one of Santa's little helpers in that red ski-suit.'

349

'Not so little anymore.'

'And that ridiculous woollen hat: where'd he get that?'

'Amy Prescott knitted it for him.' Ruth put a hand to her face. Her throat was thick.

As though he understood what she was feeling, Paul said: 'We can't worry about the future.'

'Easier to say than to do.'

'I know that.'

Ruth said softly: 'I'm so afraid he's not going to make it.' The scene in front of her was like a Wyeth painting, the white snow, the boy in his red clothes, and beyond him the dark shuttered house, no lights in the windows, no voices in the hall, no laughter falling down the stairs, closed round its battalions of ghosts, its shriveled memories.

'I can't possibly reassure you.' Paul took her hand. 'I can't wave a magic wand and make it all better for any of us.'

'I know that.'

'Let's at least try to enjoy the next few days. Give Will the best Christmas we can.'

'Yes.'

Dr and Mrs Carter arrived the following morning. While they were settling into their room, Will announced that after lunch they – *all* of them – had to go up to Carter's House and find a tree to decorate. 'And not just any old tree,' he said, 'but the *perfect* tree.' He grinned at his mother: it was what she used to say each year, wrapping the children up against the cold before they went out with an ax to search the woods.

'I think Grandad and I'll stay behind and unpack,' said Betty, glancing out at the somber sky. A few snowflakes whirled and danced on the other side of the glass. 'You don't mind, do you, dear?'

'You two can't skulk in here for the rest of the holiday,' Ruth said.

'I wasn't planning to skulk so much as put my feet up, watch the ball game, grab a beer or two,' said Jonathan.

'You're going to have to face the outdoors *some* time.'

'Why didn't you bring one of the trees up from the apartment?'

'Because in Maine you have to have a Maine tree,' Will said.

'Okay, but we don't have to look for it this afternoon, do we?' pleaded his grandmother. 'Let me psych myself up first.' She shuddered elaborately. 'Snow: I hate the stuff.'

'Me too,' said Jonathan. 'Don't forget I'm an old man, and shaky on my pins.'

'You're not that old,' said Will firmly, 'and not that shaky.'

'I can't leave your grandmother all on her own.'

'Mom'll be fine here till we get back,' Ruth said.

'I've got an idea.' Will looked at his parents. 'How about us four scout the trees first. Then we can come back and get Grandma.'

'Bad idea,' said Paul. 'If I'm going to suffer, I want everybody else to as well.'

'Much better if I stay behind and keep Grandma company,' said Jonathan cravenly. 'And if you see the perfect tree, just you go right ahead and get it. Don't bother coming back for us.'

'Grandad, you can't chicken out.'

'Why not?'

'You've *got* to come along. You always used to.'

Dr Carter allowed his gaze to wander over his grandson's face. He tutted theatrically. 'Okay,' he said. 'I'll come. But I get to eat lunch first, right?'

'Right.'

After lunch, while Paul and the Carters lingered over coffee, Will and Ruth went out into Old Port Street. The sky was overcast, the light dull, but the pure cold of the wind on Ruth's face was invigorating. Her sense of constriction had lifted, as it always did when she was up here; the fast pace of city life, the stress of Will's disease, chipped away from her like plaster and she felt a freedom she had almost forgotten.

They walked along the waterfront, bent against the wind. Overnight the temperature had plummeted. In the harbor, the water slapped hard at the wooden pilings of the dock, gray and troubled; further out, it dashed itself repeatedly against the tumbled rocks of the little bay, sending up clouds of spray. Seagulls swooped beyond the squat fishing boats, diving for scraps, squabbling over bits of refuse. Lobster traps wrapped in frosty predator nets were stacked on the dock. The lowering sky bleached everything of color except the lobster floats.

Ruth shivered. 'Doesn't it look chilly.'

'The water's always cold up here,' said Will. He had his hands plunged into his pockets. A thick lumberman's cap was pulled down over his head. 'Even in summer.'

'Want to go to Don's Donuts?' Ruth asked.

'Okay.'

Ruth brought two coffees and a donut over to the narrow table by the window where Will was looking out at the street. 'There you are.' She watched him lick a finger and touch the sugary coating, the way his sister used to do. 'Apple-cinnamon. Josie's favorite,' she said.

He shook his head. 'No, Mom,' he said patiently. 'It wasn't.'

'Yes, it was.'

'Maybe when she was like, fourteen,' he said. 'She liked the chocolate ones much better.'

'Did she?' She frowned. 'Are you sure?'

He nodded, lifting the donut to his mouth and taking a bite which left his lips covered in fine white sugar. Looking at his illness-ravaged face in the unforgiving light off the sea, Ruth was struck by a despair so profound that she could scarcely find strength to lift her mug. 'There's sugar on your—' she began, but could not finish the sentence.

As though reading her thoughts, Will smiled slightly and rubbed at the steamy glass beside him so he could see outside. 'Looks pretty, doesn't it?'

'All dressed up for Christmas.'

Lights were strung across the street, and round the eaves of the buildings. Snow lay piled up at the edge of the sidewalks: red-ribboned garlands of evergreen decorated the shopfronts. On the other side of the road, the Cabot Lodge had several small spruces set up on the roof of its front porch, trimmed with tiny white lights which blinked on and off. The shops were draped with tinsel, lights, plastic likenesses of Santa Claus and his sleigh. In the city, they might have looked tacky; here, she could not imagine it any other way.

When they had finished their coffees, Will walked back to the hotel while Ruth went into the drugstore. As she was choosing giftwrap, someone said: 'It's good to see you again.'

'Mrs Hechst . . . Trudi,' Ruth exclaimed. 'How are you?'

'Just fine.' Gertrud Hechst examined her from large pale eyes. 'And you, Ruth?'

'I'm doing okay.' Ruth nodded her head up and down several times to emphasize just how okay she was.

'I'm glad you have come back here for Christmas.'

'So are we.'

'Carter's House full again: this is good.'

'We're not actually staying up at the cottage.'

'You are not?'

Ruth shook her head. 'We're at the Cabot Inn.'

'But why? This is not home. You should not be spending the holiday in a hotel.'

'Will wanted to come, and I couldn't face opening up the house. So we compromised.'

'Such a compromise.' The broad round face was suddenly creased with concern. 'I have heard that William is not well.'

'He's very *un*well.' Ruth tried to smile but could not quite make it. 'And very happy to be up here again.'

'But he should be in his own home on Christmas Day.'

'He seems to be enjoying staying at the inn. Tyler Reed is being very kind, letting us to treat the place like our own home.'

'He is the son of my husband's cousin,' Trudi said, smiling. 'Naturally he is kind.'

'He's told Will we can put a tree up in our suite so this afternoon we're going up to Carter's House to find one.'

'Good, good. Nonetheless, this is not right, to be in a hotel at Christmas time . . .' The older woman suddenly took Ruth's arm. 'I have an idea. Ruth, why do you not bring your family to my house for dinner on Christmas Day?'

'What a kind thought,' said Ruth, somewhat taken aback.

Trudi smiled delightedly. 'A good idea, yes?'

Ruth shook her head. 'Thank you, but we couldn't possibly intrude on you: there are far too many of us. My parents are with us. And—' And besides, we hardly know you, she wanted to add. Although we have been acquainted all our lives, we do not know you.

'The more the merrier – isn't that what they say? Especially on Christmas Day.'

'I'm very touched,' Ruth said. 'It's so kind of you. But I really don't think—'

'*We* should like it very much.' Trudi stared at her with a quizzical expression on her face.

Josie's voice came back to Ruth: *To you, the year-rounders are just specimens, like something in a museum. I see them as real people, living real lives.* 'All right,' she said suddenly. 'I think that would be a wonderful idea. But only if you let us make some contribution.'

'It isn't necessary. We always have way too much.'

'We couldn't intrude unless we contribute,' Ruth said firmly. 'Wine? Fruit? Cheese? What would you like?'

'It is not necessary,' Gertrud repeated.

'We'll see.' Ruth smiled and was surprised at how stiff her facial muscles felt, as though smiling were something they had long forgotten how to do. 'Thank you, Trudi.'

Crossing the road, she went back into the hotel and up to her room. Will was sitting on the couch, earphones on, reading an Asterix book. She tapped him on the shoulder. When he looked up, taking off his earphones, she asked: 'Gertrud Hechst asked us over for Christmas dinner and I said yes. Is that okay?'

'Cool!' he said. 'I really like the Hechsts.'

'Me too. What I know of them.'

Though this small community had always played an important part in her life, yet Ruth knew almost nothing about the people who inhabited it. *Knew* them, yes. Smiled at them in the town. Stopped and chatted if she met them in the woods. Bought lobster from them, or raspberries, took jars of their preserves home to the city with her, was glad to hear of weddings or new babies, shared their sorrow when someone died. But who they were, what their background was, she had little idea. For the most part, the summer people did not really care about the year-rounders: local lives did not impinge on the city folks.

By the afternoon, the temperature had fallen even further. Paul drove them all up to Carter's House and parked in front of the barn. Icicles fringed the roof of the porch, sharp and deadly as dragon's teeth. At the side of the house, the frozen pond was covered in silvery-blue ice, thick enough to skate on.

'Okay, people, out you get.' Paul glanced at Ruth. She looked pinched and pale. Had coming up here been a good idea? Perhaps there were too many memories for her to handle. He knew she wouldn't mention them, that she would contain them, deal with them on her own, in her own way.

'Lord,' grumbled Dr Carter, climbing down into the snow, then helping his wife out of the vehicle. 'What did we ever do to deserve this?' He put his arm round her shoulder. 'Want to move back up here, hon, or shall we stay in Florida?'

Paul looked at the wide doors of the barn. Will was right: they could easily get the mastless *Lucky Duck* in there. The day after Christmas, the two of them might go down to the boatyard, ask about getting the boat moved. If Will was feeling up to it. Paul glanced across at his son: the initial euphoria of their arrival had given way to exhaustion and there were gray hollows under his eyes.

Whatever he had said to Ruth, Paul knew it wasn't enough to live for the day. For Will's sake they had to act as though there was a future as well as a present.

'Shall we get the skates out of the barn?' Will said.

His grandmother shuddered under the bulk of her long quilted coat. 'Not for me, hon.'

'Grandad says you used to be a champion skater when you were a kid.'

'That was a long time ago, dear.'

'Bet you still look good in one of those short skirts,' said her husband.

'Way to go, Gran!'

'Bet you could still do a pirouette or two,' agreed Jonathan. 'You've certainly got the legs for it.'

'Well, I'm not showing my legs to anyone at my age, especially in this kind of weather, and you just hush up, Jonathan Carter, and you too, William. Should be ashamed, making fun of an old lady.' Betty Carter wagged a finger at her grandson. 'Now, I'd be glad to watch you, Will, if *you* want to try.'

'Not today, Grandma.'

'Right.' Paul clapped his mittened hands together, issuing instructions, taking charge the way he used to do. 'Just so we don't all get exhausted, as well as soaking wet, I suggest we confine our search for the perfect tree to the area round the house. How about we meet back here in what, ten, fifteen minutes?'

'How about we just jump in the car and go back to our nice warm hotel suite,' said Jonathan.

'Silence in the ranks,' Paul said.

'Grandad, what a wimp you are.'

'My feet have turned to blocks of solid ice just standing here,' the doctor complained.

Paul knew the moans were exaggerated, part of a show put on for Will's benefit. 'Okay, Dad, quit bellyaching,' he said. 'You can manage ten minutes rummaging round in the snow, can't you?'

'Do I have a choice?'

'No,' Will said, laughing.

'Don't blame me if we catch pneumonia,' Jonathan grumbled.

'Remember we're not looking for some giant tree, we want something about three or four feet high, that's all,' said Paul. He moved to stand beside Ruth who was hugging herself against the cold, a fur hat pulled down low over her fair hair. 'Are you all right?' he asked, reaching for her hand.

'Just fine.' She pulled away. 'Let's get moving, shall we, before we all freeze to the spot?' She began trudging toward the edge of the pasture where the trees began.

Paul followed, snow crunching under his boots. Fog was drifting in from the ocean, damp and wet. He pulled at her sleeve. 'Stop, Ruth.'

'Why?'

'Look at the light on the house. It's beautiful, isn't it?'

She turned. 'Yes.'

'We had some good times here.'

'Yes, we did.'

'And could do so again.'

358

'I don't think so.'

'Different good times, Ruth.' His heart felt heavy. She looked so beaten down. If only he could have taken her in his arms as he used to do. Soothe her, tell her things would work out somehow. 'I'm glad we're going to have dinner with the Hechsts tomorrow.'

'You know what's strange,' Ruth said. 'I've lived here all my life, and I've never once been inside their house. That's part of what – what Josie used to object to, wasn't it? The way the summer folk act as though the year-round people hardly exist.'

'Josie exaggerated things, but yes, she was right.'

'We ought to be more involved.'

'How?'

'I don't really know.'

Will's voice traveled across the snow toward them. 'Here it is! I found it. The perfect tree!'

'Okay,' Paul shouted back. 'We're coming.' He took Ruth's arm again and this time she did not shrug him away as they tramped back across the frozen pasture toward their son.

After dinner in the hotel restaurant, they went back to their suite. An artificial log-fire burned in the open hearth. Dr Carter poured whiskey for the adults, gave Will a Pepsi from the icebox by the TV. 'It's almost like home here,' he said.

'And it's so beautifully warm,' said Betty.

Ruth sat on the floor, wrapping presents for the Hechsts. The room was filled with the spicy scent of fresh pine from the tree they had cut. Before dinner, Paul and Will had decorated it; now it sparkled and shimmered, its delicate ornaments and tinsel streamers lifting with every tiny current of air.

'You should have gone skating, Grandma,' Will said.

'Yes, dear.'

Ruth had a mental image of her daughter, dressed in something blue, leaving tracks across the icy pond as she spun and twirled, golden in the light reflected from the house. She suddenly felt the need, in this family gathering, to talk about the daughter she had enclosed inside herself for so long. She opened her mouth. 'Remember how good a skater Josie used to be?'

'Until she got scared off, because of that girl at her school,' said Will.

'Went skating one winter and drowned, didn't she?' Paul got up and began refilling their glasses.

'Ashley Brandon.' Will nodded his head. 'The ice broke up under her.'

'So sad,' Ruth's mother said. 'I remember Josie telling me about it.'

'Yeah: that's why she wouldn't skate anymore.'

'I'd tell her over and over she couldn't possibly fall through,' Paul agreed. 'She never believed me. Stuff'd be inches thick but she wouldn't put so much as a toe on it.'

We're talking like a normal family, Ruth thought. A sudden rush of optimism filled her. Things would turn out all right. All would be well.

Will peered between the heavy drapes which covered the window. 'It's snowing again, Grandad,' he announced happily.

'Lordy. *Please* can I go back to Florida?'

'No way. You gotta tough it out.'

The others laughed.

This is *good*, Ruth thought. We have done well here. We're making the best of things. She thought of Carter's House, alone in the snow, empty except for its ghosts.

She wished she had felt able to open up the place for Christmas. But she was too sad and dispirited for that. She saw Will watching her and forced herself to smile.

They drove along the snow-thick lanes to the Hechsts' big weathered house. The day was dull again, trees beaded with fog, sky shrouded, almost as dark as at sundown. As they pulled up by the wicket gate, the dogs began to bark, the sound echoing, thrown back to them by the mist. Lemon light spilled out onto the snow as the genial figure of Dieter Hechst stood in the doorway. 'Happy Christmas,' he called. 'And welcome.'

'Hi, Mr Hechst.' Running up the icy steps of the porch, Will slipped and ended up at Dieter's feet in a shower of snow.

'How're you, son?' Laughing, Dieter gave the boy an arm to help him back onto his feet. 'Take your things off and go on inside, where it's warm.'

As she reached the top of the steps, Dieter took Ruth's hand in both of his and pressed it against his chest. 'Welcome to our house.'

'It's so kind of you to have us.'

'It's good of you to join us.' Dieter was a handsome, placid man with a direct gaze. 'Trudi is some pleased.'

Ruth heard him greeting the others as she passed into a small cloakroom area full of snowshoes and boots and heavy winter outerwear, along with overwintering geraniums and trays of plant cuttings, apples carefully laid out so none of them touched each other, root vegetables in wooden boxes. She removed her coat and hung it up, changed her shoes and went in to where Gertrud stood waiting for her, dressed in a thick woollen skirt with a flowered shawl pinned across her shoulders.

The wood-lined living room was a single large space stretching the entire length of the house. The ceiling was wooden too, the crossbeams carved and painted in red and green. Bookshelves covered half of one wall, crammed with an eclectic collection of hardback novels, art books, volumes of popular philosophy, cookbooks, books of photography. Beautiful objects were set about the room: pieces of silver and glass which caught the firelight, wooden statues, a large swan made of cotton and paper, ceramics, hand-painted plates, carved angels with golden wings and shining faces. And everywhere there were candles, dozens of them, on the floor, on the polished surfaces, on the elaborately laid table, on the piano at the far end of the room and on the modern harpsichord at right angles to it. A Christmas tree stood between the windows, unornamented except for small creamy candles set into holders attached to its dark-green branches. Beside the wood-burning stove was a basket containing an elderly cat. Through the window Ruth could see the ruins of Gertrud's summer garden, and beyond it a snow-covered salt meadow, faintly indigo in the winter light, stretching toward a dark stand of firs.

There were other people already seated on the deep sofas on either side of the stove: an elderly lady, a man in a Scandinavian sweater, a woman with the same round face as Trudi, another man in a forest-green jacket with silver buttons, a fair-haired young woman with a baby. The long room was full of fragrances: woodsmoke, roasting meat, aniseed and oranges, wine and spices, candle wax.

Ruth opened her mouth in surprise and delight. 'How beautiful,' she exclaimed softly. 'How lovely.'

As though in a dream, she saw Will's face, its

angularity softened by the light from the candles, saw Paul greeting the other people, saw her parents come in, shaking snow off their jackets, stamping their boots on the floor, changing into indoor shoes. Paul was carrying a supermarket carton which he took into the kitchen. Her father embraced Gertrud, saying it had been a long time, far too long, and rubbed his hands together as he advanced toward the open doors of the wood-burning stove and held them to the flames.

'This is wonderful,' he said. 'Happy Christmas to all of you.'

They were introduced to each other: Dieter's mother, Trudi's sister and her husband, and their daughter, the girl with the baby, Dieter's brother. Mugs of mulled wine were passed around, hot and spicy, each one topped with a clove-studded sliver of orange peel. Will held the baby, Paul listened attentively to Trudi's sister, the fair-haired girl laughed at something Dieter's mother was saying, the man in the green jacket talked to his brother-in-law in the sweater.

Standing apart from them, observing rather than participating, Ruth was overcome by a complicated feeling of envy and sadness. *A gift from a true love . . .* Paul had read the words aloud one long-ago summer, both of them arrogant and happy under the trees, both of them secure in the belief that nothing would ever disrupt their golden lives. And now she knew what the writer had meant about coming back to Maine: it was to find this sense of shared contentment. I want what these people have, she thought. I want to be part of these warm rich lives, but I am on the outside, cut off, alienated. She visualized the sad empty house through the trees, and the spirit of Christmases now gone.

She followed Trudi into the kitchen. It was large and

warm, full of free-standing pieces of unpainted polished pine. Another cat washed itself on a chair near the window. A big table stood in the center of the room, piled with plates and pitchers, dishes ready to be filled with food, butter, cut-glass bowls, serving spoons, baskets of nuts and rosy apples, a platter of cheeses, mince pies, *stollen*, cookies, chocolate-covered stars fragrant with anise. 'Can I help?' she said, and hoped she did not sound too wistful.

Gertrud was busy lifting the lids of various pans and sniffing the contents. 'Mmm,' she said. 'This sauce is *good*. Taste that.' She held a spoon toward Ruth.

'What is it?'

'For the turkey.'

'Delicious.'

'It is a special recipe. Juices from the bird and a little flour, of course, to thicken it, and much wine, and a little dash of Cointreau, onion, orange peel, other things.'

Ruth sat on the edge of the table, swinging a leg. 'This is so kind of you, Trudi. Inviting us to join you.'

'It is nothing.'

'Five extra people is nothing?'

'We are glad to have you.'

How generous she was. How warm. Ruth recalled the way she had come into Carter's House and helped in the sad days after Josie's death.

Trudi said: 'What exactly is wrong with Will?'

Ruth clasped her arms protectively across her chest. 'He has leukemia.' The word sounded sharp and jagged in this warm room.

'Oh, my dear, that is terrible.'

'During the summer we thought he'd recovered, but it's come back.'

'The poor boy. From the way he behaves, you would hardly know he was sick. You must be a very special person, Ruth.'

'Me?' Ruth laughed a little sadly. 'I don't think so.'

'Yes,' insisted Trudi, stirring, tasting, opening the oven to look at the turkey, while Ruth began to unpack the carton Paul had dumped on the table. 'To have such wonderful children is an achievement. Josie too was very precious.'

'She was – but it was not because of anything I did.'

'Children do not grow in isolation. So much depends on what they are given by their parents. There was a lot of you in Josie, I saw it often when she was here.'

'I neglected her. Emotionally, I mean.'

'Josie was not neglected in any sense.'

'*She* thought so. She told me.' Ruth bent her head over the carton, not wanting Gertrud to see the tears in her eyes. 'We argued all the time. Especially that last summer, before she . . . before the accident.'

'This is so normal, Ruth. So usual. We have not had children of our own, Dieter and I, but we have seen it often in the families of our friends. Josie was growing up, she had found her own path to follow and it was different from yours. That is all.'

Was she right? From the carton, Ruth pulled out the bottles of wine she had brought, a bottle of Scotch, Swiss chocolate candies, a honey-roasted ham, a whole camembert. 'I believe she hated me.'

'Ruth, you must not say such things. Josephine always spoke of you with admiration and with love.'

'Did she?' The thought was comforting. She wished it was true.

'Listen to what I tell you: good children come from good parents. You must believe that.'

365

'Shall I put these under the tree?' Ruth said, holding the wrapped gifts she had brought, trying to hold back sudden tears.

'You should not have brought us anything.'

'I wanted to.' Awkwardly, Ruth added: 'Trudi, when Josie was drowned you were wonderful. I don't believe I ever properly thanked you for taking such good care of us.'

'We felt for you so much. We too loved Josie. It was like losing one of our own.'

'Oh, Trudi . . .' Ruth struggled to compose herself.

Trudi saw the things Ruth had put out on the table and held her hands up in surprise. 'What is this?'

'I told you we couldn't come unless we brought some things with us.'

'Such gifts,' said Trudi. 'So much. Cheese and wine and . . .' She smiled at Ruth, her broad face flushed with heat. 'Thank you.' She bent down to look in the oven and straightened up again. 'I think it is time to eat. This bird is telling me he is ready for the table.'

It took them more than two hours to do justice to the Dickensian feast Gertrud had prepared. The turkey was moist, the vegetables delicious, the cranberry and orange sauce outstanding. There were piles of moistly golden corn-bread, a dish of sweet potato puréed with butternut squash, red cabbage cooked with onion and apple, wild rice, roast potatoes, home-made sausages.

Paul and Dieter's brother engaged in a heated political debate with the brother-in-law about the United States' role in Latin America, old Mrs Hechst and Betty Carter reminisced about Sweetharbor in the old days, Dieter Hechst brought Dr Carter up to date on the many families whose children he had delivered over the years.

Will sat between Trudi and the fair-haired girl, with a small smile on his face, watching them all but saying very little. He was pale. Sitting opposite him, next to Paul, Ruth could see how much effort he was making not to lose a moment of this special time.

There was a lull in the conversation as they finished their coffee. Outside, the dark day was disappearing into night. Wind rattled at the windows.

'Why don't you play us something?' Dieter said to his wife.

'In a minute, Dieter,' said Trudi, smiling. 'Let me rest for a while and then we shall sing, yes?'

'Do *you* play?' Dieter asked Ruth.

'I'm afraid not.'

'I don't know why you say that,' Ruth's mother said. 'You had lessons when you were a little girl.'

'I never had time,' said Ruth, remembering how once she had loved to sit at the keys and let the music flow from her fingers. 'Not after I went back to work.'

Paul was flushed, his blue eyes crinkled with laughter. He put his hand over Ruth's. 'She used to be really good.'

Gertrud smiled at the company, swallowed the last of her coffee and wiped her mouth on her linen napkin. 'Now I will play, but only for a little.'

She went over to the grand piano and sat down. For a moment she stared at the keys. Then she began to play, her blunt work-roughened fingers moving effortlessly from Debussy to Mozart and on to Chopin.

Ruth was amazed. The music pierced her, filling her with longing for something which she could almost grasp yet which still eluded her. It had never occurred to her that such talent was to be found up here. Catching the deep calm gaze of Dieter Hechst, she blushed, ashamed, hoping he had not been able to read her thoughts. He smiled a little, and she knew that he had.

Another notion struck her: all her life she had been aware of the Hechsts simply as hardworking local people. This was the first time she had ever set foot in their house. Yet Great-Great-Grandfather Carter had also been a year-rounder. So, for many years, had her father.

'That is it,' Trudi said eventually. 'I have played enough.'

Though the others begged her to continue she shook her head. 'It is your turn to entertain now,' she said.

Dieter threw more wood on the stove and sparks flew up the chimney as the driftwood twisted and charred, tiny blue seaflames dancing along the branches. Trudi went into the kitchen and came back with a tray of glasses and a pitcher of eggnog.

'In a minute, we shall sing together,' she said. 'But first everyone must make a toast. And I will start. Here's to family.' They raised their glasses. 'How lucky we are to be together yet another year.'

'Here's to Christmas,' Dieter said.

'And to prosperity,' said his brother.

'To friends,' Trudi's sister said.

In a heavy German accent, her mother added: 'And to many children.'

'To music and laughter,' said Trudi's sister's husband.

'To roast turkey,' Paul said, patting his stomach, and everyone cheered.

Will lifted his glass. 'To Josie,' he said. 'To my sister.' He looked round at them with sparkling eyes. 'I just wish she was here.'

As the others raised their glasses to Josie, Ruth knew with sudden piercing clarity that she *was* there. The conviction was so strong that she almost voiced it aloud. She had a vision of future Christmases, of family holidays, family gatherings, and someone telling the story of doomed Josephine Connelly, the girl who had drowned in the cold waters off Caleb's Point. Josie would become another Carter legend, always young, always beautiful. She would take her place alongside drunken Preacher Downey and Great-Great-Grandmother slowly sinking in the bog. There would be continuity here. Even though Josie was long gone, she would always be part of this place.

She caught Will's gaze and smiled at him, wondering who those families would be. Not Carters, she thought. Not even Connellys.

Oh, Will . . . my child, my beloved son. Quietly pushing back her chair, she got up and went over to the window to stare out into the darkness, blinking away the tears which had filled her eyes. After a while, she felt Trudi Hechst's hand on her shoulder. She leaned her head against the older woman's shoulder and they stood together without speaking.

Eventually Ruth said: 'Trudi, I can't tell you how wonderful this afternoon has been. It's meant so much to Will.'

'It has been a valuable time.'

Ruth knew she was talking about the joining of two worlds which hitherto had existed isolated from each other. 'For us too,' she said.

'Now, we must sing,' Trudi said. 'Come, Ruth. Do you want to start?'

'Sing? Alone?' Ruth shook her head.

'You must join in.'

'No. No, I couldn't.'

'We will ask my husband, then. He has a fine voice.'

Trudi returned to the piano. 'Dieter. Please . . .' She struck some chords on the piano and Dieter rose to his feet. He beamed round at them all and then, when his wife had played the introduction, sang Schubert's *Elf King* in a beautifully rolling tenor. As the last German phrases faded away, they all applauded.

'Goodness,' Betty Carter said. 'You sound like a professional.'

He nodded. 'For a while I hoped I might be. But there were too many other young men with good voices. And my family needed what I could earn. So I became a carpenter instead.'

'What a good thing you did,' Paul said. 'You're a craftsman, Dieter. A genius.'

'Thank you, Herr Professor. And now, perhaps *you* will sing.'

'I can't sing, but I'll recite a poem,' Paul said. He stood up, harrumphed a bit, flexed his fingers, entering into the spirit of the afternoon. 'I can give you a tear-jerking rendition of "Father, Dear Father, Come Home With Me Now". Or perhaps "Little Orphan Annie", in full Hoosier dialect. Or even "Christmas Day in the Workhouse", except it goes on for twenty-one long verses.' He picked up his glass. 'But since we seem to be getting through a lot of booze at the hospitable table of our friends Gertrud and Dieter Hechst, I shall recite you an improving tale called: "The Lips That Touch Liquor Shall Never Touch Mine".'

He declaimed the ballad with much flourishing of his hands and rolling of his eyes, using such a ludicrous falsetto for the girl's voice, so deep a bass for the man's, that his audience collapsed into gales of laughter. He fits in here, Ruth thought, with a queer little ache. He belongs here in a way I never have.

'Bravo, Herr Professor,' Dieter said, when Paul finally sat down. 'Now who is next?' He looked at his mother. 'How about you, *Mutti*?'

'I have no longer the voice,' Mrs Hechst said, 'but I will sing a song from the old country, which was so lovely, even though it became a song of the last war.'

Gertrud nodded. Softly, she began to play 'Lili Marlene' and gradually everyone joined in except Will and the fair-haired girl, both too young to know the song. Listening as they harmonized, lost in the tune, Ruth found herself very close to tears again. 'Oh please,' she said, when it was over, 'play that again. It was beautiful.'

When they had repeated it, Gertrud said quietly: 'And now you, Ruth. Will you sing us something?'

Ruth shrank back in her seat, paralyzed, incapable of standing up in front of these people. 'I really can't sing.'

'Go on,' Paul said. 'Anything would do. Recite a limerick.'

Ruth shook her head and, with a sympathetic glance, Gertrud asked someone else. One by one, everyone round the table performed. Trudi's sister produced a violin and the two women played a piece of Bach together. Jonathan and Betty Carter sang 'Drink To Me Only With Thine Eyes', the fair-haired girl sang a duet with her father, Will half-sang, half-spoke a rap number while Paul accompanied him by rhythmically slapping the edge of the table.

They finished by standing round the piano singing carols, while the candles flickered on the Christmas tree and the blue dusk turned to black across the snow.

Later, as they began their goodbyes and thanks, struggling into coats and boots, preparing for the dash to the car through the deepening snow, Dieter Hechst took Ruth's hand and raised it to his lips in an old-fashioned, European gesture. 'You must not worry,' he murmured. 'Things will work out.'

She looked up at him. 'I don't think so,' she said sadly.

'Be strong, Ruth.'

Paul appeared, put his arm round her shoulders, kissed the side of her neck. 'Come on, Ruthie, you look tired,' he said. 'Better get you home.'

Driving away, Ruth carefully did not look at the path which led between the trees to their own deserted house with its shuttered windows.

Back at the hotel, they sat round the fire, opening their gifts. Betty poured eggnog for herself and Will; Jonathan and Paul moved on to Scotch. Will's cheeks were flushed, clown-patches against the paleness of his face. 'That was great,' he said.

'Wasn't it fun?' Betty said. 'I don't know when I've enjoyed myself so much.'

'Remember we used to sing together at parties?' Jonathan responded. 'We should do it more often.'

'That was back when you were expected to sing for your supper.'

'Makes a change from the TV, doesn't it?'

'Mom, you should've done something,' said Will.

'Don't you start nagging at your mom,' Paul said quickly.

'But she was the only one who—'

'Mom's tired,' said Paul. 'Wasn't it terrific when Mrs Hechst played?'

Ruth smiled at him gratefully. 'I had no idea she could play at all,' she said. 'Let alone so beautifully.'

'Almost a virtuoso,' agreed Paul.

'She used to teach piano,' said Will. 'Didn't you know?'

'I did once,' Jonathan said. 'I'd forgotten.'

'Josie used to go down there and play duets with her.'

'She did?' Had Josie deliberately kept her life hidden or had Ruth simply been too preoccupied with her own concerns to see it?

'Yeah,' said Will. 'Mrs Hechst was going to be a concert pianist when she was young. And then she met Mr Hechst and he swept her off her feet. So she says. He was really handsome when he was young, according to Mrs Hechst.'

'Still is,' said Ruth's mother. 'If I was twenty years younger . . .'

Dr Carter, his pipe lit and a glass of Scotch in his hand, sat back in his chair. 'I feel kind of ashamed,' he said. 'All the years there've been Carters living here, and Hechsts living down the road from us, and we've never invited them to our table, not once.'

'We're just summer people,' said Will. 'That's one of the things Josie always got so uptight about, the way the summer people kind of look down on the year-rounders.'

'I don't,' Paul said.

'Maybe not you, Dad. But the Trotmans, for instance. Or the Kauffmans. Or even the Steins. Like they think the Hechsts and the Cottons and the Coombs are just servants or something.'

'The Coombs go right back to the Pilgrim Fathers,' Paul said.

'I wish *we* could be year-rounders.' Will lay back tiredly against the pillows on the sofa. 'I'd *really* like that.'

'No real reason why not,' said Paul.

'Well, then. Let's do it.'

'The winters!' Ruth's mother shuddered.

'It'd need some planning,' Paul said. 'I'd have to give up my Boston job if we came up here permanently. I guess I could still manage to teach at Bowdoin twice a week, but getting down to Boston would be a killer, especially in the winter.'

It was as if he had forgotten that he had made other choices, chosen to follow different paths.

19

Just before the Easter weekend, Dr Gearin called Ruth into his office. She knew already what she would hear. It was impossible to ignore the fact that Will was not thriving. 'Will's last CBC was discouraging,' he said. The brown teddy-bear eyes were dulled by the difficulty of what he had to say. 'There's been no improvement in his blood count for some weeks. Quite the opposite, in fact.'

'What does this mean, exactly?'

'We keep on trying.'

'But you're not hopeful.'

'We're always hopeful. We never know what might not lie around the corner in terms of treatment breakthroughs.'

'But if there isn't a breakthrough—'

He gazed mournfully at Ruth. 'Then I suppose, yes, things are looking less good than we might have wished.'

Ruth had tried to pretend away her doubts and fears. Now, made concrete by the physician's words, hopelessness ran along the narrow byways of her body, leaking out into her bloodstream, saturating her with prophetic grief. Rocking forward, she put her hand over her mouth.

Gearin half-rose from behind his desk. 'Are you all right, Ruth?'

'No, Mike. I'm not all right. I'm not. I'm about as far from all right as I could be.' Harsh gasps of pain were torn from her throat. 'How can I stand by and watch him die?'

He came to stand beside her. 'It hasn't come to that yet. Not anywhere near it. As you know, your parents were not a match for Will so our best hope now is to find a bone marrow donor.'

'Even if you did, it's not going to make any difference in the long run,' Ruth said dejectedly.

'It's not like you to be so defeatist.'

'It is, Mike. It's just I've been hiding it all these months, playing at being brave and cheerful and full of hope. I've had to, haven't I? What else could I do? But now . . . I might as well face the fact that my son is going to die.'

'Do that if you want to, Ruth.' Gearin's voice was deliberately contemptuous. 'If that's how you choose to deal with it, then you must go that route. If you want Will to pick up the vibes from you, then you just go right ahead and make it even worse for him.' He tidied his case notes. 'Maybe you should change to another specialist—'

'What?'

'—because I don't think I can go on working with someone who gives up so easily. Someone who's only concerned with her own thoughts and feelings.'

There was a silence. Ruth twisted the wedding ring on her finger. 'You're right, of course,' she said quietly.

'Good.' His smile was sad. 'We're now going to undertake a serious search for a non-related bone marrow donor, since we haven't found a match in the immediate family. So we consult the worldwide register.'

'How does that work?'

'It's a register of non-related donors – people who've volunteered to provide bone marrow to someone who needs it. Their blood samples have already been analyzed and registered. There are three million names on it, so there's a good chance we might get lucky. Basically, a technician will sit down at a computer and feed the details of Will's tissue type into the database, hoping eventually to come up with a match.'

Unspoken inside Ruth lay the knowledge of how much higher Will's chances would be if Josie was still alive. The likelihood of sibling blood marrows being a match for each other was infinitely greater than anyone else's. Numbness filled her. 'He keeps telling me to leave him be, to let him go quietly.'

'I know it's tough on him.'

'What about these new "smart bombs" I've been reading about? These genetically engineered drugs. I read an article only the other day, talking about miracle drugs that can target cancerous cells but don't harm healthy tissue.'

Gearin shook his head. 'Damn media reports. One hint at something and in they rush to proclaim that we've finally got cancer licked. It's always much too soon, but they do it anyway because they know the one thing everyone wants to hear about is a cancer cure. All they do is set up false hopes. Every time there's a possible new breakthrough, we're inundated with calls, but the fact is that none of these so-called miracle cures are currently ready for human testing. It'll be two or three years before that's possible.'

'Will doesn't have that long.'

Gearin put a hand on her shoulder. 'Not the way things look right now.'

'That makes me so angry. Knowing that a cure is in sight but out of reach, that it will probably come, but not in time to save my son's life.'

'You, Ruth, and hundreds – thousands – of parents like you. We can only do our best.'

'I'd try anything if I thought it would save Will's life,' Ruth said loudly. Angrily. If only she were allowed to give in to her impulses and shriek obscenities at him, batter down the walls, smash the windows, kick the furniture to pieces.

A couple of weeks later, Dr Gearin waylaid Ruth in the corridor outside Will's hospital room. His voice was high with excitement, the words tumbling over one another. 'I spoke to our technician today. I think we've got it!' he exclaimed.

'A match for Will?'

'That's right. I think at last we're there.'

'You think, or you know?' Ruth was cautious. After Will's relapse, she was not going to allow her hopes to rise.

'I'm pretty damn sure, is what I mean. I wouldn't have mentioned it if I wasn't.'

'But not one hundred per cent certain?'

'Not yet. The transplant team is double-checking it right this very moment.'

'If you're correct, what next?' Ruth bundled the relief and delight she felt behind a screen of brisk efficiency. There was no point celebrating until they were absolutely sure. Even if a match had been discovered, it did not necessarily mean that Will would recover.

'He's only got one more dose of chemo. Let him take that, then have a period of convalescence at home. We'll build his strength up, then he can come back in and we'll go for it.'

'Please God,' Ruth whispered, the way she used to as a child, desperately wanting something to come right.

'My sentiments precisely,' Gearin said.

'When will we know?'

'Soon. Tomorrow, maybe. A couple of days at most.' He stood up and held out his hand. 'We must be hopeful, Ruth.'

Driving home, Ruth thought of the young doctor for the first time as a person, rather than as an aid to her son's recovery. What kind of life did he lead, beyond the hospital? She saw him in a neat suburban house surrounded by careful landscaping, with a barbecue out back, and a four-car garage. Was he religious? And if he had faith to sustain him, did he and his wife go to church every Sunday, trailed perhaps by two or three children who looked like them? There were no family photographs on his desk, perhaps because such a reminder of normality would seem too cruel to parents hearing the paralyzing news of their own children's disease.

Would the bone marrow transplant cure Will? She had read enough about the technique to know that even if there was a true match, there was still a strong possibility of graft-versus-host disease if the donated marrow reacted against Will's tissues. Which would mean more drugs, to reduce the risk, more needles piercing his delicate skin, more adverse reactions.

'What's the result?' Paul asked the question, even though it was unnecessary. Ruth's body language as she came toward him across the restaurant was all the answer he needed. Negative.

379

She shook her head, crushed, unable to speak.

'Oh, Ruth.' Paul poured wine into a glass and held it toward her. 'I'm so sorry.' The stress is killing her, he thought. Is killing *us*. At Christmas, he had felt her unbend toward him, he had been hopeful. But since then, with Will's condition deteriorating, she had been as distant as ever. He felt an anger toward his son which he recognized as inappropriate, but nonetheless could not help. 'Where do we go from here?'

'There's still a chance that another bone marrow match will come up which really is a match.'

He refilled his own glass. 'Shall we order?'

She set down her wine. 'What?'

'I said, shall we order?'

Under the surface of her face, emotions struggled for precedence. Anger won. 'How can you be so indifferent?' she demanded. 'How can you eat, with your son so desperately sick?'

'Don't be ridiculous. It's—'

'Shall we order? Shall we order? As if I gave a damn whether I ever ate again.' She flung down the menu he had handed to her. 'Our son is dying and all you can think about is food.'

'Calm down, Ruth.'

'No, I damn well won't calm down. My child, my son . . .' The tears in her eyes began to fall, leaving wet blotches on her blouse.

'He's my son too, Ruth.' He would have said more but he could see how tightly wound up she was.

'I never realized before how . . . how *uncaring* you are,' she said fiercely. Her body was shaking. A tic jerked under her eye.

'Oh, Ruth,' he said, wearily. 'I'm just so tired of all this.'

'There you go again. It's Will we should be worrying about, not ourselves.'

'I worry about Will all the fucking time. Taking an occasional break, eating a halfway decent meal with you . . .' He smiled at her, thinking that worry and stress had worn away the last remnants of youth from her face, '. . . isn't going to change anything for him, but it could help us.'

'Paul, I'm so afraid.' Ruth's mouth shook. She lifted her glass and tried to sip her wine but her hand trembled too much and she put it unsteadily back on the table.

Paul pressed his hand over hers. 'Right from the start, I've made myself face the fact that Will might not survive this. You know I love him, you know I feel as much anguish as you do but occasionally we need a break, Ruth. Whatever's happening to Will, we can't entirely abandon our own lives.'

'What a convenient philosophy.' She played with a spoon, not looking him in the eye. A fast pulse beat alongside her jaw.

'Listen to me, Ruth. We can't keep watch at the hospital round the clock. That doesn't mean we aren't desperately concerned about Will, just that we should recognize our own needs occasionally, as well as his.'

'I daren't,' she said miserably. 'I've let him down so badly.' She picked up her bag and pushed back her chair. 'It's hopeless, Paul.'

'Ruth, for God's sake. This is . . .'

'Hopeless,' she said again, and marched out, back straight.

He watched her go then poured more wine into his glass. He missed her. Her presence. *Her*. Scent on the pillow. A coffee cup on the counter. Papers strewn across the dining-room table. He had come to realize how much he used to resent her job, the energy she put into it, but in these months away from her, he had begun to see that her desire to succeed was as integral to her as her laugh, her walk. And that new understanding made him miss her even more.

His mind drifted back to that last afternoon, coming home from the Trotmans' party, following her into their bedroom, pushing her down on the bed under him. He had slipped his hand inside her navy blue halter top, felt her nipple harden. Maybe he'd been a bit drunk, a tad over the limit, but not very much, not enough to matter. 'No, Paul,' she had said, pulling his shoulders against her warm breasts, saying no but meaning yes, yes, 'no, we mustn't, the children . . . the picnic,' lifting her hips so he could pull down her shorts and panties. Smelling the excitement between her thighs, pushing into her, their mouths hard against each other, the taste of wine on their tongues. God, it had been good. Then Josie had called from below and he had come, emptying into Ruth while she moaned in his ear, not wanting the children to hear, writhing under him as she came too, saying God, that's wonderful, Paul, wonderful, while her body clenched and relaxed around him.

Looking back, he could see that that had been the final moment of their lives together.

Was it wrong to believe there was, there had to be, a life outside the hospital, away from Will's sad routines? It did not make him less concerned, did it, to think of something more than catheters and drugs and kids dying?

Watching the rain chase across the windows at the far end of the restaurant, he hoped against hope that Ruth would change her mind, would come back and sit down again.

A waiter hovered. 'Hi, Professor Connelly,' he said. 'How're you doing?'

'It's – uh – Jon, isn't it?' A former student, a couple of years back. Not one of the brightest, as far as he remembered.

'That's right, sir.'

'Is this just a temporary job, or are you—?'

'Saving up to go traveling. Gonna take a year off, before I settle down.'

'Lucky you.'

'I know,' Jon said. He grinned. 'Want me to tell you today's specials?'

'Not really. Just bring me something simple – how about a chicken Caesar salad?'

When it arrived, Paul looked at the big platter piled with assorted green and red leaves, croutons, Parmesan, and pushed it away. He finished the bottle of wine, watching the pale wet light outside. He could not go on like this. He was afraid that Ruth's grief would swallow him up. Unless his own did first.

Paying the modest bill, he added a twenty dollar tip. It might help Jon on his way. He wondered whether Will would get the chance to travel.

'We have to face it, Ruth. Unless a miracle happens and a bone marrow donor suddenly appears, there's almost nothing further we can do for William. The entire register's been checked and there simply isn't a match anywhere.'

Ruth listened, heard what the Chief of Hematology was saying, felt nothing but a vast emptiness.

She managed to move her lips. 'How long do we have?'

Gearin glanced at his superior before speaking. His

383

brown eyes seemed more luminous than usual, as though full of unshed tears. His face drooped. 'I can't say. The desire to live – or die, of course – is always a determining factor in these cases. I'd say – God, I'm sorry, Ruth – six months maybe. Perhaps more. The human spirit so often confounds us.' He spread his hands in an air of hopelessness, then pinched the bridge of his nose.

'But you told me you never give up,' Ruth said. 'You told me you were dedicated to the maintenance of life. Whatever the cost.'

He avoided her insistent gaze. 'What can I say? We're that much further down the track now. We've all kept on fighting this thing together.'

'What about another course of chemo?'

'I don't think his body will stand it, Ruth. Even if he himself would go for it.'

'You're telling me we've reached the end of the road?'

Gearin was silent for a while. Then, very slowly, just once, he bowed his head.

Ruth stood by Will's hospital bed. He lay asleep, flat on his back, thin arms mottled with bruises lying on either side of the flat rise of his body under the covers. So thin, she thought. So pitifully thin, except for his face, unnaturally swollen by the drugs. He has almost left us, almost slipped away. What right do I have to try and tug him back? Sunlight slanted through the window and lay across his chest. She had scarcely had time to notice that summer had come once more.

Will opened his eyes and, seeing her, tried to curve his lips into a smile. 'Hi, Mom.'

'Hi, darling.'

'The answer's no.'

'How do you mean?'

'I know what you want.'

'I want you well again. I want you fit. I want you . . .' She wanted to say 'alive' and choked on the word.

'I know all that.' He turned away. 'They didn't find a match, did they?'

'Not yet, darling.'

'Not ever, Mom. Get real.'

'You can't be—'

'Even if they find a match, I don't want any more treatment.'

'You've said that before.'

'And I'll keep on saying it until you believe me. I'm not a child anymore, I know how I feel about things.'

'Will, I know you're very mature. God knows you've had to be. But you're not sixteen yet. You don't have enough experience to look beyond the short term.'

'Short term's all I'm gonna get.'

'Don't *talk* like that.'

'It's true. And *you've* said all this before. Two treatments ago. Or is it three? But here I am, still sick.'

'You're going to get better, Will. I mean it.'

'I've had it, Mom. I'm tired. Let me go. Don't make me feel bad about it.'

'Letting go is not on the agenda, William.'

'Give me one good reason why.'

Because, she thought, if you die as well, my whole life will have been worth nothing. 'Because I'm not going to allow it.'

'Think you're that smart, huh?'

'William, I'd like to take a stick to you. Beat those thoughts out of you. Just try to be brave a little while longer.'

'I'm sick of being brave. I want to be done with all

this crap. I don't want to die, of course not, but even if I get through another lot of treatment, what kind of a life will I have? The only thing I want now is to go back to Carter's House. With both of you. You and Dad.'

'Dad's got his own life now. He doesn't seem to want to be around us much.'

'Dad's frightened.'

'What do you mean?'

'Can't you see? He thinks it was his fault about Josie. And now I'm sick and he worries that if he'd done something differently, I wouldn't be. So it's easier for him to look in another direction.'

'You'd be better off here, within reach of the hospital,' Ruth said weakly.

'I'm tired of hospital rooms and IV poles and guys in white coats, Mom. I want to go to Maine. Back to Carter's House.'

'Look, Will. You're very sick. We have to be close to a hospital. The one in Hartsfield is fine, but it's not set up for the kind of specialized care you need, the way the hospital here is.'

'I don't care. I want to go up there,' Will said stubbornly. 'It'll be the last time.'

'Don't fucking say that!' Ruth yelled. 'Just don't *say* it.' She could see herself in the mirror on his wall, hair like straw, face raw and unmade-up. She recalled how Lynda had always dressed up when she came to see Michelle.

'Okay.' Wearily he turned away from her. 'I just hope you'll remember that you refused my last request.'

'Shut *up*!'

Ruth ran from the room. She stood in the washroom, staring at herself. His last request . . . No! She pulled a brush out of her bag and tugged at her tangled hair with

386

it. Despair weighted her down, hung from her limbs so that each movement required all her strength to complete it. A world without Will. Images paraded through her head, so clear she could almost see them in her reflected eyes. His coffin. Lowered into the earth. Covered. Gone.

'No!' she howled. She pounded the heavy porcelain of the washbasin until her fists hurt. 'No!' Anguish pushed against the confines of her skin. Everything was breaking down. There would be nothing left. She pressed her forehead against the cool mirror glass and closed her eyes.

Don't die, Will . . .

A woman she had never seen before came out of the cubicle at the end of the room. As she passed, she laid a sympathetic hand on Ruth's shoulder.

Ruth took a deep breath. Will was right: how would she feel if she refused him something he so desperately wanted?

20

That evening, she called Paul. In the background people were talking, music played – he obviously had company. Since leaving him at the restaurant, she had scarcely spoken to him except to give him an occasional report of Will's condition over the phone. They had not run into each other at the hospital.

Hearing her voice, his own grew wary. 'What's up?'

'Will wants to go back to Carter's House. He wants to spend the summer up in Maine.'

'How do you feel about opening the house up again?'

'I'm not sure . . .'

In the background, a woman called his name and he shushed her. 'I don't think it's a good idea for him to be up there.'

'It's what he wants. So I'm going along with it, because – because . . . oh Paul, he's going to die. Unless there's a miracle.'

'Don't cry, Ruth. Please don't cry. Let's be sensible about this. He's too sick to travel up there. Last time I was in to see him, he was in real pain from his joints. In the hospital, they can at least make him comfortable. He shouldn't be traveling.'

'He wants to be up there,' Ruth said stubbornly. 'I've

already called Mrs Dee and told her we're coming up.'

'I don't think he should go.'

'So you won't help me by bringing him up?'

'I didn't say that.'

'You want me to go up there, open up the house, get things organized and then come back down to pick him up?'

'Ruth, I did not—'

'If I have to do that, who'll watch out for him down here while I'm in Maine? Who'd visit him? Talk to him?'

'Stop it, Ruth. It was just, I thought you couldn't bear to go back to Carter's House.'

'*Will* wants to be there. That's enough for me. He wants to . . .' Ruth's voice broke. 'He wants to *be* there. With us.'

'Is that really wise?'

Shameless, manipulative, she said: 'When he's dead, I just hope you remember that you refused the last wishes of your son.'

'I can't handle this,' Paul said.

'Do you think *I* can? Do you think it's easy for me to see my son fading away in front of me? Can't you stop thinking about yourself just for two seconds? You bastard. You *bastard*!' Ruth dissolved into despairing tears.

After listening to her for a few moments, Paul put down the phone.

He was wrong. He knew it. He walked the streets, not too steady, too much whiskey, not quite sure where he was heading. Where he was. Had to get out, walls crowding in on him, *crushing* him. Warm evening, navy sky turning velvet black, air heavy with the smell of exhaust and rubber, someone screaming abuse from a third floor apartment window across the way. Will needed him. Ruth needed him. If only she would tell him. If only she could bring herself to say it: Paul, I *need* you. Her voice on the telephone. Needing him. *Needy*.

Derelicts were setting up for the night in dark doorways, gathering their bags and carriers and newspaper round them. Eyes watched him, furtive, collars turned up round matted hair. Ripening garbage smells. Coffee shop across the road, Irish pub down the street. Had he been here before? He tripped over something, someone's feet, and heard curses, a snarl.

The last wishes of my son. It sounded so damn final. My dying son. Ruth was right. How would he feel if he didn't help? There was little enough else he could do for his son . . . didn't even have the right kind of blood.

Tears clogged his throat and he found himself choking, the whiskey he'd drunk earlier raw on the back of his tongue. Two black guys came toward him, big guys, crowding the sidewalk, laughing, eyeing him. He was too drunk to worry.

If that's what Will wanted, to travel up to Carter's House, then of course he would drive him up. Whatever she wanted. Dying. He began to weep, stumbled against the larger of the two guys. One of them caught him by the elbow. Steadied him. 'Whass up, man?'

'Cruel,' Paul said. ''S all so fucking cruel.'

'Hey, *tell* me about it.' They passed him, one on either side, wary, wondering if this was some crazy, don't need it, man, not out here on the city's night streets, already got enough trouble without looking for more, voices fading behind him.

Paul turned, walking backwards, watched them go. Tears cold on his cheeks, glinting in the light from the pub. 'So needlessly fucking senselessly cruel,' he shouted after them, and heard the faint echo of their laughter down the street.

Kid of fifteen. All the psychos, all the lowlifes, useless members of society, never contribute a thing, never do anything with their lives, nothing happens to *them*, but Will, this kid, this *good* kid, has to die. No reason for it. None.

Singing from the Irish pub. Piano tinkle. Name like Connelly, he was probably Irish himself, somewhere back in the past. *Letter from America* . . . What's it all about, really? Life, death. Big question: why are we born? Why are we put on this earth in the first place? Three-year gap between Josie and Will.

Abandoned Chinese take-out joint on the left, car easing down the street, full of Puerto Rican kids, four boys in baseball caps, two girls, looking for something, looking for anything. As they cruised by, they stared out at him, the driver flipping him the finger. He knuckled away his tears, tried to get control, drink anesthetizing his thoughts. She hadn't wanted another child, busy getting on with her career, Mrs Big Time Lawyer, heading away from him and Josie. He'd forced her. Not rape exactly, not quite, but she hadn't wanted it, especially when she found he hadn't used anything, upset, more so when she found Will was on the way. For a while there, after Will was born, she stopped being a lawyer, went back to being mom, being his wife. The way it used to be. Picnics, outings, taking the kids to the Gardens, Christmas in Maine, there for them, baking cookies.

He stumbled again, put out his hands to save himself, hit the sidewalk, felt his palm scrape raw. Pain pulled his lips back from his teeth. Dog shit near his nose, whiff of diesel as a truck went by. He got to his feet, let his head swing, tidal wave of whiskey drowning his brain. Unfair. She had a right. Every right. Make a life for herself outside the family. This wasn't the Fifties anymore. Different roles. Oh God.

He groaned, feeling nausea loose in the pit of his belly. Where did it go? What happened? The Connellys. Connellys from Ireland, a hundred years ago. Not a golden couple. Nothing special. Ordinary family, happy, doing the best they could by their kids, by each other. He staggered toward an intersection, saw lights, traffic, cab. Cab home. Take a shower.

What kind of a father . . . if that's what Ruth wanted, he'd drive Will up to Maine. Didn't approve. Wasn't the right thing, Will so sick. But if that's what she . . . 'Course he would. Of course.

'I'll go up the week before,' Ruth said. 'Open the house up, get it ready.'

'Can't the agent do that?'

'She offered, but it's more than just dusting and pulling back the shutters – which she *is* going to do. She's good but there are preparations I'll need to make. Organizing a bedroom for Will, for instance. Setting up my computers so I can keep in touch with the office, that sort of thing. I thought I'd put him in the room next to your . . . to the one you used to use as your study.'

'He'll like that. Looks over the pond.'

'There'll be other things to deal with. Part-time nursing care to arrange if he ends up . . . if he needs it. Emergency equipment. Stuff he'll want brought up from the apartment.'

'How long will you be up there?'

'As long as it takes,' she said bluntly.

'Ruth . . .' Paul stopped.

'What?'

His voice twisted. 'You don't think . . . he's not really going to die, is he? Up there?'

She was silent. Then she said steadily: 'I'll ask Dieter Hechst to come over, give me a hand with moving furniture. Anything else which needs doing.'

'I'll stay too – if you'll let me.'

'Will would be so happy if you would.'

'And you?'

'Me, too.'

Driving up, she could only think of the house waiting for her. For nearly two years it had been empty. Not neglected, but left alone. Did she have the courage to disturb at last the ghosts which flitted like moths through the deserted rooms?

At Sweetharbor she hesitated, afraid. She pulled into the parking lot behind the 7-Eleven and sat there, engine idling, willing herself onward. After a while, she turned the car in a circle and drove on.

On either side of the road out of town, new bracken had sprung up, hooks of green uncurling from the layers of winter gold. Blossom was ripe along fresh-leafed branches and the fields were brilliant with harebells and daisies. At the turn off to Carter's House, she bumped down the sandy track under the trees and wound down her windows, letting in the smell of the ocean. Coming slowly out of the pine stand to the pasture, she saw the sunlit house waiting for her, patient and unchanging, as it had waited at the start of every summer of her life.

It was this she dreaded more than anything else: that having entered it again, she would find, not the remains of the past, but the ruins.

She wanted to turn around, to flee. She did not wish

to open herself up again to the house and its memories. For a while she sat, hearing the sea-sigh from below the meadows, and the lonesome shriek of the gulls. Eventually she got out of the car, leaving the door open, as though by doing so she left herself an escape route. She walked slowly toward the porch, put a foot on the first step, looked up at the front door. If it were not for Will she would turn around right now.

Resolutely, forcing herself, she took the steps two at a time and before she could think about it anymore, put the key in the door and let herself in.

She had expected stuffiness, the smell of disuse, perhaps a sense of grievance emanating from the neglected rooms. She had certainly expected pain. What she felt instead was a deep sense of peace. Every smell, every sound, was familiar. Despite the loneliness which breathed from the walls, Belle Dee had done a good job of maintaining a semblance of current domesticity. The house felt lived-in; there was a sense of someone having just left the room, a lingering odor of recent coffee, a cushion dented as though newly leant against. Furniture was polished, surfaces shone, there were even flowers – ironically enough, a vase of freesias – on the oriental chest which did service as a coffee table. A gauzy yellowish light filtered through the blinds which had been pulled down to trap the cooler air, filling the quiet rooms with a pearly glow. The old house shifted and creaked around her, its timbers spreading like the branches of a tree to the sun's warmth outside. She walked through the empty spaces, feeling as though she were her own ghost, insubstantial, etiolated.

She could not believe that she was here again. That she could stand upright under the wooden ceilings and not be struck down with anguish. She remembered the fevered days following the accident, how she had searched up and down the coast, the salt-wet rocks under her tender palms, the smell of seaweed and driftwood, the sickening lurch between hope and despair.

The living room was more or less as it had been when they left after the accident. The piano was open, as though someone was just about to play or had just been playing. Belle Dee, or one of her refurbishment team, must have lifted the lid to dust and omitted to close it again. She pressed a few keys and was surprised to find the instrument still in tune, after so long an absence. On the stand attached to the upright lid was a song sheet – 'Mr Tambourine Man', an old Dylan song she remembered from college days. Where had it come from? *In the jingle jangle morning I'll come followin' you . . .*

As she had feared, everything was a reminder of Josie: the chipped Chinese vase, the piano which she had loved to play, books she had been reading that final summer, one of her paintings given pride of place on the dining-room wall. Ruth walked up the stairs and stopped halfway. Josie, rude and truculent – *Sorr ee, Moth-er* – had stood here. Further up, on the half-landing, she had whisked away, shiny hair bobbing under her baseball cap, saying: 'I'm glad I live now.'

Ruth had thought the memories would be impossible to cope with but, to her surprise, they were not. Time had gentled them.

She picked up her sunglasses and went out through the long windows, round the back of the house to where the trail began. These woods had not been walked for a while: the path was overgrown, almost invisible in parts. Fallen branches further obscured the way. The familiar scents of woodland terrain filled her nostrils: leaf and wet earth and rotting wood, a gentle scent of blossom. Recent rain had left puddles which glinted among the growth of fern and horsetail and bunchberry. Last winter's ferocious ice storms had caused considerable damage and there were now sunlit clearings where a year ago trees had stood.

She climbed up to where the trees opened out. In the distance, the round tops of Mount Desert Island were faint against the sky. She stood on the edge of the bluff, looking at the rocky beach below, the pointy firs beyond. The sea spread before her, blue-gray, falsely unthreatening.

Its impact doubled by reflection off the ocean, the light was brilliant. It had been the same, that last day. Such light. And the heat. Giving way to the storm. She sat down on the bench: Josie's bench. Did anyone come up here anymore? The estate was private, but the agent had said that people were sometimes seen on their land. She was too bone-exhausted to care one way or another.

She lifted her face to the skies, closed her eyes. Silence, broken only by the gently deceptive murmur of the sea, the mewl of a bird dipping above her head, the whisper of the pines behind her. She was filled with a sense of Josie's presence. She is here, she thought. Somewhere, close by. Her spirit. She is here. Which was right. The bench had been built for her, placed here overlooking the sea she had loved. Where else would a drowned ghost go except back to the place where it had been happy?

Eventually, wearily, she got to her feet. It was time to return to the house, to continue her preparations for Will's arrival. As she turned to leave, she saw something glinting in the grass at her feet. People had been up here, picnicking maybe, dropping trash. She bent and picked it up. It glittered in the harsh sunlight. Metallic. An earring.

'Oh God!' She spoke aloud, wildly staring round her. She began to hyperventilate, her heart hammering. 'Josie!'

The only answer was the throb of the sea. She sat and examined the earring. It lay in her palm like a precious insect, long legged, steel shelled. She turned it over. Silver. Square, inset with a tiny copper heart. Exactly like the ones Josie had been wearing on the afternoon she drowned. Pressing her fists against her chest, she breathed deeply, in and out, in and out.

Rationalize this, she told herself. Be logical. The earring was not, could not be, Josie's. She had noticed it immediately this time, and would surely have seen it last summer. Someone must have dropped it, one of the trespassers, a courting couple, a hiker. Someone had sat on Josie's bench, gazing out at the Sound and then gone away, leaving the earring behind. It was simply a coincidence.

'Hi, tiger,' Paul said, immediately wishing he'd chosen some other greeting. Tigers were strong, bright creatures, bounding with energy.

'Hi, Dad.'

'How're you doing, son?' Paul pulled a chair up to the high bed. He took the wasted hand in his and pressed it gently. On a table, the screensaver of Will's computer showed an endless procession of flying toasters.

'Feeling kind of zonked. Ed's been in to visit. And Dan.'

'Want me to read to you?'

'Not today.' After a bit, Will said, as though talking

to himself, 'The worst bit was when Michelle died. I couldn't hack that. Just couldn't . . .' He turned his large eyes to his father. 'Do you believe in God, Dad?'

'Tough question,' Paul said. 'I certainly believe in the need for something spiritual. I believe that we all aspire to something bigger and better than ourselves. If you want to call that God . . .' He shrugged. 'What about you? Do you believe in God?'

'I kind of used to,' said Will. 'But I don't now. Not anymore. Grandma's always talking about how merciful and kind He is. But, in that case, why'd He kill Michelle?'

'I can't give you any kind of an answer to that one,' Paul said.

'Whereas if you don't believe,' said Will, earnestly, 'then it's okay, isn't it? I mean it's just random. Not some guy with a long beard and a white gown picking you out of all the others, but like, fate. Michelle or me or the other kids here – or murdered people on the news, or accidents: it's random, it's like, it's going to happen to someone, so why not you?'

Paul was about to respond when a woman he had never seen before appeared at the door. She seemed to be dressed entirely in black leather, though when he looked more closely he could see that under her leather coat was a black cotton T-shirt. Her black hair was cut very short indeed. 'William Connelly,' she said.

'Hi, Miss Marling.' Will's lethargy faded. He pulled himself up into a sitting position.

The woman began digging in her briefcase and brought out some sheets of paper held by a clip. 'I have to tell you that this last piece of work is—' She broke off dramatically.

'Is what? Did I get a good grade, Miss Marling?'

The woman tugged at the corner of the covers on Will's bed and turned to Paul. 'Are you his father?'

Bemused, Paul said: 'I'm Paul Connelly, yes.'

'I'm Barbara Marling. William's English teacher.'

'Barbara?' Will said, his eyes wide. '*Bar*bara?'

'You got something against the name, William?'

'No, no,' Will said hastily. His pale cheeks reddened.

'You should be very proud of this boy,' Miss Marling said to Paul. 'One thing I like from my students is a one hundred per cent commitment and that's what Will's given me. This is just a fine piece of work.' She tapped the papers in her hand. 'The students were told to write a topic paper on any subject they liked, as long as it had a literary connection.'

'And what did you go for, Will?' asked Paul.

'The Isles of Shoals.'

'Off the coast of Maine?'

'Yeah.'

'And, as you surely know, Professor Connelly, America's first musicians' and artists' colony. A really interesting place.'

'Celia Thaxter,' said Paul, digging into his memory. 'And, er, Childe Hassam, wasn't it?'

'Among others, yes. Good. Well done.' Miss Marling beamed at Paul. He felt absurdly pleased.

'What grade?' Will said. 'Come on, Miss Marling, you gotta give me one hundred per cent.'

'You teasing me, boy?'

'No, ma'am. It's what I deserve, considering how hard I had to work on it.'

'Well now, William. You could be right.' The teacher looked down at the pages in her hand. 'Yes, you could very well be right.' She handed the assignment to Will.

He examined the last page then raised clasped hands

above his head. 'Yo!' he said. 'Miss Marling, what'd Ed get? Did he get an A too?'

'Wouldn't be fair of me—' The teacher darted forward and pulled a dead leaf off the houseplant which Ruth had brought in some days before. 'This plant needs watering, William. It's looking very neglected.'

'What did Ed get for his topic paper?'

'Well, I'd have to say he didn't get an A.'

'Great!' Will's eyes were shining.

Miss Marling yanked up the sleeve of her jacket and examined the heavy steel casing of the diver's watch on her wrist. 'I better go, William. I just stopped in on my way home.'

'Thanks for coming by, Miss Marling.'

At the door, she turned. Her expression softened as she examined the pale figure on the bed. 'I have to tell you, William, that although this isn't the first A you've ever had, it's the best. By far the best.'

'Thank you,' Will said, and as Miss Marling went out the door, he added quietly: '*Barbie*.'

Miss Marling popped her head round the door. 'I heard that,' she said, and made a face.

'Wow,' said Paul, after she had disappeared down the passage. 'Am I hallucinating or did a Cruise missile just whizz through here?'

'You should see her when she's not on Prozac,' said Will. 'Now you know what a hard time I have at school.'

'I didn't realize you'd started school work again.'

'I hadn't. But last time she came in, a couple of weeks back, she said my brain would atro-something and—'

'Phy,' said Paul. 'Atrophy.'

'Yeah, that, if I didn't do something with it. Said the rest of the class was doing this paper and why didn't I

400

do it too, so since I was just reading a book Mom brought in about Maine, I thought it'd be kind of fun. Especially if I could beat out Ed.' Will grinned. 'Ed'll be *steamed* I got an A!'

Maybe I do believe in God, after all, Paul thought. Just didn't realize He was into black leather and buzz cuts.

As she approached the Hechst house, dogs scrambled on the porch, watching, checking her out. She murmured soothing words, pulling open the screen to rap at the door. Before she could do so, Gertrud Hechst appeared.

'Ruth! What a pleasure this is.'

'Trudi,' Ruth said warmly. 'How are you?'

'I am good.' Gertrud examined her with her head on one side. 'And you, Ruth?'

'I'm good too. We're bringing Will up for the summer at the end of the week.'

'How is he?'

'He's bad, Trudi. The hospital has sent him home. They – they don't know what else to do for him at the moment.'

For answer, Gertrud came down the steps and held out her arms. 'I am so sorry. So very sorry. But you must not despair.'

'I can't do anything else. We seem to have run out of options.'

'You never know what is waiting around the corner.'

'No.' For a moment, Ruth drooped, then she stepped back. 'Trudi: I came to ask if your husband would be kind enough to help me move some furniture. I'd like to have things ready for when Will gets here. Christmas with you was so special for him, and he's been longing

401

to come up here again.' She hoped that the other woman would understand all the things she could not say.

'I shall speak to my husband, of course, when he comes back. I will ask him to come by first thing in the morning.'

'Thank you.'

As she stepped into the hall of Carter's House, the scent of freesias was strong, almost overwhelming. She had just closed the door behind her when the telephone rang.

'Mrs Connelly? It's Belle Dee, checking that everything's all right.'

'Very much so, thank you. The house looks very well cared for.'

'If you need someone to help in any way, you only have to call.'

'A friend is going to come by tomorrow and help me set up a room on the ground floor for my son. Other than that, it's all under control.' A friend? She had known Dieter Hechst forever, yet only now could she really call him a friend.

'That's great.'

Ruth remembered something. 'And thank you very much for the flowers.'

'Flowers?'

'So welcoming. The freesias in the living room. They have such a lovely scent. And they were my daughter's—'

'I'd like to take credit, Mrs Connelly, but I can't. We have to be careful, as I'm sure you appreciate. We never leave flowers or even groceries: our clients may have allergies or special needs, and we've found it best only to do so if specifically required.'

'How strange: I wonder where the freesias came from.'

'I'm sure there's a simple explanation,' Mrs Dee said. 'In the meantime, don't forget: if there's anything I can do for you, let me know.'

In the living room, the white flowers in their stone vase seemed too fragile, too few, to have filled the house with their perfume. She touched one of the trumpet-shaped blooms and heard Josie's voice again: *My absolute favorite flower.*

The words seemed to echo. To hang in the air: ... *favorite flower*. The effect startled her. For a long moment she stood without moving. Had she really heard the voice, or only fantasized it? Had the phrase been spoken aloud or was she imagining things? Silent, she listened for a footfall, a breath, anything which might indicate the presence of someone else, but heard only the blood racing through her veins, the tiny riffles of her own body. *My absolute favorite flower* ... her daughter's voice sounded again and this time she knew it was only inside her head.

In the evening cool, she sat out on the porch with a glass of wine and a paper knife. Better late than never, she thought, slitting open envelopes mailed two years ago, reading the stilted notes of condolence, thinking that because there is no fresh way to offer sympathy, such letters must necessarily be stilted. *Deepest sympathy, such a lovely girl, you must be so bereft, we knew her well*. Josie opened in front of her like a blossom unfurling in sunshine, a friend to people she had not met, *much missed, lighted up our home, helped me through my troubles, so much talent, her concern for others*, Josie, her daughter and yet to other people something

403

more than that, a presence, a person, *a tragic loss*.

Wiping her eyes, Ruth realized that in the time which had elapsed since the accident, the fire of her pain had abated, had finally died into embers. Reading the letters moved her unbearably. Many of them were from local people she barely knew. Recalling Josie's complaints about the way the summer people treated the year-round people, she was embarrassed once more by her own insularity.

One of the envelopes was stiffened with board and had DO NOT BEND printed on the outside. Carefully opening it, she drew out a charcoal sketch of a young girl, head bent, holding something in her hand, a flower, a paintbrush, hard to say which. Ruth drew in a sharp breath. The model was undoubtedly Josie.

The drawing was more poignant than any letter. Regarding the turn of the neck, the shape of an ear half hidden by hair, Ruth wept aloud, her sobs mingling with the sound of the sea. Josie. My lost Josie. Seeing her again at this distance in time was almost like seeing a stranger. She turned the sketch over and saw a penciled note scrawled on the back: *I thought you would like this*. The signature was one she did not recognize: *Annie Lefeau*. It meant nothing to her, did not sound like a local name. She went into the house and propped the sketch up in the kitchen where she could see it whenever she lifted her head.

She lay half-dozing in the bedroom she used to share with Paul, lulled by the sea-murmur and the whirring katydids. Annie Lefeau: who was she? Was she the person who had made the drawing? When had Josephine posed for it?

Fruitless questions. Especially when she should be

concentrating on Will. He would be here in a few days, and there was a lot to organize. She began making lists in her head. As she did so, gently, almost inaudibly, she heard the tune, Josie's tune . . . *In the jingle jangle morning* . . .

She sat up, straining to listen. Had she really heard it, or was the sound simply an extension of her thoughts? It sounded again, faint music, the notes from the piano, words . . . *upon your magic swirlin' ship* . . .

Except that nobody was singing.

She got out of bed. At the top of the stairs, she listened once more, but this time the old house was still. Not even the faintest hum of dying sound came up from the darkness below, though the flower-scent was strong.

'Is anyone there?' she called. Then, feeling idiotic, added: 'Josie?' But, of course, there was no answer.

Returning here after so long, she had been fearful of shaking up old griefs, old remembrances.

Had she disturbed something more than just memories?

Was the strength of her longing conjuring up illusions?

Back in bed, she lay under the covers knowing she would not sleep, and was surprised when she opened her eyes to the morning sky.

In the afternoon, she drove down to the convenience store in Sweetharbor for supplies. Steaks for Paul. A honey-roasted ham. Vegetables for Will. His favorite foods: those, at least, that he was still able to eat. Because of the state of his gut, the Mexican food he loved was out. So was anything highly spiced, even salt'n'vinegar chips.

In the gift shop, she bought blueberry jam, a spray of

405

dried flowers, flowered toilet paper, maple syrup, a blueberry-patterned plate. She bought a model of a lighthouse, a Turk's Head knot in white string, a carved wooden whale. Wanting Will to be happy, she spent lavishly. After stowing her purchases in the back of her car, she walked down the main street. The sidewalks were crowded with tourists, midmorning shoppers, local business-folk slipping out for a coffee. Passing Don's Donut Shop, she heard music. The sound carried through the chatter and the traffic, insistent.

She stopped, so suddenly that the people behind bumped into her. The words floated to her on the bright morning, clear as bells. The same music she had thought she heard last night. *In the jingle jangle morning I'll come followin' you* . . . She hurried down the alley between the supermarket and the dry cleaners. It led into a small square, with a circular walled flower bed in the middle of it, water dribbling over rocks, benches set round. People drifted, looking at the window display of the nautical goods store, sitting at tables outside the coffee shop, examining flowers and vegetables on the awninged stalls set up along one side. The music had ended now. She could see no one with a guitar. Had she imagined it? A group of college kids in khaki shorts and polos, bare feet pushed into salt-stained Topsiders, was sitting on the wall around the central planting. She stopped in front of them. 'Was there someone singing here a minute ago?' she demanded.

They looked at her. 'No, ma'am,' one of them – blond, sea-tanned – drawled.

'A girl,' Ruth said, hating the frantic note in her voice. 'Singing. A Bob Dylan song.'

They looked puzzled: Bob Dylan was like, ancient. Practically retro. The tanned one gestured vaguely

406

across to the other side of the square. 'Maybe over there?'

'Did you actually see her over there?'

'Who's that, ma'am?'

'The girl,' she almost screamed. 'The one who was singing.'

He shrugged. 'Didn't see anyone, ma'am. I'm sorry.'

'Oh God,' Ruth said, holding out her hands, not caring what they thought, although she could see how her intensity frightened them. They began to shift uncomfortably, look about, wishing the crazy lady would leave them alone.

She walked quickly away from them. She was going mad. Those kids had been sitting right in the center of the square and had not heard anything, seen anyone. Yet even on busy Old Port Street, the sound had been absolutely distinct. She passed a quilt shop, opened for the summer tourist trade. And a gift shop, selling shell-work and scented candles, jellies, polished beach stones with words carved into them: *Good Luck. Carpe diem. Go For It.* She peered inside but could see nothing. There was a gap between the two stores, a narrow passageway leading out of the square and back onto Old Port Street.

Josie, Josie, she thought. Even if it is just your spiritual essence, you are here. I know you are. I *know* it.

Distractedly, she stared up and down the street, not really expecting to see anyone, but nonetheless hoping for the whisk of a skirt, the toss of maple-syrup hair, a quick smile. But there was only a crowd of anonymous faces and meaningless backs. She crossed the street, pushing between cars, heedless of the irritated horns. Went down another alley, leading to the parking lot behind the convenience store. Light dazzled her, bouncing off car hoods and the green-metal glare of 7-Up cans. A car swept by and she glimpsed a woman's startled face. Not Josie, an older woman, with a dog in the back.

The town wheeled about her. Seagulls floating like white fish against the blue sky. A couple of shoppers carrying brown paper sacks of groceries. The scent of seaweed and gasoline. 'Josie!' she screamed. She turned full-circle, shouting. 'Josie. Where are you?'

Nobody answered. A few people stared at her curiously. She got into her car and drove up and down the streets. What was she hoping for? She could not have said. Eventually, heartsick, she drove home.

He was asleep when the telephone cheeped beside his bed. He groaned, his head thick with last night's whiskey. He groped for the receiver, found it, held it to his ear.

'Ruth!' He tried to clear the alcohol fog in his brain. 'What's wrong?'

'Nothing.'

'What then?'

'I don't . . . I'm not sure.' She sounded so unlike herself that he wondered briefly if it was in fact not Ruth but someone else on the other end of the line.

'What does that mean?'

'Paul . . .'

'What?' He squinted at the clock beside his bed. Jesus: it was two o'clock in the morning.

'Don't laugh but . . . do you believe in ghosts?'

'Sorry?'

'Ghosts.'

If he hadn't known her better, he might have

408

wondered if she too had been drinking. 'No,' he said, heavily patient. He coughed, tasting alcohol. 'I do not believe in ghosts. Nor goblins, nor ghouls, nor gremlins nor anything else of that—'

'I think Carter's House is haunted.'

'Haunted. What the hell are you—'

'By Josie.'

He sat up against his pillows, blinking away sleep, feeling the rough edges of his eyelids, the throb of a hangover at the back of his skull. Light bubbles danced in front of his eyeballs. Ghosts, for chrissake. He said quietly: 'Maybe you need to talk to someone, Ruth.' Ridiculously, he wanted to tell her he loved her.

'I'm not crazy, if that's what you think.'

'I know that, but . . .'

She began to talk, her voice growing stronger. He could not understand everything she was saying. A pillow on the sofa. The piano. 'Bob Dylan,' he said. 'What's he got to do with anything?'

She swept on, her voice rising. 'Her earring, Paul, the one she was wearing that . . . and flowers, freesias, the scent of them in the house, and the singing, I thought I was mistaken, but maybe it was . . .'

'Calm down, will you?' he said, struggling to pull himself together. 'The past couple of years, Will, Josie, us splitting up – the strain on you's been unbelievable. But you've got to get a grip.'

'She's here, Paul. Or something of her is.'

He sighed. 'Look, darling.' The endearment slipped out before he could stop it. 'I'll be up at the end of the week. Just hang in there until then, okay? Stay cool. We'll talk about this later, all right?'

'You think I'm mad, don't you?'

'Of course I don't.' He tried to make her smile, put

on a pleading voice. 'Can I go back to sleep now?'

'Sorry,' she said. 'Sorry if I woke you up.'

'Anytime,' he said. And realized he meant it.

Wrapped in a throw against the cool night air, she sat on the porch in the twig rocker which had been her grandmother's, holding a mug of coffee in her lap. Lightning bugs shimmered in the darkness. From beyond the salt meadow came the sea-whisper of the ocean. She adjusted the old herb-stuffed pillow in the small of her back, thinking: She is out there somewhere, I know she is.

A fox barked in the woods and the thought came suddenly, like a peal of thunder: she *is* out there. Not her ghost, not some spirit being, but the living person. She is out there. And she knows I am here. It was impossible. She knew that. Yet, having given birth to the thought that Josie might have survived, it stubbornly refused to go away. Hunched in the creaky old chair, the possibility of Josie's existence burned inside her. She flung off the throw. Stood up, walked to the edge of the porch and leaned on the railings, shivering with excitement.

Was she being given a second chance? The opportunity to put right whatever had been so wrong between her and her daughter that last summer?

All around her, the night hummed with expectation and longing. Ruth lifted her head and stared into the dark, transmitting a wordless message. Josie, come back. I'm here. I love you.

There was another thought which she could not repress. I need you, Josephine. Will needs you. Only you can help him now.

21

In the mud room, hanging from a row of brass hooks, was a pair of powerful binoculars. Ruth took them up to her bedroom and focused them on the woods which framed either side of the house. If Josie was watching, maybe Josie could also be watched. Slowly she swept the area, back and forth, looking for movement, for something which stood out among the green. She saw a ring-dove crashing about in the upper branches of a pine tree, a flash of movement which might have been a deer, three people hiking in Day-Glo vests. Offshore, small craft stood out to sea, some of them already anchored, as preparations for the daily yacht races got under way.

What had she expected? The task of looking for her daughter had all the slippery impossibility of other hopeless quests: chasing rainbows, netting moons, snaring unicorns. Finding her might require the skills of a professional.

In what had once been Paul's study, she opened the Yellow Pages and looked for *Investigators*. Of the three listed names, one appeared to be mainly concerned with business security and one offered a list of services, including fraud inquiry and video surveillance.

The third was a firm based in Hartsfield.

A gruff male voice answered her call. 'Fielding's Inquiries. Derrick Pearson speaking.'

'I'd like to make an appointment,' Ruth said.

'What's it in connection with?'

'A – uh, I suppose it's a missing person case.'

'You don't sound too certain.'

'A missing person,' Ruth said more firmly. 'My daughter. I want to find her.'

'How long's she been gone?'

'Maybe for two years.'

'Maybe? Aren't you sure?'

'Uh . . .' She cleared her throat. 'It's complicated.'

'In my experience, it always is.'

His voice was skeptical and for a moment she contemplated trying one of the other firms, but Pearson began extracting further details from her and eventually offered her an appointment for the following morning.

'Isn't there anything today?' Having made the decision to call, Ruth did not want to wait. 'It's urgent.'

After some argument, it was agreed that she would be at Pearson's office at four o'clock that afternoon. Putting down the telephone, she felt breathless, unnerved. A private eye. She would not tell Paul about it. Not yet.

Pearson had told her to bring anything she could that might be helpful in tracing Josie. She braced herself, took a deep breath and went up to the second floor. The broad-planked passage which ran from one end of the house to the other had been kept burnished; the long Turkey runners brought home by Josiah Carter stretched toward the pine door at the end. Ruth walked slowly toward it. She had run across these same rugs as a child, just as her father had done before her.

Whatever happened to its inhabitants, the house remained the same, solid and lovely.

In front of the door, she put a key into the lock and turned it. Josie's room. Shut up since the day she died. Opening the door, the smells came at her: oil paint, sun cream, old polish from the sanded boards, tired patchouli-scented air. Mrs Dee had been given instructions that neither she nor anyone else was to go into this room, so nothing had been touched in here for two years. Jeans still lay crumpled on the floor, a pair of white cotton panties hung from a half-open drawer, a hairbrush had been flung down on the bed. There was a spill of cassette tapes on a bureau top, open magazines, crumpled tissues. Dust lay over everything. There were dead moths, cobwebs, the desiccated bodies of spider-wrapped flies, even a lemon-colored butterfly, its wings frayed by fruitless beating at the windows.

She looked for anything which might be meaningful to Derrick Pearson. 'Her purse,' he had said. 'Driver's license. Date of birth. Social Security Number. Anything at all that might be relevant to the enquiry.'

She had never pried into her daughter's private possessions. Now, she did not hesitate. The table under the window was covered in a dusty mess of papers; she picked up and examined each one, searching for significance, but found none. Most were reminders to call someone, meet someone, pick up more tampons or suntan lotion from the supermarket, borrow a particular book from the tiny public library in Hartsfield. There were several scribbled phone numbers. There was an unopened box of Reese's peanut butter cups.

Ruth did not really know what she was hoping to find. A full-blown description of a love affair with someone whom Ruth could then track down would

413

have done, or photographs of Josie with someone who could have been identified. But there was nothing. No diaries, no revealing snaps, no address book. Hardy the Bear had gone, but she already knew Will had taken him. She could not see Josie's painting equipment, expensive, top-of-the-range stuff, which she thought had been carried up from the enclosed side porch after the accident, but she could have been mistaken.

She had a sudden picture of her daughter coming down the trail from the woods, taking the key from its hiding-place under the side porch, letting herself into the house after the rest of the family had gone grieving back to Boston. She saw her sitting at the piano, singing to herself. *Hey! Mr Tambourine Man, play a song for me . . .* The image was disconcerting and painful. Had she felt that her family would be better off without her, or that she would be better off without them?

Ruth raised the blind over the window, still teetering between disbelief and certainty. This had been her own room as a child: the faded wallpaper of harebells and lily-of-the-valley had been there all her remembered life – and all of Josie's. Below, the pond glinted in the afternoon sunshine. The two mallards were splashing about, raucous as they trawled for food.

Canvases were stacked against one wall. She turned them round and examined them. Local scenes. A portrait of Will. A portrait of Dieter and Trudi Hechst, done in American Primitive style. An abandoned boat. A view of the sea, with Bertlemy's Isle in the distance. A forest, thin trunks gilded with sunshine, and a man somewhere in among them, half person, half tree, solemn, hieratic. Josie had been sixteen when she painted these, but there was already a maturity of execution, a clarity of vision which was quite startling

414

in one so young. Ruth wondered why she had not noticed it at the time, why she had not encouraged Josie more. Why she had not truly believed in her.

On the shelf above the bed were books, a Bowdoin College mug holding a silk rose, a carved decoy duck, not painted in the usual bright colors but left so that the whorls of the wood melted naturally into the curves of wing and breast, the grain itself suggesting the feathers. It was beautiful, a world away from the usual tourist stuff. She turned it over and saw the initials SH burned into the wood, and a date from two years earlier. SH – that must mean Sam Hechst.

Returning it to the shelf, she wondered where Josie's purse was. Josie had not known she would never come back from the birthday picnic, which meant that it should have been on the table, slung over the back of a chair, tossed on the bed. It would have held money, credit cards, personal items which might be of help to Derrick Pearson.

Money: the thought triggered another. Ruth hurried down the passage to the walk-in linen closet and felt around behind the thick plastic storage bags in which the winter bed covers were kept. In the prudent Yankee tradition of her forebears, a contingency fund had been hidden there for as long as she could remember. Last time she looked, the box had contained five hundred dollars.

Now, when she drew it out and opened the lid, it was empty.

Empty!

It was all the confirmation she needed. Only Josie would have known where the box was kept, only Josie would have been able to go straight to it and then tidily replace it without disturbing the blankets and quilts.

415

Ruth shut the closet door. Looking up and down the passage, she smiled. 'I know you're out there,' she said aloud. 'I *know* you are.'

'You're not giving me a whole lot to go with.' Derrick Pearson raised his eyebrows. He was a large untidy man, with a weatherbeaten face. Occasionally making notes, he had listened impassively to her description of the accident, Josie being swept away, the discovery of her lifevest. He had not reacted to Ruth's reasons for believing that Josie might not after all have drowned: he had probably heard far stranger stories in his time. 'Particularly in view of the fact that your daughter has been declared officially dead. I can make some calls, access some of our databases, but I have to be honest with you: it's not going to be easy. Even if she *is* still alive, she could be going under another name – most likely is. I mean, she's old enough to be married, isn't she?'

'I can't believe she would have—'

'It seems the most likely explanation. How else would she have managed to exist for two years, a kid of sixteen—'

'Nearly seventeen.'

'—without contacting her family?'

'Married?' Ruth was not sure why the possibility was so difficult to conceive. 'She was just a child.'

'Children get married every day.'

'You said she could have adopted an assumed name.'

'She *could* have, but . . . sixteen, seventeen years old? Whatever, it's a bit of a stretch. She'd have to have been pretty resourceful. I've got a sixteen-year-old myself and I can't see her knowing what to do in similar circumstances. Unless she had friends – or more likely *a* friend

416

– to help her. Apart from a few hundred bucks, which anyway you think she didn't get a hold of for some time after the accident, she'd have been entirely on her own, poor physical condition, soaked to the skin, penniless. The more you look at it, the more it makes sense that she found someone to help her, at least at the beginning.'

'You mean some man?'

'You'd have to think so, wouldn't you? Some guy she's gotten involved with, there she is, missing, presumed drowned, ideal opportunity to run off with him, wouldn't you say?'

'I find it hard to believe she knew anyone irresponsible enough to go along with such a plan without at least letting us know she was alive.' It was harder still to imagine Josephine married, living a life somewhere, maybe with a child of her own. How desperate had she been? What sort of man would she have chosen? Was it this unknown man who had been behind Josie's distress that summer, the cause of her hostility? Was he the man who stood motionless among the trees in Josie's painting?

'She probably pitched some kind of story,' Pearson said. 'Her family's been wiped out in a car crash, or she's an orphan trying to make it on her own.' He leaned back in his chair, stared up at the ceiling. 'Or mentions these abusive parents, or some bastard of an uncle wants her to sign over her inheritance. Any one of the above. Story like that, someone would be bound to lend a hand.' He looked down at the single sheet of paper in the file he had labelled with Josie's name.

Ruth felt helpless. Although Pearson seemed entirely familiar with it, this was a world she did not know.

'On the other hand, she sounds like a smart kid,' he

417

continued. 'She'd probably have enough savvy to know she's not going to have her driver's license renewed or get an SSN if the records show she's dead.' He picked up a pen. 'Meanwhile, better give me the names of any other known associates and their phone numbers.'

'Known associates? You make her sound like a criminal.'

'People she might have turned to for help. Teachers, particular friends, places she liked to hang out.'

When he had made notes of the information, he stared hard at Ruth. 'Any chance that your daughter had friends you weren't aware of?'

Ruth shook her head. 'I don't know.'

'It strikes me, Mrs Connelly, that there's an awful lot about your daughter you don't know.'

'I agree with you, Mr Pearson. And, believe me, I regret it.'

'Any hobbies, any pet likes or dislikes?'

'What relevance do her hobbies have?'

'It's all relevant,' Pearson said. 'Or, to put it the other way around, you never know when it might *not* be relevant. Say she's a square-dance fanatic, we might check whether there are any square-dance festivals and go there, flash her picture around. Or she's crazy for the Smashing Pumpkins or whatever, and we find they're doing a gig nearby, we might have somebody on the ground, looking out for her. You can't tell when you're going to get lucky, so you cover all the bases. And in two years, there's a chance her tastes won't have changed too much.'

'I see.'

'She already had a driver's license, right?'

'Yes.'

'But no Social Security Number?'

'She was still too young.'

'We'll access the DMV, of course, and any other of the avenues open to us. Thing is, most people who want to disappear tend to leave a paper trail, however hard they try not to. Whereas this girl – if she really did survive the accident – has had two years to build a new identity, to cover her tracks, get papers in a new name. It's not like it's going to be a standard skip trace: she's too young to be tracked down via the normal identifiers. No SSN, possibly no current driver's license. Like I said, we can run a DMV check, do the usual online searches, but from what you've been telling me, I'd guess we'll draw a blank.'

'But you'll try anyway?'

'Of course. Shouldn't take too long, thanks to the technology. But I'm not hopeful about getting results, and I want you to know that before we start. Now, you say her bank account has been left untouched, and none of her credit cards used since this accident occurred. Is there anything else at all that might be helpful? Identifying features such as scars or birthmarks? A missing limb—' he saw Ruth's expression and added hastily, 'or something?'

'There's a possibility she might have broken her wrist in the accident,' Ruth said. Her certainty was beginning to wither. 'I'd forgotten about that.'

'The radiologist at the local hospital is a drinking buddy of mine. I could check with him.' He picked up the photograph. 'We can have this enhanced, age it, of course, though she could have completely changed her appearance by now. Different hairstyle, different hair color, put on weight, whatever.'

'Is there any chance at all of you finding her?'

'If she's still going by her given name, we could turn

her up by tomorrow, no problem. If she's not, then . . .'
He shrugged. 'It's almost a given that she'd have
changed her name. Otherwise you'd have known long
before this that she was still alive. I'm telling you this so
you don't get your hopes up too high.'

'I can't tell you how important this is.'

'Do our best,' he said. 'That's all I can promise you.
If we come up with anything, we'll let you know right
away.'

'Why would she have gone to such lengths to avoid
coming back to her family?'

'You tell me.'

'We're not – we weren't a dysfunctional family,' Ruth
said.

'Sorry, but I don't buy that,' Pearson said bluntly.
'There had to be something wrong. If not, how come
you're so ready to believe that your daughter – your
sixteen-year-old daughter, from a privileged background, so we're not talking exactly streetwise here –
didn't want to come back to her family? Seems to me
like she's saying loud and clear that she doesn't want
any of you in her life.'

'I don't believe that,' Ruth said. 'Whatever happened
back then, I think now she wants to be found. The clues
she's left – like the earring and so on . . .'

'If that's what they are.'

'. . . I'm sure that she's trying to tell me she wants to
come home.'

'Mrs Connelly, give me a break. All the things you've
told me about, they don't mean zip. Just random
incidents which add up to zilch.'

'Or not,' Ruth said. 'Maybe not.'

'Maybe. But if you want my honest opinion . . .'

'Yes?'

'. . . for what it's worth, I'd say that the poor kid drowned two years ago. End of story. Which is not to say that I won't do my damnedest to find her.'

'I appreciate your frankness.'

'I'll be in touch as soon as I have anything to tell you.'

Back at Carter's House, Ruth dialed Belle Dee's number and when the realtor came on the line, said: 'It's Ruth Connelly. I forgot to ask how long ago you opened up the house.'

'Three or four days before you arrived.' Defensiveness hardened the realtor's voice. 'Are you suggesting that our service is substandard? It's a busy time of year for us and we can't always arrange our schedules to match the—'

'I already said everything was fine. Just fine.'

Reassured, Mrs Dee grew friendlier. 'I'm glad you're back, Mrs Connelly. It was a real pleasure to be able to tell people that the house would be occupied for the summer.'

'Which people?'

'Well, I say people but only two, really. One was the gentleman from Montreal—'

'How would he know about the house in the first place? It's not as if it's advertised.'

'Word of mouth, maybe? Most of the locals here know the house has been empty.'

'What about the other enquiry?'

'That was from a young woman. She called only two days ago.'

'After you'd opened the place up?'

'That's right.'

'Where was she from?'

'She didn't say.'

'Did she give a name?'

'She said she was interested in renting the house for the summer and when I said the owner would be in residence, she just hung up.'

Was it far-fetched to wonder if this had been Josie? But, if so, why was she staying hidden? What was holding her back?

Later that evening, she telephoned Boston to find out how Will was doing. 'He's cheerful,' Paul said. 'He's been on a roll since he knew we were taking him back to Carter's House. He can't wait to get back there.'

'How is he otherwise?'

Paul swallowed. 'Okay, I guess. The people at the hospital seem to feel there's not much more that they can do for him.'

'You can't blame them. They've been fantastic, right from the start.' Ruth felt more empowered than she had for months. The task of tracking Josie down not only offered the illusion that she was doing something to help William, but also gave her purpose. 'If there's any chance of saving him left, Paul, I'm going to do it,' she said. 'If he dies, then at least I can say I did my best.'

'Tell you what might be good – having that English teacher of his on call.'

'Witchy Woman?'

'Is that what they call her? She certainly galvanized Will.'

'And anyone else within a hundred miles of her. But too much of her could be kind of tiring, wouldn't you think?'

'Probably. Ruth . . .'

'Yes?'

'You sound different.'

'Being away from the city for a while, being up here,

it's given me a new perspective on things. A chance to separate what's real and important from what isn't. Maybe I've been concentrating on the wrong things.'

He let that go by. 'Any more ghosts?'

'No ghosts.' She paused. 'When will you two be coming up?'

'They think Will will be okay to travel by the end of the week.'

'I'll have things in place by then.' I might even have found our daughter, Ruth thought.

She prepared a bed for Paul next to the room they used to share. There was a big old-fashioned bathroom between the two, which gave them a vestige of the old shared intimacy while at the same time keeping them apart.

She remembered how they had chosen to spend their honeymoon at Carter's House, although her mother had urged them to go to Europe.

'*Every*one goes to Europe,' she had said.

'Not me,' said Ruth. 'Not us.'

'Paris,' murmured her mother, sensing defeat. 'Vienna. Rome. London.'

'What about London?'

'Don't you want to see Buckingham Palace, Trafalgar Square, St Paul's?'

'I'm more interested in Paul than St Paul's.' Even then, she had thought: this won't last, he will not always love me though he swears he will. When he no longer does, there'll be plenty of time for Paris and Vienna and all the other places, plenty of time.

She was drinking coffee in the kitchen when Sam Hechst rapped lightly on the open door and came in. Big-chested, square-built, curly hair showing signs of gray. 'My aunt tells me you need some help,' he said.

'That's right. Want some coffee?'

'Good.'

They sat on either side of the table, taking stock of each other. Ruth started to speak but he cut across her. 'Something's happened. Do you want to talk about it?'

Ruth's hands shook; she pushed them into the pockets of her shorts. Through the open door she could smell the wind off the pines, blowing seaward. The kitchen suddenly seemed too small for both of them. 'Let's go outside. The thing is, there are . . .' She stopped. 'I don't really know where to start.'

Standing in sunshine, she watched the play of light on the pond. Expecting bread, the mallards began to drift toward her. The reeds quivered as a breeze caught them and ruffled the water. 'First of all, I know it sounds crazy, especially after all this time, but . . . I think, unbelievable or not, that . . . that Josie's still alive.' He drew in a sharp breath and she held up her hand. 'Don't say anything until I've finished.' Carefully she enumerated her reasons. In the clear, sea-sharp air, they seemed fragile, untenable. She hurried on, feeling foolish.

When she had finished, he asked: 'If Josephine survived the storm, why do you think she didn't come home?'

'Maybe she didn't want to.'

'Why not?'

'I'm not sure. Over these past months, I've realized how little I knew about her. What she thought about, what her hopes were, what she did with herself. Not even who she spent time with.'

'Isn't that perfectly natural? How *could* you know? When you were that age, did you tell your parents everything you did or thought or felt?'

424

'No, but—'

'Secrecy is an essential part of growing up.'

'I tried to be a good mother,' Ruth said anxiously. 'I thought I was. But now I can see how neglectful I was, how much more concerned with my own career than with my children.'

'We shouldn't sacrifice our own lives for our children. They're so soon gone. What are we supposed to do when they leave? We have to make preparations. We have to remember that we have as much right to our existence as they do to theirs.'

'You sound like you have children yourself.'

'Two. Living with their mother down in New York. We moved there after I resigned my job in Connecticut, but I couldn't stand living in the city and she didn't care for this kind of rural isolation.' He waved his hand. 'Especially in winter.'

'Do you see your children often?'

'As often as I can – which is less than I'd like it to be. Sometimes they come up during their vacation and stop over with my aunt and uncle.'

'I should have put myself on hold. I should have concentrated on being a mother.'

'Would that have been enough for you?'

'Maybe not.'

'Then don't blame yourself for not doing it. Stop trying to take on the guilt of the world. It's pointless to try to be something you aren't.'

'I didn't give her *time*,' Ruth said.

'Nobody could have given Josephine enough time.'

'Do you really think that?'

'I told you before, people possessed of her particular sensibilities, her creative impulses, their highs are so high, their lows so low. It makes them very demanding.

425

They want everything, *now*, they want everything perfect, all the time. It makes them difficult to live with. You can't blame yourself for that.'

'There's something else,' she said. 'If she *is* around here, then it becomes all the more important that I find her. You see, my son is . . . he's . . . dying.'

'You told me he was cured.'

'We thought he was. Late last year the disease came back.' She stared at the trees climbing up the hill away from the house. 'He's been through all the treatments available now. Our last hope is a bone marrow aspiration, but we can't find a match for his tissue. Josie might be one. If she *is* alive, then there's a possibility that Will could be saved.' She walked slowly toward the pond where the mallard pair floated.

Hechst followed. 'This is terrible.' He took her hand and held it lightly. 'I had no idea, Ruth.'

'Time's running out for him. If she's alive then she could . . . she might . . . Josie is Will's last chance. Paul's bringing him up here as soon as the hospital lets him go and he may not . . . it's . . . we'll probably, me, that is, just stay here with him until he . . . until he . . .' Ruth began to weep, clinging to Hechst's hand. 'Oh God . . .'

He gripped her arms, not moving toward her, just holding her. 'Can I do anything at all to help?'

'I'm wondering if you have any idea of where she could have gone when she . . . if she . . . after the accident. Or even who she might have gone to. She seems to have talked to you more freely than she did to me.'

'We did talk a lot. And yes, she did fantasize about running away from home. She always had this romantic notion about living with "real" people. By which I think she meant people concerned about the environment, people who didn't have the benefit of inherited money,

426

people who helped others, who made a living using their hands.'

'Unlike her parents.'

'Perhaps,' he agreed. He smiled. 'I tried to explain that never being entirely sure where the next check was coming from wasn't as much fun as she thought, but she didn't want to hear that – too much reality would have interfered with her illusions.'

'Was there a man involved?' Oh God. Why didn't she tell me? Would I have listened if she had? *You were always so hard on her . . .*

'I have no idea. But she often talked about where she'd go, if she left home. She had this romantic idea of joining a commune.' He tightened his grip on Ruth's hand. 'If – *if* – she survived the accident, maybe she saw it as an opportunity to – to test her theories. To try and see if she could earn a living from her painting. Prove herself to you.'

'By allowing us to believe she was dead?' Ruth was horrified. 'I can't believe it.'

'I don't know if she had anywhere particular in mind, but, if you're determined to look for her, I can tell you several places in the area she might have headed for. Communes: they're kind of an outdated concept these days, but they do still exist. I guess artists' colony might be a better phrase.'

'I'd be grateful for any information at all.'

'It might not come to anything but at least it would be a start.'

'I've hired a private investigator, but he's not very hopeful of finding her.'

'I can see why. There wouldn't be much documentation on her.'

'That's what he said. That's why I'm going to try a

different approach, search for her myself.' She looked up at him. 'I haven't even told Paul yet. He thinks it's completely irrational to jump to the conclusion that Josie's alive just because of an earring. I don't see that, I don't agree. There were the flowers, too. And the piano . . .' She was talking wildly now, shoulders shaking, mouth loose.

Hechst gathered her against his chest. His big hand gently stroked her hair. He smelled of wood and of turpentine. Of strength. Leaning against him, she could feel the rapid patter of his heart against her breast. She was grateful to him for not trying to argue her out of her conviction that Josie was alive. Even if he considered her search hopeless, at least he was not deriding her for wanting to undertake it.

22

Away from the coast, Maine changed, no longer the guidebook fantasy but a place undeveloped, almost primitive, where living was pared right down to the basics of water, shelter and food. Along the endless, deserted roads, Ruth passed mobile homes, fields of daisies, unexpected graveyards full of granite headstones set in the earth like rotten teeth. Abandoned wooden buildings stood beside the road; once barns or homes, they now leaned like drunks toward the ground. Faded *For Sale* signs were everywhere, planted in front yards, hanging from the sides of barns, as though everyone was looking for some place better to go.

Ruth was heading for the tiny hamlet of Colbridge. 'It's a sort of collective,' Sam Hechst had told her. 'Artists and craftspeople, getting together to market their work. Given the short season, it makes sense for them to pool their resources. Up here, you have to catch the tourists while the summer lasts.'

'How would Josie know about them?'

'She came with me once when I was dropping some of my carved pieces off. She liked the set-up they had.'

He did not know the address. 'But everybody in Colbridge knows the house. There's a core of permanent residents, but in general it's a shifting population. People show up for the summer and, when the season's over, most of them move on. Everything's kind of loose.'

'Which is why Josie liked it.'

Colbridge was off the highway, a small hamlet set round a triangular village green with an Episcopal church at one apex, a post office at another and a tiny general store on the third. In addition, there was an elementary school, an auto repair shop, a shack with a sign announcing that this was Cary's Coiffures.

Ruth parked in front of the store and went in. She picked up a jug of blueberry syrup and took a bottle of juice from the glass-fronted refrigerator case. Paying for them, she said she had heard that there was an artists' commune somewhere round here.

'Ayuh,' the woman behind the counter said. 'Just right down the road there.' She came out onto the wooden steps which led up from the road and pointed. 'See that kinda ramshackle place, the gray one? That's where they're at.' She shook her head. 'Lord, sometimes I believe that house'll fall right down, with all of 'em inside. I swear that balcony is gonna drop off one of these days. Be a wonder it don't kill someone when it does.'

Kill who? The town was deserted; apart from a single car parked beneath the Union flag above the post office building, there was no indication that anyone lived there at all. Ruth took out the photograph of Josie which she had brought with her. 'Have you ever seen this girl?' she said. 'She may have been living with them, might have come in here.'

The woman stared at it for so long that Ruth's hopes began to rise. But finally she shook her head. 'I don't believe so,' she said. 'Mind you, they all look the same to me. After a while, you can't tell one from the other.

Long hair, long skirts, rings in their noses.' Unexpectedly she laughed. 'We never did nothing like that when I was young. Looks like some fun to me.'

Ruth left her car and walked down the road. This far from the coast, the air was windless and dusty. The heat leaned on her, inescapable. By the time she had reached the gray house, her legs and face were sheened with sweat. She climbed the shallow wooden steps and pressed the bell. There was no answer. Not certain that the bell worked, she rapped at the wooden frame of the screen door. After a while, the front door opened and a man looked out at her through the screen mesh. He had a cloth in his hands. Ruth could smell the unmistakable scent of marijuana.

He smiled when he saw her. 'Yes?' He had very short hair dyed an improbable yellow, with the black roots showing, and several silver rings in his ear. His black T-shirt and cut-offs were splattered with clay.

'My name's Ruth Connelly,' she said. 'I'm looking for my daughter, Josephine.'

He had a quiet educated voice. 'What makes you think she could be here?'

'She came visiting, a couple of years ago, and liked it. I thought she might have come back here.'

'Ah. Let me guess,' he said. 'She left home, right? Hasn't been in touch since?'

'Something like that.'

He scrutinized Ruth in silence, his body completely still. Blurred by the screen mesh, he seemed guarded, wary. Then, as though some conclusion had been reached, he said: 'Okay. Got a picture?'

Ruth showed him the photograph of Josie, holding it up against the screen door. He looked at it briefly before shaking his head. 'Sorry.'

'Are you sure?' Ruth was certain he was not telling the truth.

'Definitely. You sure she's into this kind of thing, crafts and stuff?'

'She paints and I know that she always wanted to join one of these artists' communities. I've been told about a couple of others: one down near Bangor, and another in Millport. Have you heard of either?'

'I'm afraid not. The coast might be your best bet. Bar Harbor, or Northeast Harbor – that's where people buy paintings.'

'I'll try them.'

As she turned to go, the man said: 'Ever thought that she might not want to be found?'

'I'd like her to tell me that herself,' said Ruth steadily. She had thought about almost nothing else since she had first decided to look for her daughter.

'It could be more of a problem than you think. There are lots of kids like . . . um . . . Josephine. And all sorts come looking for them. So we stand by each other, kind of protect each other, know what I'm saying?'

'I think so.'

'If I run into your daughter anywhere, I'll be sure to let her know you're looking for her.'

'Okay. And thanks.'

'It'll be my pleasure,' he said softly.

As soon as the telephone chirped, Paul knew it was Ruth. 'Hi!' he said. 'How's things?'

'Fine. How's Will?'

'Okay, I guess. Anxious to be out of hospital. Looking forward to seeing you again.' He waited a fraction. 'So am I.'

'Are you?'

432

He didn't answer, the pause between the two of them lengthening but not uncomfortably and again he was reminded of their college days, the way they would sit on either end of a phone line, grinning at nothing, so lost in love that even the silence between them was exhilarating.

'Where are you?' he said. 'I tried ringing the house a couple of times.'

'I've stopped for a coffee in a place called Sawton.'

'Abandoned sawmill, polluted river, stench of urban decay, am I right?'

'Got it.'

'Of all the godforsaken places ... What are you doing up there?'

'I'm ... I'm looking for something,' she said, and he knew from her hesitation that she was lying. Or not telling the entire truth. She'd never been good at that.

'Looking for what?' He eased the phone against his jaw, imagining her in some grubby phone booth, leaning against the perspex sides, trash on the floor, dirty stretch of river dyed orange by wastes from the mill.

'I don't want to talk about it.'

'Okay. Ruth . . .'

'Yes?'

'What are you wearing?' It was what he always used to ask, when they were courting: did she remember, too?

'Green linen slacks, a white T-shirt, sandals. And this rather nice carved necklace somebody made for me. Four hearts strung on a leather lace.'

'Are you really?' he whispered.

'Yes. Really,' she said, and he heard the smile in her voice.

He picked up the phone once more and called the

nearby flower shop. Asked them to arrange for a dozen red roses to be sent to Carter's House, in Sweetharbor, Maine. Told them to write *Love, Paul* on the card.

'Anything more?'

'That's enough,' he said.

Ruth spent the night at a fine old Victorian house which had been converted to a B&B. She was tired; it had been a long and disappointing day. She had stopped at more galleries and craft centers than she could remember, but nobody knew Josie's name, nobody recognized the girl in the photograph she showed them. Time after time she had hit some small town, some hamlet, pulled into a parking space, psyched herself up to walk in and speak with total strangers. 'Do you know this girl? Have you seen her? Josephine Connelly, she's a painter, you might have come across her in the past year . . .'

And always she had drawn a blank. People seemed eager to be of help but nonetheless appeared to know nothing. Sometimes, passing round the picture, she thought that one or two people were lying when they gave it back, shaking their heads regretfully, sliding their eyes away from her desperate face, but there was no way she could force them to be more forthcoming. In a craft shop on the other side of Skowhegan, the woman in charge looked at the photograph and opened her mouth to speak. Then put the picture down, began to rearrange the pottery bowls on the shelf beside her.

'Yes?' Ruth said urgently. 'You've seen her?'

'I'm afraid not,' she said.

'But you looked as if you recognized her.'

'I was mistaken,' the woman said shortly.

Exhausted, dispirited, when the light began to fade and the craft markets were closed, Ruth drove around looking for somewhere to stay, finally pulling up in front of another B&B. Her room overlooked a shallow river. Below her window, brown water moved purposefully and she knew she must too. When she stepped out onto the little balcony, she saw a pair of ospreys hunting overhead. Like me, she thought, but with a surer chance of success.

Lying in a strange bed, she remembered the last time she had searched for her daughter and was thankful that this time she was armored, stronger, more able to cope with despair. She slept peacefully, and woke to find the room full of rainy light. The day was wet and windy, rain beating against the windows, trees bending this way and that across the river, but the dark clouds were moving swiftly eastward and there was brighter sky behind them.

After breakfast – coffee and two slices of homemade banana bread she set off again on her search through now familiar countryside, the cat-tails standing in ditches beside the road, the cranberry bogs, the gun shops and well diggers, the piled lobster traps. Long wet roads leading to yet another mill town. Pulp trucks thundering by, their big wheels throwing up a shower of spray. Signs selling *Antiques, Newtiques & Collectibles.* Signs advertising *Live Bait and Crawlers.* Rain on the windshield. Meadows of daisies and clover. Abandoned cars. Christmas tree farms. Families of mailboxes clustered beside the road. Lupines waving, pink and yellow and blue. More rain.

Toward the end of the afternoon, she found herself driving into Millport, a small town set far up one of the many inlets off the coast. The sun had broken through the heavy cloud cover and four o'clock sunlight slanted off the wet roofs of the main street. Between the buildings was water, boats, buoys. She passed a Social

Services Center, a nursing home, little cafés offering crab cakes and lobster rolls. The town was large enough to support a travel agency, housed in an elegant ginger-breaded house painted powder blue and white. Squeezed in between a small bank and a garage offering auto parts and exhaust tune-ups was a medicinal herbs store. Further on, a hand-lettered sign pointed down a short dirt track to Annie's Gallery.

Annie.

Could that be . . . was it possible that this was the same Annie who had sent her that sketch of Josephine, nearly two years ago?

Ruth drove down the track and parked. The store was clapboard-sided, with modern bow windows inserted on either side of the wooden door. Another sign informed her that the gallery sold *Fine Art and Decorative Crafts*. Tense with previous disappointment, she forced herself to relax. For a couple of minutes, she gripped the steering wheel, fortifying herself against another letdown.

The gallery's windows held none of the usual cute tourist-tempting artefacts: no dungareed dolls in lace-edged caps, no carved wooden sailors with seagulls on their shoulders or crudely made full-rigged model boats. Left of the door, there were paintings, a wooden bowl of bird's-eye maple, several pieces of hand-thrown pottery with subtle glazes. The window on the right held a spread of hand-loomed textiles, some beautiful glass jars and a wooden chest painted with folk motifs. Posters advertised a forthcoming craft show on Mount Desert Island, a music festival, an all-media art show.

Inside, the shop was bigger than it appeared, extending back through what must once have been several rooms before its conversion to a gallery. The floors were wooden and bare, the glass shelves carefully lit to show to best advantage the objects displayed.

The woman who was sitting behind a table laden with glossy art and guide books was in her mid-thirties, wearing a lowcut black top and a floor-length skirt of flimsy Indian cotton. A long braid of bright red hair hung over one shoulder; freckles across her nose offset her otherwise austere features.

'Can I help you?' she said.

'Are you Annie?'

'That's right.'

'Annie Lefeau?'

'Yes.'

'I'll just look round.' Ruth was reluctant to plunge in and ask directly about Josie. Something reticent about the woman precluded any attempt at instant empathy. She walked slowly between the intricately carved wooden boxes, the fine pottery plates and bowls, the wooden dishes, and baskets of various sizes made from local materials and vegetable dyes. At the end of the gallery, one of the walls was covered in mirrors and textile hangings. The other two held paintings.

They were mostly local scenes: seascapes, rocks, boats pulled up out of the water, weathered houses with the wide gray sky of a Maine winter behind them. At first glance, they seemed not much more than standard tourist bait, a quality souvenir to take back home, a reminder of a good vacation in a magnificent landscape. Until you looked closer. The fishing boats were not pleasure craft, designed for sunny days and holidays, but year-round working boats, oil-stained and dirty. The houses were not the bright-painted gingerbreaded cottages expensively restored by people from away, but shabby places, their shingles peeling, their lines plain and workmanlike. A graveyard, dried weed-heads, a boat turned upside-down, an abandoned anchor on an empty shore: the artist had used them to point up the reality of a community on the edge of losing its culture, as commercialism gradually eroded the traditional livelihoods. The paintings were powerful and bleak; Ruth hungered to own one.

One in particular caught her eye, a marble headstone leaning as though against the sea wind, its white surface pitted with salt. Patches of lichen burned like orange suns against the marble. Carved in elegant italic script were the words: *Death is Swallowed Up in Victory*. As though to emphasize the point, withered leaves lay piled at the foot of the stone and, among them, a single white flower.

Ruth stared at it for some time then made her way back to the front of the gallery. 'I'm interested in the paintings you have in the back,' she said.

The woman put her finger into the book she was reading and looked up. 'Any one in particular?'

'There's one of a gravestone. And another of a boat pulled up onto a beach. Some others which seem to be by the same person. I can't see a signature, though. Are they signed on the back? I didn't like to take them off the wall to look.'

Annie smiled. Her whole body seemed to light up. 'They're great, aren't they?' Getting up, she led the way to the end of the big room. Over her shoulder, she said: 'I admire all the work but I think I like the tombstone best. I love that juxtaposition of life and death, the promise of springs to come. I wish *I* could paint like that. I do try, but . . .' she spread her hands in a gesture of resigned defeat.

'Is the artist local?'

'At the moment, yes.'

'Is it a woman painter?'

Annie turned. Her gaze was suddenly wary. 'Why do you ask?'

'Partly because of the detailed observation, and partly because the sentiment the painting conveys seems to have a woman's perspective about it.'

Annie remained silent.

'Perhaps I'm reading too much into it,' Ruth said, unnerved. 'But that's how I see it.'

Unexpectedly, the other woman laughed. 'I think you're right. And yes, the painter is a woman.'

'What's her name?'

Distrust closed down Annie's face again. 'All the paintings are signed.' She stroked the auburn braid on her shoulder and narrowed her eyes like a cat.

'If they are, I can't read the signature from here.' Ruth could feel currents of emotion washing about her but was unable to determine what they were. Anger? Anxiety? Dislike? But why? This Annie was behaving more like someone anticipating attack than like a gallery owner eager to make a sale. She said boldly: 'I'd like to buy that one, the tombstone one, please.'

Silently, Annie lifted it off the wall and began carrying it back to her sales desk.

Ruth followed her. 'Where's the signature?'

'There.' Annie pointed to a dead leaf curled at the bottom left-hand corner of the picture. Ruth squinted at it, bending low over the painting, and could just make out the letters JO.

JO. Excitement swelled inside her. 'What do the initials stand for?' she asked.

Annie stared at Ruth. 'Janie O'Donnell,' she said. She folded her arms across her chest. 'You seem to be a lot more interested in the painter than in the picture. Before I give any more information away, I'd like to know why.'

The two women faced each other belligerently. Finally Ruth said, 'Because I think they may have been painted by my daughter. My estranged daughter.'

'Oh God.' Annie paled. 'You're Mrs Connelly.'

'How do you know that?'

'I'm . . . I was a friend of Josephine's.'

'You sent me a drawing of her when she . . . after the accident.'

'That was before . . . yes, I did.'

'Then you'll know I haven't seen her for two years.'

'She drowned. That's why I sent you the drawing.'

'Maybe she didn't.'

Annie Lefeau's eyes widened. They were of a curious amber brown, the pupils almost fully dilated, as though she had just come in out of the dark. 'What makes you say that?'

'Have you seen her, Ms Lefeau? I've been searching all over. Up and down the coast. Inland. Stopping in at places like this. Asking everybody.'

'Why do you think she's alive?'

'Instinct. I'm running on blind faith, nothing else.' Ruth took a step closer. 'Do you know her?'

'No.' Annie shook her head violently from side to side.

'I don't believe you.'

'That's your problem, not mine.'

Ruth clenched her jaw to prevent the angry words escaping. Writing out a check, she said curtly, 'Perhaps you'd wrap this up for me.' As she opened the door, she turned. Beside the table, Annie Lefeau stood with a hand raised uncertainly to her mouth. 'I know my daughter painted this,' Ruth said quietly. 'And I know she did it recently.'

Sitting in her car, she removed the wrapping from the painting and looked at it more closely, breathing in the smell of turpentine and oil paint. Inside the shop, she could see Annie Lefeau staring at her, drawn and somber. Ruth looked at her watch. Four thirty. Just across from here she had noticed a place called the Docksider Diner: she drove up the short track from the gallery and over the main road to park in the lot behind it. Inside, she ordered an iced tea, then sat in the window, watching, waiting.

After a while, she asked for the check and paid it, leaving a generous tip, then sat a while longer, prepared to wait for as long as it took. At five fifteen, Annie Lefeau appeared, driving a dirty green Camaro. She drove cautiously to the edge of the street, looked in both directions, then turned left. Hurriedly, Ruth stood up.

At the door of the restaurant, she turned to the waitress. 'The person who runs that place across from here. Annie Lefeau.'

The woman nodded. 'What about her?'

'Does she live far from here?'

'A couple of miles the other side of town,' the waitress said. 'Little place called Troy Ponds.'

'Right. Thanks.'

She drove fast along the road Annie Lefeau had taken. Before long, she saw the green Camaro, three cars ahead of her. Shortly after that, a sign indicated a right turn toward Troy Ponds, and Annie swung off the road, followed by one of the cars behind. And Ruth. Keeping back now, she trailed the other cars into Troy Ponds, a tiny ribbon development along a rural road. After a while, the other car peeled off. A couple of

441

vehicles came toward them on the other side of the road and Annie raised a hand to one of them, tooting her horn as she did so. If she had noticed Ruth behind her, she gave no indication.

Two or three hundred yards further, she turned off into a driveway, a rough area of gravel and grass in front of a one-storey house. There was a two-car garage on one end and a spacious porch on the other. In back, trees crowded almost to the windows. Ruth continued up the road a way, then found a place to pull off. She turned off the engine and waited for fifteen minutes by the dashboard clock before driving back again to the Lefeau house. Pulling in past the entrance, she parked on the grass at the side of the road, out of sight of Annie's windows.

Hoping she was not observed, she ran across the driveway to the front door. Before pressing the bell, she pulled the screen door open. Ms Lefeau came to the door almost immediately. She had released her rich hair from its braid and it hung below her shoulders like a fall of water. Her face paled when she saw Ruth. 'What the hell are you doing here?' she demanded.

'I have to speak to you,' Ruth said.

'I already told you I don't know your daughter.'

'And I think you're lying.' As the woman opened her mouth to speak, Ruth pushed on. 'Ms Lefeau, I *must* find her—'

'I suppose you want her to come home with you?'

'If she's willing, yes, I most certainly do.'

Annie made a sound of disgust. 'So her stepfather can go on abusing her?'

'*What?*'

'Please . . .' Annie held up her hand. 'Don't pretend you didn't know.'

442

'So she *is* alive?' Ruth put a hand against the door-post for support, afraid she might otherwise fall.

The other woman moved back. 'Don't think I have any intention of helping you find her.' She tried to push the door shut, but Ruth crowded after her.

'I don't know what Josephine's told you,' she said, 'but there is no stepfather. Nor was she ever abused by Paul, my husband, her father.'

'How do you know that?'

'Because . . .' Ruth stopped. 'Because I know my husband,' she said simply.

'I wonder how many other wives have said that.'

'Ms Lefeau – Annie. I want Josephine back. I love her more than I can say – we both do. If there's anything I can do to make up to her for what she perceives I've done to hurt her, I would willingly do it. But that's not the only reason I'm here. My son William, Josephine's brother – ' She broke off. 'Ms Lefeau, please let me come in.'

'Why should I?'

'Because I don't think you're in possession of all the facts. And if you would listen to me for a few minutes, you might view the situation somewhat differently.' Seeing Annie's hesitation, Ruth hurried on. 'Perhaps if you'd let me explain why I'm here, you would feel less hostile. So may I please come in?'

'I suppose so,' Annie said reluctantly. She motioned Ruth to go ahead of her into a pleasant sitting room where antique furniture had been skillfully combined with modern glass and wood. In front of a fieldstone fireplace filled with an elaborate arrangement of dried flowers and white-painted twigs, she faced Ruth nervously. Her pared-down face seemed suddenly much older. A tic beat in one eye. 'Go ahead,' she said. 'Let's hear what you have to say.'

In her head, Ruth assembled the salient facts, much as she would a presentation on behalf of one of her clients. 'For a start, whatever she may have told you, Josephine was a much-loved child. If she was abused, it was not by anyone in her family. If she *was* abused, she knew she could have talked to her parents – my husband of more than twenty years, and myself – about it. However, I don't believe she was abused by anyone at all, not in the way you think.'

'Go on.' Annie Lefeau narrowed her cat's-eyes.

'As you're obviously aware, there was an accident, and Josephine was lost. We all believed she was dead. We've all mourned her ever since, and missed her desperately. It's only in the past few days that I've begun to believe that perhaps she survived and, for reasons I can only guess at, didn't want to come home. What you've said so far confirms it. I'm sure you don't need me to tell you how painful it is to know that.'

Annie reached a hand toward Ruth and then withdrew it.

'My son is desperately ill with leukemia.' Ruth was pleading now. 'His only hope of survival lies in a bone marrow transplant, and so far we've been unable to find a match for him. His sister might be able to provide that match. You can see how important it is for me to locate her.'

'This is terrible.' Annie Lefeau bit her lip, nervously twisting her ringless fingers. She tossed her head so that her fox-colored hair settled back behind her ears. 'How can I believe you?' she said finally.

'How can you not?'

'I don't know what to do.'

'Ask yourself why I should come after you like this if I wasn't desperate. Josie's blood might possibly save her brother's life. As his sibling she represents the best chance Will has – the *only* chance left.' Aware of the other woman's mounting distress, Ruth pushed on relentlessly. 'If you know where she is, Mrs Lefeau, for God's sake think of my boy.'

'What have I done?' Annie said suddenly. She took a hank of her bright hair and thrust it against her mouth. 'Dear Lord, I shouldn't . . . I can't . . .'

'You should. You can.' Ruth seized the other woman's wrist and held it tightly. 'You know where she is, don't you? You know she's alive.'

Annie drew in a deep breath and then exhaled it. 'Yes. Yes, I do.'

'You do? You *do*?'

The other woman nodded.

'Where is she?' Ruth said, scarcely able to breathe, and did not mind that her voice shook.

'I told her. I said it was wrong, she shouldn't leave you in ignorance, it wasn't fair, whatever she felt about her parents, it wasn't right—'

'Where is she, Mrs Lefeau?'

'She's . . .' Annie's eyes filled with tears. 'I – uh – oh God, I wish I'd met you long ago, before all this came up.'

'Why?'

'Because then I would never have—' Annie's voice shook. 'I'm so sorry, Mrs Connelly. Truly I am. I never did think she was telling the whole—'

'*Where is she?*'

'She's been – she's been living here, right here with me.'

Blindly Ruth reached for the armchair and sank into it. The room began to waver and dim.

'She'd been into the gallery a couple of times before,

you see, we'd got on well, talked about a lot of things. Pollution, Greenpeace: we had a lot in common, even though she was so young. She was very passionate, very . . . strong. When I read about her disappearance in the papers, I was devastated. That's why I sent you that sketch. And then, later, I – I . . .' Ms Lefeau took the top off a crystal decanter and poured whiskey into two glasses, handing one to Ruth. Her hands were shaking.

'You what?'

'I went down to—' Again she broke off.

'*What?*' Ruth wanted to shake the woman, shake the information out of her trembling mouth.

Annie squared her shoulders. Took a deep breath. Gazing at the flower arrangement in the hearth, she said: 'One afternoon, about a year ago, someone came in and when I looked up – it was her. I could hardly believe it. I just couldn't—' Annie shook her head, still incredulous.

'What did she say?'

'I can't really remember, I was so taken aback. But while we were talking, she told me that for the past week she'd been sleeping in her car, some old rustbucket she'd picked up somewhere, so I offered her a room. She's used this house as a base ever since.'

'Why didn't she . . .' Ruth shook her head in bewilderment. 'One phone call would have . . . She can't have hated us that much.'

'I thought so too – until she told me about her stepfather molesting—'

'But she doesn't have a stepfather!' cried Ruth. 'And her father's a good man. A good father.'

Ms Lefeau scrubbed at her face with a balled-up tissue. 'Oh God!' she cried despairingly. 'If only I'd known . . .' She had the sad, shattered eyes of someone struggling to come to terms with grief. 'I have no family of my own. She's been like a – like my daughter.'

Ruth saw the deep hurt inside the other woman. 'She *is* my daughter,' she said gently. '*Please*, Annie, tell me where she is.'

'She trusts me. I just can't betray her. I can't even be sure that you're telling the truth.'

'You know I am.' Ruth spoke as forcefully as she dared. 'Why would I be lying? What do I stand to get out of it?'

'She told me that if anyone ever came looking for her, I wasn't to give her away. She actually made me raise my hand and swear it.'

It was precisely the kind of melodramatic gesture Josie would have gone for. 'If she doesn't want to see us or be with us, that's her choice and however hard it is for us, we'll respect it. But for Will's sake . . .'

'She doesn't know about him being ill,' Annie said softly.

'If she did, wouldn't she want to help?'

'I'm sure she would.'

'Then tell her that Will needs her.' Ruth raised her voice a little: 'And that I do, too.'

Annie lifted the weight of her hair in both hands and let it fall against her neck. 'I can't do that.'

'Why not?'

'Because – I don't know where she is. She's taken off again. She does that. She'll call me eventually, but I have no way of knowing when.'

A choking despair swept over Ruth. To have come so close to her daughter, only to lose her again . . . she buried her face in her hands.

Annie put a hand on her shoulder. 'Don't give up now,' she said.

23

When the telephone rang, he was watching some crap on the TV, not really watching, just thankful to have the bright images to focus on rather than the thought of his son's white face. Still staring at the screen, he reached over and lifted the receiver. When he heard her voice, he hit the mute button on the remote. 'Ruth . . . Did you find what you were looking for?'

'Almost,' she said.

'Want to tell me about it.'

'Maybe.'

'What do I have to do?'

'Listen, Paul. Just listen, okay?'

'I promise.'

'It's about Josie.'

'But—'

'You promised.'

'All right.'

'She's alive, Paul. She's really alive.'

He had not the slightest doubt that Ruth was making a terrible mistake. Once, he might have said this to her, been rational, logical. But he understood the pressures she was under. He wished he was with her, could hold her in his arms and gently explain how life didn't work

448

like that. Drowned daughters didn't just show up after two years, however hard you might desire them to.

He tried not to think of Josie, the way her hair fell round her face, her thin dark eyebrows, much darker than her hair ever was, her passionate approach to life. So like her mother, and yet so much her own person. 'Where is she now?'

'You don't believe me, do you?'

'I do.'

'I think,' Ruth said, and he could tell she was choosing her words with extreme care, 'I think she needs me to find her.'

'I worry about you, Ruth.'

'Thank you for thinking of me.'

'You wouldn't believe how often I do.'

'And thank you for the roses you sent. They're beautiful.'

'You know what red roses mean?'

'Yes,' she said quietly. 'Yes, I do.'

Putting down the phone, he thought: I'm falling in love with her all over again.

Paul rang the following day as she dispiritedly drank coffee in the kitchen. 'We'll be with you by six tonight,' he told her.

'Good. Everything's ready. How's Will?'

'Glad to be coming up to Maine.' Paul sounded bleak.

'What's wrong?'

'He seems to be getting worse by the day. It's almost more than I can bear.'

'At least we'll be able to support each other when you get here.'

'True.' He sighed heavily. 'Have you heard anything

449

from – from Jo—' He broke off and she knew he could not complete the sentence because he still did not believe that Josie was alive.

'Not yet,' she said quietly.

'Will, his illness, it's going to take every ounce of strength we have to get through the next few months. Or weeks.'

'At least we'll be together.'

Will seemed in much worse physical shape than when Ruth had last seen him a week ago. The pallor of his drug-swollen face, and the gray shadows under his eyes, belied the temporary animation he displayed as he moved heavily from room to room, checking the place out, making sure that everything was as he had remembered. Trying to hide the grief she felt, Ruth followed him, not wanting to let him out of her sight.

'It's great,' he kept saying. 'It's just so great to be back here.'

'I've put you downstairs.'

'But I wanted to be in my own room.'

'I thought you'd like to be able to step directly onto the porch. I've brought all your things down from upstairs.'

'But I . . .' He was about to protest some more, then saw her face and stopped. With an effort, he said: 'Thanks, Mom.'

'Come and talk to me. I'm going to make supper.'

They walked together down the passage to the kitchen. 'Where did that come from?' Will asked, nodding at the sketch of Josie which Ruth had tacked to a cupboard door.

'Someone gave it to me.'

'It's good.'

'I know.'

'You've changed, Mom.'

'Have I?'

'A year ago you wouldn't have allowed yourself to mention Josie's name, let alone had her picture up.'

'I chose the wrong way to come to terms with what happened,' Ruth said. 'I realize that now.' Should she tell him what she had found out or should she wait until he was rested from the journey?

'Ed and his family'll be up on Monday.' Will sat on the edge of the table. 'It's going to be great to sleep in a proper bed, instead of that hospital thing with sides, like I was a baby in a crib.' He stood up again. 'Mind if I go down to the shore?'

'Just don't overtire yourself.'

'I'm not a kid, Mom.'

'I know you're not.'

From the front porch, she watched him walk slowly and with obvious effort across the meadow toward the stony strip of beach below it.

The day had started out warm and blue, sunlight dazzling on the water, the tranquility of intense heat pressing down on them, but since nightfall it had grown progressively colder.

'Fog's coming in,' Will said, looking out into the darkness.

'Which means it'll be cold tonight,' said Paul.

'I like the way it wraps itself round the house. Sort of like a blanket.'

'What do you say we start a fire?'

'Great idea.'

'There's wood stacked on the side porch.'

Will fetched the big two-handled wicker basket from

its place beside the fieldstone hearth in the living room and together they started to fill it.

'Hey, *Dad*,' Will said, reproachfully, after a few moments.

'What?'

'You can't just drop the logs in the basket. You gotta shake them first.'

'Why?'

'There's all sorts of creatures've been living there all this time – sowbugs and spiders and centipedes and stuff. You don't want them to fry, do you?'

'I guess not.' Solemnly, Paul began shaking each log, inspecting it, squinting at the end, until Will started giggling and Paul too, both of them staggering about, bent with laughter, shaking the wood above their heads, to the side, between their legs, shimmying around as though the logs were clumsy maracas. Finally, breathless, still snickering, they lugged the basket back into the living room, and Paul laid and started a fire while Will sat back on the couch and closed his eyes.

For the first time since the second onset of his illness, Paul was truly frightened. Will looked so worn out. The small effort of gathering the logs, of laughing, seemed to have completely exhausted him. Once the fire was going, he sat in front of it, holding his hands to the flames. The firelight gleamed through and around them; to Paul's panicked eyes, they seemed almost transparent, as though the life force was gradually but inexorably being extinguished.

'How about a game of Scrabble?' he said after supper. 'Ruth?'

'Good idea.'

'Okay,' Will said, but once they had started, he couldn't concentrate, his eyes drooping, so deeply sunk that the reflections of the flames in the hearth scarcely reached them.

No, Paul thought, trying not to let his anxiety show. Not my son. Don't take my son.

But he feared that the God he didn't believe in was not listening.

When Will had gone to bed, he sat opposite Ruth, watching the firelight play on her hair. She was wearing some musky perfume which, enhanced by the heat of the flames, filled the air around her.

'What's wrong?' Ruth smiled at him.

'You look so pretty,' he said.

'Me?'

'Like you did when I first met you.'

'Oh, sure.'

He got up and went to sit beside her. He lifted her hand. 'You're still wearing your wedding band.'

'That's because I'm still married.'

'Tell me about Josephine.' He slipped an arm around her shoulders and felt her yield, melt into the curve of his body, lift her face toward him and open her mouth to speak.

Then the telephone rang, and she pulled away, suddenly frantic, scrambling for the receiver, her face tight with anticipation.

Annie Lefeau was on the other end of the line.

'Janie – Josephine – called me this morning,' Annie said. She sounded tense. 'I told her about her brother being sick. She was terribly upset.'

'Did she say where she was?'

'No. She was calling from a pay phone. We didn't get a chance to talk for long. I told her about the bone marrow thing, that she might be a match, and it was Will's last chance. She was distraught,

Ruth, crying and sobbing on the phone.'

'Did you tell her I'd been looking for her?'

'She knows.'

'Did you tell her how much I need to see her?'

'Yes.'

'Did you tell her I love her?'

'She knows that too, Ruth. She said she'd be in touch.'

'That's all?'

'Yes.'

'Did she say when?'

'No. I told her over and over she should call you right away.'

'Thanks for trying.'

'Ruth, I'm going to be in Sweetharbor tomorrow,' Annie said slowly. 'After what's happened, I'll absolutely understand if you say no, but – but would it be okay for me to come by and visit with you? Just for an hour – I can't stay long. I'd like to meet Will. And your husband.'

'Good idea,' said Ruth, trying to reassure, reminding herself that, with Josephine's departure, Ms Lefeau too had been deprived of something precious. 'I haven't told Will yet about his sister. If you're here, you can at least confirm to both of them that I haven't totally lost it.'

'There's something else. Something I need to talk to you about.'

'What sort of thing?'

'I'll – I'll explain when I see you. I'll be with you early afternoon, then, okay?'

'Okay.' Hanging up, Ruth closed her eyes, exhausted.

'Tell me about Josephine.' Paul tried to pick up their conversation where it had been broken off. For the length of a heartbeat, she gazed into his eyes, wondering

454

if the lost mood could be recaptured and deciding it could not.

'Maybe tomorrow,' she said.

Was Josephine really alive?

Staring into the not-quite-darkness, Paul didn't dare allow himself to hope.

He hadn't slept in this bed before, nor in this room. It smelled of herbs and lavender water. Reminded him of his grandmother, who never went out of the house without wearing gloves. Wavy shadows played across the ceiling, as though reflected off the sea, though he didn't know how that could be since it was dark outside.

Ruth and he had started their married life here at Carter's House – and maybe ended it. Coming up here with Will, he'd hoped – he didn't quite know what he had hoped, but he knew it involved holding Ruth in his arms. He could hear her moving about in the bathroom, the spurt and hiss of water from an air-locked faucet as she ran a bath, the clink of a bottle against the glass shelf above the basin. He could imagine her in the tub, lying in scented bubbles, her eyes closed. He was aware of a desperate longing, fierce as a flame, an absolute desire for her.

'I'm starving,' Ruth said, when Will appeared in the kitchen the next morning. 'Are you up for breakfast at the Cabot Inn?'

'You betcha.'

'Let's go.'

'What about Dad?'

'He's gone down to the boatyard. Wants to take another look at the *Duck*.'

'We were going to try and rebuild it,' Will said. 'Before . . . all this.'

'You still could.'

Tyler Reed, the hotel manager, was standing by the reception desk when they came in and at Will's request he seated them at a table overlooking Old Port Street. Will stared avidly out of the window. 'It's so good to be back,' he said. He gazed at his mother over the rim of his glass of milk. 'I really wish we lived here all the time.'

'I'm thinking', Ruth said slowly, 'that maybe we should.'

Although the thought had only just come into her mind, she immediately saw how right it was. Up here she could start again. Striving hard for cheerfulness, she smiled at him. 'I should have thought of it long before now.'

'If we did move up here, what would happen with your job?'

'These days it's much easier to work from home. Anyway, I'm about ready for a downsize. Or even a change. If we moved, I'd probably try to find something closer to home.'

'Really? Honestly?'

'Why not?'

'That's so *cool*.'

'Isn't it though?'

'And we'll drag Grandad and Grandma up from Florida for Christmas. Boy, will they hate that!'

'You're telling me.'

'Everything'll be great again.' He sighed with pleasure as the waitress placed a stack of pancakes and a jug of blueberry syrup in front of him.

'Will . . .' Ruth leaned across her coffee cup, closer to

456

her son. 'I don't know if this is the right place or time to do it, but there's something desperately important I have to tell you.'

The joy ebbed from his face. 'Is it about my cancer? 'Cause if so, don't worry. It doesn't bother me anymore. It did at first, dying and stuff, but I'm okay about it now, I really am.' He cut into the pancakes and lifted a forkful to his mouth.

'You break my heart when you talk like that.'

He looked directly at her. There was a smear of blueberry syrup by his mouth, and the specter of death in his eyes. 'I'm not frightened, Mom, if that's what you think. I've had plenty long enough to get used to the idea.'

'Don't, Will. I can't bear it.'

'Okay. What's so important? You can tell me. I promise not to faint.'

'Will, it's . . .' she began, then shook her head.

'Tell me, Mom.'

'It's about Josie.'

'What about her?'

'She's alive,' Ruth said.

Eyes wide, he stared at her. She saw his hand tremble as he put down his fork. He looked down at his plate. 'Don't, Mom. Please.'

'Don't what?'

'Dad told me you'd got this idea that . . .' He raised his head again. 'C'mon, Mom. Let it go. She's dead. We had a funeral and everything.'

'It was a service, Will, not a funeral. There wasn't a body. And there wasn't a body because she didn't drown that afternoon.'

'Jesus, Mom. Don't drop this on me. I can't take anymore.'

She reached across for his hand and saw him force

457

himself not to pull away. 'Will, believe me. I'm not dreaming this up. It's true.'

'How do you know?'

'Because I've spent the past week looking for her, and I finally found where she's been living for the past year.' Ruth described what she had learned from Annie Lefeau.

He listened without comment, then said: 'Where did she go at the beginning? How did she handle it all?'

'I don't know. Not yet. She'll tell us.'

'It'd better be good,' said Will. He sounded angry. 'I thought – I kind of kept hoping that she'd made it okay, after the accident. But when she didn't get in touch with us, I realized she must have died after all. Otherwise she'd have called us. She'd have let us know she was okay. She'd never have left us hanging like that. Never in a million years.' His eyes filled. 'I knew it was all my fault—'

'No.'

'—and that was *so* terrible.' He turned his head away so she could not see his face. 'Is this Annie woman playing with a full deck?'

'I think so.'

'And Josie's really truly alive?'

'Yes, she really truly is.'

'Oh, Mom . . .' There was a break in Will's voice. 'Are you *sure*?'

'I'm sure. Annie Lefeau is coming to visit this afternoon. She can tell you herself.'

'Do you think Josie knows we're back in Carter's House?' Will pushed at the tears in his eyes.

'Yes, I do. Oh, darling Will, if only she'd get in touch with us.'

There was a flush lying along Will's over-prominent

458

cheekbones. 'Josie alive after all! That's my last wish come true.' His eyes filled again.

As they drove home, he said: 'Maybe Josie and I can take the boat out when she comes home. I really want to go sailing, and I know you're not up for it.'

When she comes home . . . How ordinary it sounded. 'I could try if you like. Crew for you, I mean.' Ruth's stomach began to churn. The sea, just the two of them, in a small boat . . . 'If that's what you want.'

'That's okay. I don't want you getting worried. Dad and I can go. Or I'll wait until Josie can take me.'

'Oh, Will. I'm so terribly proud of you.'

'Hey, you're not so bad yourself.'

Mother and son smiled at each other. Unspoken between them lay the treasure of a Josie refound and all it might mean.

Annie Lefeau arrived at four o'clock. She had piled up her fierce hair on top of her head and anchored it insecurely with colored combs. She seemed less austere, the lines of worry smoothed from her face, as though she could relax now that the burden of Josie's problems, real or supposed, had been removed. She would not meet Ruth's eyes.

She shook hands with Paul, greeted Will with delight. 'I'm *so* happy to meet you,' she told him. 'Your sister talked about you such a lot.'

'You really know her?'

'I really do. She's something special.'

'Mom said she's been living with you.'

'That's right.' Reaching into the leather pouch slung over her shoulder, Annie took out a package. 'I brought you this.'

'Thanks,' Will said. He undid the wrapping to reveal

a small picture of a freckled boy leaning against an upturned boat and laughing. He stared down at it. 'Hey, it's me.'

'Janie – Josie, I mean – she painted it on your birthday last year,' Annie said softly. 'She kept it in her room.'

'Oh, Mom . . .' Blindly Will passed the little painting to his mother.

'She did it from memory,' said Annie.

'It's beautiful.' Ruth showed it to Paul.

He looked at it with a mixture of surprise and pride on his face. 'I'm impressed.'

'You have a very talented daughter, Professor Connelly.'

'*Have*? Are you really sure you mean what you're saying, Ms Lefeau?'

She drew in a deep breath and clasped her hands together in her lap. Looking above their heads toward the sea, she said: 'I need to tell you something. I hope that when you've heard me out, you'll be able to forgive me.' Shaking her head, she took another breath. 'This is so hard . . . I guess . . . I better just get on and say what I've come to say.'

'Which is what, exactly?' Paul said.

'I . . . uh . . . I own a cabin in the woods, down by the shore, round the coast a ways from here. It's a sort of extra studio. Unless you knew it was there, you'd never find it. If I'm working on a painting I sometimes stay there overnight – it's kind of primitive but there's packaged food and cans, an oil lamp, candles, a sleeping bag. Even water, rainwater, collected from an old cistern.' She leaned toward Paul and Ruth. 'After the sailing accident, a week or so after Josephine's disappearance, I went down there to work on a canvas I'd started a while ago. And—' She broke off.

'And what?'

'She . . . she was there.'

'Josie was?'

'Yes.'

Ruth looked at Paul and then back at Annie. '*What?* I can't – she was in your cabin?'

'I couldn't believe what I was seeing. She was dead, I knew that – I'd read the papers, I sent you that drawing of her – and yet there she was, alive, in my cabin.'

'I knew about the cabin along the shore, and the food and everything,' Will said. 'I did kind of wonder. It was just the sort of place she'd have headed for.'

'Why didn't you tell us?' demanded Ruth.

Will turned his large eyes on her. 'How could I? You wouldn't talk about her. And anyway, people were looking everywhere for her. I thought that if by any chance she'd ended up there, she'd have been found.'

'When I first saw her, she looked like a wild animal,' Annie said. Her hands jumped about in her lap and she pressed them against her thighs. 'Hair straggling over her face, bruises everywhere, a half-healed gash down one of her arms, a filthy strip of something tied round her wrist. She was feverish, rambling, not really there at all. She'd been living there ever since your accident. She told me that when she was swept away, the current was much too strong to swim against, all she could do was let it carry her. The sea was crashing over her, she was choking, semi-conscious, certain she was going to die. And then she found herself flung forward by a wave and before she was sucked back, realized there were rocks under her feet. The third or fourth time she was washed up, she managed to grab onto a spar of rock and eventually to crawl higher up on to dry ground. She said it took her nearly two days to make her way to my cabin.'

'But . . . I don't understand. Why didn't you let us . . . why didn't she . . .?' Ruth pressed her hands against her temples. 'Why didn't you let us *know*?'

'Ever since you showed up on my doorstep yesterday, I've asked myself that a thousand times.'

'Did you have any idea what we were going through? How we suffered?'

'I do now.'

Ruth hardly heard her. 'I could understand that *she* had some wild idea of not coming home again, but you . . . *you*—' She swallowed. 'You're a responsible adult. How could you have done this?'

Annie's hands leaped and she held them close against her breast. 'There are no excuses, Ruth. None. But at that stage I didn't know you and I did know Josie. So I believed her when she told me that her stepfather . . . that she had been molested . . .'

'Josie said that?' Paul's eyes had grown smoky with suppressed anger.

'I can see now that she was lying, but at the time . . . If you'd seen her . . . she was hardly rational, raving and hysterical. She kept pleading with me not to let anyone know. In the end, I agreed.'

'A phone call,' Ruth said helplessly. 'That's all it would have taken. One call to say she was all right.'

'I told her that. She said . . . she said foolish things, hysterical things. That you wouldn't miss her. That you didn't care about her.'

'That wasn't true,' Will burst out. There was color in his pale face. 'We loved her. All of us.'

Ruth stood up. Anger rushed through her. 'All this time you knew she wasn't drowned, after all.' Raging, she turned away from Annie. 'Christ! How could you have behaved like that? How *could* you?'

462

Annie drew in a shuddering breath. 'I *couldn't*. I moved her in with me, so I could take care of her while I decided what to do. We had so many arguments about it, over those first few days. In the end, she said she'd call you. When I came back the next day, she'd gone.'

'Where to?'

'Ruth, I swear I thought she'd gone back to Boston, taken up her life with you again. I sometimes thought about you, how happy you all must be.'

'And when you saw her again, what did you think then?' Paul asked coldly.

'I . . . I don't really know. I was so happy to see her back again.' Annie fiddled with the combs which held her russet hair back from her face. 'I've behaved so . . . terribly badly.'

'Yes, you have,' Ruth said.

'So has Josie,' said Will.

'If what you've said is true,' Paul agreed, 'then you've caused more pain than you can possibly imagine. If this really is our Josie you're talking about.'

'You still don't believe she's alive, do you?' Ruth said.

'I'm exercising my right to feel skeptical. For instance, if she was who she said, why did she run away from Annie's house?'

'She was always taking off,' said Annie. 'When she had enough paintings, she'd load up that old car of hers and go out on the road to sell them.'

'Making her living from her work, like she always said she would,' Will said softly.

'I knew she'd come back again, so I didn't worry.' Annie looked from one to another. 'I'm sorry.'

'There would have been people who recognized her. At the time, the papers were full of the accident: if she'd

463

been seen, someone would have contacted us, wouldn't they?'

'She deliberately kept away from Sweetharbor and Hartsfield,' said Annie. 'From anywhere she might be recognized. Besides, she looks different now. And Millport is miles away from here.'

'This is all extremely painful for us,' Paul said angrily. He reached across and took Ruth's hand.

Annie stood. 'I can only say that I'm desperately sorry.'

'I should damn well think you are!'

'I don't suppose we shall meet again,' Annie said humbly.

'If I have anything to do with it, no, we won't,' said Paul. He was breathing heavily, his nostrils white and pinched with rage.

Ruth, aware of the other woman's distress, wondered how she herself might have handled the situation. Better than this, she was certain. One phone call – surely just one phone call could have been made.

When Annie had left, they sat silently on the porch with glasses of iced tea. None of them wanted to discuss what they had just been told. They waited. Hoped. Any moment now the telephone would ring and it would be Josie. Or a car would come bumping up the track and she would be home again. Now that she knew about Will's illness, she would surely come as soon as she could. In the distance the sea shimmered and winked. A breeze stirred the tops of the pointed trees and tugged at Will's thin hair. Every now and then they heard the sound of the bell on the buoy out in the channel.

One phone call, Ruth thought, over and over again. How different our lives might have been.

* * *

That evening, they lit another fire and played cribbage for a while with the ivory-inlaid set which had belonged to Ruth's great-grandmother. Again, Will found it difficult to concentrate.

Ruth put her hand on his. 'She'll come,' she said softly. 'Don't worry.'

'I wish she'd hurry up,' he said fretfully. His breath rattled inside his ribs. The firelight threw long shadows across his face as he put down his cards. 'I'm tired. I'll go to bed, guys, if you don't mind.'

'That's okay, son.'

'I'll come and tuck you up,' added Ruth. The bedtime ritual of childhood seemed to calm him a little.

'Ten minutes,' he said.

Later, having kissed him goodnight, Ruth was about to close his door behind her when Will called out. 'Mom!'

'What, sweetheart?'

'Are you angry with her? With Josie? For not getting in touch.'

Ruth wondered what she should say. 'I – I don't know.'

'Because I am,' Will said.

'I think we're going to have to just concentrate on the future and forget about what's happened,' said Ruth carefully.

'Just like that? I don't think so.' The smudged shadows beneath Will's eyes lay like puddles in the pallor of his face. The picture Josie had painted was propped against the wall at the end of his bed, where he could see it from his pillow. 'When she comes, you'll wake me up, won't you?'

'Of course I will.'

'Even if it's really late?'

'I promise.'

'Even if I'm dead asleep?'

She shuddered inwardly at his choice of words. 'Whatever time it is, I swear I will wake you up,' she said. 'Okay?'

'Okay.' He smiled the gaunt, pale-gummed smile she had grown used to over the past months. 'Please don't think I'm frightened, Mom. About dying. Because I'm really not.' He lifted his arms. 'Mom.'

'Yes?'

'Give me a hug.'

'As many as you like.' Tears pooled behind Ruth's eyes as she walked back across the hooked rugs and put her arms round her son. His bones felt as fragile as breadsticks, as though they would snap under the slightest pressure. She screwed her face up to prevent herself from weeping.

Will pushed his naked head into her shoulder, snuggling like a puppy. 'I love you, Mom.'

'And I love you, William, oh, with all my heart.'

In her head, she heard Josie's voice again: *Would you love me, no matter what?*

Would she? Could she?

Paul lay in bed, leaning on his elbow, pretending to read but in reality listening to Ruth getting ready for bed. It had been a craggy sort of day, shredded by the un-fulfilled anticipation of his daughter's return. He thought about the painting of the lichened tombstone, *Death is Swallowed Up in Victory*, and the date – this year – underneath the two-letter signature.

If it really was Josie, what would she look like now? How would she be? Anger and pain simmered under his ribs. How could she have . . .? Why hadn't she . . .?

466

Tears gathered in his throat and he snorted them away.

In the bathroom, water ran into the large old-fashioned basin. He heard Ruth brushing her teeth. Intimate sounds, domestic sounds. He wished he dared call her. He wanted to invite her into his bed, to be reassured by her smell again, her feel, but was afraid that she would stare at him from her large solemn eyes and then turn away. As he had once done from her. He had realized too late that she was telling him that the shell she had built round herself had shattered. Even now he burned at the thought of what she must have felt at his rejection.

Before getting into bed, Ruth stood at the balcony rail. The fog was clearing at last, backing away from the house toward the horizon. A bright sliver of moon hung against the intense lavender of the summer sky, its fragile reflection floating on the black glass of the deeper water beyond the bay. She could hear the ocean breathe and sigh at the foot of the pasture. Across the Sound, lights flickered among the branches of the firs on the shore.

Josie would come.

She would come. For Will's sake, she had to

24

Fog had crept in during the night and now lay heaped across the front pasture. The house felt damp, as though the pale sea-mist had seeped in through the screens and under the door; a thick white light filled the rooms.

Paul had to pick up something from the bookshop in Hartsfield and suggested that Will drive over with him, but Will preferred to stay at home. He spent the morning walking slowly from room to room, as though, if he tried hard enough, he could force his sister to materialize at the kitchen table, on the living-room couch, in his bedroom. 'When do you think she'll get here?' he asked, standing at the windows, gazing into the fog.

Ruth put an arm round his shoulder, grieving at the way his bones pushed against the thin flesh which covered them. His face was bloodless, the eyes deeply shadowed. There were bruises on his neck and down his arms.

'Soon.' Carefully, she hugged him.

'But *when*?' He put a hand against the wall, as though he needed support to remain standing. '*How* soon?'

'The minute she can, sweetheart.'

The hours went by, and Josephine did not appear.

'But she will, darling,' Ruth said to Will, now lying on the sofa in the living room. 'She will.'

Will lifted his head. 'I just wish she'd hurry up, that's all.'

Around noon, Carmel Stein called. 'What a dreary day,' she said. 'Why don't you bring Will over for lunch? The kids can do boy stuff together while you and I dish the dirt.'

'Let me just check with Will,' Ruth said.

This time she found him huddled miserably on the porch, still gazing toward the invisible sea, his hair and clothes pearled with mist. 'Want to go over to the Steins'?'

'We have to stay here,' he said. 'In case she comes.'

'But—' Ruth broke off when he turned his face to her. His eyes were like those of a trapped animal. Shaken, she went back to the phone.

'We can't make it today,' she lied. 'Maybe another time.'

'How's Will?'

'He's – he's a bit tired but fine.'

'Are you okay, Ruthie? You sound kind of stressed.'

'No, I'm okay. Honestly.'

'Call me if you want anything,' Carmel said.

'I will.'

Ruth made sandwiches but Will barely touched his. It was difficult to keep up any pretence of normality. The seconds, the minutes, sluggishly changed into hours.

As the afternoon began to fade, she found Will lying on his bed. 'I thought I'd drop by the Cottons',' she said. 'I bought some candies for Marietta. Peanut butter cups. I know she likes them.'

'You've never done that before.'

'Maybe I should have,' Ruth said. 'Want to walk down to their house with me?'

'Marietta'll be some glad,' he said, in the voice he kept for Maine, an attempt to belong to the place he loved best.

'Come with me, Will.'

'Suppose Josie calls?'

'We won't be long.'

'Is Dad coming too?'

'Let's go ask him.'

Paul was at the edge of the woods, chopping logs from a sapling birch which had fallen during the winter storms. His face was flushed. Seeing them coming, he stopped and wiped his forehead with his arm.

'Getting ready for winter already, Dad?' Will asked, giving his ghostly grin.

'Can't start too soon,' Paul said.

'We're going to visit the Cottons,' Ruth said.

'On second thoughts, Mom . . . maybe I'll stay here. Give Dad a hand.'

'Are you sure?'

'In case there's a phone call.'

Paul and Ruth exchanged glances. 'I've got my cell phone,' Paul said gently to his son. 'You can sit and talk to me and we'll hear if anyone telephones.'

Tucked up against the edge of woods, the Cottons' house was painted the same red as Ruth's barn, its woodwork picked out in white. The side porch looked out over an abundant vegetable patch and a red-painted, white-trimmed shed like a smaller version of the house. The property stood lower down on the same inlet as Carter's House. Ben's skiff was tied up to a jetty, alongside a salt-pocked old lobster smack called *Mari*.

Ben's rusty pickup truck was parked alongside a tractor worn down by wind and weather to the bare metal. Beside the shed, lobster traps were neatly stacked, together with a bright tumble of pot buoys. Pink and purple lupines stood beside the steps leading to the front door; more of them spread toward the trees. Glossy brown chickens scratched in front of an unpainted wooden chicken coop.

Ruth banged at the door but it seemed the Cottons were not home. She sat on the porch of their weathered little house and waited for a while, enjoying the solitude, the peace. On the rough grass behind the house, laundry was pegged to a clothes line, billowing and filling with the fresh breeze off the water. She remembered Josie demanding to know why she too didn't hang the laundry out to dry in the fresh air and could not recall what her response had been. Something to do with not having enough time, probably. Back then, time had constantly slipped past her, carried away on a tide of meaningless and self-imposed duties. Now, with every second precious, she saw how important it was sometimes to do nothing except appreciate the privilege of being alive.

Eventually, she wrote a note, using large plain letters, thinking that Ben's old eyes might not be able to make out her normal tight script, knowing that Marietta was not good with writing. She said she hoped the arthritis was better now the warm weather had come, that she would drop by again very soon. She found a rock and used it to weight down the note on the box of candies, then set off to climb up through the woods toward Carter's House.

The fog had finally begun to roll back. Wisps of it clung to the trees like cotton-candy and then were suddenly gone. Although the sun was not yet visible, the thinning mist took on a golden glow, promising late afternoon heat. Where the trail forked, Ruth hesitated.

471

I'll only stay a couple of minutes, she promised herself. Just a few minutes.

Up on the bluff, the miniature garden in the dip of the big boulder was flourishing. Someone had added five or six tiny white stones, making a wandering path through the little ferns and flowers. A glossy flock of grackles had landed on the rough grass, but lifted into flight as Ruth approached, their purple wings gleaming across the sky before they disappeared behind the trees.

A breeze blew fitfully off the sea, not quite cold. She stood behind the bench, tracing the letters of her daughter's name on the brass plate set into its back. Josephine Carter Connelly. The sea was flat calm now, the color of the lead-foil which used to line the big wooden tea-boxes in the grocery in Hartsfield when she was a child. A steady certainty possessed her. Today, Josie would come home. She knew it as surely as she knew that tomorrow the sun would rise.

The garnered images of Will's and Josie's childhood crowded into her mind and suddenly, despite herself, despite her defiant optimism, she was overtaken by a tide of grief. Confronted by the indifferent sky, the unfeeling sea, she could not hold back her tears.

'Don't cry . . .'

The voice behind her was so low she thought she must have dreamed words into the sound of the wind.

'Mom . . .'

Slowly she turned. For a moment, she wondered whether she was seeing real flesh and blood or merely a mirage conjured up by desperation. 'Josie . . .' she whispered.

'Mom . . .'

'Josie!' Ruth held out her arms and her daughter came running and the two women wrapped themselves

472

around each other, clinging together tightly, tightly, for moments that seemed to last forever.

At last, Ruth thought. My daughter, at last. Lost and found. The miracle of this reunion was almost overwhelming. The swell of love inside her threatened to break through the frail barriers of body as she drew into herself the youthful scent of skin, fragility of bones under flesh, smooth slide of hair. 'I love you,' she murmured, her lips fierce against her daughter's cheek. She remembered how she used to crush the little girl Josie had once been against her, lost in a welter of passion. 'I *love* you.'

'Mom,' breathed Josie. 'Oh, Mom.'

'We've missed you. *Missed* you, Josie, more than . . .'

'So have I.'

'How I've longed . . . ached to . . .' Ruth stopped. What she wanted to say was beyond words. She held her daughter away from her. 'How did you know I'd be here?'

'This has always been our special place.'

'You look so . . .' Josie was taller than she had been at sixteen. And very different. The long-legged slimness of girlhood had given way to feminine curves. She had cut her hair short. Her eyes were older, wiser: examining the detail of her face, Ruth did not want to know just yet what they had seen. The scar on her wide suntanned forehead shone like a tiny crescent moon. 'Josie . . .' Ruth said softly.

'What?'

Ruth laughed. 'It's so good to be able to say your name. To see you. To . . . have you here.' There were so many questions to ask, so many blanks to be filled in. Stepping back but not letting go of her daughter's arm, Ruth said as calmly as she could: 'Shall we go

473

tell the rest of the family you've come home?'

Josie did not move. 'Mom, please forgive me.'

Forgive? 'You're back now,' Ruth said. 'That's all that matters.'

'Please, Mom. We have to talk about this,' insisted Josie.

'Will's desperate to see you. And your father . . .'

'I don't want to see them until we've discussed this, Mom. You and me. It's so important. Why didn't I call? That's what you want to know, isn't it?'

'Now isn't really the—'

Josie's gaze was direct, anxious. 'How could I have let you go on believing I was dead? You can't push the question away, Mom. It lies at the heart of everything.'

'Okay. You're right,' Ruth said. 'I'll try to say something of what I feel.' She could feel her heart knotting inside her. She was terrified of reacting wrongly, of scaring Josie away again, yet at the same time there were things it seemed important to say. Forgiveness was easy. But behind the flame of love renewed lay something more complex – the need to understand. 'I've learned so much about you that I didn't know – how kind you are, how compassionate, how thoughtful of others. Yet to the people who ought to matter most in the world . . .'

'You don't know how many times I wanted to call you,' Josie interrupted. Her voice briefly failed and she cleared her throat. 'Not at first. But then, after a while, it got so difficult. The longer I left it . . . what would I say? After what I'd done, how could I expect to come back into your lives?' She lifted her shoulders. 'I don't know . . . I guess I was afraid.'

Fog still lay at the far edge of the sky. Below them, the sea moved slowly. Josie walked to the edge of the bluff and looked down at the rocks. 'I've thought about it so often. At first, I was just mad. At you, mostly. Then I was hurt. When I fetched up on the beach, coughing up seawater, aching all over, I felt such hurt . . .'

'But why?'

'Because—' On the edge of the bluff, she turned. Tried to laugh. 'It sounds so petty – because you'd called out for Will, but not for me.'

'He was younger, smaller . . .'

'I know.' Josie caught her lip between her teeth. 'I guess the truth is, I wanted to punish you.'

'It's enough that you're back,' Ruth said gently. 'I don't need to know anything else.'

'You *have* to know. Because I want to tell you that I realize there was nothing to punish you *for*. It was just . . . I didn't appreciate how lucky I was to have you for a mother. I keep asking myself how I could have been so – so unfeeling. How I could have let you suffer.'

'Josie, it's not necessary—'

'Listen to me, Mom . . .'

'As I never used to.'

'. . . I need to say this. Now. Before we go back to the house.' Josie shook her head. 'You're so strong, you see. And I wanted to be like you. I admired you so much for being made a partner, for doing so well. For succeeding. And yet, at the same time, I wanted you to be home in an apron, baking cookies and apple pies, the all-American mom.' Josie gave a laugh that was almost a sob. 'It's only recently I've begun to see that nobody can do everything. And then I remembered that you *did* do all that when we were little kids, and it was only when we got older that you picked up your own life again.'

'Josie, you don't have to—'

'I want to. I *need* to. I was so unfair. So hard on you.'

475

'Your grandmother thinks *I* was hard on *you*.'

'But that's *good*, Mom. Don't you see? You set standards for me – for all of us. And I also see now that part of your strength lies in the fact that you do what you do in the way you do it.' Josie ran her suntanned fingers through her hair. 'I just couldn't see it then. Any of it. So when I finally kind of came to, after the accident, I thought . . . I thought you probably wouldn't mind that much, after the way things were between us that summer. And you'd said you were going to send me off to one of those behavior-modification places . . .'

'I never meant it, not for a single moment.'

'. . . and you were refusing to let me leave school, and then the last thing I heard, when that wave crashed over us, was you yelling for Will, not for me.' Josie walked slowly toward her mother and then stood with her hands hanging at her sides. She began to cry. 'Mom, I'm so ashamed of myself.'

'Sweetheart, it's all right.'

'It's *not*. All I thought about was my own feelings. I didn't give a shit about anyone else's.'

'Everything I know about you, Josephine, everything I've come to realize, hearing what people think of you, has made me so proud . . .' Ruth tilted Josie's face toward her and with her finger wiped the tears from her cheek. 'I only wish I could be as proud of myself.' They were both silent for a moment. The wind off the sea blew through Ruth's hair, cold enough to tighten her scalp. 'Losing you . . . I didn't handle it well.' She hesitated. 'Dad and I split up.'

'It's all my fault,' sobbed Josie.

'It just seemed less difficult for us to cope alone than together.'

'You guys were so close.'

'We still are,' Ruth said quietly.

'I often used to think how lucky I was, having parents who were still together after such a long time, when so many of my friends' parents were divorced.'

'We've kind of gotten back together for the moment.'

'Mom . . .'

'Hush,' said Ruth. 'I love you more than I can say, Josephine. I always have. I always will, whatever you do. You're my child. It's a bond which can't ever be broken.'

'I realize that now.'

'When Annie Lefeau told me that all along you were—' The sentence lost itself somewhere at the back of her throat.

'Don't blame her. She kept telling me it wasn't fair to you and Dad, that I was being callous, inhumane. All sorts of things. I knew she was right.'

'If you hadn't left the earring,' Ruth said, 'even now, I'd never have thought for a minute that you were still alive. I'd never have gone looking for you.'

'Which earring?'

'The one you put right here for me to find. One of the pair I gave you, silver, with a copper heart in the middle. You remember – you were wearing them when you . . . on the day of the accident.'

'I've still got them. Both of them.'

'But it's because of the earring that I first started to—'

Josie shook her head. 'It wasn't mine.' Out on the water the bell buoy clanged once. She clutched at her mother's hand. 'I used to go into the house from time to time. I took my painting gear away. And some money. The contingency fund. Sometimes I'd play the piano, sit, be there where we used to be happy and just wish that we . . .'

'Oh, Josie . . .' Ruth said softly.

'And I used to ring Mrs Dee, pretending I wanted to rent the house, to find out if you were coming back at Christmas or in the summer. Thought I might sneak around, you see, try and catch a glimpse of you, check out how you were all doing.'

'We were here at Christmas.'

'But not at Carter's House.'

'No. I – I wasn't ready for that.'

'Oh, Mom . . . what have I done to you?'

'I bought a picture of yours. *Death is Swallowed Up in Victory.*'

'Annie told me.'

'I think it's amazing.'

'I've learned a lot in the past year or so.' Josie stared steadily at her mother. 'And not just about painting.'

'So have I.' Ruth squeezed her daughter's hand. 'Come on, darling, let's go find the others.'

They began to walk down through the woods. As they passed the boulder, Josie touched the scar on her forehead. 'Do you remember, Mom?'

'Of course.'

In single file, Josie in front, they crossed the log bridge. 'When I found out you were opening up the cottage for the summer, I put some flowers there for you,' Josie said over her shoulder.

'Freesias. Your absolute favorite flower . . .'

'That's right.'

Consumed with love, Ruth luxuriated in the new-found details of her daughter: the strong line of her back, the way her long legs strode so confidently down the trail, the toss of hair over her scalp. Everything is going to be all right now, she thought. We can go back to being a family again.

Skirting the cranberry bog, Josie stopped. 'Mom. How sick exactly is Will?'

'He's going to die,' Ruth said. 'Unless . . .'

'What?'

'Unless we're able to find a tissue match, so he can have a bone marrow transplant. There's a world-wide register, but so far nothing's come up. His best chance is from within the family, but none of us is a match.' Ruth expelled a deep breath. 'He'll be *so* happy to see you, Josie.'

'Mom, I never said this enough, if I ever did at all, but . . . I love you so much.'

'As I love you.'

For a long deep moment they held each other's gaze. What is she thinking, Ruth wondered? The young woman in front of her was Josie, and yet not Josie. There was a distance between them, made up not of antipathy now, but of time. Whatever they had been two years ago, both of them were different now. Stronger. Better. They would need time to learn each other again.

When they emerged from the woods, Will was standing at the edge of the pond, staring toward the trees, as though he already knew that his sister had returned. When he saw them, he began an awkward limping run toward them, arms outspread. 'Josie!' His face seemed to be one enormous grin. 'Josie, Josie! You're back.'

Watching her, Ruth saw Josie's shock at the first sight of her brother and how fear drew the color from her face as she hugged him, kissed his pale cheek, carefully reached up to pat the top of his head. 'You've grown,' she said.

'It happens,' Will said.

'Where'd you get the ear stud?'

'Mom bought it.'

'C'mon,' Josie said, glancing over at her mother, digging into herself for the strength not to exclaim over Will's appearance. 'Get real. Ruth Carter Connelly bought her son an *ear* stud?'

'It's true.'

'Things must've changed round here.'

'You can say that again.'

Josie touched her brother's arm. 'You aren't going to believe this, but I've really missed you.'

Will sighed. 'It's been so great not having a big sister to boss me around. But I guess I could get used to it again.'

'Did you get the picture of you I painted?'

'Ayuh. And you know what?'

'What?'

'I hate to admit it, but you're *some* good.'

'Think so?'

'Know so.' Will put out his hand and Josie took it tenderly in hers.

'Anybody want anything?' Ruth asked, her eyes misting over. 'Because I'm going into the house to pour myself some lemonade, take some to your father.'

'I'll come and . . . and see Dad in just a minute,' said Josie. To Will, she said, 'How about a walk down to the shore?'

'Great.' Clumsily, Will turned. Every movement he made seemed to hurt him. 'You'll have to go slowly, though.'

'As slowly as you like, Will.'

As they disappeared round the side of the house, Ruth went into the kitchen and poured a glass of lemonade which she took out to Paul.

'Do you think she's going to show up today?' he said as soon as he saw her.

480

'Paul . . . she's already here.'

'Josie is?'

'She's just gone down to the shore. With Will.'

'Why didn't she come and—'

'She's ashamed, Paul. And a bit afraid.'

He slammed his ax into the tree-stump so that it stuck there. 'I'll go and—'

Ruth held him back. 'Give her a few moments alone with Will first.'

'But I want to—' He broke off. 'I suppose you're right.'

'Paul.'

'Yes?'

'I can hardly believe it that we're all together. A family again.' Wounded, broken, but a family.

Paul nodded. 'I guess.'

'Tomorrow, Josie can go to the hospital and have a blood test and, if we're lucky, we'll find a match. Then maybe everything will be all right again.'

'Maybe it will,' he agreed. He wiped his hands on the front of his shirt. 'Sorry, I can't wait. I'm going to find them.'

He ran across the rough grass of the pasture toward the little slope leading to the shore. He could see them standing facing each other down by the water's edge. Coming closer, the breeze carried toward him a sound so unusual he barely recognized it. Will, angry? Will, yelling at his sister? Paul wanted to rush forward, stop him, put a hand across his mouth, warn him to take care, in case she vanished again.

'. . . not fucking fair!' Will was shouting.

'I know that—'

'Do you have the faintest idea what you've done to

us? Mom and Dad, *me*? We thought you were fucking *dead*.'

'I'm sorry.'

'Sorry's not good enough.' Will was weeping now, picking up pebbles from the beach and lobbing them into the water. 'You even told that Lefeau woman that Dad was – was feeling you up. That's disgusting. Gross.'

'I know, I know. But it was the only thing I could think of that would stop her contacting them. And don't call her "that Lefeau woman" – she's been a good friend to me.'

'I just don't get it, Josie. Why'd you let us go on believing you were *dead*, for fuck's sake?'

'I – it sounds so stupid now – I guess I wanted to punish them, just for a bit. Especially Mom. I can't really explain it.'

'But it was such a *shitty* thing to do. Can't you see that? It was like you didn't give a fuck about us.'

'I didn't feel like anyone gave a fuck about *me*. I wanted to leave school, go to art school, and I knew Mom wouldn't let me in a million years, even if I could persuade Dad. And neither of them seemed to have the faintest idea of what it meant to me. Nor . . . nor how *good* I was.'

'So you were going to make them pay, is that it?'

'Sort of, I guess.'

'That's so horrible, Josie.'

'I know. I hate myself. I'm not at all the person I thought I was. Not strong, or – or kind – or *good*. It was like I'd dug myself into a hole. It just got harder and harder to get out of it.'

'And me, what about me, what did I ever do to you?' Will's thin body twisted as the sobs were wrenched from his chest. 'Why'd you let *me* think you were dead?'

'I couldn't have told you and not them.'

'I've had this fucking awful time, being sick and all, and the whole time I'm worrying about you not being around and what it'd do to Mom and Dad if I wasn't either.'

Josie too was crying. 'Will, you're not going to—'

'I hate you, all right? I hate you for what you did.' Will stopped and knuckled the tears from his eyes. He bent down and picked up a driftwood branch and threw it into the water. As it floated away, he said quietly: 'Which doesn't mean I don't – I don't love you, too.'

'Oh Will . . .' Josie put her arms around her brother and rocked him against her chest.

After a moment, Paul cleared his throat.

Josie broke away from Will and looked up at him. 'Dad.'

He stared at her. It really was her, standing below him, hair riffled by the wind lifting off the water, his daughter, his Josie, his little girl. Restored to life.

'Dad,' she said again. 'I'm home.'

He held his arms wide. A pulsing rush of joy filled him as she ran toward him and flung herself into them. 'Josie,' he said. He felt her heart leaping against his and knew, with unstoppable certainty, that here, now, everything at last was put right. Tears sprang from his eyes and he suddenly began to sob. 'Oh God. Josie . . .'

'Dad, I'm sorry, I'm sorry.' Josie wept too.

He wanted to tell her it was okay, but his voice would not function.

'I'm *sorry*,' Josie said again.

He held her tighter, never wanting to let her go again. He had a sudden flash of her, two years old, tottering toward him on chubby legs, and how he had swept her up into the air, listened enraptured to her breathless

483

laughter as he held her high above him. Tears ran down his face, dropping into her hair – so clean, so well remembered – while the pain of the last two years dissipated, vanished as though it had never been.

'I *love* you,' he whispered, but could not have said whether he spoke the words aloud or simply felt them. Then Will walked slowly across the beach to join them and they stood together like that, clinging to each other.

That evening, he couldn't take his eyes off his daughter as they sat round the table. Celebrating, Ruth had laid a formal table in the dining room, taken the heavy silver-gilt candlesticks from their hiding place in the linen cupboard, unlocked the glazed commode and taken out the best crystal. The return of the prodigal daughter. She that was lost is found again.

She'd changed so much. Her hair was cut close to her head and dyed a darker brown, her face was thin, far too thin, the bones much more clearly defined than they had been two years ago. How slight she looked. How beautiful.

Josie was talking to Will. 'So this total *prick* asks me to paint a mural all round his indoor swimming pool. Offers to pay me a small fortune.'

'How much is that?' asked Ruth.

'Enough to live on for a month or two. Anyway, he says he wants something to remind him of his mother, who's originally from Greece, right? So I spend hours and hours painting this scene with olive groves and grapevines and, like, the Acropolis in the background.'

'Greek gods, of course,' Paul said, gazing at his daughter as though his eyes could never have enough of her.

'More than you could count,' said Josie. 'Zeus and Apollo and Poseidon and all the rest of them. Mount

Olympus. Wine-dark sea. I boned up on the whole shtick before I started. You never saw anything so Greek in your life. Took me weeks. And then, when I'm finished, know what he says?' She picked up her glass and drank from it, keeping her eyes on Will.

He shook his head. 'What?'

'He says, where's my mom? I don't see my mom. Didn't I tell you I wanted something to remind me of my mom?'

'So what did you do?'

'Told him I hadn't realized he wanted his mother scoping him out every time he stepped under the pool-side shower. And anyway, since he hadn't given me a picture, how did he expect me to know what she looked like?'

Listening to her, Paul realized that they were a family again. It felt strange and yet entirely natural. 'What did he do then?' he said.

'He finked out. Refused to pay me. Said I hadn't carried out the commission. Then I discovered he does that all the time. Gets people to do things for him and then refuses to pay. Wanna know what I did?'

'What?' said Will.

'The guy spends half the year at his house in Pacific Palisades, right? So next time he was out in California, I got into his house one night—'

'Broke in, you mean?' Will's eyes were round.

'Sort of. And then I painted over the entire mural. Painted it white. Two coats.'

'Wow!'

'Takes guts to obliterate a piece of work like that,' Paul said.

'It was the principle of the thing, Dad. I didn't see why he should have something for nothing. Annie

Lefeau told me he did the same thing to a woodworker she knows, who's in a wheelchair and really needs the money. And to a small local builder. What're they going to do? How're they going to get justice?'

'Sure showed him.' Will's over-prominent cheekbones were flushed. His hand, as he lifted food to his mouth, shook slightly.

Where had Josie learned how to force her way into someone else's house? What other dubious skills had she picked up in the time she had been away from them? Where had she been? Was there a man in her life? How had she survived? There was so much Paul wanted to know. Smiling at her through the candle flames, he found that he wanted – *needed* – the answers. Why? *Why?*

Josie caught his eye. Her expression changed. 'I can't explain, Dad,' she said quietly. 'I just can't. Like I said to Mom, by the time I came to my senses, it seemed almost easier just to keep silent.'

'Your mother and I . . . your brother . . .' But what was there to say? It wouldn't alter anything; the lost years couldn't be replaced. He glanced across at Ruth, wondering if she, too, felt this tiny brake on happiness. He poured more wine, guessing that in the future it might simply have to be enough that Josie was back. He tilted his glass to her in a toast. 'To you, darling heart. You don't know how happy we are to have you home.'

She bent toward Will, saying something Paul didn't hear. And seeing the familiar little Josie-smile on her face as she spoke, he felt the hard lump of incomprehension begin to thaw.

Sam Hechst telephoned. 'I promised to take Will out in my boat,' he began, but Ruth cut in.

'Josie's home,' she said.

'Thank God. Oh, that is truly wonderful news.' His voice was warm with pleasure. 'You must be so happy. How is she?'

'About how you'd expect.'

'How are *you*, Ruth?'

'I think you can imagine how we feel.'

'No doubt you'll find it a little strange to have her back, as well as joyful.'

'Well . . .' She did not want to lie. '. . . maybe a little. But it's all going to work out just fine.'

'Let's hope so. Now, I wondered if I could pick Will up tomorrow morning?'

'He'd love that, Sam. Especially since . . .' Ruth lowered her voice. 'Josie's going down to the hospital in Hartsfield to have blood taken, see if it matches her brother's. I know he won't want to be there.'

'I'll be at the house by nine thirty, okay?'

Paul lay listening to Ruth in the bathroom. It had become a nightly routine for him, to lie there imagining her undressing, recalling the way the knobs of her spine swelled beneath her skin as she bent to remove her clothes, the line of her leg as she stepped into the scented water, her full breasts. It was a kind of self-inflicted torture, as though he were pressed against the locked gates of a lost Eden. He knew precisely how she would look lying in the tub, the way she would reach for the towel when she was through, the smell of her warm skin.

What would happen if he went in to her once she had gotten into her own bed? If he slipped under the covers, aware that she might reject him, prepared to have her turn away from him, but hoping nonetheless that she would not? Maybe she wanted him to do that. Maybe she was waiting for him to make the first move.

He switched off the lamp and lay on his back under the thin summer quilt which Ruth's grandmother had pieced some sixty years ago. The uncurtained window was a rectangle of silvery blue against the larger darkness of the room. He could hear the faint swish of the waves down on the shore, and the rustle of pine trees. A scrap of tissue-thin moon hung in one corner of the sky. From the woods the katydids endlessly called.

He was half asleep when he heard quiet footsteps across the wooden floorboards. Before he could sit up, the quilt was gently pulled back and Ruth slid in beside him.

'Ruth . . .' He opened his arms and she came into them, tucking herself in close as she had always done. She was naked, still damp from the bath, and holding her he recalled all the years of their marriage, all the nights they had gone to sleep curled together like this, two bodies molded into a single entity. She placed a hand on his chest, above his heart and he drew in a long deep breath. The feel of her fingers against his skin was like a valuable gift which he had thought lost forever.

'Ruth . . .' With a hand low on her buttocks, he pulled her even closer. 'Oh, Ruth, I want you so much . . .' He traced the line of her jaw with his lips, enraptured, dazed with longing.

Her breasts were pressed against him. He moved his hand slowly about her body, feeling each separate and particular change of her skin, the soft curve of her breast, the nubbliness of the area around her nipples, the delicate jut of her hip, the thick pelt at the base of her stomach. He shifted, feeling her naked body all along his. He wanted to possess her, to taste her, to *be* her. Or rather, that the two of them be one again. He pressed his mouth into the soft place under her arm.

Ruth shifted, lifting a leg over his so that she could move in even closer to him. She gently squeezed his erection and he groaned. She kissed him, thrusting her tongue into his mouth, pushing against him, her body speaking its need. 'Anything else you want?'

'This.' He moved down the bed and lowered his head to the dark sweet space between her legs, tasting it, breathing it deep into his lungs. 'This is what I want.' Outside, the sea beat against the shore, in time with the blood which coursed through his body. Behind his eyes, a thousand other lovemakings shared with this woman fused and condensed into this single one. He lifted his head. 'Or this.' He touched her delicately with the tip of his tongue, hearing her gasp. 'Or this.' Slowly he slid his fingers inside her, feeling the damp red lusciousness of her. 'Or I could even—'

'Come into me, Paul. Now. Quickly.'

He moved over her, positioning himself, giddy with the prospect of being inside her again.

'Be there, love me, fuck me, quickly, quickly.' She spread herself to his strong urgency, throwing back her head, moaning. 'Just love me, Paul.'

'I do, my darling, I do,' he said, entering her in a swift sure surge, knowing it would be over quickly this time, because the ecstasy of the long drive toward the center, toward the very heart of her, was already causing him to expand, to erupt, to explode into a million whitehot shattering stars.

Outside the window, the sea crashed and roared, the wind raged in the trees, thunder cracked and lightning fizzed across the sky as she grabbed his hips, kept him tight inside her, moved against him, swelled and bloomed around him. He heard her soft cries as she arched beneath him, cresting toward her climax until she fell back, while the core of her leaped and shuddered and he felt the convulsive gush of her at last.

'I love you, Paul,' she said.

'And I love you, Ruth. More than you'll ever know.'

Later, much later, when he had thickened once again and she had urged him into her and they had spent an hour as long as a lifetime in relearning each other, she sighed happily. 'We're a family again, aren't we?'

'Yes.'

'And everything's all right, isn't it?' She sounded like a little girl.

He kissed her forehead. 'Everything's as all right as it can be.'

25

'Sure you don't want to come along, Will?' Josie asked.

'I've had enough of hospitals to last me for a lifetime.' Will's spectral grin lengthened across his pale face. He seemed very frail this morning, as though drained by the excitement of yesterday. 'Besides, I've got better things to do.'

'What time did Sam say he'd come for you?' Josie was nervous, picking at a thread in her jeans, tapping her foot, constantly trying to push her hair behind her ears although it was far too short.

'About nine thirty,' said Ruth.

'Here he comes!' Will said. For a moment excitement glowed in his eyes, then dimmed, as though it was an emotion too strong for him to sustain for very long.

Sam's pickup bumped its way along the track and up through the meadow to park in front of them. He swung down from the cabin, adjusting a deep-crowned baseball cap on his head. He had another in his hand.

'This is for you, William,' he said, his brown eyes sweeping over Ruth's face, lingering for a moment on Josie's. 'Nobody steps on my boat without one of these.'

The cap had a multi-clawed lobster embroidered on it and underneath, the word LOBSTERMAN.

'Hey, *cool*.' Will settled it over his skull. 'Whadda ya think, Mom?'

'You look like a real professional,' Ruth said. She wanted to fuss over him, ask if he had brought a sweater, tell him not to get overtired, beseech Sam to take proper care of him. Instead, she came down the shallow steps of the porch and put her arms round the big man. 'Thank you, Sam. You will remember that Will's very frail, won't you?'

He nodded. 'Don't worry, Ruth. He'll be safe with me.' He sketched a little bow to Josie. 'Good morning, Miss Connelly. I heard you were . . . back with us. What can I say?'

'Best say nothing. After all this time, guess I can say it all for myself.'

'I'm some glad you're home,' he said.

'So am I.'

Sam helped Will into the pickup and drove away while Josie stood with her hands in the back pocket of her jeans watching them go.

'It'll take us a while, won't it?' Josie said. 'To get back to where we used to be.'

Paul twisted the wheel to overtake a semi which was thundering down the road toward Hartsfield. 'Think people can really do that? Go back, I mean?'

'If you . . . if you're mad at me, I'd understand.'

'I'm not mad.'

'I feel so guilty. The pain I've caused you. Mom won't admit it, but I know I have.'

'Josie. Honey. You're grown now. You've lived without us for two years. What we think or feel doesn't matter.'

'It matters to *me*.'

'We can't pretend that the last two years didn't happen. But it's all irrelevant, now that you're back—'

'It's not, it's not.'

'In one sense, maybe. But in the most important sense, it doesn't matter a damn.'

'I ruined your lives.'

'That's not true.' Paul eased his foot on the accelerator. 'The crucial thing is that we found each other again.'

'But it's my fault you ever lost each other in the first place.'

'If it's yours, it's ours too, Josie. Maybe, in some dreadful way, we needed something like this to happen. All of us. Your mom and I – yes, we broke apart under the strain of losing you, but looking back I can see that, for all sorts of reasons, we were already becoming a fragile kind of partnership. Which we aren't now. Not anymore.'

'Forgive me, Dad.'

'Why don't we make a pact,' Paul said. 'We'll accept that all of us could have done things differently. That we all love each other. That we're together now and that's . . . that's *wonderful*! Okay?'

'Dad . . .'

'And that anyone who keeps apologizing is going to be sent back to the city in chains.'

Josie laughed.

They sat holding hands, huddled together on a leatherette couch in a side room. Under the harsh light from the neon strip hanging from the ceiling, their faces looked gray and haggard. Other anxious people had obviously waited here before them: the cheap table was

493

dotted with cigarette burns, and the box of tissues on the windowsill was empty. A pile of children's building blocks stood in one corner, the bright colors crudely garish.

Neither of them was able to talk about what really occupied their thoughts. Every time someone passed the door they tensed. 'God, I wish they'd hurry up,' Josie said. 'I can't stand much more of this.'

'I'm sure they're rushing the tests through. They know how urgent it is.'

Josie glanced up as a white-coated doctor paused at the door, looked at them then continued on down the passage. She leaned toward Paul. 'Can you understand how desperately I want this to work? If it did, it'd be like making up for all the harm I've caused.'

'Josephine, I want you to understand something very clearly.'

'What?'

'If you can provide a bone marrow match for Will, that'd be fantastic. It would be more than . . . than . . . But that's not why we're so terribly happy you're home. We love you because you're Josie. Our daughter. Remember, whatever you've done, whatever you do, we love you.' Paul looked down at her hand, softly ran a finger across the knuckles. 'You do realize that the chances of this working are pretty slim, don't you?'

Josie's face crumpled. She took a sharp breath and squeezed her eyes shut. 'I don't want to think about that.'

'If it doesn't work, it's not your fault, okay?'

She nodded.

'At least you tried.'

'Dad, whatever the result, let me be the one to tell Will.'

494

'Don't you think he'll know?'

'Just let me do this, Dad.'

'Okay.'

Down the hall, a baby began to cry. A little red-headed boy ran into the room and, after a cursory glance at them, began to throw the plastic bricks about.

'Will used to look like that,' Paul said softly.

A young woman came through the door. She stopped when she saw them. 'Hi,' she said. Her gaze lingered on their faces for a moment. She turned to the child: 'Now, listen up, Max. You just better stop that. You're disturbing these people, can't you see?'

Max threw a blue brick at her and laughed.

'Ooh, you're such a bad little boy,' said the woman, smiling. She bent to pick up her son and swing him into her arms. 'Such a bad, bad little boy.'

Max laughed again, beating at her with his fists. 'Bad boy,' he said delightedly.

'Good thing I love you,' his mother said. At the door, she smiled apologetically at Paul and Josie. 'Sorry about my son.'

And I'm sorry about mine, Paul thought. 'Did Will tell you that we were going to try and fix up the *Lucky Duck*?' he asked Josie a little later, breaking into the silence.

'Can I help?'

'Of course you can.'

'It'd be good to do some sailing again. I kind of . . . went off it.'

There was another pause. 'Wonder if Will'll bring some lobsters home for supper tonight,' Paul said.

After a while, Josie leaned her head against Paul's shoulder. He rested his cheek on her hair. They sat again in silence.

Another white-coated doctor stood at the door. 'Josephine Connelly?' he said, looking down at the clipboard in his hand.

'That's me.'

'If you'd like to come with me, Ms Connelly . . .' He stepped back and stood waiting in the passage outside.

Josie stood up. She turned to look down at her father, her expression anguished. 'Dad . . .'

'You'll be fine,' Paul said. He pressed his lips together to stop the tremor in them.

'Suppose it doesn't work?'

'Suppose it does.'

She hesitated as though about to say something more, then joined the doctor. Paul heard the sound of their footsteps receding down the corridor. Even though he knew she was an adult now, he wanted to be with her when she heard whatever news the doctors had to give her. After a while, he got up and walked slowly along the passage, looking in at the windows of the side rooms as he went. Halfway down, he saw Josie. She was listening with head bent, hands clasped tightly in her lap, as the doctor pointed to a sheet of printout, tapping it here and there with a pen. His lips moved though Paul could not hear what he was saying.

But he knew anyway.

Ruth left Paul sleeping and went downstairs. There was a linger of coffee in the empty kitchen. Early morning sun slanted through the windows, golden and hopeful. It was going to be another glorious day. There were two mugs on the table and a milky cereal bowl.

'Will!' Ruth called. 'Where are you? Josie?'

No answer.

'Are you okay?' There was still no reply. She stepped

out through the open door of Will's bedroom onto the side porch. 'Will?'

Expecting food, the mallards on the pond began to drift toward her. The reeds quivered as a breeze caught them and ruffled the water. 'Will? Josie?' Her voice floated up into the astringent sea-sharp air and was lost. Maybe they had both gone for a walk.

Slowly she went up to her bedroom. She had been surprised at her reaction to the news of Josie's tests. Having pinned all her hopes on there being a match between Josie's blood and Will's, she had expected to be crushed if the results proved negative. Instead, her mind was already spinning ahead, turning over the possibilities that might still remain. More chemo, a sudden match discovered on the register, another remission, a miracle.

On the balcony, she lifted the binoculars she kept there, swept them round, across pink rock and pale water and blue spruce, their colors distorted by the sun-glare off the Sound. Out on the water, a lobster boat was pulling up traps: when she focused she could see Dieter Hechst at work and, with him, Sam. She swept the glasses round once more. There was nothing out there except trees, grass, boulders thrusting up from the ancient earth. And the sea. All along the rocky shore was a dark line left by the receding tide. A couple of sloops lay at anchor, hardly moving on the still surface of the water. Apart from the Hechsts, it was still too early for anyone to be about.

Where would Will have gone?

She slipped the strap of the glasses over her neck. The sun was still low as it danced and dazzled across the water; the scattered pot buoys swayed in the glare. Josie could not possibly appreciate just how weak Will was.

And they might not even be together. Perhaps they had had an early coffee then she had driven off somewhere while he decided to go for a walk. Or a sail in the Beetle Cat, as he had done many times before.

A jolt of alarm shook her. Suppose he had collapsed, suppose he was lying somewhere, unable to help himself, waiting for them to find him. She ran into their bedroom. 'Paul!' She shook his shoulder.

'Mmm,' he said sleepily. Eyes still shut, he reached for her. 'I love you, Ruth.'

'Darling: Will's gone. And Josie.'

'They've probably gone down to the shore together,' he murmured, stretching lazily, opening his eyes to look at her, lust kindling in his face as he saw her bending over him, her breasts loose inside her robe. 'God, what a gorgeous sight to wake up to.' He stretched out a hand to fondle her but she pushed him away.

'I'm worried, Paul. Suppose Will's in trouble.'

Hearing the anxiety in her voice, he pulled himself up, swung out of bed, walked toward the chair where his clothes had been flung the night before. 'Let's both of us get some clothes on and we'll go look.'

Ten minutes later, standing on the porch, a second pair of binoculars around his neck, he said: 'Where do you think he'd go?'

'Up to the Point. Or sailing.'

'Is he strong enough to take out the cat boat on his own?'

'I don't know.'

'Then let's go up to Caleb's Point.' Paul put his arm round Ruth's shoulder. 'Don't worry, Ruth.'

She kissed his cheek. 'It's so hard not to.'

Hand in hand, they walked along the edge of the pond. Bluets and pondhawks hovered, the high neon flash of their bodies like sudden jewels amongst the reeds. They turned off past the cranberry bog, and took the trail up into the trees. Sunlight slanted between the fog-dampened branches; the ground underfoot was still soggy from the rain earlier in the week as they climbed toward Caleb's Point.

The Hechsts' lobster smack had gone and it was still too early for the boats from the yacht club to be out, but one little dinghy already bobbed on the water, haloed by the brilliant light. Ruth focused on the white sail, gilded by the sun behind it.

'There they are,' she said, relieved. She raised the glasses again. Out on the water, the Beetle Cat skimmed along against the sky, its sail full of golden wind, a wake forming a line of white behind it. Small waves glittered. She could see Will leaning back in the cockpit, one arm spread along the gunwales, the other lightly on the tiller. He was smiling at his sister.

'Paul.' She took his hand. 'Seeing them together again, our children . . . it's wonderful.'

'A true miracle, darling.'

In the little boat, Josie was talking, apparently exhorting Will, one hand slapping through the air as she made whatever point she was trying to convey. And Will, still smiling, kept shaking his head.

'She looks well, doesn't she?' Paul said. He raised his own glasses.

'She looks *lovely*.'

'She always did. Takes after her beautiful mother.'

Ruth looked at Paul. 'It's what he wanted most of all, to go sailing with her.'

Staring out to sea, he said: 'Look at your children, Ruth.'

'*Our* children.' Ruth laughed aloud. She leaned

499

against her husband. Josie was back. She felt as though she were a new mother again, holding her first baby in her arms. 'Aren't they something?'

The little boat tacked between the pot buoys then veered away across the calm surface toward the open water. It sailed between the wooded arms of the bay before turning and tacking back again, while brother and sister sat, scarcely moving, and talked. The sun glinted, catching lines of light along the gentle waves. Beyond the trees rose the whale-humps of Mount Desert Island.

'In spite of the test results, I feel happy,' Ruth said. 'Something's going to turn up, I just know.'

'It's so peaceful up here.' Paul sat down on Josie's bench.

Ruth sat beside him. She lowered the glasses to her lap and closed her eyes, turning her face up to the sun. The breeze brought the fresh tang of salt and kelp off the water below them. Gulls screamed distantly out in the bay.

'Should we do something about this bench?' Paul asked.

'Leave it here,' Ruth murmured.

'As a reminder?'

'That's right.'

They sat quietly, hand in hand, the air between them rich with promise. Happiness filled her like water. Every now and then she lifted the glasses to watch her children talking while the Beetle Cat drifted gently between the pot buoys and the water danced. A yellow-gold light shone across the bay, the color of honey, the color of hope.

'I wish this day could last forever,' she said lazily. 'Just this bit of it, with them out there and . . . us here.'

500

She lifted her glasses again. Josie had now moved to sit beside her brother. She put her arms around him for a long moment, hugging him tightly. She rubbed her face against his, touched his cheek with her hand. Will took her hand and held it. He talked earnestly for several minutes, while Josie heard him out, her head bent.

The little boat came in right below the bluff, so close to shore that Ruth could hear the *clunk* as the boom swung over. Neither Josie nor Will looked up, however, too engrossed in their conversation. She saw Will lean forward and kiss his sister. As they headed out into the bay again, Ruth's contentment began slowly to dissipate. What were the two of them discussing so earnestly? Although the scene seemed idyllic, somehow it was off kilter, something was dragging it awry.

Through her glasses, she saw Josie speak and then turn away, her face grim. At the same time, Will let go of the tiller and stood up. He had the anchor clasped against his chest, the chain wrapped round his wrist. He rested one hand on the edge of the cockpit, sat down and swung his legs over the side.

'What's he doing?' Ruth asked. A wave of fear engulfed her. Something was wrong. Even at this distance, she could see how white his face was.

'What's he doing?' she demanded. 'Paul . . . is he going swimming?'

Will turned his head toward his sister, said something and smiled. He was wearing shorts and a black T-shirt, with the LOBSTERMAN baseball cap covering his bald head.

'Why's he holding the anchor like that?' Alarm drummed, louder now.

'Ruth,' said Paul suddenly. 'Ruth.' He closed his hand

tightly round her arm as Will took off the cap and then slowly, slowly, slipped over the side of the boat into the sea. As he hit the water, a silent splash of spray rose, sparking a brief rainbow as it caught the sun, and then he was gone. Disbelieving, Ruth watched him disappear beneath the surface of the sea, remembering the bitter chill of the water, the numbing cold that burned like fire.

'The water's so cold,' she said in a reasonable voice, while fear clutched at her heart and threatened to freeze her lungs. 'Why would he want to swim out there?'

Paul's grip on her arm was painful. 'I don't think that he's—'

'What's he doing?' Ruth cried. Will had not yet surfaced. 'Paul, what is he . . . Why hasn't he . . .'

Paul stood up, holding the glasses to his eyes. 'Oh God,' he said. 'Oh no.'

Below them, Josie resolutely sailed away from the spot where Will had disappeared.

'Where is he?' Ruth said loudly. She too rose to her feet. 'Why has she left him alone? He hasn't come up, Paul. Why isn't she helping him?'

Paul said nothing.

Ruth stared at the spot where she had last seen her son. Will did not reappear. Josie, her head bent, steered across the water toward the open sea.

Understanding finally came. And horror.

'No!' Ruth screamed. 'Will . . . Oh, my God. Oh Will, my darling, no!' The words flew across the water and mingled with the cries of the seagulls. 'Will! Will. I love you. I love . . .'

She turned and began to run downhill to where the bluff grew less steep and it was possible to gain access to the beach. Paul ran too, pounding along behind her, calling her name, but she paid no heed. If she could

502

swim out to the spot where he had disappeared, she could find him, she could save him, her sad sick child, she could breathe life back into him, resurrect him, turn back the clock. *Will* . . . But even as she scrambled across the rocks, slipping on the seaweed, splashing into rock pools – *Will!* – she knew it was useless.

One part of her mind insisted that this was not happening, that somewhere another Ruth still stood at the edge of the bluff and looked across the water to where a little boat bobbed and her children laughed together. As she plunged into the waiting sea, straight into the oncoming waves, and began to swim out into the bay, the only message her distraught brain could process was this: he had chosen his own path and there was nothing now that she could do to prevent him from following it.

As she swam further and further out, she screamed Will's name and the sea poured through her, swamped, deluged her. The gasp, the choke, clutching at water which slid through her fingers: she remembered it still, the purity of her panic in that long-ago moment as a child when salt had stung her eyes, burned the back of her throat, and she had been aware of death, oblivion, nothingness.

Would you die for me, Josie had said. *Would you give your life for me?*

Encumbered by her clothes, heart bursting with terror, salt water heavy in her mouth, the answer was so blindingly clear that Ruth wondered why Josie had needed to put the question. Oh *yes*, without any doubt whatsoever. If it was necessary, I would gladly give my life for you. For both of you. But neither of you ever asked.

* * *

Shivering, she stood passive while Paul silently removed her wet clothes and guided her into the shower. She felt his hands on her body, washing away the salt, washing away the sea. A cold numbness filled her, blotting out all feeling except grief. Will . . . She would never see him again, never joke with him, never hold his hand again or kiss his rough hair.

Paul toweled her dry, found her robe on the back of the door and wrapped her in it. He began to weep and she took his head in her hands and held it against her breast, as though he were her child, not her husband. The two of them stood there together, stunned with grief, each seeking comfort from the other, each giving comfort, too.

'Paul,' she said, tears sliding ceaselessly down her face. She gripped him tightly. 'This time we must treasure each other.'

'Yes.'

'Not be careless of the richness we have together.' She bent her head over his, the seaweed smell of salt still on her skin, and began to weep, her shoulders bowed over the sobs which came ripping up her body in an explosion of grief and pain.

He could not speak. Tears flowed across his face, pulsing out of his eyes. He nodded slowly. Together they went downstairs to the kitchen where Josie was sitting at the table, staring at her clasped hands.

Seeing them, she hesitated for a moment then got up and stood between them, touching them lightly on the shoulders, like a bridge. 'He was going to die anyway,' she said.

'But not like that. Not drowning.' While Paul walked toward the back door and stood looking out, Ruth sank down on a chair and buried her face in her hands.

504

Despair ate into her body: a skeleton of grief had formed beneath her flesh. 'Will,' she moaned. 'Oh Will.'

Josie put her arm around her mother. 'He said he had hoped he'd have the whole summer. But he was getting weaker and weaker. This morning he could hardly stand. He didn't want you to know, but he was afraid he soon wouldn't be able to get up. Said he was damned if he was going to spend a perfect downeast summer lying in bed, looking out the window.'

'Oh, Will. My poor boy.'

'I told him the results of the tests this morning. He said he'd already guessed. He asked me to take him out in the boat and I knew he was planning something. He didn't say so, but I could see it in his eyes.'

Sorrow pushed against Ruth's heart, cold as a winter sea. She felt as though she was going to suffocate. It was what he would do. What, somewhere in the very bottom of her heart, Ruth had always feared he might do. But not yet. Not yet. 'He was so young . . .'

'He didn't want to live. He told me this morning. He was tired of being ill. He didn't want any more treatments. Just a few last days up here and then finished, over, ended. The way he wanted to go.' Tears gathered in Josie's eyes but did not fall. 'We talked for hours this morning. I'm so glad about that. My poor little brother. He was just waiting for me to come back so he could go himself.'

'You didn't try to stop him?'

'Not once I realized it was what he wanted. What he'd planned.'

'I thought he wanted to spend the summer here.'

'He wanted to *die* here, Mom. He told me he had had a wonderful life and that he knew it wasn't going to get better, only worse.'

505

'He's like you, isn't he? Both of you are so ... strong.'

'We get that from you.' Josie put her arms around Ruth again. 'Will asked me to make sure you got this.' She put a piece of folded paper on the table beside Ruth's arm.

Ruth opened it, scarcely able to see the letters through her tears.

> *Mom, Dad, don't be sad. I couldn't take anymore. I wanted to be in control, not like the kids in the hospital, like poor little Michelle.*
> *Thank you for all the things you gave me.*
> *I love you all. Please don't cry.*
> From your loving son William

Ruth thought of his swollen-knuckled fingers struggling to hold the pen to write the words. Grief welled up again. But now, as well as anguish, she felt a sudden kind of peace. She turned to Josie and rested her head on her daughter's shoulder and felt her daughter's hand on her hair. Heard her husband's footsteps across the kitchen, and the comfort of his arms around them both.

They sat on the bench at Caleb's Point, looking out to sea. Bertlemy's Isle lay on the water, the tips of the spruces at its center gilded by the setting sun. Out of sight, on the strip of stony beach below them, the sea whispered, sucking at the pebbles and falling away with a sigh. A single star was already out, low on the horizon.

Ruth stared at the place where she had last seen Will. I gave birth to him, she thought, I gave him life and raised him, my sunny, funny Will and now there is nothing left of him. In her mind she saw Will's face when they took him from the water, and the way his pale lips were curved into a little smile.

'Mom,' Josie said. Heartbroken, she began to sob.

'It's all right.' Ruth forced herself away from thoughts of her dead son to the business of comforting her living daughter. Of being a mother. 'It's okay. It's . . . okay.'

Thank you for all the things you gave me, Will had written. He had endured so much and yet he still thanked them . . . Ruth too wept, quietly, hopelessly. This death was irremediable. This death could not be reversed.

'He said he thought you'd be happier up here than in the city,' Josie said.

'I think he's right,' said Paul. His arm tightened around Ruth's shoulders. 'We'll have to think about it.'

For so long Ruth had not had time to consider the simple matter of happiness. Now, tentatively tasting the idea, she realized that somewhere, out beyond the edge of now, a kind of contentment waited for them. Along the way, she would find it. And Paul, too. Josie. The three of them.

'One of the awful things, when we thought you were dead,' Ruth said, 'was that I couldn't talk about it. The grief, the sorrow . . . I tried to pretend it had never happened. I refused to let anyone mention your name.'

'We mustn't do that with William.' Paul tightened his hold on his family. 'We'll have to tell you all about it. All the things he did and said while you were away.'

'There was this little girl called Michelle,' said Ruth. 'Such a cute child. Will was kind of taken with her sister. Kelly. She made him a pink gingham hat to cover his bald head.' She smiled at the remembrance, looking across the water. One child had been exchanged for another. For the rest of her life, whenever she came up here, she would see, in slow motion, tiny and foreshortened, the figures of her children in the little boat out on the water. Her resurrected daughter. And her doomed son, bending, slipping, falling slowly into the welcoming sea.

All her life she had feared death by water, but until that moment, she had always imagined that the death would be her own.

THE END

Acknowledgements

A book such as this could not have been written without help from a number of sources. Among the many who have contributed in various ways, I should particularly like to thank the following:

For faith and support from the very beginning, R. D. Zimmerman.

For medical details, Rosemary Herbert and Mary Small and all the parents of children suffering from the kind of terminal diseases mentioned in this book, whose anonymous stories I read and wept over so many times.

For sailing expertise, Bernard Cornwell and Captain John Crabtree, Ocean Yacht Master.

For always believing, and promises made good, Nicki Kennedy of ILA.

For local insider information and crab rolls, Marilyn Mays.

And, in particular, for devotedly responding to my constant cries for help with every kind of esoteric information, including all of the above, Jim Napier.

Above all, I must categorically state that without the

prodding and encouragement of my wise and wonderful agents, Araminta Whitley and Mark Lucas of Lucas Alexander Whitley, this book would never have become what it is, and I thank them unreservedly for remaining (fairly) calm when I did not.

THE LOOP
by Nicholas Evans

'Drama . . . power . . . passion'
The Times

Helen Ross, a twenty-nine-year-old biologist, is sent to a sleepy Rocky Mountain ranching town to defend a pack of wolves from those who want to destroy them. For in Hope, Montana, a century ago, the wolf was slaughtered to extinction and though now protected by law as an endangered species, the old hatred runs deep.

Alone in this hostile place, bruised by a broken love affair, Helen struggles for self-esteem and survival, embarking on a dangerous alliance with the son of her most ferocious opponent, the brutal and charismatic rancher, Buck Calder.

From its heart-stopping first chapter to its devastating climax, *The Loop*, set in the same vast landscape as *The Horse Whisperer*, is an epic tale of primal passion and redemptive love.

'*The Horse Whisperer* . . . conveyed a genuine and personal emotional charge which resonated with millions of readers. *The Loop*, Evans's second novel, confirms that he is that rare phenomenon, a natural storyteller'
Mail on Sunday

'As good as Evans's first novel, *The Horse Whisperer* . . . total entertainment'
Daily Telegraph (Australia)

0 552 14495 9

A SELECTED LIST OF FINE NOVELS
AVAILABLE FROM CORGI BOOKS